Also available from
Gena Showalter
and HQN Books

And look for more hotly anticipated novels
from Gena Showalter

coming soon!

GENA SHOWALTER

THE *Hotter* YOU BURN

HQN™

HQN™

ISBN-13: 978-0-373-77969-7

The Hotter You Burn

Recycling programs
for this product may
not exist in your area.

This book would not be what it is without my amazing editor, Emily Ohanjanians, who once again went above and beyond, pointing me in the right direction anytime I lost my way. Thank you! I thank God, the giver of all good things, for bringing you into my life.

A huge shout out to the magnificent Katie McGarry— an author I admire and adore—who spent precious time on the phone with me, helping me with my research (any mistakes are my own). You are a treasure!

A special thank you to these fantastic ladies and authors: Lori Foster, Carly Phillips, Jill Shalvis and Kristan Higgins. You guys rock on so many levels!

And to all the wonderful folks at Harlequin Books for taking a chance on this series I've been foaming at the mouth eager to write.

CHAPTER ONE

HARLOW GLASS STOOD on the porch of a hundred-year-old farmhouse that had more character than most people, waning daylight wrapping the structure in its loving embrace. Exterior walls once covered in chipped cream-colored paint that revealed crumbling, weathered wood now boasted new slats of paneling and a fresh coat. The broken seal on the bay window had been replaced, no more sheets of moisture collecting between the panes. Ivy used to climb all the way to the roof, but every stalk had been cut down.

She scanned the driveway. No cars.

She listened at the door. No suspicious sounds.

A smile stretched from ear to ear. After months of bad luck, something had finally worked in her favor.

Here's hoping it lasted.

Trembling, she inserted her key in the door lock. Hinges whined as the thick, wooden entrance brushed open, homey scents—fresh bread, vanilla and some kind of caramelized fruit—wafting out and making her mouth water. Her empty stomach grumbled and twisted painfully.

"Hello," she called.

No one cried out a startled rebuke.

She shut the door with more confidence and entered the living room, breathing a sigh of relief. *I'm ba-ack.*

Her childhood home creaked out a welcome, and for a moment, one of her favorite memories played at the forefront of her mind: Martha Glass pushing the sofa to a new angle, while Harlow straddled one of the arms, pretending to ride a bucking bronco. Her dad hadn't been home to sneer insults, thank God—*you're pathetic, you're stupid, you're such a disappointment*—so a relaxed, almost giddy atmosphere had pervaded.

But the cherished recollection withered against the depressing heat of realization. This might be Harlow's childhood home, but it no longer belonged to her; technically she'd just committed breaking and entering. But only technically! She'd just...well, after all the work that had been done, she'd *needed* an inside look at the place. And if a few items of food happened to leave with her, she'd be doing the new owners a favor, saving them from nasty fat grams.

"You're welcome, everyone," she muttered.

The owners were the newest residents of Strawberry Valley, Oklahoma. Bachelors she'd watched from a distance for weeks. Lincoln West, the one she'd dubbed Most Intelligent. Beck Ockley—Most Beautiful. And Jase Hollister—Most Fierce. Men she'd never spoken to and never wanted to speak to, really. In Harlow's heart, the house still belonged to her, would *always* belong to her, making the guys the trespassers. She had been born here, and if all went according to her life plan, she would die here. Just hopefully not today.

This was her first time inside the house since the bank had kicked her out roughly seven months ago. Spinning slowly, she drank in the only love still part of her life. *Too many changes.* Gone were the scuffed, stained wood floors, the "imperfections" sanded away.

What was wrong with a few flaws? In a home, or even in a person, flaws proclaimed, "Life happened here."

The wallpaper had been peeled, Sheetrock repaired and painted the color of a caramel latte. Once decrepit crown molding and wainscoting gleamed with new life. There were a few feminine touches here and there to save the place from being a total man cave—throw pillows, bowls of potpourri and lace doilies—but she missed the cat portraits her mother had hung, random displays of china, knitting baskets, porcelain dolls and the gaudy lamps that once rested on lace-covered side tables.

Harlow braced for disappointment and headed for the bedrooms. Up first, the former guest room, now a man cave on steroids. A king-size bed with dark brown sheets dominated one side, while the large flat-screen suspended above a ginormous console stuffed with DVDs dominated the other.

How was a person supposed to relax in here?

The next bedroom—hers—boiled her blood. The princess paradise her mother had created for her as a child, which she'd never had the heart to change, even as she'd grown up, had been transformed into a man-child's playpen. Multiple gaming systems cluttered a tiered platform, the controls scattered across the floor. In front of a gargantuan unmade bed towered a floor-to-ceiling projector screen. The walls where she'd once lovingly painted a magical forest were now beige. Beige!

Sure, the mural had come with defects, but she'd loved every inch of it, had spent weeks etching different designs, mixing colors, learning and adoring the entire process while allowing her imagination to sweep her away. Of course, she'd ruined the fruit of her efforts long before boring beige had done so, throwing handfuls of mismatched paint at the images in a fit of temper. Still. The sea of monotone was worse.

Before she gave in to the urge to find a marker and draw something to liven up the room, most likely a pair of hands with both middle fingers extended, she backed out and shut the door.

The master bedroom had been converted into a nerdy workaholic's dream, all traces of her parents gone. Computers and computer parts were stacked on the desk, on the bed and scattered across the floor, and oh, she couldn't stand this.

She made her way to the kitchen…where the wallpaper had been removed. But okay. No big deal. This change she understood. The design had been so faded the different clusters of strawberries had looked like swollen testicles.

The matching red laminate countertops had been swapped for sparkling white marble, but at least the cabinets were the same, even though they'd been sanded and painted black. Not bad… Just different.

A pang over what should and shouldn't be cut through her and might have broken what remained of her heart if she hadn't spotted the blueberry pie perched on the stovetop.

Jobless, penniless—homeless—she hadn't eaten a decent meal in forever. And a decent dessert? Not since Momma died.

Another pang, this one sharper, but again, the lure of the pie distracted her, and she moved forward, as though in a trance. Trembling, she traced her fingertip over the rim of the pan and caught a warm glob of juice.

One taste... Just one.

The moment the sweetness hit her tongue, her plan to make a sandwich with ingredients the Bachelors Three wouldn't miss completely upended. She rushed around, digging through drawers for the necessary supplies, growing indignant when she discovered nothing in its rightful place.

Gravel crunched. A door slammed.

Chilled to the bone, she dashed into the living room and threw herself on the couch to peer out the window.

Beck Ockley, Most Beautiful himself, helped a woman from the passenger side of his car. Beck...the man who reminded her of the shed out back, polished on the outside, crumbling on the inside.

He was a little over six feet and lusciously muscled, with an intriguing mix of light and dark brown hair, the strands always in a state of disarray. His just-roused-from-bed eyes were the color of melted honey and framed by the longest, thickest black lashes she'd ever seen. But even a man like him should need a few hours, at least, to reel in a new fish.

Then again, he rocked serious man-magic, and with a single smile, he could probably drop a thousand pairs of panties.

Harlow's heart galloped, a racehorse in her chest as she returned into the kitchen to swipe up the pie. Probably best to eat the evidence of her impromptu house tour. *Hurry!* She sprinted to the back door...only to grind to a stop. Beveled glass revealed Jase and his fiancée, Brook Lynn Dillon, cuddled on the porch swing.

How had she missed them on her pre-break-in perimeter check?

Hinges on the front door whined. Crap! Beck and his

date would enter any second. She darted into the living room, the hall, the first bedroom she came across—but the lock on the window was new and complicated, and no matter how much she jiggled it, she couldn't open it. Suspecting all other locks were the same, she headed for the living room. If she stood beside the door, she'd be hidden when it opened. If Beck forgot to close it, she could sneak out as soon as he—

"Now that you've got me here," a woman said, breathless with longing, "what are you going to do to me?"

Too late! Fear settled like thousand-pound boulders in Harlow's feet, and she wrenched to a halt in the hallway, blood rushing from her head, her lungs hemorrhaging air as if survival had just become enemy one.

Tawny Ferguson walked backward. If she looked to the left, she would see a wild-eyed Harlow, pie in hand. *Don't look left. Please, please, don't look left.*

Beck slowly, leisurely prowled after the girl, radiating sultry heat and a carnal, predator-prey determination. He pinned Tawny's hands over her head, saying, "I'm going to do whatever I want."

Tawny arched her hips, rubbing against him. "Should I be afraid?"

"Honey, you should be grateful."

The sensual impact of his voice sent heated shivers through Harlow's veins, and she hated them almost as much as she loved them.

He leaned down, his mouth hovering over Tawny's to tease her with what was to come. "You're going to like every second of our time together. That I promise you."

Tawny quivered, a woman on the verge of ecstasy. "Oh, I know I'll like it. But what happens afterward?"

Crickets.

He stiffened, even as he nuzzled his nose along the line of her jaw. "Afterward, you'll be so weak in the knees you'll have to crawl home."

Tawny giggled. "No, I meant relationship-wise. I know your reputation as the one-night-stand king. Will you still want me in the morning?"

A moment rife with tension as Beck cupped her chin to ensure she wasn't able to look away from him. "I told you. I've never offered anyone more than a single night. There will never be an exception."

"But why?" Tawny asked with a pout, even as she played with his zipper. "I'd make a very…good…exception." With every word she uttered, she opened those metal teeth another inch.

His smile didn't quite reach his eyes, making it a cold, bitter thing. "A girl like you should have a happily-ever-after with a man carrying far less baggage."

"I don't mind baggage."

"Doesn't matter one way or the other." He ground against her, distracting her. "All that matters right now is whether or not you want *me*."

Tawny moaned, her eyes closing. "Don't stop. Please, don't stop."

No, no, don't stop, don't you dare—a slap of harsh reality brought Harlow back to her senses. While Tawny—and even Harlow—had lost sight of everything but Beck, he'd had no problem retaining his wits. He'd deflected masterfully. And she should know. She'd done the same in high school. Multiple teachers and counselors had pulled her aside to ask a single question.

Why do you insult your peers?

Her reply? *I'm not insulting them. I'm helping them by pointing out flaws in need of work.*

Meanwhile, a dirty secret had festered deep inside her. The insults she dished—and they were indeed insults—were nothing compared to the words her father hurled at her.

The only thing you're good at, little girl, is making my day worse.

She cringed even now.

One day, a switch had just sort of flipped inside her, and she'd lashed out at a friend, making the girl cry. It was then Harlow realized she could affect the emotions of others, and with the realization had come power. Soon, verbally knocking down her peers had become the only thing capable of making her feel better about herself…for a little while, at least. Because that feeling of power had been nothing but an illusion, a house of cards kicked down daily by guilt and sadness, in constant need of rebuilding.

True power came not from tearing others down but from building them up.

"Beck," Tawny said, "let me have you. Tonight… and tomorrow."

"Once is for the best." The flatness of his tone caused Harlow to blink in surprise. No matter whom she'd heard him speak with—male, female, young or old—she'd only ever heard him tease and flirt. "Trust me."

"But—"

"Once or nothing," he said, every inch of him intractable steel. "Your choice. Decide now, or I'll decide for you and take you home."

If Tawny continued to push for more, would he truly

do as threatened? Principles before pleasure, no matter how warped those principles might be?

The starch dissolved from the girl's shoulders, and she sighed, defeated. "Once."

As a reward, Beck tilted her head the way he wanted it and dived in for a scorching, earth-shattering kiss. Tawny melted against him, clutching his shirt, wrinkling the black cotton. Harlow almost covered her eyes. Almost. She had lost the ability to move, much less to breathe. Beck clearly knew what he was doing, and oh, he was hot. Licking, sucking…his hands doing delicious things to a woman who already sounded on the verge of orgasm.

A surprising ache throbbed low in Harlow's belly.

Beck and Tawny created a perfect study of passion: seductive, erotic and wanton. The very thing missing from her own life. But then, the man had created a perfect study of passion with *every* woman she'd seen him with.

She'd watched Beck perform this same routine many times before, only with different women, in different locations. The porch. The backyard. Even on the roof.

No one had ever turned him down.

He cupped Tawny's rear and commanded in a husky growl, "Wrap your legs around me."

Tawny complied, as they all complied, and Beck turned toward the couch, away from Harlow.

Sweet relief swept through her. *In the home stretch now... Just a couple more minutes...* And oh, crap, the sugary aroma of the pie ruthlessly taunted her.

Ever the traitor, Harlow's stomach chose that moment to rumble.

It was enough.

Beck's head snapped in her direction, his body going taut. He set Tawny on her feet and stepped in front of her, acting as her shield.

The gesture of protection proved hotter than the kiss.

Recognition lit his features. "You," he said, and he sounded awed rather than angry.

Confused, Harlow blinked at him. "Me?" He knew her?

"What are you doing inside my house?"

My house! But Harlow didn't stick around to correct him. Nothing would placate him or save her stupid hide, so she bolted around him, remaining just out of reach as she headed for the door, yanked it open and at last soared outside.

"Hey!" Beck called. "Stop."

She quickened her pace, aiming for the bank of trees ahead: a giant oak, several mature pecans and two magnolias in full bloom. Locusts buzzed. Grasshoppers sang. Birds squawked. The three created a macabre soundtrack as the familiar scent of wild strawberries and dewy roses lodged in her throat, forming a hard lump.

Almost there... Just a little farther...

While the fifty-two-acre spread had come with a greenhouse, a small dairy, two barns, three work sheds and multiple vegetable gardens Harlow had tried and failed to tend, there was a shadowed section in back filled with gnarled trees, sharp sandburs and crunchy brushwood where snakes and scorpions liked to nest. A section none of the guys had ever dared venture. It would have been the perfect place to hide if she hadn't set up camp there.

Once she passed the embankment, she veered in the

opposite direction, whizzing by the towering oak she used to climb…the weeping willow where she'd experienced her first kiss…the tire swing her father had made during one of his rare moments of affection.

"Stop," Beck commanded. "Now."

He sounded close, too close, but he didn't sound winded. She clutched the pie closer—*try to take it from me, I dare you*—and glanced back. Crap! He was almost on her. She picked up the pace…until several burs lodged in her heels, causing sharp spikes of pain to slow her down. Any second now, Beck would overtake—

Hard hands snaked around her waist, two hundred pounds of muscle bearing down on her. As she fell, the pie went flying.

"Noooo!" she shouted.

Impact emptied her lungs. Tears welled in her eyes, but she wiped the droplets away with a shaky hand, a whimper escaping when she spotted the dark blueberry splatters now streaming across rock and dirt, the crust now sprinkled with dirt.

"Pie killer!" Hello, dark side. "If there's any justice in the world, you will fry for this."

"Really? *That's* what you say to me?" He sat on his haunches, freeing her from the bulk of his weight.

"You tackled me. I should sue you for everything you own."

"Yes, please do so. Meanwhile, I'll press charges for trespassing. Now tell me what you were doing with my pie."

My pie! She'd stolen it fair and square. But the trespassing reminder sobered her. "If you think about things like a reasonable adult, you'll see your crime is worse.

Your actions led to the painful death of an innocent dessert." Now she would go hungry for yet another night.

Her stomach, the whore, grumbled in protest.

"The pie was going to die one way or another tonight. I just assumed my mouth would be the weapon of mass destruction, not a dirty little thief determined to blame someone else."

He stood, then surprised her by offering her a helping hand. A trick, surely. She declined by pushing to her feet under her own steam. Besides, she'd seen some of the places those hands had been. And, really, she didn't need to know what they felt like. If they were callused and rough…hot enough to make her burn and quiver the way Tawny and countless others had.

"What are you doing here?" he asked.

Why not tell him the truth? He had only to ask the townsfolk about her to hear a thousand stories detailing her reign of terror in high school. Perhaps some kind soul would even mention the time a poll was pinned to the corkboard in the town square: "If given a choice, who would you rather torture? The devil or Harlow Glass?"

Harlow had won by a landslide.

"I'm Harlow Glass, and I used to live here."

His gaze raked over her once, then again far more slowly. "I'm honored. Harlow Glass in the flesh. A sighting rarer than Bigfoot."

How did he know? It wasn't as if he'd ever had a reason to look for her.

And oh, wow. His voice. He'd pumped up the smoke, making it even better than before, captivating and temping, sending cascades of pleasure rippling through her.

Danger! Danger! She widened the distance between them.

"Oh, no, you don't. We're going back to the house." He waved her forward.

Stay strong. "How cute. You made a funny."

His expression hardened, promising severe consequences if she refused him a second time, and yet his tenor softened, no longer quite so menacing. "My apologies for not being clear, sweetheart. You're coming with me, and that's that."

"No, that's not that. I have no desire to watch another mouth-to-mouth sesh with Tawny. Let's just conclude our business here."

The smile he unveiled lacked any sort of humor, and yet it utterly devastated her senses, leaving her reeling. "You have two options. One—we discuss the theft and destruction of my pie within the privacy of my home, and just how you're going to make it up to me. Or two—I call Sheriff Lintz."

Dang it! He had her by the lady balls, and he knew it. "Look. You could waterboard me, but I still won't confess—"

"Good to know I have your permission to waterboard."

"—to a crime, so why don't I say I'm sorry for interrupting your evening, and we call it good?"

"Does that sorry come with a side of pie?"

"No," she said through gritted teeth.

"Then we won't be good."

Figured. "So…what? You expect me to bake you another one?"

"Yes, ma'am, I surely do."

"Are you going to ask me a thousand questions about

how I did what I allegedly did, or why I did what I allegedly did?"

"Do I look like a guy who cares about how and why?"

No. No, he didn't. He looked like a guy who didn't care about much of anything—except pleasure. "Okay. All right." Anything to (1) continue to keep him away from her camp, (2) speed up their parting and (3) appease him so the matter stayed between the two of them. But he was in for an unpleasant surprise. Her mother hadn't given her the title of Worst Chef in History for nothing. "You win."

Head high, she marched past him. He didn't lag behind for long, was soon keeping pace beside her, his hand light on her lower back. The action was meant to ensure she stayed the course, but the heat of him pricked at her, made her itch for…something.

"You do know baking a pie takes several hours, right?" At least, it had for her mother. "Are you going to trust me in the kitchen, alone, while you and Tawny conclude *your* business?"

"Tawny will have to wait. In a contest between sex and pie, sex will lose every time."

"Wow," she said, rolling her eyes. "No wonder panties drop in your presence. Your words are poetry."

"Are you trying to tell me your panties have already dropped?"

She peered up at him, incredulous, then stunned. Waning sunlight hit him just right, stroking him with muted golden rays, making him almost inhumanly beautiful. Definitely otherworldly. The ache returned to her chest.

"The day my panties drop for you," she said without

any sharpness, "is the day I want to be taken behind one of the sheds and shot."

"Because you'll know you'll never have me again and you won't be able to live with the pain?"

She snorted, oddly charmed by his warped sense of humor.

No. Not oddly. He knew what he was doing.

"Yeah," she said drily. "Something like that."

Mirth glittered in those golden eyes, the corners of his mouth twitching. "Very well. I promise to make it as quick and painless as possible."

How kind. "Let's backtrack. Earlier you looked at me as if you knew me. You also hinted you'd searched for me. Why?"

His amusement drained in a snap. "Perhaps you're mistaking shock for familiarity."

She wasn't the greatest at reading people, but she wasn't the worst, either. "The two aren't even close to similar."

"You find the thought of meeting me and forgetting me more plausible?"

Well. That was certainly a good point, wasn't it?

As they passed the line of trees, Tawny came into view. The girl waited on the porch, her hands braced on the railing where the initials *H.G.* were carved, her upper arms pushing her breasts together. As if she really needed the help. She was short and curvy, a real live pinup compared to Harlow's too-slender frame.

Eyes of the coldest steel narrowed, and Tawny hissed like a rattler about to strike. "I was hoping I'd had a waking nightmare." A gust of wind lifted strands of her punk-rock hair as she flew down the steps to meet them at the railing. "But nope. Here you are. A demon in the flesh."

Harlow remained silent. The formerly overweight Tawny had once been a victim of her cruelty, so Harlow accepted the insult as her due.

Looking back, she knew there was no excusing the hateful things she'd said to *anyone*. A bullying dad? A desire to feel better about herself? Please.

At least she'd gotten hers in the end.

Out of habit, she rubbed the scars on her torso, proof she'd gone from bully to victim in a blink.

Beck wrapped an arm around her waist, the contact electric, jolting her from her thoughts. Tawny noticed and cursed.

Harlow stepped away from the playboy. When it came to repaying the sins of her youth, she couldn't give Tawny much, but she could give her an open playing field for the affections of the town he-slut.

Problem. Beck refused to let her go, putting his delicious muscles to good use to hold her steady. The connection unnerved her, an instant, undeniable and almost unbearable high.

Get it together, Glass.

"If you know what's good for you," Tawny said to Beck, "you'll cut out her viper tongue and leave her on the side of the road to bleed to death."

Ouch.

"Maybe later," he said. "Right now, she and I have some business to discuss."

At the top of the steps, he paused to wrap his other arm around Tawny. The blonde gave another hiss, clearly not wanting to be linked with Harlow, even through association.

Very well. At the door, Harlow wrenched away from him under the pretext of tying her sandal that had no laces.

Beck, who was proving stubborn to his core, simply stopped and waited for her to rise, then once again pulled her close to herd her into the kitchen.

"Stay," he told her with a pointed glare. "If you run, I'll catch you and you won't like what happens next."

Her heart skipped a beat. "Is that a threat?"

"Honey, it's a promise. I'll be on the phone with Sheriff Lintz so fast your head will spin."

Sheriff Lintz, who had every reason to hate her. In tenth grade, she'd publicly dumped his son, and none too nicely. "I'll stay," Harlow vowed.

As he dragged a protesting Tawny down the hall, Harlow picked up the muffled sounds of their conversation—her whining, him placating—until she more clearly heard him say the words "Wait here."

A door closed. Footsteps echoed. He rounded the corner, reentering the kitchen, then stopping to lean against the marble, his hands flattening on the surface. His gaze locked on Harlow, hot enough to burn.

She licked her suddenly dry lips.

"Now then," he said. "This is the part where I don't have to ask you a thousand questions about how and why—because you're just going to tell me. Or else."

CHAPTER TWO

BECK WOULD RATHER make a jump rope from his small intestines than accept a change. Change sucked. Even moving to Strawberry Valley, Oklahoma, a few months ago had been a special kind of mental and emotional torture for him, and only at the urging of the friends he loved like brothers had he managed it.

He was still adjusting. In the city, he could go to the grocery store or bank without being hassled. Here, everyone stopped him to ask for a favor, or advice, or simply to inquire about what he was doing, as if they had a right to know.

Though Miss Harlow Glass had no idea, she'd already changed his life in more ways than one, and it had nothing to do with her visit today.

"I told you I wouldn't admit to anything." She shifted from one sandaled foot to the other. "I meant it."

He admired her refusal to buckle under the pressure of his narrowed gaze. But every word she uttered was a stroke of sin and heartbreak, and he wasn't quite prepared for the instant, intense effect she had on him.

"I don't care what you told me, honey. You don't make the rules. I do."

"Rules were made to be broken?"

"Were they? You don't sound very sure."

She raised her chin, a pose he recognized.

He knew her, this black-haired beauty with features so feminine, so delicate, his deepest masculine instincts pawed at their cage, ready to be unleashed. She'd invaded his dreams for weeks.

When he, Jase and West had first moved into the Glass house—as everyone in town still called it—Beck had found an old box of photos left behind by the previous owner. In them, a girl ranged in age from infant to adult, every image fascinating him. As a child, Harlow Glass had been sad, haunted and haunting. She'd kept her chin down and her shoulders tucked in, a position he'd adopted far too many times at the same age. An involuntary way of making himself a smaller target.

As she'd grown into a teenager, the sadness had faded, overshadowed by calculated sharpness. A loss of innocence. As she'd blossomed into a woman, her eyes—the most beautiful ocean blue—had projected guilt, sorrow and pain. Emotions reflected back at him every time he looked into a mirror.

A sense of possessiveness had taken up residence inside him, and he'd kept the photos a secret. Not exactly a surprise. A former foster kid, he'd had his toys and clothes taken every six to eight months, causing him to develop a keen distaste for sharing.

In a way, this girl was his.

He'd watched her life unfold. He'd wondered about her, constantly playing host to curiosity and obsession, even scouring the town for her. Now here she was, a gift from heaven dropped straight into his lap, more luscious than he'd imagined.

"I hold your fate in my hands. You might want to give sugar, spice and everything nice a try, honey."

Peeking at him through the thick shield of her lashes,

so beautiful it almost hurt to look at her, she nibbled on her plump bottom lip. "Are you going to call Sheriff Lintz?"

Beck crossed his arms over his chest, pretending he needed a minute to think things over, letting her fret. He didn't like the thought of this girl in trouble with the law. And yeah, okay, he doubted Harlow would receive more than a slap on the wrist, maybe a little community service for what she'd done, but the stain on her record would follow her for the rest of her life.

"No," he finally said, making sure to grumble. "I'm not calling the sheriff."

Relief danced through her eyes, reminding him of cottonwood in the wind. "How do I know you're telling the truth?"

"Honey, I'm sure I'm being as honest with you as you've been with me." Let her stew on *that*. "I only want answers from you, not a pound of flesh."

He might be a "cold, unfeeling bastard," as some of the women he'd slept with had called him when he'd stuck to his word and refused to commit the morning after a one-night stand, but he wasn't heartless. Harlow used to live in this home, and the foreclosure obviously hadn't changed her sense of ownership. It wouldn't have changed his, either. He'd been here only a few months, but he'd have to be pried out with a crane. The fifty-plus acres boasted pecan, cherry and sand plum trees, as well as wild strawberries, blackberry and blueberry patches. Everything Brook Lynn, Jase's fiancée, needed for her pies.

There was a pool he and his friends had restored, two ponds, one loaded with crappie and bass, and a shed/safe house now fully equipped with weapons and food just in case the zombie apocalypse kicked off. Something Brook Lynn actually feared.

Also, there was the whole theft thing. Harlow didn't strike him as the law-breaking type. Considering everyone in town hated her and no one would give her a job, she had to be broke and starved.

The thought drove him to the fridge, where he slapped together the ingredients for a turkey sandwich.

"Here," he said.

"No, no. I couldn't." She backed away, though her gaze remained on the food, longing darkening in her eyes.

"You can steal my pie, but can't accept my sandwich?"

"Allegedly stole. And maybe I learned a lesson about the perils of taking from others."

"Maybe I don't want to eat alone." Though he'd had dinner with Tawny, he made a second sandwich. "Did you ever think of that?"

"Oh! In that case." Harlow nabbed the offering so fast she probably had whiplash. At first, she tried to eat daintily, a nibble here and there, but she soon gave up the pretense and ripped into the bread with a savagery that broke his damn heart.

Why had she stuck around Strawberry Valley so long? True, the rolling hills and colorful Main Street could have come straight out of a Thomas Kinkade portrait, and the public barbecues, block parties, swim parties, festivals and celebrations for everything from a kid's orthodontic work to a teenager's first date were charming enough to seduce even someone like Beck. But Harlow couldn't support herself here, so why hadn't she moved to the city and started fresh?

Roots? Something he was only just beginning to understand.

As a young kid he'd lost his mother to cancer and, soon afterward, his father to plain ole selfishness. Daddy Dearest had dropped him off with an aunt and just never come back. After Aunt Millie got tired of him, she'd passed him on to *another* family member. Rinse and repeat five times over until there was no one left, the entire lot refusing to take him in permanently. He'd become a ward of the state, shuffled from one foster home to another. While some had been nice, others had been bona fide hellholes.

The back door opened, hinges creaking. Jase Hollister stepped into the kitchen with Brook Lynn in tow, the two pink-cheeked and breathless.

"Hey, man." Jase bumped fists with Beck.

"Hey."

Jase and West had been stuck in the system with him, and they'd understood him in a way he hadn't understood himself. They'd bonded at meeting one, and they'd become each other's only family, sticking together through good times and bad. He loved them. Hell, he would die for them.

Brook Lynn noticed Harlow and frowned. "What's *she* doing here?"

Harlow must have endured her limit of insults for the day, because she flipped her hair over her shoulder and said, "Beck saw me and chased me down. He *insisted* I spend private time with him here at the house."

He rubbed his fingers over his mouth to hide his grin. "This is true."

"Beck." Brook Lynn radiated concern. "You don't

know her or the evil she's capable of. Don't sleep with her, please. She's—"

Jase spoke over his girl, saying, "This is where we part ways," as he dragged her away.

The past few months had softened him, the man many would call "a hardened criminal." For once, Beck had to admit a change had been for the best.

After Jase's nine-year prison stint, he'd needed a fresh start in a new place. He'd picked Strawberry Valley, enamored by the wide-open spaces and community support.

Moving with him had been a no-brainer for Beck, despite the challenges. Being without his friend for so long had been bad enough, but he and West owed Jase more than they could ever repay. And really, that debt was the reason Beck had never complained when Jase renovated the ramshackle farmhouse. The reason he grinned as his surroundings were altered bit by bit.

"I should be going," Harlow announced.

Beck focused on her. "Nice try, honey, but we still have unfinished business. How did you get inside the house?" He hadn't seen a single sign of forced entry. Not that he'd been paying much attention before or after he'd chased her down.

"Well…I kind of have a key." She plucked at an invisible piece of lint on her shirt, adding, "Is now a bad time to mention I don't like the repairs you've made on the house?"

"You do not have a key. Jase changed the locks our first day here." The guy was distrustful of strangers. They all were. They'd learned to be.

"Well…he may or may not have left the new keys on the porch while he ran to the backyard to get his tools."

And she'd just happened to be nearby, watching? And none of them had noticed? "As of tomorrow, your key won't work."

A flash of fury in her ocean-blues, quickly extinguished by defeat. She put her chin down and hunched her shoulders, the same pose she'd struck in so many of the pictures. "Yeah. I figured."

Damn it. His chest began to ache. How many knocks had this girl taken in her young life?

And why did he even care? Yes, her pictures had intrigued him. Yes, she was hot as hell. But devoting so much time and energy to one woman wasn't his MO.

"If you were hungry, why didn't you come to the door and *ask* us for food?"

She went ramrod straight. "I didn't—I don't—need your help."

Ah. Pride. The downfall of so many. He'd once tried to convince himself he didn't need anyone, either, that he was fine on his own. Meanwhile, anytime he'd spotted a happy family, he'd felt as though he were being run over by a car.

"You did—you do—need my help, or you wouldn't be here." As she glared at him, he added, "How'd you lose the house, anyway?"

"That's none of your business," she stated flatly.

"You blew through your mother's insurance money. Got it." The day of the purchase, the broker had prattled on about the Glass bully losing her mom earlier in the year and refusing to lower herself by getting a job. Beck had only half listened at the time and had regretted it with every fiber of his being since finding the box of photos. Now he tried to dredge up any other information he might have heard without any luck. "What are you, Harlow Glass?"

Her lips pursed, drawing his gaze and holding it hostage. Those lips were better than the pictures had promised. Plump and red, the kind every man fantasized about devouring…and being devoured by. She shifted from foot to foot, more nervous now than when she'd first arrived.

"What do you mean? What am I? What kind of question is that?"

"The legit kind. What do you do for a living? Are you a life coach? Accountant? Underwear model?" He looked her over, careful to avoid the dangerous beauty of her face—but the rest of her proved just as detrimental to his mental health. "Femme fatale?"

"I'm not a heartbreaker, that's for sure. Not like some people I've recently met."

"Meaning me?"

"Yes, you," she said with a nod. "Who else? You've never dated the same woman twice. Not since you've been here, at least."

Or ever. "So?" Yes, he slept around. But why not? Sex felt good and for a few hours, he could drown himself in pleasure. No thoughts. No problems. No worries. His version of therapy.

"So. I wasn't finished. You've got a woman in your bedroom right this second, but you're still out here—" she waved her arm around the kitchen "—flirting with me."

"This isn't flirting, sweetheart. This is an interrogation."

"Ha! An interrogation implies I'm being threatened,

but the only part of me currently in any danger is my mouth. You're staring."

Was he? "Am I scaring you…or exciting you?"

Her eyes widened. "N-neither."

A stutter. Adorable. "Let's find out how you react to actual flirting." He prowled his way around the counter.

She stepped back, once, twice, and would have again but the stove stopped her retreat. A sense of triumph overtook him as he placed his hands at her sides, caging her. He leaned in and brushed the tip of his nose against hers, the heady scent of strawberries and pecans teasing him. "If every guy you've ever met hasn't looked at your lips with animal hunger," he said, his voice low and husky with need he couldn't hide, "I'd be shocked."

She traced her fingertips over the lips in question, the action so inherently sensual, so damned innocent, he would have given anything to corrupt… To steal a taste.

Tit for tat, one dessert for another.

"Prepare to be shocked," she whispered.

"Foolish men." Up close, he could see little details the pictures had missed. The curl in her midnight lashes. The smattering of freckles on her nose. The rose-colored flush under her cheeks. "But let's get to the heart of the matter, honey. You owe me, and not just for the food. For the mental anguish I've suffered."

"Mental anguish," she echoed.

"That's right." He leaned forward the barest inch, drawn by a force he could not control, and his chest brushed against hers.

She inhaled sharply, exhaled fast and shallow, an instinctive action born of awareness, and just like that, he was as rigid as steel.

"A part of me died with that pie," he said, caressing the side of his nose against hers.

"Died." Another echo.

"Mmm." His lips hovered just short of kissing hers, their breaths intermingling, and damn. How was *not* touching this woman more carnal than getting another naked? "I asked what you are because I need to know how I can devise a sufficient payment. Do you know how painful it is to crave something with every fiber of your being? To want it more than you want water to drink?"

"I do." She melted into him, all her softness fusing to his aching hardness. "I really, really do."

How close was she to surrender?

He cut back a curse. The answer didn't matter. It couldn't matter. She wasn't here for sex, and what she'd said before was true. Another woman waited in his bedroom. While he had the morals of an alley cat, he refused to make out with one female while another waited in his bed. It was a line he never wanted to cross.

Back on track. "That's how badly I want…the pie."

Horrified realization dawned, and she pushed him away. A puny action, but he willingly stepped back.

"Thanks for the taste of your flirting," she said with a sneer, "but as you can see, it left a foul taste in my mouth."

No. She'd gotten lost in the moment. Hell, *he'd* gotten lost in the moment.

She opened her mouth, closed it. "Look. I'm sorry I stole your pie. Okay? I guess… Well, I was resentful. You're living in my house, where I'm supposed to be, and I just… I'm sorry. I won't do it again."

"I accept your apology."

"Great. I guess I'll be going now." She attempted to circle him, but he stretched out an arm, stopping her.

"You'll find all the ingredients in the fridge and pantry, and the dishes in the cabinets beside the sink."

She sputtered for a moment. "Forgiveness shouldn't come with strings."

"I'm giving you a chance to put words into action, to prove you mean what you say and help ease the pain of my loss."

"Fine." She pinched the bridge of her nose. "I'll bake for you."

Sexiest. Phrase. Ever. "You can start with a pie and finish with a cake, a dozen cookies and cupcakes."

"Wow, that's quite a bit of interest."

"Did I mention I'm feeling quite a bit of pain?"

She glared daggers at him. "I hope you like your pies, cakes, cookies and cupcakes with char. I've never baked a dessert I haven't burned."

"You can't be that bad."

"Want to bet?" Her hips swayed seductively as she ambled to the far side of the kitchen and pointed to a smear of black on the fan over the oven, the one thing Jase had yet to replace. "What has two thumbs and ruins everything she touches?" She hiked her thumbs at her chest. "This girl."

Well, hell. "Forget baking. What do you suggest you do to balance the scales?"

She twirled a strand of her hair and said, "I can... I don't know... Garden? I couldn't help but notice the disgraceful appearance of the roses."

"Neither could we. When we moved in." For weeks the guys had bugged him to hire a landscaper, a task he was responsible for rather than Jase because he expected everything from mowing to weed pulling to be done a certain way—his way—or done again. But he'd put off the hire, not wanting to deal with the chaos of yet another new person in his life.

But…as Harlow tended the overgrown rosebushes out back, he could stealthily question her about her past, assuage his curiosity about her and finally move on. Moving on was familiar. He liked familiar.

"All right," he said, punctuating the words with a nod. "You can start tomorrow morning. Unless you have a job I don't know about?"

"I don't. I'll be here bright and early."

His suspicious nature came out swinging. "How do you pay rent? For that matter, *where* do you rent?"

A flash of panic, quickly gone. "Look. It's late. I'm exhausted." She peered longingly at the exit. "I need to leave. Okay?"

Not okay. Alarm bells clanged inside his head. "Where are you living, Harlow?"

"Well, you see, when I said I didn't have a job, I meant I didn't have a job I was proud of." She laughed almost manically. "I'm, uh, well… I'm a stripper. Yep, that's right. I take off my clothes and dance on a pole for a living, and I make lots of money. Tons of money. *So much.* I have the most amazing apartment. In the city. Right by the strip club. Where I work."

"What's the name of the strip club?"

"Boobie Bungalow," she offered without missing a beat, more confident in her story now.

He nearly choked on his tongue. Liar, Liar.

"What?" She glowered at him. "It's very exclusive."

"I should know. I'm a very exclusive man, and I've been there."

"You have?" she squeaked.

"I have." Clients sometimes preferred to do business while doling out singles. "I don't remember seeing you, and you're not the kind of woman I'd forget."

"Well, uh, I just started."

He offered his most innocent grin before going in for the kill. "I have an idea. Why don't we work off your debt another way? You come over tomorrow, as planned, but rather than gardening, you'll give me a lap dance."

The color drained from her cheeks as she pulled at the collar of her shirt. "No. I've got my heart set on gardening."

"You're sure? I can score you afterward, give you pointers on how to do a better job next time."

"Very sure."

He released an exaggerated sigh. "All right. But if you change your mind—"

"I won't."

"But if you do, my answer is yes." He escorted her to the front door. "Until tomorrow, Harlow Glass."

She gulped. "Until tomorrow, Beck Ockley."

As she raced onto the porch, he noticed there were no cars in the driveway and called, "How are you getting home, honey?"

She stopped, but kept her back to him. "Just because you can't see an adorable little Camaro down the street doesn't mean it's not there, does it?" She raced off then, as quick as her feet would carry her.

Something was off. He had to curb the urge to go after her as he shut the door. Holding a woman against her will would only cause problems, and not just the

moral variety. He and his friends could not afford another run-in with the law.

Jase had paid dearly for the last one.

Ten years ago, West's girlfriend had been assaulted
at a frat party. Tessa's tearful confession had sparked
an unstoppable rage in all three of them. Jase and Beck
had loved her like a sister.

Together, they'd hunted down the bastard responsible and beat him into blood and pulp. They should
have walked away, let him heal and the system punish
him for his crime, but they hadn't been the most emotionally stable guys at the best of times and they'd continued whaling.

Thoughts that seemed to have no bearing on the situation had bombarded Beck. Thoughts of the foster mom
who'd introduced him to sex at the age of fourteen. He'd
remembered how every illicit touch had filled him with
guilt and shame, but had also made him feel good, even
special. How he'd told himself time and time again that
pleasing her would earn her love; she would keep him,
and they would be a family. And later, when she'd let
him move on to the next house with a smile and a wave
goodbye, how he'd cried. As he'd punched and kicked
Tessa's assailant, he'd poured his frustration, betrayal
and anger with his own past into every blow.

The rapist—Pax Gillis—had died on the blood-
soaked ground.

Beck had never forgotten his name, had never quite
shaken the tide of remorse.

He should have paid a terrible price for helping end
someone's life—even if the life belonged to scum. But
he and West had been spared, Jase taking the fall on
his own, wanting his friends to have a chance to pursue

their dreams, demanding they stay quiet. Because they operated by a single rule—what one demands, the others do, no questions asked—they'd acquiesced, but over the years their guilt and remorse had only deepened.

Beck should have come forward at some point, if only to try to reduce Jase's sentence. A dime to a nickel, maybe. Finally doing something good with his life. Under his watch, Tessa had ended up dying in a car crash after a fight with West, and West had ended up high on coke, losing his scholarship to MIT.

Beck wasn't even the one who'd helped West get clean. The guy had done it all on his own, going on to create a computer program Beck, a born salesman, was able to unload for millions, allowing them to split the shares three ways, investing Jase's portion for him to enjoy upon his release from prison.

And damn, Beck needed a beer. No, he needed a distraction from his troubles. Thankfully one waited in his bedroom.

He stalked down the hall, opened the door. Feminine clothing littered his floor, leading to the bed…where Tawny reclined, naked and ready.

"I've missed you." She ran a fingertip between the heavy weight of her breasts. "Tell me you got rid of the wicked witch of the Southwest, and I'll do bad, bad things to you."

"She isn't a witch, and we're not going to talk about her." He kicked the door shut. "But you are still going to do those bad, bad things."

CHAPTER THREE

HARLOW LOOKED FROM her bleeding hands to the mangled remains of the bush she'd just "pruned" and whimpered. For three hours she'd worked harder than she'd ever worked in her life, baking under the death glare of an angry summer sun, and *this* was the result?

Hardly seemed fair.

"Thirsty?"

The woman's voice cut through Harlow's pity party, and she glanced up to find the blonde and very beautiful Brook Lynn Dillon standing before her, so happy with life she actually glowed. Envy clawed at Harlow, but she paid it no heed. Brook Lynn was worthy of her happiness.

For years she and her big, golden heart had chased after her party-girl sister, Jessie Kay, while working two full-time jobs just to pay rent—and she'd done it all while dealing with an inner ear disorder. Harlow wasn't sure what the disorder was called; she only knew the devices in the girl's ears prevented her from hearing whispers as loudly as screams.

While Harlow had never turned her evil sights on Brook Lynn—even a bully of her magnitude had lines she wouldn't cross—Jessie Kay and Kenna Starr, the sisters' best friend, had not been so lucky.

"Are you offering arsenic or bleach?" Harlow quipped.

"I didn't ask if you wanted what everyone in town would like to serve you," Brook Lynn said staunchly, making Harlow flinch. "I asked if you were thirsty."

"I am," she said, standing. "Thank you."

As an old, ugly dog playfully nipped at Brook Lynn's heels, she held out a glass of ice-cold water.

Harlow tried for ladylike, taking a dainty sip, but the taste of heaven snapped the tether to her control and she chugged the rest, draining every drop. No liquid had ever been cooler or more soothing, wetting her tongue and moistening her dry-as-the-desert throat.

"Thank you," she repeated, feeling human again.

Brook Lynn confiscated the glass. "Actually, you shouldn't thank me. You should thank Beck."

His name alone caused her heartbeat to pick up speed and knock against her ribs. She'd stared at the back door for hours, willing him to come outside and check on her. Surely she'd built up the intoxicating effects he'd had on her.

"Is he here?" Was he still in bed with Tawny? Her hands curled into tight little fists.

"No," Brook Lynn said. "He was called in for a meeting, but he told me to take care of you while he was gone."

A contented thrill—followed by an irritating realization. He hadn't cared enough to see her? Wow. Well, screw him. He disturbed her, rendering her breathless and shaky with a simple glance, but so what? Physical attraction never lasted. And neither did he! One and done, the king of the one-night stand.

Harlow had no interest in being used and tossed

aside, nothing but an afterthought to the man she'd welcomed into her body. She wanted affection and love, the kind she'd read about in books and seen in movies. The kind where couples fought to stay together, even during the worst of times. The kind that protected. Defended. Cherished.

A pang of longing razed her. There'd be no name-calling. No shaming. No being made to feel worthless.

Before dropping out of high school in favor of being homeschooled, she'd had boyfriends. A *lot* of boyfriends. She'd dated and dumped them at Beck-speed, searching for someone, anyone, to fill the void inside her. A void somehow made bigger when a machine exploded at Dairyland, the milk plant just south of town, killing half the workforce—including her dad.

As horrible as he'd been, she should have rejoiced, right? All of her problems should have vanished in a puff of smoke. But that couldn't have been further from reality.

Brook Lynn turned and, without uttering another word, walked away, the dog prancing behind her.

"Brook Lynn," she called, and the girl stopped without spinning around. "I'm sorry for the way I acted. In the past, I mean…and recently." RIP, blueberry pie.

"That's great, I'm glad" was the response, "but actions mean more than words, and so far you've proved nothing."

"I know. But I'm still here, subjecting myself to this, so that I *can* prove I've changed."

"Please. This, as you call it, is payment." Brook Lynn glanced over her shoulder, looking very much like an avenging angel. "But I wonder. Are you ruining the garden on purpose? A way to strike at Beck for…what?

What supposed crime did he commit against you? The same crime as the rest of us? Simply existing?"

Her chin fell and her shoulders drew inward. *I deserve this. I really do.* "He didn't do anything wrong. He's wonderful." And he was. As a boss, or whatever he happened to be to her—debt holder?—he totally rocked. He wasn't hovering but allowing her to do her own thing, and knowing he wouldn't be here, he'd taken steps to ensure she had everything she needed.

But Beck, the guy? Him, she wasn't so sure about. There was the one-and-done thing, of course, but also the fact that he'd bought Harlow's ancestral home even though she hadn't sold it. The bank had forced her off the property, voiding her claim to it, all because her mother had taken out a small loan a few years before, using the house as collateral. When her mother died, Harlow had tried to get a job.

She'd visited every business in town and asked to paint murals on store windows, or to do portraits of family members. Even to paint houses. When those requests were denied, she'd applied for basically any position available—trash collector, bird-poop cleaner, bunion scraper—but everyone had turned her away. Most had laughed. Moving to the city would have been wise. No one knew the old Harlow, and someone, surely, would hire her *somewhere* to do *something*. But her heart beat for Strawberry Valley. Her mother had grown up here. *She'd* grown up here. She trusted the townsfolk not to hurt her, despite their hatred of her, which was far more than she could say for a city full of strangers.

Plus, she had a five-step plan. Up first? Proving she wasn't the incarnation of evil. So far no luck, but as she'd learned, circumstances could change in a blink.

"I don't know how to garden," she admitted, "but I'm trying."

One of the blonde's brows winged up, her expression total disbelief. "Well, then, I guess you should try harder."

"Angel?" A husky male voice drifted across the daylight, followed by squeaking hinges as the back door opened.

Brook Lynn skipped over to greet her fiancé, Jase. He nodded at Harlow, his green eyes shrewd and curious, before he focused on Brook Lynn.

"I missed you," he said, uncaring that Harlow could hear. He brushed his fingers through the girl's pale hair.

"I was only gone a few minutes," Brook Lynn replied with an adoring smile.

"A second is too long. Maybe it's time to have that surgery we talked about and finally get you attached to my side."

Brook Lynn chuckled. "Adding an extra two hundred and fifty pounds to this body will make it harder for me to kick zombie butt."

"I'll protect you."

"Actually, I'm pretty sure you'll be one of the first to be bitten."

He nipped her lips. "Fine. Let me show you what I'll do to you when I'm turned into a zombie."

The two lovebirds reminded Harlow of *Beauty and the Beast*. Romance at its best. Jase was a big man, tall and muscled, his dark hair styled in bad-boy spikes. Rumors claimed Brook Lynn had mentioned liking the style, and boom, the next day he'd changed his. He had tattoos running from the base of his neck to the waist of his pants. Maybe other places, too. Harlow had only glimpsed him shirtless as he worked on the outside of the house; she'd marveled that a man like him actually existed.

Brook Lynn, on the other hand, appeared fragile and as useless as a doll, though everyone knew she was as far from a child's toy as possible. Not only had she tamed the town's new dragon—a feat in and of itself—but she'd started her own flourishing catering business.

Their love had inspired Harlow's dream of happily-ever-after, and if canvas and paints hadn't been out of her zero-dollar budget, she would have immortalized them in a portrait.

As they disappeared inside, she dusted the dirt from her hands. No more of this, she decided. Not today, at least. Not until she'd done a little gardening research. Which meant heading into town…facing ridicule…

She rarely ventured far from her property—even before she'd been ousted from her home, but especially since. Her job search had led her into town on a few occasions, but she'd quickly learned she had to pay a hefty price for daring to go where she wasn't wanted.

Suck it up. Take your medicine like a good girl.

Head down, shoulders in, she made her way to the side of an unpaved and narrow road. It wasn't long before a car slowed down, allowing the driver to rubberneck.

The attention unnerved her, and she found herself rubbing the scars on her stomach. Sometimes she thought she could still feel the flames licking all the way from her navel to her collarbone, using her shirt as kindling.

But she wasn't going to think about the worst day of her life. Distraction wasn't her friend any more than the next driver who passed her, rolling down his window and leaning out to snicker at her. She quickened her step, breathing a sigh of relief when the vehicle finally disappeared beyond the hill.

The third car to come along actually pulled up alongside her, keeping pace.

"Harlow Glass," the driver said with a sneer.

She suppressed a moan. Scott Cameron. In high school, he'd been Popular Jock Boy and one of the first to receive the infamous "Glass Pass." Her special brand of cruel dismissal postdating. It had been especially cruel in Scott's case because he'd dropped his longtime girlfriend to be with her, yet Harlow had dumped him the day after their first date.

Yes, she'd been *that* girl.

Someone must have called and told him she'd been spotted in the wild. "Gotta say, Glass. You're not looking so good."

Truer words had never been spoken. She was sunburned, sweaty and wearing as much dirt as clothing. "Well, I can't say the same to you." Under the brim of his hat, his golden hair looked perfectly coiffed. His white shirt was crisp, without wrinkles, and his skin tanned to a glimmering bronze. "You look great."

His eyes narrowed, making her think he'd heard sarcasm in her voice even though there'd been none.

She sighed. "And yes, I've been better."

"You headed to town?"

She nodded as she kept trudging forward. "I am."

"That's about four miles away."

"Yes."

"About an hour's walk in the intense summer heat."

"Yes," she said again. The reminders were unnecessary.

"Bet you'd like a ride."

As a matter of fact—

"Good luck finding one." Laughing with glee, he put the pedal to the metal and blazed forward, flinging dirt and gravel at her.

Coughing, she waved a hand in front of her face. *Can't complain. Just another dose of medicine.*

She hit Fragaria Street by late afternoon, fatigue threatening to turn her limbs into jelly. This time of year, the scent of strawberries always coated the air, wafting from hundreds of acres of wild patches.

A handful of cars motored by, and multiple people meandered along the sidewalks. The buildings around her were different colors, from blue to yellow to red, and different sizes. Some were tall, some short. Some were wide, some thin. Some were made of brick and others of wood. A true hodgepodge of design, and she loved every inch of it.

Virgil Porter and Anthony Rodriguez each sat in a rocker, playing checkers in front of Style Me Tender, Mr. Rodriguez's salon. Harlow stuck to the shadows and most people never noticed her, which she preferred, but as usual, those two managed to spot her right away.

"How you doing, Miss Glass?" Mr. Porter called. He owned Swat Team 8—"We assassinate fleas, ticks, silverfish, cockroaches, bees, ants, mice and rats"—and he was one of the few people who actually seemed to care about her well-being, but she had to be mistaken. Back in her heyday, she'd called his son terrible names.

"I'm well, thank you," she muttered, discouraging further questions. Lying always made her feel guilty, but the truth was never palatable. *Well, you see, Mr. Porter, I'm homeless, I've been found out as a thief on my own property, and I'm currently unemployed. How about you? Still having trouble with your liver spots?*

"I'm willing to listen if you'd like to rephrase your answer, Miss Glass. We can talk over a nice glass of sweet tea." He shook the one in his hand, ice rattling. "Maybe we can even eat the strawberry scones Brook Lynn brought me."

Her mouth watered, her stomach twisting with painful hunger, but she forced herself to say, "No, thank you." The sooner she got out of the town square, the sooner her spirits would rally.

"Harlow?"

The familiar male voice came from across the street. As she turned, her nervous system nearly blew a gasket—there he was, Beck Ockley. And, oh, it so wasn't fair. He looked good enough to eat. The gold streaks in his hair gleamed brighter in the sunlight, and his flawless sunkissed skin somehow appeared painted on by a master artist. Did he even have pores? He'd rolled up the sleeves of his white button-up, revealing muscled forearms with a slight dusting of hair.

"Uh, hi," she said, offering the lamest wave.

He grinned at her, both wicked and virtuous, stealing her breath.

Lincoln West stood beside him, slightly taller but just as well muscled—just as gorgeous—with the smoldering intensity of a man on death row, whose last meal would be the females he trapped in his sights. Not that he'd ever made good on the silent promise. Unlike Beck, he practiced restraint, not going on a single date since coming to town.

The two were with an unfamliar man and woman dressed in business-formal clothes. Both were attractive, and though the male looked to be in his late thirties, the woman, an elegant redhead, looked to be in her late twenties. Roughly the same age as Harlow and yet a thousand times more successful.

Talk about a knife through the heart.

Was Lady Successful a new conquest of Beck's? Or a soon-to-be conquest? Did she know he'd move on in the morning?

Beck muttered something to the group, and Harlow took off. No reason to stick around, and every reason not to. But he shocked her by racing across the street and keeping pace beside her.

"I'm surprised to see you out and about," he said.

Oh, his voice! She'd forgotten how deep and husky it could get, every word he uttered a promise.

Gaze drawn to him by a force she couldn't control, she looked up. He was peering at her, too, and between one moment and the next, the air charged with electricity. Whispers of sensation brushed over her skin, leaving goose bumps behind.

"Expected me to still be slaving away in your garden?" she managed.

"Something like that." Heavy-lidded eyes swept over her, powerful, sensual…almost possessive. "Are you headed into the city for your shift at the Boobie Bungalow?"

Her cheeks burned as she remembered the story she'd told him. It wasn't a lie if she believed it, right? As a lover of romance novels, she'd often fantasized about being a woman down on her luck—could be a stripper, why not—rescued by the prince of some distant land.

"Maybe I've got the week off. Maybe the other girls lose money when I'm there, and I thought I'd give them a chance to make rent."

"How kind of you." The corners of his mouth curled up, his amusement as seductive as the rest of him. "Where are you headed, sweetheart?"

Sweetheart. Her heart skipped a treacherous beat, her blood heating dangerously, making her sweat, and dang it, she hated herself for reacting so strongly to something that meant absolutely nothing to him. He called every woman he met by an endearment. Which irritated her because… Just because.

He needed a spoonful of his own medicine, the way she was often forced to taste hers.

"I'm going to the library, sugar tush. Why?"

"That's my question." He flattened his palm between her shoulder blades, sliding it down the ridges of her spine, stopping just above the curve of her bottom. The touch was innocent, nothing overtly sexual to it, and yet it frazzled her nerves. "Why are you going to the library?"

As she opened her mouth to respond—what she would say, she didn't know—Tim Whatson sidled up to Beck's other side.

"Hey, man. Can we talk?"

Beck stiffened before fisting the hem of Harlow's shirt, forcing her to stop with him. The backs of his knuckles brushed against her, skin to heated skin, and tendrils of something hot and dark shot through her.

Need more. Now.

"Hey," he said to Tim, whom he obviously knew. Was he oblivious to the cravings he'd just stirred inside her? "How's it going?"

"Not so good. I need your help. My girlfriend is tee-icked. I forgot our three-month anniversary, and she's threatening to leave me. What should I do?"

Beck, the new Dear Abby? "You should give her a thoughtful, personal gift. There's nothing more thoughtful or personal than a portrait, and I happen to have an opening in my schedule. I could—"

"What do you think, Beck?" Tim said, interrupting her.

"Give her a thoughtful, personal gift," Beck replied. "There's nothing more thoughtful or personal than a portrait."

Tim nodded as if he'd just received the answer to every prayer, and Beck released her to gently push her forward.

"Now," he said. "Where were we?"

Your skin against mine... "Uh, I was telling you how I ruined your rosebushes this morning—by accident!— and how I'm headed to the library to learn how to fix them. You were in the process of forgiving me."

"Hold up a sec." He darted in front of her.

Unprepared, she slammed into his powerful chest and ricocheted backward. His arms wrapped around her to cage her and hold her steady.

"Whoa. I've got you."

Her every pulse point suddenly leaped, and as she peered up at him, the rest of the world vanished, every second revolving around Beck alone. Her chest pressed against his, her breath coming faster and shallower, as if the air between them had somehow thickened.

"You okay?" he asked, the gleam in his eyes anything but concerned. Instead, the hot and dark thing she'd felt earlier was now reflected back to her.

"No. I mean yes. Maybe. I don't know."

His hand swept up, up, his fingers soon toying with the hairs at her nape, tickling. "I think you mean *yes, Beck, you make everything better.*"

She shivered and grabbed a handful of his shirt. The hard line of his body shifted subtly but definitely, ensuring he consumed what remained of her personal space. He stared at her lips…

Did he desire her?

She wanted him to desire her.

No. No. He wasn't the man for her, wasn't steady or reliable. Fortifying her resolve, she stepped away from him, and in an instant, the world crashed back into focus. She sucked in a mouthful of strawberry-scented air, only then realizing she'd been breathing in the man's heady musk—a musk that had clearly drugged her.

He shook his head and frowned. "Let's backtrack. You ruined my roses?"

"Yes. So now you know my newest crime. You should return to your meeting. Don't let me keep you."

Beck, ever the ladies' man, winked at her. "Why would I want to have lunch with business associates when I can pore through dusty old books and learn how to garden with the cutest little pie stealer in town?"

Said without a crumb of resentment. Said with relish. Had he truly forgiven her? Did he actually *want* to spend time with her? Excitement bloomed—only to be dashed by disappointment. He had a knack for making every woman he met feel special, and she couldn't forget again.

"Sorry," she said, "but I work better alone."

"You only think so because you've never worked with me. Come on." He looped an arm over her shoulders and urged her forward, the contact almost too much to her touch-starved senses. The handful of women they passed peered at him with longing, then glared at Harlow, but he didn't seem to notice. "When we finish at the library, we'll grab lunch and you'll tell me all about your childhood."

"You'll be bored."

"I'll be riveted, guaranteed. You're an incredibly interesting subject, Miss Glass."

A line. Surely. Just to be contrary, she said, "Should I start with my first period?"

"See?" The low, gravelly tone had returned. He squeezed her tighter, and she just couldn't help herself; she rubbed her cheek against his shoulder. "I'm already foaming-at-the-mouth eager for the details."

"Only fair to warn you. My childhood will make you cry. And if it doesn't, you need prayer."

"That bad, huh?"

Worse. "Will you tell me about *your* childhood?"

"Does my childhood include stories about you?" he asked good-naturedly.

There he went, deflecting. "Maybe it does. For all I know, you're boy who visited Strawberry Valley every summer and spent his nights peeping inside my bedroom window."

"Hardly. I never would have been content to remain outside. I would have climbed in. And yes, you would have invited me. I would have made sure of it."

"So sure of yourself." She tsk-tsked despite her breathlessness. "I was an ice queen. I would have ignored you."

"I was a blowtorch. I would have melted you."

She snort-laughed, then sighed. *He's charming me*

too easily. "If you want to know about my childhood, fine." The thought of food was too heady to resist. "As long as I get to pick where we eat and you pay for everything." Besides the sandwich he'd given her yesterday, she'd only eaten what she'd managed to forage—two pecans the squirrels left behind.

He ran his fingers up and down her arm, saying, "You're not even going to make a token play for the check?"

Ignore the earth-shattering tingles. Ignore the delicious burn. "Are you kidding? Never!"

He chuckled, and a moment later they reached the library, a little red-and-white building in the center of town. A set of cement stairs led to French doors, and four columns held up a wraparound parapet. An American flag flew proudly at one side while the town banner flew on the other, the latter showcasing a bloom with white petals and a bright yellow center.

"Wait." A flare of panic overshadowed her good humor as Beck tried to escort her inside. She dug in her heels. "I need a moment to prepare myself."

"For what?"

For what would surely be a humiliating experience. One he would witness.

Oh, crap! She tore away from his grip. The thought of being subjected to people's ire in front of this perfect man was simply too much to bear. "I'll wait out here. You go in and get the books, okay? *Then* we'll eat."

"And do all the heavy lifting myself?" Beck shook his head. "No. We do this together."

Sweat beaded over her brow and upper lip, even dripped down her nape, which was odd since ice crystals had sprouted inside her veins. "I'm just… I'm not going in there. Okay?"

"What, you don't want to be seen with me?" He arched a brow at her. "What if I promise to make it worth your while?"

He didn't understand. A guy like him, so blessed in every area of his life, would never understand.

She backed away from him, saying, "I'm sorry, Beck, but I just remembered I'm needed at work. Private party." She turned and rushed away, never looking back.

CHAPTER FOUR

THE NEXT DAY, Beck had a meeting in Oklahoma City. He decided to use the opportunity to find a new distraction.

He'd tossed and turned all night, his mind a volcano of activity. He knew he wasn't good enough for long-term anything with anybody, but Harlow had taken it to a whole other level by refusing to be seen in public with him. She'd actually run away from him.

He wished he'd never seen the photos of her, wished he'd never spied her across the road yesterday, looking adorable with dirt streaked on her cheeks and arms, her hair so black it gleamed blue in the sunlight, her skin rosy, the smattering of freckles more evident than usual. She'd been fan-freaking-tastically adorable. A Country Girl Gone Wild fantasy he hadn't known he'd had.

Her white shirt had been so thin, so damp with perspiration, he'd seen the outline of her bra. A sensible white cotton somehow sexier than red lace just because it nestled against *her*. It hadn't helped when her nipples puckered before his eyes.

Desire for her had come swift and sharp, strong enough to make him crazy, to make him pant like a dog. His mouth had watered at the thought of tasting her, and his hands had itched to touch her. If she'd given him any encouragement at all, he would have gladly spent the rest of the day feasting on her.

But she hadn't encouraged him, and now he was glad. Harlow Glass was nothing like the women he usually pursued; she wasn't looking for a good time, and she wouldn't go quietly in the morning. She'd already expressed curiosity about his past and would have demanded stories about his childhood as soon as she'd told stories about her own.

She was a complication he didn't need, so, he'd find someone else. Easily. And he'd do it today.

The pencil in his hand snapped in half.

Dane Michaelson's newest assistant… Sarah? Samantha? Whatever. She rushed over to pick up the pieces and give him a new one. He looked her over. She was understated but pretty, with brown hair and piercing green eyes. Not that it mattered. A woman was a woman. And he could have this one. She would take him however she could get him, and for the few hours he spent between her legs, he could fool himself into believing everything was okay. No thoughts. No problems. No worries, he reminded himself. Only pleasure.

He smiled at her, and she smiled back. Good. This was good. This was familiar.

"That will be all, Sasha," Dane said. "Thank you."

She sauntered out of the office, casting Beck a final peek over her shoulder. He winked at her.

"You surprise me. Flirting? At a business meeting?" Dane sat across from him, relaxed behind an elaborate desk constructed from salvaged wood. For a billionaire oil tycoon, he was absurdly young. Twenty-eight, Beck's age. They'd known each other for…what? Close to six years now? Though they'd merely traded phone calls up until recently.

The guy had grown up in Strawberry Valley and

even though he'd moved to the big, bad city for a number of years, he'd never been able to cut ties with his hometown, even tattooing his arms with wild strawberries.

"And now you ignore me," Dane muttered. "We've been sitting in silence for a full ten minutes. You want to tell me about the new security program or not? That *is* the reason you're here, isn't it?"

"We both know you're going to buy it no matter what I say. West does quality work and you won't find a better system anywhere else."

"Can we at least pretend to negotiate?"

"No. I'd rather talk about Harlow Glass. Do you know her?" Damn it. What happened to washing his hands of her?

What the hell made her so special? Yes, he'd seen pictures of her during childhood. Yes, he had an insane need to know more about the girl she'd been and the woman she'd become. But this seeming obsession with her did not fit his character.

"Know?" Dane said. "No. Know of? Yes. She went from shy and sugar-sweet to barbwire-mean overnight, eventually becoming the meanest girl in elementary school." He worked his jaw. "She used to make Kenna cry."

Kenna, Dane's fiancée, was as tough as nails, so it was hard to imagine her breaking down, and equally hard to imagine Harlow the wannabe stripper as a school-yard terror. But then, most people probably didn't look at him and see a murderer.

Dane eyed him thoughtfully. "Why the interest in her?"

"She and I have unfinished business." He offered no

more, his feelings too personal—too raw. "What else do you know about her?"

"Not much. I once overhead Kenna and Brook Lynn talking about her, and from what I gathered, she dropped out of public school her junior year in favor of being homeschooled and after that, she rarely left her house." Dane leaned back in his chair and tapped his pen against the edge of his desk. "I must admit, your curiosity surprises me more than anything else."

"Why?"

"For the first time in our history, you've turned a business meeting into a personal gabfest."

He had, hadn't he? Damn it! It was a small change, but a change nonetheless.

He adjusted his tie before standing a little too swiftly. "All right. Meeting adjourned. I'll tell West you want his new program as soon as possible, and you'll be paying full asking price."

"You could at least give me the friendship discount."

"Full asking price *is* the friendship discount. Everyone else will have to pay double." He strode out of the office before he did something stupid, like ask more questions about Harlow.

The assistant spotted him and leaped to her feet, smoothing her skirt. "Leaving so soon, Mr. Ockley?"

Not just the perfect distraction, he decided, but the perfect means to an end. Harlow *wasn't* anything special to him, and she wouldn't usher in any more changes; he would prove it. "Now that my eyes are on you," he said, leaning against the counter in front of her, "leaving is the last thing on my mind."

She batted her lashes at him, playfully twirling a

lock of her hair around her finger. "Thank you. I'm flattered."

"Then I'm pleased." But was he? He'd said the words by rote, with a definite lack of enthusiasm. Where was his enjoyment? His sense of victory?

Or was this yet another change to place at Harlow's door?

"Will you have dinner with me?" he asked, his hands fisting.

Green eyes widened, a cherry-red mouth forming a small O. "I… Yes. When?"

"How about tonight? The sooner I see you again the better." *That* he meant with every fiber of his being.

She practically hummed with excitement as she rattled off her digits.

"I'll be counting the minutes."

By the time Beck made it home, the farmhouse was empty. West was at the office, while Brook Lynn and Jase were out delivering sandwiches for her catering business, You've Got It Coming.

Beck threw his briefcase on his bedroom floor and sank into the chair in front of his desk, where pictures of Harlow were scattered. He went still. Sad ocean-water eyes stared up at him, holding his gaze captive, silently beseeching him to help…to save. His gut knotted. He was no one's savior. He was too screwed up.

Look at him. He bounced from moment to moment without any thought for the future. He broke into a sweat at the mere thought of commitment. He had an all-consuming hatred for change. His first sexual experience had been with a married maternal figure. He'd helped kill a man in a fistfight, and then allowed his best friend to rot in prison for nine years.

Beck anchored his elbows on his knees and rested his head in his upraised hands. Clearly he needed someone to save *him*.

As if he could be saved.

But…maybe it wasn't too late for Harlow. While he wasn't a savior, there *were* things even a guy like him could do to help. Like set her up financially, maybe even move her into the city where she wouldn't be reviled at every turn. And bonus for him: she would be out of sight, out of mind.

Yes. He picked up the landline and started making calls, putting the wheels in motion to set up a trust in Harlow's name, telling his real estate agent what kind of home to search for in Oklahoma City. Then he called West.

"You in front of a computer?" he asked in lieu of a greeting.

"Are you a top contender for banging the most women in any given year?"

"I'll take that as a yes. Work your magic and tell me how Harlow Glass has been making money." To survive as long as she had, she had to be bringing in a little cash from somewhere.

"All right." Fingers click-clacked over a keyboard, one minute bleeding into another. "Okay, this is strange."

"What?"

"My superpower is finding information—nice trust you're setting up for her, by the way—but I can't locate Harlow's place of employment. Or where she's been staying. She has no known address and hasn't paid taxes. She has zero credit cards and no checking account. She doesn't have a tag registered for a vehicle."

Damn. "Thanks, West."

"Anytime, my man. Sorry I couldn't be of more help."

"No worries. Just…do me a solid and keep digging." He hung up, mind racing. Where the hell was Harlow staying? How was she getting around? How was she eating?

The answer to that last one seemed an unequivocal *she wasn't*, and for a moment, his vision went black, rage boiling to the surface. No one should have to live that way, and whether Harlow liked it or not, he wasn't going to stand for it in her case.

LATE THE NEXT AFTERNOON, Beck was ready for a strait-jacket and a padded room. They'd make a nice vacation. Harlow hadn't shown up to work on the garden that morning, and he'd had no luck finding her in town. He'd asked around, but no one had seen her. A couple of people had offered to round up a lynch mob and go hunting for her, and he'd had to curb the urge to respond with his fists. She seemed to have disappeared into the ether.

Now he racked the balls on one of the most expensive pool tables ever made, the outer shell a limited edition 1965 Shelby GT 350. Normally he took great care with every inch of it. *My precious.* Today, he wanted to rip out the felt and pull the metal and wood apart piece by piece.

His date with Sandra…Sally?…could have made a Worst Ever list. He'd thought about Harlow all evening, wondering where she was and what she was doing. Frustrated with the lack of answers, he'd turned up the heat with *S* girl until she'd practically begged him to stay the night at her place. There was no better distraction than sex, but as she'd undressed, his mind had returned to Harlow yet again. He'd thought of the nice steak dinner he'd just enjoyed and wondered if she'd had any dinner at all.

Little surprise he'd failed to get an erection while a beautiful woman writhed on his lap.

He'd left without doing the deed, and the humiliation still lingered.

"Your turn," Jase said, snapping fingers in front of his face.

Beck swiped up his cue and nearly broke the wood in two, so tight was his grip.

"Careful. What's with you?"

"I'm fine." No way he'd dump his problems in Jase's lap. The guy had carried too many burdens for too long. Beck would die before he added another.

"Don't lie. Not to us."

The statement came from West, who rose from the bench press Jase had installed earlier in the week. Though he'd built a workout room in the back of the house, more and more equipment was migrating into other areas of the house, allowing anyone in the mood to exercise to spend time with those who weren't.

Dark locks of hair were plastered to West's face, and he used the shirt he'd discarded to wipe his brow. Sweat dripped down the ropes of muscle and sinew in his chest, bypassing his only tattoo: the name *Tessa* etched over his heart.

He snatched the cue from Beck. "Bad boys don't get to play the greatest game ever invented."

At six-two—two inches taller than Beck—West was his staunchest competition in the meat market. Not that they'd ever competed. West only dated for two months out of the year, picking one female and staying with her the entire time, only to dump her for some made-up reason when the clock zeroed out.

He had his reasons, so Beck didn't fault him. "Okay, all right." Beck held up his hands, palms out. "You got me. I'm not fine, but I will be. There's no need to worry."

"We'll worry if we want to worry," Jase said. "We haven't seen you this worked up since you went parking with Kara Bradburry in the tenth grade."

West barked out a laugh. "Dude. You were so nervous, shaking so hard, you couldn't even unhook her bra."

At the time, his only experience had come from a woman more than twice Kara's age, who'd told him what to do every step of the way.

Great. Now he needed a drink.

He grabbed a beer from the minifridge and downed half. "Like you guys did any better with your dates." Back then, the three of them had seen nothing wrong with semipublic make-out sessions, because they were teenagers and teenagers were stupid, the males most of all; they had two brains and the one down south usually made the most important life decisions. It went something like: *Her. Her. Not her—fine, she'll do.*

West lined up a shot and with his gaze on Beck, sank a solid in the corner pocket. "Let me guess. This is about Harlow Glass."

Just the mention of her name proved last night's limp-wood experience had been an anomaly, and it pissed him off as much as it relieved him.

"She's pretty," Jase said, his tone conversational.

Pretty? Like calling an ocean a puddle. "She's gorgeous."

West straightened and grinned. A genuine grin, and it was good to see. The past few weeks had been rough for him, the anniversary of Tessa's death taking a toll. "Are you about to wax poetic about Harlow? Because I don't have bad poetry penciled into my schedule."

West lived by the clock, and if he had his way, he would die by it, too.

"I wax poetic about nothing," Beck said. "Except pie. And cake. Maybe cookies in a pinch, but that's only on a case-by-case basis. Anything with raisins should be stuffed in a box and delivered to hell with Return to Sender stamped over the top."

Jase snickered. "How's this for poetry? 'Roses are red, violets are blue. Beck wants Harlow, I know this to be true.'"

Beck, in the process of lifting the bottle to his mouth, went still, nearly swept away by a tide of shock. Jase hadn't cracked a joke in damn near forever, and until that moment, Beck hadn't realized how much he'd missed the playful side of his friend.

"Beck, my man," Jase said, frowning at him. "Don't look at me like I'm some kind of mythical creature. Not after I told you to let go of the past. I have."

"I know. I'm sorry. I freaking love you, that's all." Beck set his beer aside and swiped his cue from West. He lined up his own shot…and like a loser, failed to sink a solid. Usually he could win the game blindfolded with both hands tied behind his back.

Yes, he was *that* good.

"I freaking love you, too." Jase patted him on the shoulder before going for one of the only remaining stripes. "But I still want you to admit you're into Harlow."

Guy didn't know his own strength and nearly pounded Beck into the floor, but damn if Beck didn't adore every second of it, the affectionate gesture somehow drilling through all kinds of dark emotion.

"I'm into her, okay," he said. "Happy now? I'm curious and concerned about her. I can't get her out of my head."

"Well, that's new," West said.

"You're telling me. But she wants nothing to do with me."

"Dude. You sound just like Jase when he first met Brook Lynn." West hit another shot and of course, two solids flew into their slots. "You're all 'woe is me' with zero nut power. Just suck it up and make a play for her. She'll fold. They always do."

Maybe. But then what? He would casually mention he planned to finance the rest of her life, before walking away from her? He would forget her like all the others and move on to his next conquest, his next moment?

That was where things got tricky. He didn't want to forget her. He wanted to hang around her, wanted the right to check on her anytime the urge hit, to make sure she had everything she needed… Damn it, he wanted the right to protect her.

Protect someone other than himself? Please.

The ache in his chest returned, a pesky fly he couldn't kill. He wanted her to have what he never would: a happily-ever-after. But as he well knew, money and security could only do so much. Women like her usually wanted more. They dreamed of falling in love, connecting emotionally as well as physically. Something he'd never done and wasn't even sure he could do.

He saluted his friends with the beer bottle, then drained the contents.

Jase took pity on him and changed the subject. "You'll be pleased to know Brook Lynn has claimed responsibility for the soccer banquet."

"We're in good hands, then." The best. For the past eight years, Beck and West had financed and coached a soccer team for underprivileged kids, always ending a season with a big blowout celebration. While they loved the interaction, they hated the planning.

"Brook Lynn is pretty much a unicorn at the end of a double rainbow," West said. "And since we're on the subject of parties, I should warn you. I got a call from Charlene Burns. She's in charge of the annual Berryween Festival, some kind of Strawberry Valley play on Halloween. She asked us to set up a booth."

"For?" Beck asked.

"Kissing. And if not that, anything we want."

"Someone doesn't know us very well," Jase said. "Otherwise she would have given us a ten-page list of restrictions. To start."

"I told Charlene we wouldn't be setting up our own booth, but we would be happy to pay for *all* the booths," West said, "as long as You've Got It Coming is allowed to cater the event exclusively."

Jase gave West a pat—drill—on the shoulder. "Good man."

West tried to play it cool, but his ear-to-ear smile gave him away. "You're just now noticing? You kind of suck."

The front door creaked open and closed, a patter of footsteps soon following. "Jase?" Brook Lynn called.

His friend lit up so brightly Beck actually had to look away. "Back here, angel."

The footsteps quickened, and Jase moved forward. The couple met in the doorway, their arms winding around each other automatically. Beck and West shared a moment of unspoken envy, but also of contentment. Jase deserved this kind of happiness and it was amazing to see.

"Finished with your breakfast deliveries?" Jase asked her.

"Finally. We had eleven more than usual."

"Word is spreading."

A part of Beck hated the resounding success she'd made of her business. The more she worked, the less time she had to bake for him. Like another casserole named Just for the Halibut. *Mine!* A selfish mentality, sure, but anyone who'd ever tasted her food would understand.

If only Harlow could bake...

What the hell did that matter?

"By the way," Brook Lynn said, peeking around Jase. "I saw Harlow Glass in town."

Beck lost all interest in the game. Not that he'd had any to begin with. "Where is she?"

"Well, well. I thought you might be interested," she said and shook her head. "I just hoped I was wrong, that you'd—"

Beck spoke over her with a clipped "Where?"

"She was snooping around the library."

The library again? He raced out of the game room, grabbed his wallet and called, "I'll be back in a bit."

He didn't need keys. His car had a push-button start, which activated with his thumbprint.

His friends' laughter followed him all the way outside, but he didn't care. He drove so fast he left skid marks on the road, breaking speed records as lush trees, rolling hills and wild strawberry patches whizzed past, nothing but a blur. Only when he reached the town square did he slow to a crawl. Pedestrians strolled along sidewalks, and kids too young for school played chase underneath a large red-and-white-striped umbrella.

Everyone who spotted him smiled and waved, and it did something odd to his insides.

He parked in back of the library, the lot empty. There was no sign of Harlow. If she'd already taken off…well, he might just tear the town apart looking for her. He stormed around to the front—and finally felt as if he could breathe.

She stood at the door, muttering to herself. "I can do this. I can. I have lady balls, and they're big. Huge."

He fought a grin. Lady balls?

She hadn't yet noticed him, so he took a moment to drink her in. The gleam of her dark hair. The glow of her skin, now scrubbed free of dirt, revealing more freckles for him to count…to trace with his tongue. But her cheeks had hollowed a bit, he noticed with a frown. Had she eaten today?

There went what remained of his amusement. She wore another too-thin shirt, and a pair of jean shorts too big for her, bagged low on her waist. Her sandals were frayed at the buckles.

Just how poor was she?

"Harlow," he said, loving the taste of her name.

Nothing. No reaction from her.

"I can do this," she muttered.

He closed the distance, ghosted his knuckles over the heated satin of her cheekbone. A mistake. Not only because she gasped and swung toward him, one of her palms fluttering to her chest while the other extended to push him away, but because the contact jacked him up. Made him desperate for another touch. *Any* touch, as long as it came from her.

Her panic morphed into consternation as his identity clicked. "Beck." She took a minute to control her accelerated breathing. "What are you doing here?"

"What do you think I'm doing here? I've come to continue my study on the art of seduction."

"Please." Those gorgeous baby blues seemed to cut through a veneer he'd worked years to perfect, reaching the black soul he would have done anything to cleanse. "You're already an expert, and you know it."

"So you've succumbed to my charms already?" A man could hope.

"Me? Succumb to you? Never!" She flicked her hair over her shoulder, saying defiantly, "You're like a brother to me."

Careful to moderate his tone, he said, "Is that why you ran from me yesterday?" He even managed to adopt an indulgent expression as he leaned his shoulder against the doorpost. "Because I'm like a stepbrother you can't stop dreaming about?"

A pretty blush bloomed in her cheeks and even extended down her neck, under her collar. A blush like that gave him ideas. Bad, bad ideas. "I didn't run from you," she admitted, "but from what was going to happen once I passed through those doors."

Relief drove him to reach for her. He couldn't have

stopped the action if he'd tried—*Have to touch her.*
He twined their fingers, the feel of her skin tantalizing
and teasing him. Though she resisted at first, she soon
stilled, a tangible spark erupting between them, bur-
rowing into him, whirring through him. He shuddered
with awareness and unwittingly erased what remained
of her personal space, needing to be closer to her on the
most primitive level. To take from her. To give to her.

"Beck?" she whispered, suddenly panting. "What
are you doing?"

He didn't know. He couldn't seem to control his reactions to her, his body burning for hers.

Frustrated by her—and himself—he released her
and stepped back. "You had a shift at the Bungalow last
night? Is that why you didn't come over this morning?"

She rubbed at her wrist, as if she could still feel him
there, and it only made him want to touch her longer,
harder. "Uh, yep. That's right. Had trouble with one of
the regulars."

"He get grabby during one of your famous bump-
and-grinds?"

"Yeah. Thankfully the bouncers kicked him out before he ever made contact."

At least she was sticking to her story. "I promise to
keep my hands to myself...at least for a little while...
if you've changed your mind and want to give me that
lap dance."

"Sorry, but I still plan to garden for you. After I *learn*
how to garden."

"Why not research in the privacy of your own home,
on a computer? You do have a computer, don't you? Or
at least a phone with internet access." *Tell me the truth,
sweetheart. For once.*

"Maybe I just prefer the old-fashioned way. Did you ever think of that?"

A supposition rather than a lie. *I'm on to you now, honey.* "Let's go inside, then."

She nibbled on her bottom lip. "The librarian hates me for something I did as a teenager."

"Ah. Fixing public relations problems just happens to be my specialty." He flung his arm over her shoulders, ignored the rightness of having her softness pressed against his hardness once again and urged her forward. "Give me five minutes, and she'll love you."

"Impossible," Harlow said, but this time she allowed him to lead her past the door.

He felt the sweet intensity of her gaze lingering on his profile, and like everything else about her, it affected him deeply. "What will you give me if I succeed?"

"My eternal gratitude."

"Well, that's certainly a good start."

The room was small and crammed with dozens of shelves. The scent of old books and dust assailed him as a short, round woman with silver streaks in her slicked-back hair walked around the checkout desk with the precision of a military commander. Glasses hung around her neck, bouncing with her every step.

"Harlow Glass." Her features pinched with displeasure. "You are not welcome here. You've been told repeatedly not to darken—"

"Ms. Cavanaugh," Beck said, reading the name tag pinned to the collar of her dress. "It's so lovely to finally meet you." He claimed her hand, kissed her knuckles. "Had I known a woman such as yourself guarded these precious tomes, I would have come much sooner."

"Yes. Well." She cleared her throat and returned

her attention to Harlow. "You know you're not supposed to—"

"I hope you don't mind our intrusion, but Harlow hoped to take a moment of your valuable time and sincerely apologize for any and all trouble she once caused you," he interjected smoothly. "As a woman who values knowledge, I know you'll be interested in hearing what she has to say."

Different emotions played over the older woman's features, but in the end she nodded stiffly. "Very well. Speak."

Harlow did just that. "I am so, so sorry for organizing a Students Against Stupid Books protest ten years ago. Someone caught me reading a romance novel, and I was embarrassed. The protest was my way of earning cool points, but I felt like I needed to shower on the inside the entire time, especially while the books were burning. Books are awesome. Go books!"

Students Against Stupid Books? Dude.

"Yes, well. Time will prove all truths," Ms. Cavanaugh said, the starch staying with her.

"That it will." Beck gave her knuckles another kiss. "Harlow, honey, why don't you tell Ms. Cavanaugh about the books you'd like to read and treasure."

"That won't be necessary." Ms. Cavanaugh placed her glasses on the bridge of her nose and stared up at him. "As Harlow is aware, she is forever banned from having a library card. I cannot change our policies. No card, no books."

"I understand," Beck said with an indulgent smile, "which is why we'll put the books on *my* card. After I fill out the proper paperwork, of course."

Several beats of silence passed before the librarian

gave another stiff nod. "I hope you know what you're doing, young man."

As she walked away, Harlow peered up at him, wide-eyed with awe. "Beck," she whispered, and threw her arms around him, hugging him.

He didn't hug her back, not at first. The softness of her breasts pressed against his chest, and an instant blast of heat suffused him, his entire body practically going up in flames.

"Thank you. You're the best. Thank you," she repeated.

Slowly he wound his arms around her and held on tight, probably too tight, but she didn't seem to mind. "Anytime, sweetheart." The hoarseness of his tone embarrassed him. When he began to tremble like a puss, he knew he had to end the contact. He set her away with a swift, almost jarring movement and cleared his throat.

A bell tinkled over the door, saving him from having to come up with an excuse for his behavior, and a feminine voice suddenly called out, "Beck! You're really here." An attractive brunette strolled toward him, grinning. "I noticed your car out back and came in to say hi."

How did he know her?

Well, one guess. "Hey, pretty." He winked, reassured as he sank back into an old habit.

Harlow snorted. "While we're here, you might want to check out a few books on the consequences of he-sluttery."

"You mean extreme fun and temporary pleasure?"

Her mouth curled with distaste. "When it comes to matters of the heart, the only thing you should want to be temporary is an STD."

Deep down, he'd known she would balk at anything fleeting. Now he had to bite the inside of his cheek to combat a blistering surge of something akin to disappointment.

The brunette reached him, scowling at Harlow before schooling her features and raking her nails down his tie. "A few weeks ago you asked me out. Do you remember?"

"Do you really think I could forget?" he replied smoothly, still drawing a blank.

She shook her head, relieved, and said, "At the time, I told you no, but I've regretted it ever since."

The words jogged his memory. That's right. She'd played hard to get, turning him down flat, and he'd moved on to someone else. No harm, no foul.

"You two deserve each other. I hope you're happy... temporarily." Harlow kept her attention squarely on Beck, glaring daggers at him. "Meanwhile, I'll be outside. I'll give you ten minutes to get your card and whatever books you want me to follow while tending your garden, and then I'm gone. I have places to be."

He didn't want her to leave, didn't want her out of his sight, but he said, "If you want to leave, leave. I won't stop you." Not now, not ever.

As he spoke, the brunette linked her arm through his, a clear attempt to stake a claim. He almost shook off her hold, but the feeling was so new, so unexpected— so different—he locked his limbs in place.

Harlow looked from him to the girl, the girl to him, the severity he'd noticed in the later-childhood pictures soon masking her features. "Forget the books, and screw you," she spat, turning toward the door. "Screw you both."

He knew. In that moment, he knew beyond any doubt. She liked him, and not as a brother. Jealousy was the only reason she would lash out this sharply.

"Harlow," he called.

"What?" she snapped.

"Stay close. I'll be coming for you."

CHAPTER FIVE

HARLOW PACED BACK and forth in front of the library's front door. Old wood planks creaked and whined, a warm breeze actually cool against her damp neck. Her mind churned.

How dumb was she? Suzie Quaid had walked into the library, and Harlow had nearly erupted into flames of jealousy. All because Beck had smiled and turned on the charm. But the great he-slut of the Southwest *always* smiled and turned on the charm. He'd even softened the hard-as-stone Ms. Cavanaugh.

Why should Harlow care that he'd stayed true to form and paid attention to the girl once voted Most Likely to Become a Professional Jell-O Wrestler?

Beck might be gorgeous, and nice, and gorgeous, and charismatic, and gorgeous, but he still wasn't the man for Harlow. He would never be the man for her. Even temporarily. *Especially* temporarily. Learn the bliss of being his woman, only to lose him? No, thanks.

Her eyes remained on the prize: stability. Falling in love, creating a home and starting a family. Her desires would never align with his. Best to tend to his garden, as owed, and then move on.

Right on time, he sailed out of the library and smiled his most devastating smile. He handed her the books he'd checked out.

"Catch you later, honey." He ambled away, whistling a happy tune. Sounded like "Baby Got Back."

Seriously? That was it? He was just going to leave her here?

Had he made a lunch arrangement with Suzie? Or maybe dinner—followed by bedroom dancing?

Irritation flourished, and in an effort to distract herself, Harlow hugged the books to her chest. The three hardbacks had to weigh a thousand pounds each, and her arms began to shake. As she motored forward, she did her best to remain in the shadows. Mr. Porter and Mr. Rodriguez were no longer playing checkers. Jessie Kay Dillon and her sidekick, Sunny Day, occupied the chairs, drinking whiskey from a bottle and scoring men as they walked past.

Jessie Kay whistled. "Oh, baby. I'm giving you a ten. You look like you're into commitment. Come give me a taste of that!"

"Oh, sugar, sugar," Sunny called. "I bet you've got a healthy relationship with your mom. Marry me?"

While the guys soaked up the attention, Harlow did her best to escape unnoticed.

She failed.

"Look who just entered my territory." Sunny fist-pumped the sky. "Catfight, anyone?"

Keep walking. Harlow wasn't male, but she was given a score anyway. Both girls held up big fat zeros.

I wrote the word slut *all over Jessie Kay's locker on more than one occasion. I dated Scott, Sunny's ex-boyfriend, only to dump him a day later. This is deserved.*

Bad choices, nasty results. No exceptions.

"You're lucky we don't have negative numbers, Glass," Jessie Kay shouted.

Maybe if Harlow tried being nice for once, she'd see better results? "You look real pretty today, Sunny," she said, flashing a smile. Forced, yes, but also sincere. The blonde was a knockout. "And Jessie Kay, I think you're more beautiful every time I see you."

Sunny gasped. "You dirty, rotten *bitch*. How dare you imply we're ugly!"

Ugly? *You've got to be kidding.* Would no one ever give her the benefit of the doubt?

Her five-step plan might need a little tweaking.

Head down. Shoulders in. Gait fast. When she turned a corner, she noticed Mr. Brooks struggling to hang an oversize 10% Off sign in the window of his antiques shop.

Harlow hurried over. "Here, let me help you." She placed her books at her feet and reached for the sign.

Mr. Brooks nearly fell over in an effort to keep her hands off his property. "Trying to steal from me again, Harlow Glass?"

"No, no. I just wanted to—"

"Desecrate the sign and stake it in someone's yard. *I know.*"

"Give me a break," she practically begged, picking up her books. "I'm not that girl anymore. I just wanted to help you."

"Oh, I know exactly who you are. Now get. Get!" He kicked at the air.

"Fine. Enjoy your back strain." She tromped off, spotting the elderly Mrs. Winthorp carrying a bag of groceries across the street.

Their eyes met. Mrs. Winthorp turned and walked in the other direction.

Nice.

Maybe Harlow should have stayed in school rather than choosing a home-study program. By the time she'd dropped out, she'd already changed, and the kids would have been forced to spend time with the new Harlow and eventually, they would have grown to like her. Physically, however, she'd been unable to sit still for long periods of time. She'd been in too much pain.

Her fingers itched to rub her scars, the habit ingrained. Think about the attack, feel the proof she'd survived it. But all she could do was squeeze the books tighter.

By the time she'd been strong enough to venture outdoors, her friends had wanted nothing to do with her.

They just need time, her mother had told her. *You're a good girl who was raised in a volatile home, and that's my fault. I should have left your father the moment he showed his true colors. But I didn't, and you paid the price. Now I'm going to make it up to you. As long as there's breath in this body, I'm going to do everything in my power to take care of you.*

True to her word, she'd woken Harlow every morning with breakfast and a hug. She'd encouraged Harlow in her studies and praised her every accomplishment. She'd left notes on Harlow's pillow every night, positive affirmations meant to build her confidence.

You are a bright light.

There is nothing you cannot do.

You are a true beauty, glowing from the inside out.

"I miss you so much, Momma," she whispered to the sky.

Martha Glass had fallen from a stepladder, and though she'd merely seemed bruised at the time, the impact had knocked loose a blood clot and she was dead by morning.

Harlow's chin trembled, a lone tear streaking down her cheek, as hot and stinging as the sun. As much as she looked forward to a cooldown in temperature, she wasn't looking forward to a cooldown in temperature. There were four seasons in Strawberry Valley, but unlike the rest of the world, those seasons were classified as "hotter than hell," "tornado," "a brief moment of intense, icy cold" and "the warm-up before hotter than hell." Her tent often felt like a sauna, but when the snow and ice came, it would feel like a freezer.

Footsteps sounded behind her, and she swung around, arm lifted to defend herself. A scowling Scott Cameron barreled in her direction, and she stepped out of his way. He simply angled toward her, giving her shoulder a purposeful shove with his own.

"Watch where you're going," he spat.

She stumbled, saved from falling flat on her face by the wall of the post office. "Why don't you grow a pair of testicles and act like a man," she called, unable to hold back the words. A girl could be a punching bag for only so long before she had to start punching back, no matter the consequences.

Scott swung around, the muscles in his shoulders bunching, and for a moment she thought he would return to her and…what? Hit her? She didn't want to think the worst of him, but he wasn't giving her much choice. In the end, his gaze moved behind her and widened, and he spun to motor on.

Finally, something had gone in her favor, but it only

depressed her more. The fact that a guy hadn't punched her or called her a horrible name was the highlight of her day? Wow.

She made the trek out of town, stopping occasionally to pick up trash on someone's lawn while mosquitoes—aka flying vampires—attacked her in droves, hungry for a little Harlow dinner. As she slapped her arm to kill one of the fiendish suckers, a prickle at the back of her neck suggested she had an audience. Tensing, she studied the tangled landscape—trees, thick underbrush, dead piles of crispy leaves—but she found no sign of a pursuer.

Her brain must be melting. She continued on, not stopping again until she reached Virgil Porter's house. A pile of brushwood had blown in front of his mailbox, and Mr. Fritz, the postman, was the cranky sort who wouldn't make a delivery if he had to step out of his vehicle.

Ten minutes into her work to clear it away, movement in Mr. Porter's living room caught her attention. Her heart banged a song of panic against her ribs as she met Daniel Porter's gaze, Mr. Porter's son.

He'd left for the military a few years ago and, according to whispers, had only returned to Strawberry Valley a few days ago. And oh, wow, he was shirtless, ripped with muscle and tattoos, standing with his hands on his hips, watching her. About to storm outside to rail at her for trespassing?

Harlow grabbed her books and dashed off. About halfway home, her legs began to tremble so intensely she feared she would go down and never get up. Somehow she found the strength to troop onward, on the lookout for scorpions, listening for the telltale hiss of nearby snakes.

At long last, she reached her destination, dropping the books in front of her tent as her arms finally gave out. Her biceps trembled and burned, and she knew they'd be sore tomorrow. Sighing, she sank in front of the tomes and surveyed her home of the past however many months. A small blue tent with a faulty zipper sat beside an even smaller pond. She'd stacked a circle of rocks around a stack of twigs to create a fire pit where she boiled water in the only pan she had. There were gopher mounds everywhere, dirt flung in every direction, but at least multiple oaks offered shade…and branches for birds to poop from.

She imagined Beck showing up for "tea." Sanitized pond water.

Oh, how far the queen bee has fallen. From the highest of highs to the lowest of lows. The lap of luxury to *this*. No real home. No security of any kind. No way to eat or drink whenever the urge struck. No comfy bed or modern conveniences of any kind.

She turned her attention to her new books…and blinked in shock. *Gardening for the Super Ignoramus. 101 Ways to Seduce Your Dream Man. The Male Penis: What You Really Need to Know.*

But…but…when had the small-town library begun carrying books like *that*? They'd nearly banned a paranormal romance series about supersexy demon-possessed warriors for being too racy!

She reached for the gardening book, really she did, but her fingers somehow curled around the spine of *Seduce Your Dream Man* and riffled through the pages—and oh, wow! There were pictures. She ended up "reading" until the last tendril of sunlight vanished.

Now, back to work. She started a small fire with the lighter she'd found—no one would notice the smoke at this time of night—and set a pot of water to boil. After she drank her fill, she called it a day and nestled in her tent. The tear in the top allowed her to gaze up at the stars, diamond pinpricks in a sea of black velvet. One of God's finest creations, second only to Strawberry Valley. And speaking of Strawberry Valley, it was time to face the facts. Her five-step plan didn't just need tweaking, it needed scrapping. At this rate, a hundred-step plan wouldn't work.

If she wanted different results, she had to do something different. The most obvious choice was simple. Finally make the heart-wrenching move to the city.

Panic and heartache instantly converged. No. Not that. Not yet. This was her home, and the man of her dreams lived here. He had to live here. They would fall in love and raise their kids here.

But who would want her? As a military man, Daniel Porter was used to dealing with hostile people and situations. Could he forgive the past?

A few years ago, Jeffery James had moved to town. He'd heard rumors about her, sure, but he had no personal experience with her. Of course, she wasn't attracted to him, but what did that matter? Love could grow from support, affection and stability.

There was that word again. *Stability*. The mother ship. The holy grail.

Who could give her something so precious? Lincoln West, maybe. Handsome, sweet and, like Jeffery, she had no real personal experience with him. Plus, he lived in her ancestral home. If they happened to fall in love, she could move back in. And promptly kick Beck out, she thought with a smile.

What she knew about West: he hadn't dated anyone in town...which was kinda odd, now that she considered it. He wasn't just handsome, he was *handsome*, and he had as many admirers as Beck. He just didn't jump their bones at every opportunity. He was over six foot, leanly muscled and he was nice. He had a smile for everyone he came across, and he worked like a fiend, creating different kinds of computer programs.

She knew about his business only because she'd visited his office in town the day after it opened. His assistant from the city had been there, and Harlow had asked questions, submitted a résumé. And it had been a doozy. Past jobs: zero. Experience: none. Strengths: still searching. She'd hoped to decorate their walls with murals or, barring that, become their receptionist. Surprisingly enough—har har—she was never called in for an interview; she'd listed the number to the only pay phone in town and camped by it for days.

But maybe she didn't need a job from West...maybe she just needed *him*.

What kind of women did he prefer?

If the answer was sometimes mousy, sometimes feisty homeless girls, she had this in the bag. If not, well, she would just have to earn his interest another way.

Which shouldn't be a problem. Thanks to Beck, she was now equipped with an instruction manual.

For the first time in months, she was hopeful as she drifted off to sleep. Unfortunately, it wasn't West's face she saw in her dreams...

WEST AND JASE tried to speak with Beck as he stalked through the house.

"Sorry, guys, but I can't," he said. "Not now."

They asked no questions, and for that he was grateful. He locked himself in his bedroom and plopped onto the end of his bed, resting his elbows on his knees and his head in his upraised hands, just trying to breathe, align his thoughts, maybe shake off the worst of his emotions. What he'd just witnessed...

He'd followed Harlow, hoping to unearth a few of her secrets. Maybe he shouldn't have invaded her privacy like that, but he'd wanted answers and she'd been unwilling to give them, and though he'd tried, he'd realized he wasn't going to get them any other way.

He'd done what was necessary.

Of course, he'd almost veered off track when a brute of a guy purposely bumped into her. In some of the foster homes Beck had stayed in, he'd seen girls and women abused mentally, emotionally and even physically, and it had always infuriated him.

Not on my watch.

Only the thought of going after the guy at a later date allowed him to continue following Harlow.

She lived on his land in abject poverty. People treated her like trash, and she took it, every bit of it, as if she had to do penance. And yet, tired and hungry, she still found the strength to help those who now hurt her.

He wondered how she cleaned her clothes, how she

showered, because he knew she somehow managed to do both.

He wondered what she ate, *when* she ate. He'd spent hours trailing her, and she hadn't consumed a single bite of food. The only water she'd had was what she'd boiled. He wondered what she planned to do during the upcoming winter months, if she would allow herself to freeze to death before she came to him for aid.

He wondered—and he got pissed. The little girl from the pictures shouldn't be living that way. The woman she'd become shouldn't be living that way. He had a home with plenty of rooms. He had a refrigerator filled with food. He had unlimited access to fresh water. He had stacks of blankets, a closet full of coats. Hell, he had everything the girl could ever need or want. And yet she suffered out there?

Her stupid pride, he thought, jaw aching as his molars gnashed together. If he went to her now, she would spurn him. No doubt about it. Time to plan.

He'd hated leaving her out there, almost hadn't managed it, but he'd consoled himself with the thought that this would be her last night in that tent, her last night exposed to the elements and wild animals. Coyotes, snakes and scorpions lived out there, and the fool woman would make a mighty tasty meal.

So what that she'd survived this long. Tomorrow her life was going to change *drastically*. And there was nothing she could do to stop it.

CHAPTER SIX

BRIGHT MORNING SUNLIGHT streaked through the tears in Harlow's tent, waking her before she was ready to rise. She pried open tired, gritty eyes, caught sight of puffy white clouds and a flock of blackbirds twirling overhead. A cheery sight mixed with an ominous one. Yay.

She struggled to sit up, her body as sore as she'd predicted. Actually more so.

Plan for the day: read about gardening for an hour, apply what she learned to Beck's roses, find and flirt with West.

Foolproof.

She gathered her basket of meager supplies—toothbrush, toothpaste, hairbrush and a dwindling roll of toilet paper—and crawled from the tent.

A high-pitched scream split her lips. Intruder!

Beck, only Beck, she realized a moment later, flattening a hand over her racing heart. He sat on the boulder she'd managed to roll next to the fire pit when she'd first moved out here, staring at her through narrowed eyes. The blaze she'd started last night had long since died, and there was no hint of smoke in the air to shield her view. She saw every inch of the man who had tormented her dreams, from his harsh, intractable expression to his big, strong body. Gone was the charming facade he usually displayed so readily. Now, iron-hard determination pulled his skin taut around his eyes and his mouth.

The change was startling and beautiful. He was a work of art, and he made her yearn for the impossible—or a few hours in his bed, no matter the cost. His hair stuck out in spikes, the strands seemingly a thousand different shades of gold and brown, from the palest flax to the darkest sable. His eyes were sensuously tilted, his cheekbones sharp and his jaw squared with resolve. His wide shoulders looked as if they could carry any burden, and she wished he were the kind of man who would hold her with one arm while protecting her with the other.

But he's not, so he's not for me.

"I'm not sure I like how you're looking at me," he said. "But it doesn't matter. Get out here and talk to me."

Gulping, she scrambled the rest of the way out of the tent. "How did you find me?"

"How else? I followed you," he replied, his tone hard and inflexible. "You should have asked me for help long ago."

Humiliation burned her all over. "I just woke up. I need a moment of privacy. If you'll excuse me…" *I will take off like a bullet, hide out and regroup.*

A muscle jumped underneath his eye. "You'll get your privacy, all right, but you'll get it at my house."

Mine! "I would rather—"

"There's food. A feast."

"—continue with my day the way I originally— A feast?" A whimper escaped her.

"One way or another, you're going with me. I'll carry you if I have to." His lids narrowed to tiny slits, his lashes hiding the sudden dark anticipation in his irises. "And, Harlow, as angry as I am, I kind of hope I have to."

She didn't understand what was happening right now. But then, why would she? Her experience with the male species was limited to boys, those who had received the Glass Pass in junior high and high school.

"Okay. I'll go with you. But I'll walk." Having his hands on her would be her undoing. "Is West there?" she asked, deciding to use this as an opportunity to kick-start her Ever After plan. The sooner the better.

His frown deepened. "Yes. Why?"

"Just because," she replied, both excited and nervous. She set her basket of goodies in her tent. The toothbrush, however, she pocketed.

Beck motioned her forward.

"I should have asked permission to camp here, I know," she said, marching onward, "but you'd forgive me if I told you it was only for a night, right?"

"It wasn't one night, and we both know it." He stayed beside her, careful not to touch her. "Don't lie to me. Not ever again."

The challenging tone had returned, demanding more than she was willing to give.

"You are not a stripper," he said.

"I am, too! In my imagination," she muttered. She'd been a lot of things in her imagination. A divorced mom supporting five kids…who happened to catch the eye of the richest CEO in town. A skilled surgeon given three more weeks to live…who happened to catch the eye of her handsomest patient—who happened to be a brilliant scientist willing to risk his career to save her life. She'd even been a princess from a distant world where lands were ravaged by war…and she happened to catch the eye of the enemy army's leader, ushering in long-desired peace.

Without a TV or a computer, she'd had to entertain herself, and as an unrepentant bookworm, she'd had a lot of inspiration.

"Be that as it may—" Beck pushed a branch out of her path "—you don't live in the city. You don't own a car or have a job. You've been living on this land since you were kicked out of the farmhouse. And by living, of course, I mean existing. Have I left anything out?"

"No." She surged forward and because of him, she wasn't sliced by thorns. For a jerk, he sure was considerate. "Thank you."

"You're welcome."

He still sounded angry.

At the house, he opened the front door for her. She entered the living room, and the second she caught the scent of breakfast, she picked up speed. A feast was indeed spread across the kitchen table, plus two empty plates and two glasses of orange juice. Her stomach rumbled, her knees going weak, her mouth watering.

"Sit." He flattened his hand on her lower back and gave her a gentle push forward.

The moment she obeyed, he began piling her plate high with heaping spoonfuls of every dish. Scrambled eggs. Bacon. Sausage patties. Sausage links. Pancakes. Waffles. Biscuits and gravy. The contents began to spill over the side. After he set the plate in front of her, he took the seat next to her.

"Eat," he said.

She did, and oh, wow. The taste! Even better than the blueberry juice she'd filched from the pie.

"Good, right?" he said, and she heard the pride in his tone.

"You cooked this?" she asked around a mouthful of eggs. She couldn't force herself to stop chewing long enough to pretend to be feminine and proper, a girl with manners.

"It's my specialty."

Breakfast. Of course. For every morning after one of his sexcapades. "Well, I commend you on your perfect consolation prize."

"I don't think I know what you mean, honey."

"It's what you give your women instead of a relationship, right?"

His fork clattered against his plate. Which still had food on it, while hers was basically licked clean.

"Are you going to eat that?" She pointed to the waffle dripping with butter and syrup.

"It's not a consolation prize. It's breakfast. Nothing more, nothing less." He pushed the plate in her direction, and she dug in.

"What's your problem with long-term relationships?"

"Relationships leave scars," he said.

"Sometimes."

"Always."

"Well, those scars can be healed."

"Sometimes," he said, mimicking her. "But why risk any kind of mental or emotional harm when I can give something far better?"

Flushing, she said, "What could possibly be better than a relationship?"

"I believe we've discussed this. Pleasure. Lots and lots of pleasure."

The huskiness of his voice invited her to lean close and experience everything he had to offer...

Doing her best to ignore a cascade of shivers, she focused on her bacon. Every bite proved better than the last, and when she finished, she almost ate the plate. So good! But also threatening to come back up.

Whatever. Every bite had been worth it. She rubbed her new food baby, saying, "Thank you, Beck. Really."

"Done?"

"Yes."

He stood and held out his hand. She hesitated, but in the end, there was no denying the man who'd just taken such good care of her. She curled her fingers around his, the calluses on his palms creating a delicious friction against her skin.

She tried to play it cool as he helped her stand to shaky legs. He led her into the hallway, to the second room on the right. Her old bedroom. How had he known?

"My room," he said.

"Seriously?" As she'd done the last time she'd been here, she took a moment to mourn the loss of her queen-size bed with its floral comforter, her antique nightstands, and the vaulted ceiling with crumbling crown molding and the distorted images she'd painted.

Harlow flashed back to the emotional breakdown she'd suffered soon after her mother's death, when she'd splattered the different colors of paint across the magical fairyland, leaving a chaotic mess.

"Were you the one who ruined the murals?" he asked.

She'd been staring up, she realized, and he'd easily guessed the direction of her thoughts. "Yes. The day of my mom's funeral."

"I'm sorry for your loss. I'm also sorry you did what you did. I liked the images and hoped to preserve them, but you'd made sure nothing could be salvaged."

The words shocked her. "You actually liked my art?"

"*You* painted them?"

"Well, yeah. Why so surprised?"

He paid no heed to her question, saying, "Your talent is amazing, honey."

"Thank you." Glowing at his praise, Harlow took in the rest of the bedroom. "I never would have guessed you were a fan. I mean, you decided to go with beige walls."

"You don't like beige?"

"Beige is boring."

"The house I lived in before this one had beige walls."

"And now you can't live with a little color?"

A flash of annoyance in those golden eyes, quickly replaced with the flirtatious glint she was so used to seeing. "Did you see my sheets? They're blue."

Will not look at the bed.

"Why don't you take a shower and relax?" he said. "There are towels in the cabinet by the tub and clean clothes next to the sink. And, honey? If you crawl out the window, I will hunt you down. You won't like what happens afterward." He paused, smiled slowly, wickedly. "Or maybe you'll like it a little too much."

How embarrassing. He knew the effect he had on her. "Beck—"

"Shower." He shut the door, sealing her inside.

Fine. She made her way into the bathroom. Once upon a time, the walls had been tiled in pink, her favorite color. Now everything was white, black and chrome:

sleek and sexy for a modern man. But the changes didn't bother her so much anymore. Maybe because they reminded her of Beck.

She brushed her teeth once, twice for good measure, then stripped and stepped under the hot spray of the shower. Steam filled the air, the scent of Beck—masculine and sultry—joining it as she shampooed and conditioned her hair. She'd gotten used to cold showers, having to sneak them from the outdoor hoses of nearby homes after the owners sped off to work, and she'd come to prefer them. At least, that's what she'd told herself. Here, now, she admitted she'd only been fooling herself, trying to make herself feel better about her situation.

While the water continued to rain on her, she settled on the stall's black-and-white floor. Would Beck want to chat with her when she finished? Yeah. Would he kick her off the land for good?

He had every right to do so, but…but… Hot tears scalded her eyes. Why couldn't things go her way for once? Just once?

BECK PACED IN the living room, trying not to picture Harlow naked, soap and water trickling over miles of delectable skin he would sell his soul to touch. Trying, and failing. He wanted his hands on her, doing things. Bad things. Sweet things. Making her squirm and gasp and beg for more. Always more.

The desires were heightened, just like his reactions to her. But then, anger he'd rarely ever allowed himself to feel had burned away what remained of his restraint. Harlow lived as she did to punish herself, whether she realized it or not, and that crap ended today.

From now on, she would know only pleasure.

For the first time in his life, he craved a specific woman, and no one else would do until his desires for her were sated. Another change, one that bothered him, but not enough to stop him. He wanted her, she wanted him, and so he would have her.

"She here?" Jase asked as he entered the room.

"Yeah. Did you find out what crimes she supposedly committed as a teen?" Last night, after a little prompting from Beck, Jase had done his bro-duty and questioned his girlfriend in-depth about Harlow's past.

"Typical bully stuff. Called people awful names, made fun of them, made them cry. Stole boyfriends from other girls, only to dump the guys soon after. Everything stopped halfway through her junior year when she dropped out."

"Why, exactly, did she drop out?"

"Brook Lynn didn't know. No one does, apparently."

Something must have happened to her. Kids didn't just drop out for grins and giggles. Especially the ones who ruled the school with an iron fist.

"You want me to hire someone to look into what happened to her?" Jase asked.

"Already done." He'd made the call last night.

"Yeah, but your people aren't my people. My guys will look places yours don't even know about."

Illegal places. "I don't want to go there." He trusted Jase, but he didn't want Harlow brought to anyone else's attention. "But thank you."

"Not a problem. Just let me know if you change your mind."

"Will do." Pipes whined, signaling the shower had just been shut off. He had to tamp down his excitement.

"I know Jessie Kay is on her way over to help Brook Lynn with her sandwiches, but have your girl call her and tell her to cage the rage. No name-calling. No insulting." Seeing the way Jessie Kay and Sunny had gone for Harlow's throat yesterday had sharpened his shiny new protective instincts into razors. "If Jessie Kay can't manage civil, she needs to stay away from Harlow."

"You're putting me in the middle of a shit storm, my friend. You know that, right?"

"I do, and I'm sorry." He hated asking Jase for *anything*. "I'm also grateful."

"Hey, I wasn't complaining," Jase said with a grin. "I like make-up sex."

"Then I guess you owe me."

Jase snorted and strode from the room. Right on time. The faint pitter-patter of bare feet echoed from the wood floor. Harlow rounded the corner—and Beck reacted as if he'd just been kicked in the gut.

Her fingers twisted in the hem of her shirt, a nervous gesture. For what he had planned, she should be *very* nervous.

Wet hair clung to her neck and arms. Her white T-shirt was damp in spots, revealing the outline of her lacy crimson bra. He'd had to guess her size: small, but perfect.

He couldn't wait to get the little plums in his hands.

The shorts she wore had been cut from his most comfortable sweatpants, revealing mile-long legs that would wrap around his waist and hold on tight till the end of the ride.

"Have a seat," he said, motioning to the couch.

She shifted from one foot to the other, remaining in place. "Beck, I don't want to talk about my past."

"Then you won't." Again he motioned to the couch. "Sit. Please."

Frowning, she walked over and eased down. He settled in the chair across from her, wanting distance, hell, needing it to clear his head. But it didn't help. Her scent had changed subtly, the strawberries now dusted with sandalwood, saturating the air, filling his nose, going straight to his head—and his groin.

"Whether you want to or not, we *are* going to talk about your future. You, Harlow Glass, work for WOH Industries, effective immediately." Yet another change. Too much, too fast, like everything else about her, and enough to make his head spin. But there was no better way to take care of her and keep her close.

"Wait." She shook her head, as if she were certain she'd misheard him. "Come again."

"Your talent is incomparable. Which is why—"

"But you've only seen my ruined murals. How do you know my talent is incomparable?"

"I can't believe you have to ask. While your superpower is painting, mine is X-ray vision. I saw beneath the splatters to the bones of the picture." And, okay, there were photos of her amazing work in the box. "May I continue now?"

She nibbled on her bottom lip and nodded.

"You are going to design the sets and characters West uses in his games. You'll do it on paper, which he will then scan digitally. An RV will be delivered to my front yard later today, and you will live in it. A signing bonus for your services, one I would give to anyone I hired." Probably. "We don't always work normal hours."

"But...but...you haven't even seen my résumé.

Which, to be fair, I submitted to one of your assistants when you first opened up shop here."

"The assistant stayed long enough to hire a receptionist from Strawberry Valley, not an artist. And I don't need to see your résumé. Your work speaks for itself." When she continued to gape at him, he decided to forge ahead. "Say thank you, but don't make the mistake of thinking your job will be easy. You will be at our beck and call twenty-four hours a day, seven days a week. If we want you to draw a character sketch at two in the morning, you will."

"Do you even *need* an artist on staff?"

"Yes. West works way too much, and constantly recruiting freelancers takes a ton of time. This will take a major burden off his shoulders."

"So why haven't you hired an artist before today?"

Rather than admitting the truth—new hires usually gave him hives—he said, "Maybe I hadn't found the right slave. I mean, the right *person* yet."

Her lips twitched at the corners, as he'd intended.

Then the slam of a car door registered, and she stiffened. "Expecting company?"

"Just Jessie Kay."

The color drained from Harlow's cheeks. "She's going to be *so* mad I'm here. I should probably sneak out the back before you're forced to break up a catfight."

"First, I would never break up a catfight. I would watch it. Second, don't be silly. This isn't her house, and you're my guest. She'll deal."

The awe she leveled at him made him uncomfortable—and hot as hell.

Jessie Kay stopped to glare at Harlow, then at Beck. Then she beat feet to the kitchen, calling, "Brook Lynn.

Let's get to cookin' before I put a brick through a window."

The stiffness gradually abandoned Harlow. "Well. That went better than I expected."

A shirtless, sweaty West charged out of the workout room, and there was no need to guess why. He'd hoped to catch a glance of Jessie Kay.

West was like a starving man at an all-you-can-eat buffet around that girl. Problem was, he refused to buy a ticket to the meal.

Upon first arriving in Strawberry Valley, Beck had asked her out, slept with her, and when they parted on friendly terms, she ended up hooking up with Jase. Another one-time deal, but the damage had been done. To West, whose attraction to her had only developed after Beck and Jase's association with her, the statute of limitations would never run out. She was forever off-limits.

"Hi, West," Harlow said, smiling and waving at the guy. "We haven't been officially introduced. I'm Harlow Glass, and I would love a chance to get to know you. Join me? I'm certain Beck was just about to leave."

Excuse me? "I wasn't."

She flushed but didn't rescind her flirtatious invitation.

West glanced between them before smiling and walking over. "Well. This should be interesting."

CHAPTER SEVEN

HARLOW PRETENDED TO sink more comfortably into the couch as West eased beside Beck. Meanwhile, she wasn't freaking comfortable. This might just be the most nerve-racking experience of her life. The man she wanted to want was side by side with the man she shouldn't want, the first watching her with amusement she didn't understand, the other with an angry glower she didn't appreciate.

Trying to dredge up the confidence she'd had before the scarring incident, she batted her lashes at West. According to the seduction book, she had to be bold, and she couldn't be afraid to show interest. She had to let the object of her affections know he had a chance with her, and just how far she would go to be with him.

"Tell me about yourself," she said with a forced smile. "I'm interested in every detail, and I would enjoy nothing more than sitting here and listening."

Beck gave his friend's shoulder a hard shove. "All right. You are now officially dismissed."

West leaned back, crossing his arms at his middle and an ankle over a knee. "Why would I leave? My schedule is wide-open right now, and I've got a past to unveil."

Beck ran his tongue over his teeth and focused more intently on Harlow. "A new company policy has just been instated. No flirting with the staff. Ever."

"But I wasn't flirting." *Trying* to flirt would be a more accurate description. "Learning about my new employer will give me an idea about what to expect on the job." The one at WOH now, and later the one as West's (possible) forever girlfriend.

"Since it's for the job *I* just hired you for…" Beck shifted, his knee brushing against hers, making her gasp. "How about I tell you all about *me*?"

"You? Talk about yourself?" Her breathless tone embarrassed her, but she continued anyway. "Don't be ridiculous."

"Yes, Beck," West said, no longer fighting the smile. "Go ahead and tell us all about your life. We are figuratively *dying* of curiosity."

A soft animallike growl rose from Beck, the intensity of it baffling her. "Aren't you needed elsewhere, Westley?"

What was his deal? He was acting like a jealous boyfriend who'd—

She fought another gasp, this one steeped in shock. *Was* he jealous?

No. No, of course not. As a one-and-done man, such an emotion was beneath him. Right?

"Schedule's wide-open, remember?" West rubbed his hands together. "Start with your first memory as a child and end with your secret crush on—"

"Go." Beck pointed toward the door.

"Me," West finished with an outright laugh. He tried to cover the sound with a cough, then glanced at his wristwatch. "Well. I might have overstated my availability." He cleared his throat and stood, already walking away. "I think I hear— What's that, Jase?" he called, though no one had said anything. "You need me? No problem. I'm on my way." He paused in the doorway to wink at Harlow. "We'll have to do this again sometime."

"Yes, please." Had it been love at first sight? No. Was it a romance in the making? Maybe. As far as first interactions went, it wasn't the worst she'd ever had. *Go, me!*

Beck peered at her for a long while, silent and brooding. "Want to tell me what that was about?"

"No, actually, I don't." He would just rat her out to West, maybe even warn him away.

The purr of a very large engine registered, followed by the sound of crunching gravel. Through the crack in the curtains, she caught a glimpse of a brand-new, luxurious RV. Beck had been dead serious about the signing bonus.

Tides of excitement boosted her to her feet. "That's really mine? No matter what?"

"Are you accepting my job offer?"

And see her dream of becoming a paid artist come true at last? "Yes!"

He slowly unfolded from his seat, towering over her, both menacing and protective. "Then it's yours. No matter what."

"Thank you, thank you, a thousand times thank you, Beck." She wanted to hug him. She wanted to climb him like a mountain. She settled for patting his shoulder. "I will be forever grateful."

His gaze locked with hers, flames practically dancing in those golden irises. "I don't want your gratitude, Harlow."

The rough tone of his voice made her breath catch. She waited, staring up at him as her heart drummed out of control, but he never told her what he *did* want.

HARLOW MARVELED. In a single day, her world had been dumped upside down and turned inside out. Again.

After months of sleeping in a patchwork tent, she'd finally slept in a real bed, utter softness enveloping her. She'd taken a hot shower in a bathroom all her own, lingering until the steam died out. She'd eaten her fill anytime a hunger pang hit, and had drunk a tall glass of juice anytime her mouth went dry.

Life was suddenly, amazingly perfect, and in the bright light of the new morning, sprawled in her new bed in her new RV, she laughed. The queen-size bed consumed the back of the vehicle, the sheets a decadent caress against her skin. No more fearing the coming winter, warmed by old clothes, ratty blankets others had discarded, fires she'd started, and finicky rays of the sun.

A brand-new cell phone rested on the nightstand. An actual phone with apps and everything. The fridge was fully stocked, even though she'd devoured enough food to feed an army.

She lacked only one thing. Someone to share her good fortune.

She imagined Beck lying beside her, his strong arms embracing her, his warm breath tickling her hair, and tendrils of electric heat curled around her. Silly Harlow. He might be her benefactor, but there was no white knight lurking underneath his beautiful he-slut shell. He was temporary. She was forever.

"Knock, knock," the male in question said as he entered the RV *without* knocking. "Rise and shine, thornbush."

"Thornbush?" She sat up, not bothering to clutch the comforter to her chest. She'd fallen asleep with her clothes on, for which she was suddenly grateful. Seeing him set off a chain reaction of sensations inside her. Tingles along her flesh, a conflagration in her veins, both stealing the air from her lungs.

"I'm trying out different nicknames until I find the one that works for you," he said with a shrug.

"What's wrong with the usual *honey* and *sweetheart*?"

"They don't fit you."

Wow. Okay. Talk about a major punch in the gut. But she sucked it up and offered him the brightest smile she could manage.

He rolled his eyes. "It's a good thing. You're memorable. The others were not."

Oh.

"Well, here's an idea," she said in an effort to mask her delight. "Try *Harlow*. It's easy. Say it with me, Harrr-looow."

"Hayyy-booow."

She giggled. He laughed, then held out two paper coffee cups, the scent of caffeine, sugar and cream wafting from the rims. "You want one?"

"Yes!"

He placed both on the granite countertop in the small kitchenette. Just out of her reach. A clear incentive to "rise and shine."

"You are a cruel, cruel man."

"I do what I must." He propped his shoulder against the frame of the open doorway, looking inhumanly beautiful in a dark pin-striped suit, his hair brushed back from his face, a slight glint of stubble on his jaw.

My heartbeat is not quickening. My blood is cooling, not growing hotter.

"This is your first day working for me," he said.

"You mean for WOH Industries."

"No. I mean me." He arched a brow, daring her to contradict him a second time. "Are you nervous?"

"Hardly."

"You should be. Your boss will yell at you if you're late."

"You're my boss *and* my ride."

"Exactly. I'm always late."

There would be no understanding him today. Noted.

"Before we head off, I should probably go over the ground rules." He didn't give her a chance to respond. "At the office, I'll call you Miss Glass. You will call me Mr. Ockley." A gleam of mirth brightened his expression, somehow doing the impossible and making him more beautiful. "Or you may call me *sir*. Yes, definitely go with *sir*."

"No way. We are not part of an erotica novel," she said.

"Erotica, hmm?" His grin was wide, devastating. "Tell sir all about the naughty things you've read."

She laughed, trying not to be utterly enchanted by him. "Well, just last night I read about the mating habits of penguins. Did you know they have—"

"Way to ruin the sparks we had going."

"We had sparks?" she asked, just to be contrary.

"Get dressed," he said. "Or not. Yeah, probably not. We've got a big day, and I could use a little eye candy as inspiration."

For a moment, she wanted to bask in the glow of his praise. He considered her eye candy? Then she remembered he hadn't seen her scars. "I'll ignore your early start at sexual harassment and get dressed just as soon as you exit my bedroom."

"Why? You don't have anything I haven't seen before."

"Actually, I do," she said, throwing a pillow at him. It thudded against the wide expanse of his chest and fell harmlessly to the floor. He laughed, the sound as beautiful as the rest of him. "For all you know, my *anything* is better than any other you've seen." It wasn't. It soooo wasn't. She was so scarred even a man of his nondiscriminating taste would be sickened.

"You think so?" His gaze dropped to her chest. "Show me." A croak. But was it a demand—or a plea?

Desire mingled with panic, and she gulped. "Not even if you begged me."

"I've never begged before." His voice went low, husky. "But there's a first time for everything, isn't there?"

The air between them began to thicken, becoming heavier, making it harder for her to breathe, a sensation she was getting used to. She ached. She craved what only he seemed capable of giving her.

She'd made a tactical error, she realized. She'd challenged a playboy. "Just…get out," she managed. "Please."

His gaze roved over her slowly, heating, hotter and hotter. "Are you sure that's what you want?"

No. "Please," she repeated.

"Very well. I'll allow you to retreat. This time." He stepped out of the room, shutting the door behind him.

BECK GRABBED A beer from Harlow's fridge. He hadn't slept, so, technically this morning was merely an extension of last night. He took a long, deep swig while glaring at the cubbies and shelves. He saw his favorite beer. His favorite sandwich meat. His favorite cheeses. He hadn't known what she liked, and he'd refused to leave the thing empty, even for a day. Now a sense of possession rose. *My food, her fridge. Our stuff. Together.*

He banged his fist into the door. He didn't need this.

He remembered Harlow's reaction to seeing the items. She hadn't cared about name brands or that he'd made sure each of the four food groups properly represented. She had rejoiced over the simple fact that she would be eating. Period. And it had broken his freaking heart.

So. Yeah. Alcohol goggles had never sounded like a better idea. He took another swig of the beer. The situation with Harlow grew more complicated by the second, and something had to give. Soon. He'd been building to this point for a while, a man who hated change on the brink of one he couldn't stop—didn't want to stop. He was a pressure cooker set to explode any day…minute…second…

That happened, and he would be on her. But what accompanied an explosion of any kind? Destruction. Old habits would die hard.

There were so many things he wanted to do to and with her. One night would never be enough.

Despite what most people thought, his one-night stands weren't just about sex. Or even his own brand of therapy. For a little while, he wasn't a piece of trash easily left behind; he was a man worth begging for. A man without a past, without faults or failures. And when he left, he was a fantasy worth remembering.

What would he be to Harlow? Heartbreak?

He drained the rest of the beer and tossed the glass bottle in the recycling bin with more force than he'd intended. Normally he could take or leave a woman. If one didn't want him, fine. Another soon came along. But he couldn't leave Harlow, despite the complications. Despite the torment of *this*. He wanted her too desperately. Wanted her even though she'd given him no real encouragement.

But damn if she hadn't given West plenty.

When she'd flirted with his friend, every muscle in Beck's body had tensed. His blood had morphed into fuel, a lit match dropped inside his veins. Hello, wildfire. He'd nearly started a fight. Over nothing.

West's interrogation this morning hadn't helped.

"Why was your girl trying to interview me?" his friend had asked. "And for what position?"

Jase had been there, too. He'd grinned. "Did she ask you to name your biggest weakness?"

"You mean my inability not to be awesome?" Beck had quipped. "No. Because she didn't ask *me* anything. She asked West. I have no idea why." Was she attracted to the guy?

Well, too bad. Beck had found her first. She belonged to him.

Damn it. He could have her, but he would not claim her.

Harlow exited the bedroom looking fresh, adorable and young in a plain white T-shirt and jean skirt. Last night he'd burned her tent and collected her meager possessions from the campsite, feeling like an ass for throwing out everything that had been in the house when he and the others first moved in. Everything but the photos. The items had been hers, all she'd had left from her childhood, and he'd thoughtlessly had them destroyed at the city dump.

"What do you think?" she asked.

"You are…" *Stunning, worth anything, worth everything.* "You'll do." Worth anything? Everything? Hell, no.

"Not exactly office-appropriate, I know," she said, smoothing the sides of the denim. "But it's the best I've got."

Her unease gutted him. This amazing woman should only ever be confident and assured. And damn it, he needed to find a way to detach from her. Fast.

"Like I said, you'll do."

She frowned at him. "For an incurable flirt who always has a kind word for the women in his life, you kind of suck right now."

She was right. Flirt was his default, compliments his currency. He should be doling out praise rather than insulting her while staring at her with hopeless longing, but he simply couldn't quite manage it. If she smiled at him, if she laughed, her face would light up. Bye-bye, what little remained of his control.

"Come on. Let's go." He preferred to be inside the office well before eight, when the rest of the town came alive and accosting him on the sidewalk became a sport.

The ten-minute drive passed in silence, and he was glad. He used the time to calm the hell down.

Cora, the receptionist, sat at her desk in the lobby and smiled when she spotted him. "Good morning, Mr. Ockley."

"Morning, Cora. This is—"

The older woman hissed. "I know who she is. She's the bully who caused many of my students to cry."

Cora was a former schoolteacher, with the index finger from hell. Whenever she pointed it in your direction, you felt the flames rise up and lick at your feet. "Now, Cora," he said.

"I'm sorry," Harlow interjected, stepping forward on her own. "I regret my childhood actions every day, and I hope you'll give me a chance to prove I'm a different person now."

Beck liked that she made no excuses. She copped to her wrongdoing and accepted full responsibility.

Cora wasn't so easily convinced. "Time will tell, Miss Glass. Time will tell."

"I agree."

He draped his arm around Harlow's waist in a show of support, but immediately regretted the decision. She fit him perfectly. Too perfectly. "If you need us, we'll be in my office." Beck led her through the building, saying, "What do you think of West's nerdatory?"

"The walls are beige," Harlow said, and he barked out a laugh.

He should have known she'd focus on the lack of color.

Once he had her settled on the couch in his office, and himself behind the desk, he said, "Why were you a bully as a kid?"

Up went her chin, a stubborn action he recognized and was coming to hate. But she also rubbed her fingers over her stomach, as if tracing a familiar pattern. "Maybe I was born rotten to the core."

On to her tricks now, he shook his head. "I had Jase ask around. Also, I've seen pictures of you when you were little." No reason to lie, every reason not to. There was a shaky trust building between them, and a single untruth would cause it to crumble. "Once upon a time, you were a sweetheart with sad eyes."

"Pictures?" She blinked as realization struck. "You found my box. In my—your—closet."

"Yes."

"But…why didn't you throw them away, like everything else?"

He shifted in his seat, suddenly uncomfortable. "Maybe I hoped I'd find a nude of adult Harlow."

The prettiest pink brightened her cheeks. "Yes, well, I'm sure the people in town gave Jase an earful about all the times I *wasn't* such a sweetheart."

"They did, but I don't care about what you once did, only why. I have an interesting childhood myself."

In a small voice, she said, "Really?"

Hoping she would soften if she knew a little about him, he admitted, "I ran away from several foster homes. I was involved in multiple fights and a few other unsavory exploits. I left a trail of broken hearts in my wake."

She opened her mouth, closed it. Opened, closed. "You were in foster care?"

"Yes. Now, what happened to you?"

Plucking at the hem of her skirt, she said, "Nothing original, really. My dad called me names, and I called other people names."

The thought of little Harlow subjected to verbal and mental abuse enraged him. "Your dad is gone now?"

"Yes."

Too bad. Beck would have enjoyed dishing his own brand of abuse. "Why did you *stop* being a bully?"

She looked away, licked her lips. "What do you want me to do first, boss?"

Damn it, he'd pushed too soon for too much. What would it take to get her to open up? And why did he even care? It wasn't as if he had to know her secrets to enjoy her delectable little body.

"Just sit there and look pretty while I get some work done," he grumbled, focusing on his computer screen and the thousand emails waiting to be answered. "I haven't seen the set or character descriptions on the latest game contract."

He was able to block Harlow out...until she shifted on the couch. Her jean skirt rode higher up her thighs. *Such lovely thighs.* He was going to love trailing his tongue up, up from her knees to the edge of the denim. With a slight push of his fingers, his tongue would be able to complete the journey and find—

"Beck," she said, breathless. "Whatever you're thinking about..."

He was staring at her, he realized, gripping the edge of his desk, seething with the need to pull the blinds over the glass walls and dive on her. "You'd like it. Ask nicely, and I'll show you."

The building's front door opened, sunlight pouring inside along with Mark and Kimberly of S&S Financial. Right. His eight-o'clock meeting. A welcome distraction.

"Never mind." The company had only recently signed up as a client, and now Beck had to explain the operating systems more thoroughly.

"Mr. Ockley." Cora's voice spilled from the speakerphone. "Mr. Timberlane and Miss Potus are here to see you."

He picked up the phone. "Send them back."

As the pair made their way to his office, Harlow asked, "Should I step outside?"

No longer have her within reach? "You need to familiarize yourself with the inner workings of the business. Stay and take mental notes."

"Yes, sir." Her ocean-water gaze lingered on Mark as he entered, and Beck tensed, a curse brewing at the back of his throat…until she turned her attention to Kimberly, giving the young woman a once-over, abject longing overtaking her expression. She looked herself over, too, and plucked at a bit of lint on her T-shirt.

Beck's heart melted at the self-conscious gesture. She outshone the other woman by miles, but she had no idea.

Mark cleared his throat.

The meeting. Right. Beck stood, walked around the desk, and shook hands with both. "Good to see you again."

Kimberly smiled sweetly. But then, everything about her was sweet. She'd reminded him of sugar since the moment they'd met, kind to everyone she encountered. He'd thought about asking her out, but was now glad he hadn't. He was coming to realize he preferred his women with a little spice.

Harlow stood. Kimberly nodded a welcome at her, and Mark arched a brow in question.

"Our newest hire," Beck explained. "She'll be listening in, learning the ropes. Don't hesitate to stop and ask her to repeat everything we've said."

Harlow paled, and Beck had to swallow a laugh.

"Nice to meet you both," she croaked.

Everyone took their seats, and for over an hour Beck explained the ins and outs of West's newest program. He wondered what Harlow thought of everything, watching her more than he watched his associates, but her expression gave nothing away.

"Please, don't take this the wrong way," Kimberly said, smoothing a strand of hair in place, "but I'm a little lost. There's so much information to take in."

"I know, which is why it would be best if one of you spent the week in Strawberry Valley." Most companies like his would send an employee to train those at S&S Financial, but that wasn't the way Beck worked. The change in his routine on top of the change in his location would finally push him over the edge. "I can train you more thoroughly."

Kimberly nodded. "Thank you. I would be happy to stay."

"Wonderful." He looked again at Harlow. Her nails dug into the arms of the couch, her knuckles bleaching of color as she glared daggers at Kimberly.

She was angry?

Impossible. The emotion made zero sense. He would be training Kimberly, nothing more. But to train her, he would have to spend time with her. Was Harlow jealous?

Beck's head spun. He'd never been with a woman long enough for her to feel threatened by another potential conquest, or for her to view him as a prize worth coveting long-term. The thought of Harlow determined to win him…it intoxicated him, playing havoc with an already primed body.

This couldn't be the right reaction. This kind of intensity couldn't be normal. He swiped up a pen and drummed it against his thigh. Or, hell, maybe it *was* normal. Jase certainly couldn't function without Brook Lynn. To be fair, however, Jase was in love.

Love. Alarm bells suddenly clanged. Beck wanted

Harlow, but he'd be damned if he allowed himself to fall for her. To need her or anyone. Need was nothing but a barbed cage. It trapped you, cutting you into bleeding shreds anytime you tried to escape it.

I've got to get out of here. He pushed to his feet, his chair skidding behind him. "I'll show you to the Strawberry Inn," he said to Kimberly. "Miss Glass will stay here and type up notes detailing everything we've discussed."

"I will?" Harlow cleared her throat, nodded. "I mean, I will. Yes."

He offered a hand to Kimberly. "Shall we?"

"Yes. Thank you." She cupped her fingers around his and stood.

He led her and Mark out of the office and felt a prickle at the back of his neck. He turned to glance back at Harlow; he just couldn't stop himself.

Their gazes met, the moment utterly electric. A shock to his system, one he experienced bone-deep. Holding on to Kimberly suddenly felt wrong. Racing to Harlow's side seemed like a good idea. But he didn't release the redhead, and he didn't return to Harlow.

Leaving was for the best. If he didn't protect himself from a potential loss, who would?

CHAPTER EIGHT

WHAT A DAY. Harlow paced the confines of her RV, desperate for some kind of distraction, finding none. Her mind returned to Beck again and again, tormenting her.

He'd left the office that morning and had stayed gone for over three hours. Judging by the way his arm had easily slipped around the elegant Kimberly's waist on the way out the door, Harlow could guess what the two had done once the hooker—uh, lady—had a room at the inn.

Not that Harlow cared who Beck did. The bastard!

After she'd typed up her notes about what had been said during the meeting—blah blah firewall and blah blah HTML blah blah—she'd spent the remainder of her time writing letters to West, per the seduction book's instructions. And, okay, yes, she'd also brooded, growing angrier by the second. How dare Beck abandon her on her first day at work!

At least he'd returned with food. Cartons of beef stroganoff from Two Farms, the only "fine dining" experience in town, said its owner, and only its owner. And though Harlow had searched for wrinkles in Beck's clothes and lipstick stains on his skin—a good employee made her sure boss always looked presentable—she hadn't found either, and some of her tension had drained. But only some, and only for a few seconds.

"Do you have to be such a flirt?" she'd burst out, immediately wishing she'd kept her mouth closed. It was just, right before he'd left, he'd peered at her as if he couldn't wait another second to get inside her. But he'd still walked off with Kimberly clinging to his arm.

"I didn't flirt with Kimberly. I businessed her. And yes, I just used *businessed* as a verb. I'm brilliant like that." He'd flattened his hands on the desk and leaned toward Harlow, aggressive and almost angry, as if *she* had done something wrong. "Do you need another example of what *is* flirting?"

Indignation had struck. "Keep your example to yourself. I know where it's been."

He'd glowered at her. "Careful, sweetheart. You sound jealous."

"Your mom is jealous," she'd snapped. Like a child. But he'd called her *sweetheart*. What happened to her special nicknames?

Eyes narrowing, he'd flicked his tongue over an incisor. "You're seriously going with a mom joke right now? You need to get laid, Harlow."

She'd gasped at his crudeness.

"But here's the good news," he'd added. "I'm willing to help you out."

It was the first full-on let's-have-sex advance he'd ever made toward her, and she'd sputtered in response, "Get over yourself! You've been crowdsourced far too often for my taste. Besides, I told you. I want a relationship."

"A relationship?" Beck had scoffed. "You mean extended pain and suffering?"

"Because pain and suffering is all I bring to the table?" She'd thrown her notes on his desk, gathered her letters and lunch and stomped out of the office. And okay, yes, she'd abandoned ship at midpoint her first day on the job. Not exactly appropriate employee behavior. She sucked as bad as Beck.

The whole way home, she'd wondered why she'd been so upset with him. He'd done nothing wrong. Not really. He was her boss. Her friend. The only friend she had. They weren't boyfriend and girlfriend, and she had no right to castigate him for his life choices, no matter how bad they were.

Her fingers twitched, and suddenly she *ached* to pick up a brush, to pour her emotions into her art. In the past, no matter her riotous state of mind, the task of creating something from nothing had soothed her. But she had no supplies. Only pen and paper. The papers on which she'd written her letters to West. Whatever. They would do.

She sat at the kitchenette, flipped a page to its blank side, and grabbed a pen. As she allowed her imagination to guide her, she wasn't sure what she was drawing... until she recognized the square curve of Beck's jaw.

Made sense, she supposed. He was a beautiful subject and in the past few days—despite her better judgment—he'd taken over her thoughts and utterly consumed her desires.

When she finished, she surveyed her handiwork with a critical eye. Not to pat herself on the back, but yeah, she was totally going to pat herself on the back. She'd nailed every detail. From the fall of his hair, to the arch of his brow, to the fiery, determined expression he revealed whenever his affability was stripped away.

A knock sounded at her door, startling her. She

jolted upright, thrusting the incriminating picture behind her back.

"Harlow?" Brook Lynn called. "You in there?"

Not Beck, she realized, releasing a breath she hadn't known she'd been holding. *I'm not disappointed.*

"Just a minute." She stuffed the picture in a cabinet and hurried to the door, opening it to sunlight—and more than just Brook Lynn. Jessie Kay and Daphne, the woman Jase used to date, flanked the girl's sides. All three women held multiple bags of…clothing?

"Hobo chic might be good for a Saturday-night barbecue, or not—yeah, probably not—but it definitely isn't good for the office." Jessie Kay pushed her way inside, forcing Harlow to back up or be mowed down. "It's time for a makeover, Dillon style."

Hobo chic? *I'll cut a bitch!*

Whoa. Calm down. Why was she so defensive? Jessie Kay was right. The only way Harlow would be further from office-appropriate would be if she took Beck's suggestion and showed more skin.

Wait. Backtracking. They'd come to help her?

Harlow flattened a hand over her heart, touched in a way she wasn't sure she could articulate.

The others followed Jessie Kay in.

"Beck told us not to go inside," Brook Lynn said to her sister. "To just hand over the clothes and leave."

"Beck ain't my boss. Not that he couldn't be for the discount price of a million dollars a year."

"That's quite some discount," Daphne said. "Last week it was two million."

"Economy," Jessie Kay said, as if the single word explained everything. "By the way." She focused on Harlow with laser-sharp intensity. "Dillon style means by force if necessary, so do yourself a favor and get to moving."

Brook Lynn hit her sister on the arm. "Rude!"

"The way she's keeping us waiting?" Jessie Kay said with a nod. "I *know*."

The disdain Harlow heard caused her spine to stiffen. The trio might be here to help her, but they weren't here willingly. "If you're going to insult me," she said, a little of her old spirit returning, "you can leave."

"We're not here to cause trouble, I promise." Daphne, a beautiful brunette with kind eyes and a welcoming demeanor, smiled at her. "We haven't been introduced. I'm—"

"Oh, I know who you are." The mother of Jase's nine-year-old daughter. For weeks, all anyone in town had talked about was how she'd run out on Jase without telling him she was pregnant, how he'd only found out about his child recently. But Daphne had since done everything she could to right the wrongs of her past, and she'd succeeded, which was why Harlow admired her. "I'm happy to meet you. And, uh, was Beck the one who picked the clothing you brought?" Would she find nothing but bras and panties in the bags?

"He sure was. Adamant about it, too," the brunette added. "But he had to run, and I'm glad. Ever since Jase mentioned you've been hanging out with Beck, I've been desperate to chat with you."

"Really?" she asked, surprised. "Me?" In a "see the bully up close" kind of way, or in a "let's become friends" way?

Daphne's head tilted to the side, her brow furrowing with confusion. "Why not you?"

Harlow struggled to form a proper response. *Shall*

I count the ways? "For starters, I've been likened to the devil."

"It's true," Jessie Kay said. "I know because I have likened her to the devil."

"Well." Brook Lynn cleared her throat. "How about our Mighty Stallions, huh? I hear our illustrious high school is going to take State this year."

"How'd you meet Beck?" Daphne asked Harlow, ignoring the sisters.

Jessie Kay hiked a thumb in Harlow's direction. "She's been camping in the woods by the house. Which isn't as amazing as it sounds. Even I could survive in the wild…with credit cards, a bag of feminine products and a bottle of painkillers."

Brook Lynn rolled her eyes. "Yes. You're a true survivalist. Now that introductions are over, let's get down to business. How about you start trying on these clothes?"

An excuse to lock herself in the bedroom, take a moment to collect her thoughts and get her emotions under control? Yes! She snatched up the bags, along with the letters she'd left on the counter, glanced nervously at the unlocked cabinet holding her picture of Beck and retreated. Curious, she dumped the contents on her bed. Not a bra or pair of panties in sight. Just dress suits, summer dresses, purses, jewelry and shoes. Everything in her size.

Her hands trembled as she stroked soft cashmere, softer silk and the prettiest patterns she'd ever seen. Most of the items were different shades of blue—to highlight her eyes?—though several boasted ribbons of pink.

Why would Beck do this for her? Especially after the way she'd acted today?

"We want to see," Brook Lynn called.

Harlow stripped, catching a glimpse of her reflection in the mirror and cringing. It was like looking at Frankenstein's sister. Her numerous scars were pink, jagged and unavoidable, each forming a square with grafted skin inside. The damage stretched from her collarbone to her waist, and to say it was ugly would be kind. Her soul mate, whoever he was, would have to fall for her personality first and learn to live with the rest of her.

Trembling now, she donned the prettiest of the summer dresses; it was of Grecian design with spaghetti straps, a plunging neckline and pleats falling from a cinched waist. In front, the skirt hit just above her knees, but in back, the long, sheer train flowed to her ankles. Never had she felt so feminine, not even back in her heyday, and yet there was no way she'd ever wear the dress in public. Too many of her scars showed.

Feminine instincts screamed in protest as she changed into the most modest of her choices. A dress with capped sleeves and a scooped neck. At least the azure material clung to her curves.

She placed her hand on the knob, noticed she wasn't trembling as badly and perked up. The girls might have been coerced into helping her, but they were here, and they weren't setting the place on fire. Hope filled her as she exited the bedroom, her step lighter than it had been in years.

THAT NIGHT, BECK sat in his new chair—a plush black leather beast he'd had delivered and placed by the window in his bedroom. He peered outside. The moon was high and round, but also eerie as clouds swept past, obscuring the stars, offering no light to illuminate the RV parked in the front yard.

What did Harlow think of the clothing he'd purchased for her? What did she favor? What did she have on right this very second?

He would not be finding out.

I want a relationship, she'd shouted at him earlier today.

He squeezed the arms of the chair. She wanted the one thing he couldn't give her. And with the dreaded *R* word now in play, his desire for her should have cooled at last. Commit to one person? Trust one person to stick with him through even the worst of times? Hell, no. Never. But his desire *hadn't* cooled. It clawed at his insides even more diligently, desperate to be let off its leash.

He should have made a play for Kimberly. She might be too nice, and his tastes might run toward spicy, but she was a woman and they could have had fun. He could have experienced a moment of pleasure without drama or worry. Instead, he'd politely kissed her knuckles and left her at her hotel door. His body, the traitor, wasn't interested in a substitute for Harlow. Which made no damn sense!

Part of him hated the black-haired witch for doing this to him, for making him feel twisted up and wrung out. Turmoil sucked ass. He'd had enough of it in his childhood.

And damn it! He should have cut Harlow out of his life the first time he'd experienced a blip of unease. He should have done everything in his power to return to the way things used to be. The way he needed them to be. His life had been fine without her. Easy and uncomplicated, just the way he liked.

But he hadn't cut her out, and he now had a new reality. One where his every mood revolved around a woman he craved more than water to drink. It scared the hell out of him. It unnerved and panicked him. He wasn't sure how much longer he could go on like this.

With a grunt, he kicked the wall in front of him, leaving a crack behind. Harlow had changed more than his desires. She'd changed his oldest rule: don't do anything to draw the attention of law enforcement. While she'd tried on her new clothes, he'd finally paid a visit to Scott Cameron, and the conversation had nearly ended in assault and battery.

"Stay away from Harlow Glass," Beck had said the moment the guy opened his front door. They were roughly the same height, though Beck had him by at least fifty pounds of muscle—and a whole hell of a lot of skill. Cameron knew it, probably noticed the scars on his knuckles as he stroked two fingers over his jaw. "You don't, and I'll make you regret it."

Cameron had sneered at him. "You chasing after her now, city boy?"

"She works for me, and I protect what's mine. I saw the way you pushed her, and if it happens again, you won't be walking away. You may not even be crawling."

Cameron had narrowed his eyes. "If you live in the Glass house, you shouldn't throw stones. I'm no woman beater, but if ever there was one in need of a good flogging, it's that one. She only wants the guys she can't have. But you think you're different because you want her so bad, and I get it. Just like I get that you're not really here to warn me about my behavior. You just want an open playing field."

"What I want doesn't matter right now. Only what you do in the future."

"Man to man, I'll give it to you straight. She's poison, and she'll ruin your life."

"Man to man-child, your bitterness is showing. You need to get over the past, and you need to do it fast." The past only served as an anchor, dragging you down, down, and only when it was too late did you realize you were drowning. Wasn't that what Jase had tried to tell him every time he'd urged Beck to move on? To let go of his guilt and shame and grab on to hope…to the future. "What she did to you, she did a long time ago. She's not the same person."

Cameron had laughed. "You're a goner, there's no question about that. When you get the Glass Pass, don't say I didn't warn you." He'd shut the door in Beck's face.

He'd nearly ripped that thing from its hinges to get to the guy. Harlow deserved a flogging? Them be fightin' words. But as much as Beck protected what was his, she wasn't his—not really—so he'd walked away.

He downed the rest of his beer in a single gulp, his mind jumping to another incident. A few weeks ago, Jase had had too much to drink and prattled on and on about the difference between sex and making love. How making love was an expression of deep and abiding affection, that it meant something, that it was an act of importance with an extreme emotional payoff.

Leaves you vulnerable in the best way, Jase had added. *You adore the woman you're with. She's your partner, that one special person, and she adores you right back.*

If that *one special person* had the power to drive you insane, then Harlow was certainly Beck's. But for every healthy relationship like Jase mentioned, there were a thousand terrible examples. Could someone like Beck really be one of the few lucky ones?

Was it worth trying, just for the chance to be as happy as Jase?

A hard rap at his door. "Beck," West called. "You got a moment?"

For his friends? "Always." He switched on the lamp next to him and set the empty bottle aside. "What's up?"

West entered, wearing his new favorite attire. A pair of sweatpants. He'd been working out again. Trying to keep his mind off a certain blonde? He eased onto the edge of the bed, saying, "I've been thinking about your girl."

"She's not my girl." But the words left a bitter taste in his mouth.

Did he want her to be?

"Stop lying to yourself. You would give up your left nut for a taste of her and you know it," West said.

"You're right. I would." Staying away from her hadn't done him a bit of good. Maybe it was time to give in and go to her.

"Well, that's a start."

He noticed the wrinkled-up piece of paper in his friend's hand. "Whatcha got?"

Tension radiated from West as he said, "Before I show you, you need to know I haven't encouraged her."

Beck went still. No. Damn it. No! If West claimed to have interest in Harlow...

I won't be able to walk away.

"Jessie Kay went snooping through her things and gave this to her sister, who gave it to Jase, who gave it to me." West held out the paper. "Now I'm giving it to you."

Beck snatched it up and fell back into his chair. He unfolded it and found an etching of his face. A very lifelike rendering.

Harlow had drawn this, no doubt about it. And the expression she'd chosen to render? The one he'd thrown at her while they were in his office, when he'd had to fight to remain in his seat, hungry for a taste of her.

Satisfaction filled him, and he grinned.

Then West said, "Turn it over."

He obeyed and discovered a letter. As he read, he lost his grin, a low growl rising from his chest.

~~My dearest~~ West. Meeting you has the potential to be the greatest thing to ever happen to me. You seem to be a man of unparalleled ~~sexiness~~ character, and I'd love the chance to get to know you better. How about ~~dinner a movie~~ coffee? ~~Yours~~ Talk soon, Harlow

Rage unlike anything he'd ever known consumed him. She desired West.

"I'll meet with her, but only to tell her I'm not interested," West assured him.

Can't force the one you want to want you back. Can't convince a woman determined to leave you to stick around. The reminders grounded him, even as they reopened wounds that had only just begun to heal.

"Wouldn't matter to me if you were interested," he managed to grit out. "You deserve to be happy."

"I won't be. Not with her."

He said that now. But if Harlow came after him with all she had, West would eventually give in. She wasn't the kind of woman a man could resist for long.

Beck almost kicked the wall again. *Not grounded, after all.*

West stood, patted him on the shoulder. "I love you, man, and I would never do anything to upset you."

"I love you, too. Don't worry about me. I'll be fine."

Unconvinced, his friend said, "Nothing is more important to me than your happiness. You stood by me when I was nothing but a junkie. You supported me every time I tried to get clean and cheered me on when I finally found the strength. There is nothing I wouldn't do for you."

Beck stared into his friend's concerned gaze a minute longer, certain the guy had romanticized their past. Help? Him? No. Then he cut the tension with an insolent shrug. "Right now I'm going to need you to get lost. If you think a mug this gorgeous happens naturally, you're wrong. I need my beauty z's."

West lingered as if he had more to say, sighed, then finally left, quietly shutting the door behind him.

CHAPTER NINE

SLEEP NEVER CAME. Beck tossed and turned for hours before finally giving up, climbing out of bed with a dark curse and dressing. He had to get out of here.

He drove without a destination in mind, ending up in the city, at his favorite hotel bar. He drank way too much whiskey and flirted with every woman who approached him. His go-to type of woman. The kind he'd always preferred. Easy and fun. No muss, no fuss. But after a while, the strangest thing happened. The women began to irritate him. They coyly played with locks of his hair while leaning into him to give him a whiff of too much perfume and a glance at ample cleavage. Predators determined to use him for his goods and services.

Eventually he became gruff and rude, and they scattered. Good riddance!

He threw back a few more shots of whiskey before acquiring a room. He sobered by morning and called West to mention he wouldn't be making it into the office. Then he phoned a woman he'd once hired to try to get Jase out of prison early. A woman he'd never slept with, putting business first.

Patricia, a thirty-five-year-old defense attorney, had always seemed as leery of commitment as he was. She wouldn't make him feel as if he teetered on the brink of collapse. She wouldn't demand a relationship, and she wouldn't make him feel as if his entire world was careening out of control.

Harlow wanted West. Fine. She could have him. Beck wouldn't stand in her way. He would return to his old ways. What he preferred.

He picked Patricia up at her condo in the heart of Oklahoma City. Her walls were beige, and seeing them made him want to put a fist through them. But he merely flirted as they ate dinner at Mickey Mantle's, keeping things nice and light. Afterward they walked through Bricktown. Gold, pink and purple lights shone from multiple buildings, reflecting off the canal as ducks swam past. The air was cool, the perfect temperature, but missing the scent of wild strawberries.

The scent of home, as necessary as his heart or his lungs.

When had that happened? At first, he'd hated the inherent sweetness and had actually missed the smell of car exhaust, clashing perfumes and colognes.

"Whoa there, tiger. Your grip is crushing me." Patricia shook free of his hold, then withdrew an electric cigarette from her purse. She took a drag, vapor wafting on the breeze. "Something wrong?"

Get it together. "I'm with you. What could possibly be wrong?" How easily those words would have fallen from his lips in the past. Tonight? He cringed inside.

Patricia studied him, her eyes shrewd. "I know you're only telling me what you think I want to hear, but that's okay. I like what I'm hearing." She straightened his tie, and he almost backed away—like a puss—as if even that much contact was a betrayal to Harlow. "Let's go back to my place and forget the rest of the world exists."

A moment of bliss, nothing more, nothing less.

A moment without Harlow. The only woman he really wanted.

The ache in his chest, the one that had plagued him since he'd first met her, returned full force. Damn it, if he wanted to get over her, he had to get inside Patricia. But using another woman as a substitute was as ugly to him now as it had been with Kimberly.

Why? Sex was just sex. Right?

How can I know the truth when I've never experienced something better?

"Shit," he snarled. He pulled Patricia off the redbrick path and onto cement, out of the way of passersby. "I can't do this. I'm sorry. I want to, but I can't."

Her eyes rounded. "You're kidding me, right? I've seen you in action. You've never said *can't* before."

"I know, but things have…changed." Just saying the word was more painful than taking a double right cross to the jaw.

Patricia sputtered for a moment. "You, Beck Ockley, are committed to someone?"

He tried to think of something to say to lighten the mood—*there's no one else in the world when I'm with you, sweetheart*—but much as he tried, he didn't have the energy to charm and flatter. He released his breath and accepted the truth, finally nodding. "She doesn't want me, and right now, I'm not even sure I like her, but still she has this pull on me."

A sad smile curled the corners of Patricia's mouth. "Don't worry. I get it. I've been where you are."

"What happened?"

"What always happens when the fairy tale ends, I suppose. I lost him."

Beck's heart pumped faster, his breath coming in

short pants. Then she made everything worse by adding, "I've never recovered."

SOMETHING WAS WRONG with Beck. For the next three weeks, he spoke very little to Harlow. Every morning at seven, he knocked at the RV's door. Two hard raps, that was all, but he never came inside, and he never complimented her on the new clothes. He remained silent as they drove to the nerdatory, and while there, he just handed her pages typed with instructions. Draw this set and that character. He would then leave her in his office while he worked inside West's, pretending she didn't exist.

Despite his current abysmal treatment, she found herself watching him interact with others. On a purely scientific basis, of course. She had to acknowledge he was an even better guy than she'd realized. He coached a youth soccer team. He donated money to charity and time to town members who came in looking for advice. He checked on Cora to make sure she had enough sweet tea. He was even nice to his discarded conquests.

When Tawny came to visit him, hoping to rekindle their flame, he'd kindly said, "Any man would be lucky to have you, honey, but you deserve to be the center of his world, and that's just not my style."

Kimberly had eavesdropped—the slag—and given Beck a hug. "That was considerate of you," she'd told him.

Harlow had mentally flipped them both off and thought they should run away together and have a thousand considerate babies.

Hate myself. Kimberly was everything Harlow was

not, everything she wished she could be, and envy was eating her up inside.

She hadn't had a chance to continue her seduction of West, mainly because she hadn't gathered the courage to present him with one of her letters; but then, she hadn't yet written the right one. Something was off about all of them. And she hadn't been able to forget the way West had pulled her aside not too long ago, blurting out, "We're going to be friends, nothing more. Get used to the idea, fast."

At the time, she hadn't been worried. Friends? Awesome! As a dedicated lover of romance novels, she knew a great passion could bloom from a friendship. But nowadays West left a room anytime she walked into it, as if she were toxic waste.

Hope was dwindling fast.

The door to her office sprang open, startling her. Beck entered, his stride as graceful, powerful and sleek as a panther's. He wouldn't look at her as he said, "Hungry? Brook Lynn is here with lunch."

"Really!" Harlow was on her feet and racing around him a second later. Her shoulder brushed against his chest, the heat of him instantly spearing her, all her girlie parts singing at once.

Keep walking. Just keep walking.

Brook Lynn clutched a basket filled with sandwiches, telling everyone in the office, "I need test subjects for a few of my new recipes, and you guys are going to be my guinea pigs. So. I've got honey and cheese, turkey and cranberry chutney, peanut butter and banana, marshmallow and bacon, and salmon with pickled tomato. Take your pick."

"I want the bacon and marshmallow!" Harlow rushed

out, reminding herself of a hungry dog who'd spotted the only bone in miles. Brook Lynn created the best foods out of the weirdest ingredients, but nothing could beat bacon. Ever.

But Kimberly had said the same words at the same time, and they ended up staring each other down, willing the other to cave. Nice did not exist in a battle for bacon.

Five step plan, remember? "I'll take the turkey and cranberry," Harlow said, her disappointment keen but hopefully hidden. "Unless someone else wanted that one?"

No one spoke up.

Brook Lynn's gaze stayed on Harlow a second longer than was probably polite, an odd—confused?—expression on her face as she handed over the sandwiches.

"Thank you," Harlow said.

"After you eat," Brook Lynn announced, "I'd like everyone to tell me if the sandwich was totally awesome, on the border of awesome, or not even close to awesome."

"Will do," Harlow said, clutching the precious sandwich to her chest. What did she have to complain about, anyway? One bite of this one would blow a gasket in her mind, no doubt about it, making her forget bacon ever existed.

Too far!

Rephrase: making her forget bacon for a moment or two.

Better.

She turned and discovered Beck watching her with the same befuddled look as Brook Lynn, as if he didn't know what to think about her. Which she totally didn't understand! She hadn't done anything wrong.

She forced a smile. He was the reason she had any sandwich at all, really. Without the job he'd given her, Brook Lynn never would have spoken to her, much less gifted her with a morsel straight from heaven.

"I'll, uh, be in my office," she said.

"I think you mean *my* office," he corrected.

"I think you gave up your rights the first time you refused to enter because I was inside." She sauntered around him and kicked the door shut.

Kimberly came in behind her, smiling yet rueful. "I thought we could have our lunch together. You know, do a little girl bonding."

Harlow wanted to hate the woman with the passion of a thousand suns, but couldn't quite manage it and motioned to the couch. "I'm a little rusty, but I'm willing to try."

The redhead reclined on the couch and dug into her bacon sandwich, moaning with delight. Harlow bit into her own sandwich—and had an instant mouth-gasm.

What happened next would have embarrassed both of them if they'd been aware of anything but the food. They attacked the sandwiches like savages, no hint of manners, and they did not come up for air until the last crumb was consumed.

"I have to ask you a question, and I hope I'm not overstepping," Kimberly said, wadding up the wrapper and tossing it in the wastebasket.

"Go for it."

"Is Beck seeing anyone?"

Harlow tensed. "Define *seeing*."

"Dating."

"Define *dating*."

Kimberly chuckled, as if they were playing a fun new game. "Is he sleeping with anyone?"

"No. I don't think he does much sleeping when he's with his girls." Harlow tapped her chin and added, "I see him more as a wham-bam, out-the-door-the-moment-the-sex-ends-without-a-thank-you-ma'am."

Kimberly sighed. "I suspected he was a player. I'd hoped otherwise."

"You…want him?"

"I do. He's just so *delicious*."

Attack!

No, no. "Yeah, well, you're actually perfect for him." Harlow's nails dug into her thighs as her gaze landed on Beck, who stood in the lobby with Cora. His sleeves were rolled up, his hands in his pockets. A man without equal. Strong, beautiful and unattainable. A dream that would flitter away with the rising of the sun.

Don't water a dead flower, her mother used to say.

Wise words. If only her body cared.

"You like him," Kimberly gasped out. "Oh, Harlow. I'm so sorry. I didn't know, didn't realize…"

She sputtered for a minute. "I don't… He's not… He's my boss. And my friend." Or rather, he used to be. Before he'd started giving her the silent treatment. "I'm interested in West."

Kimberly blinked, shook her head. "West? Seriously? But… I've never seen you look at him the way you just looked at Beck."

"You're wrong." The girl had to be wrong. "What do you think about Strawberry Valley?" she asked, changing the subject.

Though it appeared she wanted to protest, Kimberly went along with her, saying, "It's hot, but pretty."

"Pretty? It's gorgeous. Exquisite!"

Smiling, Kimberly brushed a sandwich crumb from her skirt. "You're right, you're right."

"That would be a first," Beck said as he entered the office.

Every nerve ending Harlow possessed jolted in sudden awareness.

"Kimberly, honey." He used his most devastating tone, pricking Harlow's hackles. "I need a moment alone with Miss Glass." He waited at the door, holding it open. "If you'll excuse us…"

"Of course." Kimberly cast Harlow an encouraging smile before pushing to her feet and walking to the door.

"I think you've gotten what you need for the day," Beck told her. "Why don't you head out? I'll pick you up at seven."

The moisture in Harlow's mouth dried. "Seven?"

"For our date," Beck replied.

Kimberly's gaze darted to Harlow. "I, uh, really need to talk to you about that, Beck."

"I'm afraid that's gonna have to wait, honey. My meeting with Miss Glass is urgent." He gave her a gentle push from the room and shut the door.

"Date?" Harlow croaked.

His features were blank, revealing nothing. "Earlier today she asked me out. I said yes."

"She's sweet," she said, her voice hollow. "You'll have a great time."

"I don't want to talk about her." He claimed the spot Kimberly had vacated, and Harlow felt a stab of something dark inside her, not liking the fact that the girl's lingering body heat now radiated around him. "I noticed you've been wearing your new clothes, but only the same ones over and over, and not any of the others." He draped an arm over the top of the couch and leaned back, a pose of rugged relaxation and total seduction. With so many glass walls and windows, sunlight was able to stream inside, catching on the rich hues of his hair. "Why?"

Her fingers automatically sought her scars, tracing, tracing. "They're too revealing."

One corner of his mouth curved into an adorable lopsided smile. "Why, Miss Glass. Are you a bit of a prude?"

When it came to the hideous marks on her body? "Yes, sir. I am."

"Well, now. That surprises me."

"Why exactly does that surprise you?" She'd resisted his allure at every turn. He should wonder if she wore a chastity belt.

"You're beautiful. I want to see you draped in beautiful things. That's all."

Reeling...

Suddenly agitated, as if he'd revealed too much, he stood and strode to the wet bar in the far right corner, where he poured himself three fingers of whiskey. "So. The reason I'm here. West has been hired to design yet another new computer game."

Okay. All right. Time to get down to business. "Congratulations are in order, then."

"Yes, but there's no time for a party. I'm in the process of composing a cast of characters for you."

Excitement sparked. "Could you hurry? I mean, I'm not complaining, but I finished the last drawing you requested days ago." And she'd been itching to create another.

"I'll have it done later today. I was also thinking I would have paints, brushes and canvas delivered to the RV. I'd like to hire you to paint my portrait."

She almost bounced out of her seat, but caught herself with a single thought. *Can't appear too hasty.* "Okay," she said, playing with the edge of a piece of paper. "If you insist. And if the price is right." She'd drawn countless images of him, but the thought of painting him to scale and seeing him in full color intoxicated her. She could play with different shades of gold, brown and bronze, and even a wealth of greens to get the emerald flecks hidden so deeply in his eyes just right.

Maybe Kimberly had nailed it. Maybe Harlow *had* stared at Beck for reasons that had nothing to do with the job.

"Name a figure." He slowly, leisurely, walked back to the couch and eased down, the whiskey in hand. "Whatever it is, lollipop, I'll pay it."

The new endearment startled her, considering he hadn't used one these past three weeks. The fact that he'd gone with *lollipop*, something sweet and edible he'd never called the others…

I'm special to him.

Oh, no, no, no. Red alert! Red alert! That was the true danger of him. Somehow, he made *everyone* feel special.

"That's a daring thing to say," she stated quietly.

"But true nonetheless."

She placed her elbows on the desk and leaned forward. "Very well. The price is…" Inspiration struck, and she smiled evilly. "You can't have sex for a week."

His eyes narrowed to tiny slits, but he appeared far from angry. "Why do you care about my sex life?"

"I care about *you*, and I think abstinence will help build character."

He didn't miss a beat. "Very well, I accept." No time to celebrate. "With two caveats," he added. "The week won't start until the painting is done." *He* smiled now, and it was a wicked one. "Also, I want the painting to be a nude."

Her breath caught in her throat, only to exit on a gust. "I… You… Excuse me?"

"A nude. Meaning I won't be wearing any clothing. If you want to strip down, that'll be okay, too."

This was punishment for daring to impede his sex life, wasn't it? "I've never actually painted or even drawn what you're suggesting, and I'm not sure I have the skill." Or if she would survive.

"I have complete faith in your ability. And as an artist, a *professional*, I'll expect you to view me strictly through objective eyes. You can do that, can't you?"

"Of course," she said. She could absolutely, 100 percent view him through objective eyes…if he wore a cloak of invisibility. But even then it would be iffy. "Why do you want a nude?" she demanded, hoping to shame him into retracting his request.

"Maybe I enjoy the thought of disrobing for you." His voice had gone low and husky, a caress of unfettered temptation, making her shiver. "Maybe I like the thought of your eyes on my bare skin and your hands forming the shapes of my body."

She gulped. Having only ever dealt with boys, never with men, she had no idea how to respond to so blatant a statement.

"Or," he said, his voice returning to its normal fun, flirty tone. "Maybe I'm narcissistic and want to immortalize every inch of myself. How is one to know?"

How, indeed. "When would you like to start?"

"Tonight."

I'm going to hate myself for reminding him of this, but... "What about your date? I can't—won't—hurt Kimberly."

"I think we both know she was about to cancel on me. Which makes me wonder what the two of you were discussing."

Shifting uncomfortably, she said, "I will never betray a confidence."

"I could change your mind, but I won't. I admire your mind-set." His gaze dropped to the pulse fluttering in her neck. "I'll arrive at seven, and I'll bring dinner."

"Yes. I'd like that." A lot. And it wasn't the thought of food that made her heart race, but the thought of having him in her space. Alone... Naked. Within reach.

She sucked in a breath. Oh...crap. The worst had happened, hadn't it?

Kimberly had figured it out, but Harlow had done her best to deny it until the truth practically vibrated in her bones. How had she *ever* fooled herself into thinking she could fall for West...when she'd already fallen for Beck?

"What's wrong, dove?" he asked gently. He came around the desk and sat at the edge, turning her chair to trap her between his legs. "You were twinkles one moment, sullen the next."

He always read her so well, while she always struggled to make sense of his moods. Life wasn't fair. "It's nothing I want to discuss right now," she said, refusing to lie to him. But she *had* to talk to someone about this.

Who? She had no confidants, and any secrets she revealed to others could be used as a weapon against her. A game of "humiliate Harlow for sport."

"What will it take to get you to trust me, hmm?"

Was he serious? "Beck, for the past three weeks you've treated me like I'm a carrier of cholera. Why do you *want* my trust?"

"You're my friend."

But I want to be more. "Yes," she said, and cleared her throat. "You're right. I am."

"So talk to me like a friend. Share your past with me. Tell me what changed you in high school."

Her mouth went dry. Always they circled back to this. "Forget I agreed to be your friend. We're enemies."

"You'll tell me what's easy, but nothing that's hard."

"I don't like to think about what changed me. It hurts."

"Pain fades. Rip off the bandage and give the wound a chance to heal."

"No." If she told him, she'd have to show him. If she showed him, he'd never want her again. And right now he wanted her. He had to. The way he was looking at her...

He leaned down until his nose almost brushed against hers. "One day, Harlow, you'll open up to me."

"One day," she whispered. "Maybe. But probably not."

He cupped her nape, the heat of him making her gasp. "Definitely. And in more ways than one. I'll make sure of it."

CHAPTER TEN

BECK KNOCKED ON Harlow's door. This might be the biggest mistake of his life, but he suspected it would also be his favorite.

He'd kept his hands to himself for nearly a month, even as the hot little piece paraded around the office in the sexy summer dresses he'd bought for her, the material clinging to her perfect body in a way that should be illegal. He'd done his rock-solid best to ignore her. She desired West. Or at least she thought she desired West. Beck had watched her more and more closely with every day that passed, seeing nothing romantic in her dealings with the guy and everything awkward.

Then, of course, there was her undeniable attraction to Beck. As many lovers as he'd had, as much experience as he'd garnered throughout the years, he could detect a woman's desire for him even if he were blindfolded. Every time Harlow looked his way, her electric blues projected longing hot enough to make him think total-body third-degree wounds would be fun. And when he neared her, her breathing altered. When he touched her, goose bumps broke out over her skin. When he'd talked about posing nude for her, her expression had gone slumberous, as if they were already in bed together.

She wanted him the way he wanted her. And despite

all her talk of relationships, she would settle for what he could give her—a night of passion so hot they'd forget their own names. Temptation demanded its due.

She opened the door, wearing a tank and a pair of shorts, and smiled nervously in welcome. "Right on time."

His skin burned for contact, but he kept his arms at his sides. "Always."

"Except for the times you're late, right?" As she stepped back, he prowled inside and handed her the dish of food he'd brought.

Her eyes widened with delight. "I smell bacon."

"I had Brook Lynn make you some kind of stuffed peppers with your drug of choice."

"Seriously?"

At his nod, she ripped the foil off the dish and squealed with delight.

"It's not bacon and marshmallow, I know, but she ran out of marsh—"

"It's perfect!" She threw herself against him, wrapping her arms around him. "Thank you, Beck. Thank you so much."

The softness of her body conformed to the hard, masculine planes of his. She was curvier now that she'd been eating properly, and he liked it. A lot. Her strawberry scent overshadowed the smell of the peppers and bacon, fogging his brain, and her warmth stroked over him, heating him, reminding him of the first rays of sunlight after a long, harsh winter. He held her tighter than he'd intended, anticipation building inside him, the burning only growing worse—and better.

The urge to pick her up and set her on the kitchen counter nearly overwhelmed him. One button on those shorts. Probably one hundred and fifteen teeth in that zipper. A tug of his wrist would leave her in a pair of panties. One strip of cloth separating his fingers…his mouth…from her sweet spot.

Not yet. He forced himself to release her. He'd thought about this, about her reclusiveness and the hatred of the townsfolk, and he doubted she'd been on a date since high school. He wasn't sure how far she had gone back then, only knew boys her age wouldn't have known their way around an orgasm with a map and a flashlight. He had to take this one step at a time.

Still smiling, glowing so brightly she made his chest ache, she skipped to the kitchen table. Did she have any idea how much he wanted her?

Earlier, the perpetually sweet Kimberly had finally revealed a pair of claws—for a bacon sandwich. Harlow, who had seemed to covet the item more than lottery winnings, had graciously relinquished her claim. The girl who had spent the past however many months starving had willingly given food to the one who had never known lack. It was that second, that moment, that slice of life, that Beck's icy facade had melted.

After that, there'd been no denying the truth. No holding back, his reserve nothing but a crumbled heap. He wanted Harlow, and so he would have her. No matter the consequences.

"Aren't you hungry?" Harlow asked, offering one of the peppers.

"Starving," he said, his voice low, nothing but gravel. At the table, he claimed the seat next to hers, making sure their shoulders and thighs brushed together.

He heard a hitch in her breath, saw a scatter of goose bumps on her arms—felt yet another fire ignite in his veins. In unison, they turned their attention to the food. Probably for different reasons. They ate in silence, the air between them still crackling with ever-sharpening tension. She'd missed so many of his cues today, but this closeness…this she couldn't deny.

Her hand trembled as she took a drink of water. She licked a drop from her bottom lip, and he hardened painfully, imagining the other things she could lick up with that little pink tongue.

"What are you thinking about?" she asked, folding the edge of the sandwich's wrapper.

"Honestly? You're not ready for the answer." He tugged on the end of her hair. "Besides, I'd rather talk about the lies you told me when we first met."

Shame caused her shoulders to hunch in. "I'm sorry about that. But I promise you, I will never lie to you again, no matter how painful the truth is."

"Good. Prove it by telling me something about your past." When she opened her mouth to protest, he added, "Start with a favorite memory of the farmhouse." The need to learn more about her had yet to lessen.

"A favorite memory…" A faraway glaze appeared in her eyes as her mind drifted. "Christmas, about a year after my dad died. My mother and I decorated the entire house with ribbons and bows and afterward she baked pumpkin spice cookies. For the first time, we weren't afraid of anyone finding fault with our efforts."

"You were afraid before?" he asked gently. "With your father?"

Her nod was reluctant, but it was a response and it was progress.

"I know you mentioned he called you names. Did he ever hurt you physically?"

"He didn't have to. His words did enough damage."

Beck took her hand and twined their fingers. "Sometimes that's worse. Physical damage heals. Inner wounds can fester."

She held on tight, and the ache returned to his chest. But he was used to it now. It was almost like an old friend. "You were hurt, too," she said, a statement rather than a question.

Oh, no, she didn't. They weren't talking about him. "Haven't you heard?" He smiled as he released her and gripped his knees. "I'm Superlover. Stronger— and harder—than steel."

She rolled her eyes. "You're also deflecting."

"No, I'm stating facts. Now, what's your favorite food?"

"Bacon. Isn't everyone's?"

"Your favorite drink?

"Lemonade. What about you?" she asked. "Your favorite memory of the farmhouse, I mean. And don't try to flirt or tease your way out of answering. I'll kick you out of my RV."

"Harsh, Harlow. Harsh. But okay, fine. I enjoyed finding a blueberry pie thief in my hallway." When she pointed to the door, he said, "I mean it. You looked both scared and determined, like you were defenseless, but you would kill to protect the pilfered dessert."

"I would have," she said, a smile teasing the corners of her mouth. A smile he wanted to taste.

"Bunny," he said, reaching out to finger the hem of her shorts, the need to touch her born from his most primitive instincts. "Have you thought long and hard about what position you'd like me in for the painting?"

Color bloomed in her cheeks, her breath catching

in her throat. "Yes. You should be bent over the couch, your bottom red from a recent spanking."

"In to pain and punishment, are you? Good to know. Grab the supplies I sent over, and we'll get started," he said—and while she sputtered for a response, he began unbuttoning his shirt.

ONCE AGAIN THERE was something different about Beck. Only, this change came from the opposite end of the spectrum, and it was making Harlow nervous. He was charming, more charming than usual, and he was clearly bent on seduction. Did she have the strength to resist?

"Wait," she said. "I've been thinking. I should paint you with your clothes on first. You know, to make you feel more comfortable."

"Trust me. I'm always comfortable naked."

I'll bet you are.

He popped open another button. His nimble fingers had already worked halfway down the shirt, and what she saw of his chest captivated her. Well-defined pecs with a dusting of black hair that was golden at the tips. Tanned, unmarred skin. An eight-pack capable of intoxicating her after a single glance. He was altogether flawless and utterly divine.

His past lovers were probably equally flawless. Look at Tawny. Kimberly, whom he hadn't slept with but had considered dating. And then there was Harlow. Up top, she was like a patchwork quilt. "Don't you want to make sure I can get your upper proportions right before you trust me down below?"

A wicked sparkle in eyes now tilted with languid desire. "Do you think I'll be too big for the canvas?"

Kill me. Kill me now. "Just leave your pants on!"

He shrugged out of his shirt, saying, "You're sure?"

Not even a little, but she forced herself to nod.

He gave a heavy sigh, as if he were doing her a huge favor. "Very well. The pants stay on. For now."

"Sit on the couch," she instructed, pulling the easel, paints and brushes from the cabinet. Earlier she'd given him a list of everything she would need, and she'd had to make a split-second decision about acrylic paint or oil-based. In the end she'd opted for oil-based. Acrylic dried too fast, even when mixed with a retarder, making the blending of colors more difficult.

"I don't want to hurt your feelings by being truthful about how wrong you are," he said, "but even I know the bed will make a more visually appealing background."

The bed. He reclined on it, lounging against the pillows.

Tremors plagued her as she set up shop. "You'll have to be still."

"I can do anything you need me to do, lover." His voice had gone low and husky again, stroking over her with the power of a caress. "All you have to do is tell me, and it's done."

Her hand trembled even harder as she picked up her brush. "You're not supposed to flirt with staff."

"It'll be our secret," he said. "You've done portrait work before."

She began to etch his silhouette. "Yes. My mother was my favorite subject."

"What happened to the canvases? Because there weren't any in the house when I moved in. I would have seen them."

Why not tell him? "I burned them." Watched them smolder to ash.

He frowned, suddenly as serious as a heart attack. "Why?"

"I didn't like how I felt when I looked at them."

"I thought your mother was kind to you."

"She was, but every time I spotted her image, I remembered I never became the woman she expected me to be. I remembered the years I kept her bound to the house, and I just... I guess I decided to finally set her free."

"You loved her. And she loved you," he said, his voice weighted with an emotion she guessed was envy.

"Yes. Very much." Tears welled in her eyes, the lines on the canvas blurring. She paused for a moment, calmed herself with a few deep breaths, and continued. "What about your parents?"

He remained silent. Of course. He could prod into her life, but she had no business poking into his.

"Biological? Foster?" she prompted.

More silence.

"You know," she said, not trying to hide her irritation, "you insist I tell you all kinds of stuff about me, but you shut down anytime I question you. It's really not fair. I'm not going to do anything with the information but know you better."

Another minute passed before he said, "My mom died when I was five. My dad pawned me off on relatives for a while, and after I'd worn out my welcome, good ole Dad relinquished his rights to me."

"Oh, baby. I'm so sorry." Wait. *I called him baby?* The embarrassing slip had come out so naturally it scared her.

Thankfully, Beck hadn't seemed to notice. He merely hiked up his shoulders and said, "It is what it is."

"No. I refuse to think that way. What happened clearly hurt you. What was shouldn't have been." He'd lost a parent, only to be rejected by the other one. Harlow couldn't imagine what she would have done if Momma had cast her away as soon as Dad was buried. "You deserved better."

Beck cleared his throat. "Artists work by inspiration," he said, steering the conversation in a different direction. "What's yours?"

She didn't protest the change, saying, "Pretty much everything."

"Tsk-tsk. Harlow told her first lie of the evening. I'll give you that one, but the next one will cost you."

"I didn't lie," she said, earnest. But...*what will the next one cost me?*

"If everything inspired you, you never would have stopped painting in the first place."

"I was too poor to buy the supplies."

"Poor or not, if you'd wanted to paint, you would have found a way."

He had a point. "Allow me to amend my statement." She traced her brush over the canvas, beginning to bring him to life with color. "Everything inspires me...when I'm feeling safe."

"*Safe.* Interesting word choice, considering you have a shirtless man in your bed."

As if I need the reminder. "Hmm," she muttered, unwilling to commit to an actual response. And for a heartbeat, maybe an eternity, she became utterly lost in her art... Lost in Beck. In his beauty and charisma. His carnality. It was there in his eyes, staring at her from the bed as well as the canvas. Soon she was panting as if running a brush through paint were somehow a physical workout. Her skin hot with fever, her limbs not just trembling but buzzing with electricity.

"You okay over there?" he asked. "You look a little flushed."

"I'm fine," she said, breathless. "Just fine."

"You lying again?"

"No."

"My Spidy senses tell me otherwise."

"You're Superlover, remember? You have X-ray vision, not overdeveloped senses. But what if I *was* lying? What would you do then?" The impish side of her had to know.

He shifted, resting at a higher incline, his legs open and bent at the knees, creating the perfect cradle for her. "Let me show you," he said and wagged a finger at her. "Come here."

Self-preservation forced her to reply, "No way."

"Come here," he insisted. "Please, Harlow."

Please…

Her limbs acted the traitor, moving without her brain's permission. She set down her brush and stepped out from behind the easel. When she was halfway across the room, she realized what was happening and stopped.

Suspicious, she asked, "What are you going to do to me?"

He smiled slowly. "Everything I've been dying to do."

Red alert! He clearly planned to give her a night of pleasure…only, true to form, he would end things in the morning.

"If you'd rather keep working, fine," he said. "Let my body be your canvas and your tongue the brush."

So blatant. Anger flared, a halogen lamp in the forest of her conflicted emotions. *He really does want me. Me! But he will still discard me.*

Would he fire her afterward?

Her nails dug into her palms. Was this the routine he used on every woman? Hook her with a little romance, line her up with a slight baring of his soul, then sink her by convincing her to touch him?

Bastard! He needed to be taught a lesson.

Welcome to Miss Glass's classroom.

"You know, Beckham," she said with a sunny smile, wishing she could think up a more original nickname— and maybe one that insulted rather than praised, "I can think of a few things I'd like you to do for me." As she finished the journey to his side, being sure to sway her hips, raw hunger gleamed in his eyes, the green flecks brighter than ever. It threw her, made her stumble.

This is a game to him... Of course it's just a game.

She sat at the edge of the bed and cupped his hand in hers. Tingles, heat. She ignored both.

He went still, the pulse in his neck quickening. She fought the urge to lean over and lick it—an urge she'd never before entertained. In high school, the hickey had been something of a specialty for her, but it had never been about passion. She'd simply marked the guys as her property.

"Your hands are placed awkwardly," she said, getting back to business. "This is what you should *always* do with them." She folded one of his fingers, then another, another and another, leaving only one. The middle one. "Yes, that's right. I want you to go screw yourself!"

His gaze jerked up to hers and narrowed.

"I know what you're doing," she said. "You're lining me up to be your next one-and-done, and I won't stand for it."

"Now, now, dumpling. You're hurting my feelings."

"As if you actually have any feelings!" She slapped at his chest. "But guess what? I do. And you want to know what isn't nice? Using a girl for sex and ignoring her afterward!"

When she drew back her elbow to deliver another strike, he caught her wrist. He didn't grin, he didn't smirk, just flashed raw desire at her. "You want the sex, too. Admit it."

At least he'd dropped the pretense. "I admit to nothing."

"Back to that, are we?" He tugged her forward, at the same time swinging her around. She hit the mattress and bounced, Beck moving over her. "First, I wouldn't ignore you afterward. We'd remain friendly. Second, if I took these fingers," he said, waving them in her face, "even the one you seemed to favor, and tunneled them under your shorts...your panties...I'd find you wet. Wouldn't I."

The bastard didn't even pose it as a question.

"No!" *You'd find me soaking.* "Don't you dare do it. I... I want someone else."

"West?" He shook his head, adamant. "I know that's what you think, baby, but you're wrong. You want me."

She'd figured out she didn't really want West, thank you, but she wasn't going to give Beck the satisfaction of admitting the truth aloud. Well, not the full truth, anyway.

"I want a dream man, and you're not him."

Far from angered, he said silkily, "Tell me about

him, then," while tracing his knuckles over the curve of her cheek.

Fighting to gain control of her treacherous body, she lashed out. "For starters, he's interested in marriage, not a fling."

Beck laughed. Actually laughed. "And you think West is the marrying kind?"

"Why wouldn't I think so? He hasn't been banging his way through the female population."

Low blow. He flinched, his good humor gone in a blink. "You are not a Victorian maiden, Harlow. You don't have to get married to have sex."

"You're right. I don't have to, but I want to. Or at the very least, I want to know I'm on that path before I take such a big step. I want to be part of a family again."

The scowl he flashed was dark and lethal. "Have you *practiced* before marriage?"

"That's none of your business," she muttered.

"I'll take that to mean *very little*."

"Or a whole hell of a lot." Or not at all. Whatever.

"And you think you want your family to include West?" he said. "Fine. Come on, then. Let's get this over with so we can move on." He stood, pulled on his shirt and buttoned it halfway up his chest before yanking her to her feet. He held on tight as he tugged her toward the door.

"Where are we going?"

"To the house. Friend that I am, I'm going to help you get to know West better."

Had his voice hitched there at the end? Or was that wishful thinking on her part? "I don't need your help."

"You do, or you'd already have nailed him down."

"There's nothing wrong with taking things slow."

"But there's everything wrong with procrastinating. Just remember," he said, continuing to drag her through the night as crickets sang and locusts buzzed, "this was what *you* asked for."

CHAPTER ELEVEN

BECK HAD OVERPLAYED his hand tonight, but there was no going back now. He had to continue playing or he had to fold, and he wasn't even close to being ready to fold. Harlow was a sickness, and bedding her was the only cure. If the only way to win her was to show her just how mistaken she was about West, then so be it.

He hauled her to the porch, moonlight and lamplight spilling over her, paying her delicate features nothing but tribute. Just then she was a woman who'd stepped straight from his sweetest dreams—and his worst nightmares. Someone who changed the rules of the game. She was lovely, almost ethereal, and her eyes the only glimpse of morning sky. Endless, fathomless. Breathtaking. His gut twisted with a sharp blend of anger and desire.

"I hope you're ready for this," he said. He sure wasn't. He opened the door, heard voices streaming from the kitchen and wound an arm around Harlow's waist, just in case she considered bolting. The way she fit him…

"I don't have to be ready. I'm not going along with it." She contradicted her words by snuggling against him, as if starved for contact, and damn it, need for her burned away his anger.

He had to have her. Soon. This was the way.

The dogs were asleep in the living room, though Sparkles—Brook Lynn's shadow—woke up at the thump of his boots on the wood floors and lifted his head, his ears twitching. He gave Beck the evil eye.

"Keep moving," he told Harlow. The mutt from hell might decide it was time for dinner. Or time to pee on his shoes again.

Conversations ceased as their grand entrance was noticed.

"Hi, Harlow," Daphne said. "It's good to see you again."

"Thank you," Harlow said, trembling against him. "You, too."

"Uncle Beck! Guess what?" Hope, Jase's nine-year-old daughter, bounced in her seat, her pigtails swinging back and forth. "We played Monopoly, and I won."

"Only because you're a tyrant," West said with affection. His features darkened as he focused on Jessie Kay. "And you're a sore loser."

"Because I refused to stay at your hotel and risk a flea infestation?"

"I stayed at yours even though there's no telling what *I'll* come down with."

Jessie Kay hissed at him.

"And that's our cue to leave. Go get your dog, Hope." Daphne placed an empty glass in the sink, saying to Harlow, "Steve, the hellion—I mean, the prince—used to live with Jase, but Hope can't stand to be parted from him, even though he hates me."

"All dogs hate you," Beck reminded her.

"This is true."

"But, Mah-mah." Hope stomped her foot. "Uncle Beck just got here, and he brought a friend, so—"

"Steve," Daphne insisted. "Now."

"Fine." Hope pushed to her feet. "But I'm adding this to my growing list of your grievances."

Jase clasped the little girl's hand and kissed her knuckles. "Don't forget you promised to spend the day with Brook Lynn and me tomorrow."

"Only babies forget, and I'm not a baby," she groused.

"But you *are* tired, hence the reason you're more prickly than a porcupine," Brook Lynn said.

"That's *not* an insult," Hope proclaimed as Daphne escorted her from the kitchen. "Porcupines are cute."

Jessie Kay stood. "Well. That's my cue to leave, too." She leaned down to kiss Brook Lynn on the cheek. "See you later, sis. Jase, give it to her good tonight." She scowled at West, then quickly averted her gaze. When she walked by Beck, she patted his cheek.

West faked a yawn. "Well. I've scheduled an early bedtime tonight and—"

"Stay," Beck said before looking at Jase and motioning to the exit with a tilt of his chin.

Jase took the hint and helped Brook Lynn to her feet. "All right, time to pay your rent, angel. I haven't forgotten how many times I let you spend the night in my hotels."

"Let me? You charged me double!"

"Yes, but all the money bought you was time. You still have to pay interest."

Brook Lynn chuckled huskily and waved before following Jase out of the kitchen, calling, "Night, guys."

"Night," everyone returned.

Finally. West, Harlow and Beck were alone.

Beck leaned down to whisper into Harlow's ear, "Go

ahead. Show him your best." He gave her a little push toward the table.

"Someone clue me in," West said. "What's going on?"

"I'm leaving, that's what," Harlow said. Determined words, snotty tone. She attempted to wrench herself from Beck's grip.

"Oh, no." Beck merely tightened his hold. "We're going to have a glass of sweet tea while you two crazy kids get to know each other better."

Harlow anchored her hands on her hips. "You know what? You're right. We *are* going to get to know each other. But your presence is unnecessary, Beck. Leave."

"Not gonna happen."

"We don't need—"

He cut her off, whispering, "If you and West get married and live happily ever after, you'll have to get used to having me around."

She snapped her mouth shut, then lifted her chin and grumbled, "That's a very sad point." She flashed a too-bright smile at West and eased into the chair Jase had vacated. "I'm game if you are."

Beck vibrated with irritation as he carried a pitcher of tea and three glasses to the table and settled between the pair. "My girl here has certain ideas about the kind of man she wants to end up with," he explained, "and I'd like to know if the two of you are compatible."

Understanding dawned on West's features, a smile nearly breaking free. He cleared his throat and donned his most uncaring expression. "Sure. Whatever."

Beck poured the tea, handed out the glasses, and Harlow clutched hers as if it were a lifeline.

"Kick us off, sweet pea," he said. "Tell my good

buddy Lincoln—that's his first name, in case you didn't know—a little about yourself."

"Well." There was a slight tremor in her voice. "I'm twenty-six, and I've never been married."

"Would you like a medal?" West muttered, while staring down at his cell phone, playing one of the games he'd created.

She glared at Beck, but he merely arched a brow.

Don't make plans with men you don't know.

"Yes, actually, I *would* like a medal, considering I'm hot but don't realize it, which makes me even hotter." The tremor had vanished, the snotty attitude firmly in its place. "It's a miracle no one's snatched me up. But then, most men are idiots, so…"

West smiled, realized his mistake, and glowered at his screen.

Beck braced elbows on the table. "You're suggesting outward beauty is all that matters."

"Hardly. My personality is hot, too. But Beck, darling." Sugary-sweet tone now. Too sweet. "You aren't part of this get-to-know-you session, even though you insist on being a total third wheel, so do us all a favor and zip your stupid lips."

Then, she dismissed him. Looking to West, she traced her fingertips over the collar of her shirt, so feminine Beck's every masculine instinct growled, hungry for the next meal. "So. Lincoln. How old are you?"

West played the video game a little longer before deigning to answer. "I'm twenty-eight, but I've got the stamina of an eighty-year-old coma victim. Horrible lover. Even worse cuddler."

"Well, those skills can be taught," she said, reaching over to caress his shoulder. "Anyway, you're quite young to be so successful. It's impressive."

It *was* impressive. Beck wasn't sure where he would have ended up without the guy.

West shrugged. "I work hard," he said, then added, "probably too hard. I tend to ignore the people in my life. Especially women."

"Well, I understand how taxing such a busy work schedule can be, and I commend you for it." She gave his shoulder another caress, and Beck almost jerked the two apart. "I hope the lucky ladies in your life are as understanding as I am."

"I guess," West said and shrugged again.

"Wow, just look at these muscles, West. You are amazingly strong, aren't you?" She cast another narrowed glance Beck's way, presumably to make sure he was watching as she scooted her chair closer to West's. "You know," she said, the tip of her finger toying with the rim of West's glass. When she caught a bead of condensation, she brought it to her lips and sucked, causing Beck's groin to twitch behind his zipper. "I have a skill of my own, but it's quite naughty."

West glanced up, phone forgotten. "Do tell."

"Yes. Do." Beck simmered with renewed anger— even more desire. He smoothed a lock of hair from Harlow's face. One touch, but he was greedy for more.

Her breath caught, but she leaned away from him, getting closer and closer to West, until her mouth was poised at the shell of his ear. In a husky voice low enough to be considered a whisper but loud enough for Beck to overhear, she said, "I'm *super* good at parking."

Stick a fork in me. I'm done. Done with the conversation. Done with watching the object of his obsession doing her rock-solid best to arouse another male. "West doesn't need to hear about that. Let's go—"

"Even boys from two counties over dreamed of making out with me in the backseat of their trucks," she continued with an effortless sensuality. "I'm very bendy."

Beck slammed his glass on the table, tea sloshing over the sides of the rim. "Harlow here is looking to settle down forever," he barked. "She thinks you'd make an awesome groom."

"Marriage?" West sneered with distaste. "Me? Hell, no. Never."

"He's all for others tying the knot, but when it comes to himself he thinks *The Newlywed Game* should be called the Dig Your Own Grave game," Beck explained, relaxing now that the conversation had taken a new direction.

Harlow unveiled a brittle smile. "Maybe you just haven't met the right person, Lincoln. You don't mind if I call you Lincoln, do you?"

"Call me whatever you like, but I *have* met the right person." His voice cracked. "She died." He stood, his chair skidding behind him, and strode out of the kitchen.

Harlow rounded on Beck, all hint of supple, willing female gone. "I hope you're happy with yourself. You did this."

"Me?"

"Yes, you." The words were nothing more than a hiss. "You wanted me to know I can't win the affections of anyone else, that I'm stuck with you, destined to be your newest conquest."

"Stuck with me?" he snarled.

"Yeah, that's right. You aren't the prize you think you are, Beck Ockley, but maybe West is. Maybe he's worth fighting for. Maybe, unlike you, he has a heart and the ability to care for someone other than himself."

"I have a heart. I care."

She didn't seem to hear him, plowing ahead. "You know, there are plenty of guys in town. Why focus all my efforts on just one? I'm sure *lots* of guys would like a chance to get to know the new me. I can bring them back to my RV—"

"*My* RV."

"—and practice being married, just the way you suggested."

Beck would burn the RV to ash first.

Too far gone to fight his sense of possession, he hooked his foot around the bottom of her chair and forced her chair closer, closer still. Their thighs touched, and she gasped, perhaps at the force he'd used, perhaps with a desire of her own.

He grabbed her by the waist and easily hefted her onto the table, on his feet and between her legs a second later, glaring down at her.

"I want you, and it's past time I showed you how much. You'll keep your sweet ass *parked* on this table and you'll show *me* your skills. Me. No one else." And then his hand was cupping the back of her neck, drawing her forward.

WHAT THE HECK was happening?

The question echoed inside Harlow's mind as Beck smashed his mouth against hers. She lost her breath, shook with need, desire and heat, so much heat. Two seconds ago, she'd wanted to lash out at him for his part in tonight's debacle. Now? She just wanted to melt into his arms.

The mint-and-sugar taste of him tantalized her, and she instantly craved more. Her head swam, their tongues dueling, and even though she clutched at his shirt for balance, she still felt off-kilter. *Been so long since I've been the center of a guy's world, but never like this.*

He worked her mouth expertly, the pressure fierce but not stinging, as if she were a treasure he wanted to enjoy and protect at the same time. His fingers curled through locks of her hair, angling her head, allowing him to take her mouth even deeper.

Pleasure burned through her, nerve endings she'd never known she possessed coming alive with sensation. Her blood fizzed in her veins, and sitting still became impossible. She ran her hands up the strength of his chest, around his back, desperate to touch more of him, greedy for it.

She felt knots of tension as hard as rock and dug her nails in deep, urging him closer to her. His chest brushed against hers, creating the most delicious friction, sending waves of heat deep in her belly.

"Beck."

He bit at her bottom lip, and like that, a kiss she'd already considered wild spun completely out of control, tearing through any resistance she might have still harbored. He caressed his hands down the ridges of her spine and cupped her rear. When he squeezed her, skin to blistering skin, she realized the hem of her dress had ridden up.

"You feel so good, Harlow."

He'd said her name rather than a silly endearment, and somehow that was ten thousand times sweeter. He'd just made it clear he knew the woman he held in his arms. He knew who he kissed as if his life depended on it.

"More," she demanded. "Please, more."

"I'll take care of you." He tilted her back and nipped his way along her jaw. He licked and sucked on her neck, leaving a trail of fire in his wake. He laved at her hammering pulse, and she nearly shot off the table. The heat of his mouth on her skin…the wet…

Moaning, purring, she tunneled her fingers through his hair to hold him in place.

"The sounds you make…they're killing me, baby."

Only fair, since parts of her were dying brutal deaths, as well. The loneliness. The heartbreak. The guilt and shame for a past she couldn't redo. Here, now, there was only Beck. And his mouth. And his hands. She existed for pleasure, his pleasure, aching to the point of pain.

Led only by instinct, she had no finesse, no defense as she grabbed hold of his belt and pulled him forward, arching her hips. The long, hard length of him ground into the apex of her thighs, and she gave another low, needy moan.

"You said you'd…take care… Beck, please."

This time, she didn't have to urge him physically. He ground against her again and again, every point of contact making her gasp and plead for more. If he decided to rip away her panties and take her here and now, she would let him. It didn't matter that anyone could walk in on them. Didn't matter that they'd had no discussion about what this would mean, or how this would change the foundation of their relationship. She'd reached a place of no…yes, yes…*like that…there!*

He rocked into her harder, faster, causing the table to inch backward, banging into the wall. One of the pictures rattled, threatening to fall.

"Wrap your legs around me," Beck commanded.

The words yanked her out of the moment. He'd said them before—*wrap your legs around me*—but not to her... To another woman. To Tawny the night Harlow had broken into his house.

One and done.

She was about to give herself to a man who'd made no promises beyond tonight.

It mattered, she thought, cold realization slapping her. This night would mean something to her, but it would be one night in a long line of nights for him. She would want more—always more—but he would be finished with her. One and done. No exceptions. She would have to watch him move on to his next conquest.

Harlow pushed against his chest. He was too strong to budge, but he did lift his head. In the light, his eyes were molten gold, his lips pink, moist and kiss-swollen, and as the tension she'd felt in him revealed fine lines around his eyes, he'd never looked more devastatingly beautiful. A warrior straight from battle, determined to enjoy his prize.

"No," she said, shaking her head. "No. We can't do this."

"We *can*."

"We shouldn't."

"You want me. I want you. I don't see a problem."

He wouldn't, would he? "You *never* see a problem, Beck. Not with anyone. And *that's* a problem for me."

Releasing her as if she'd just sprouted horns and fangs, he ran his tongue over his teeth. A cry of disappointment bubbled in her chest, but she swallowed it back.

"I don't want to have a one-night stand with you," she whispered, wishing she would stop trembling. West wasn't the man for her and never would be—she got that—but neither was Beck, even though he drew her with invisible chains, and oh, crap, the urge to curl into a ball and sob bombarded her.

"We'll enjoy ourselves, Harlow. That I can promise you."

"I know. But to taste what you have to offer and then have it taken away? No," she said, shaking her head. *I've lost too much already.* "Give me forever, or give me nothing."

He gazed at her with longing.

He gazed at her with terror.

He gazed at her with fury.

He backed a step away, and the nerve endings he'd awakened within her stopped singing, suddenly screaming in protest. They hadn't gotten nearly enough of him. *She* hadn't gotten enough.

His features shuttered, hiding his emotions. "I don't know what I can give you, but however long we last, it won't be forever. The future is too unpredictable."

"Then it's nothing," she said, tears welling. There was a part of her, deep inside, shouting for her to girl-up and fight for him. Walking away would be easy. Emotionally gut-wrenching, but easy. And really, "easy" would be her only reward. Fighting for him would be difficult, but the potential for payoff would be far greater. But the potential for hurt and failure, losing what little she'd gained in her life… It scared her to the bone.

"It's not enough," she said.

He laughed bitterly. "That's the thing, sweet. I never am."

CHAPTER TWELVE

HARLOW TRUDGED OUT of bed and dressed in a pair of frayed jeans shorts and her high school cheer shirt—go Stallions! Very little else in the RV belonged to her. She hadn't paid for anything with the weekly checks she'd earned as a WOH employee because she hadn't needed to; Beck had always given her cash plus bags of groceries, toiletries and clothing, allowing her to build a small savings. So, suspecting she would soon be kicked out, she didn't bother packing. She wondered if Beck would knock on her door as usual, not to tell her to "rise and shine" so they could leave for work, but to tell her to take a walk of shame off the property. Or maybe he just expected her to head off on her own without being told.

She'd been watching the clock… Any second now the answer would become clear…

Two hard raps sounded at the door. "Harlow," he snapped. "Get up. Let's go."

She yelped and tugged at the knob, not sure why she was surprised, considering she'd been waiting an eternity for this moment to arrive. He stood in the sunlight, his dark/light hair brushed back from his face, his lids narrowed, the tension from last night seeming to have doubled.

He looked her over and frowned. "That's how you want to go to the office today?"

He wasn't firing her *or* kicking her out? "Well…I wasn't sure I'd be welcome at the office."

His gaze flipped to hers and narrowed further. "Always thinking the worst of me."

Guilt gave her a good old-fashioned kick in the heart. "I don't always think the worst of you. I think the worst will happen to me. There's a difference."

"Whatever you need to tell yourself, honey. Let's go."

For once, he didn't open the car door for her, and all vestiges of his flirtatious side were gone. He switched on the radio, discouraging further chatting, but the hard rock soon grated at her ears.

She turned off the radio and said, "Are you—"

"I don't want to talk about last night."

"Good. Neither do I." She was still too raw. Still reeling. One kiss had ripped away her every defense, making her forget her long-term goals. "I was simply going to ask if you were coming over tonight so I can work on your portrait."

"No. I'm going out."

"With whom?" The question whipped from her before she could stop it, and she considered jumping out of the car. Eating asphalt would be less painful than this conversation.

"That isn't any of your business."

She dug her nails into her thighs, cutting into skin. Just last night he'd had his tongue in her mouth, and now he treated her as if she were nothing special. Because—let's be honest—she wasn't. Not to him. But how much worse would it have hurt if she'd actually had sex with him, and then had to go through this same routine today? *Count my blessings.*

"You're right. Forget I said anything," she managed with a carefree tone. She turned the radio back on.

When they arrived at the office, she didn't wait for him to come around the car—or not. She got out on her own and as casually as possible walked inside the building. The supplies she needed to sketch the new cast of characters were waiting in her office, as promised. The descriptions, the pencils and the notepads. There was a note from Kimberly, as well.

Dear Harlow,
I never meant to encroach on your territory! I truly had no idea you were interested in Beck. For your peace of mind, you should know we canceled our date. Also, I'm heading back to S&S Financial. I'll be rooting for you. If anyone can tame a playboy, it's you. You're like a rose, thorns and all. You leave a mark. (And that's a good thing!) Make sure to send me an invitation to your wedding.
Kimberly

Harlow's heart skipped a treacherous beat.

She heard Beck come into the room, the clunk of his briefcase as he set it down, the thump of his shoes as he left the room. The swish of the door as it closed. Her heart drummed. She glanced up in time to watch him enter West's office, which was currently empty.

Disappointment and despair washed over her. Beck hadn't fired her or kicked her out, but he sure had written her out of his life. And she wasn't sure why. She'd told him she didn't want a one-night stand, and before that, he'd known she was interested in a long-term relationship. Why act as if she'd ripped out his heart and trampled on it?

Maybe Kimberly was right. Maybe Harlow had left a mark.

Shouldn't get my hopes up. Letting the descriptions of the character profiles play through her mind and guide her hand, she worked for several hours. One image after another came to life on the page, but none of them satisfied her. There was no spark. The images fit the narratives but lacked any sign of life. When she found herself subconsciously adding Beck's features to the hero of the game, well, she decided to call it quits for the day.

She had to talk to someone about what was going on. She desperately needed advice, her inexperience cloying, choking her. She'd never get anything done, otherwise. But who could she call?

Beck was her only real friend, but the only advice he'd give her was *get naked and get in bed.*

Brook Lynn might be willing to listen. While they weren't bosom buddies, they didn't hate each other, either. At least Harlow hoped not. There was only one way to find out...

Harlow picked up the phone and dialed. Beck had given her a list of names and numbers soon after she'd begun working for him, just in case she had questions about something when he wasn't around.

Brook Lynn answered on the third ring. "Hey, Beck. What's up?"

"Uh, it's Harlow."

"Oh. Um. Hi."

"Listen. I know it's weird I'm calling, and you will

never be my biggest fan, but I have nowhere else to turn, and I need help."

One beat of awkward silence, two. "Are you calling to discuss your plans for the zombie apocalypse?"

"No. Nothing like that." Harlow peered through the glass into West's office. Beck had a phone to his ear. He threw back his head and laughed at whatever the speaker had just said. Confirming plans with his date tonight? A knife of jealousy stabbed at her chest.

"Then what do you want, Harlow?" Brook Lynn prompted.

"Harlow? As in Harlow Glass?" Jessie Kay said in the background. "What's she doing calling you?"

Ignore her. "Well, the problem is Beck, and I—"

"I'm going to stop you right there," Brook Lynn said. "I won't give you any dirt on him."

"She wants dirt on him?" another voice gasped in the background. Kenna Starr, maybe.

"I don't want dirt," she rushed out. "Besides, I already know about his past."

"How?" Brook Lynn demanded.

Okay, so, this call had been a mistake. Noted. "He told me. How else?"

"He *told* you?"

"Yes." But that had nothing to do with her problem. "Look, I shouldn't have—"

"What did he tell you?"

Curses! Would the girl always interrupt? "You'll have to forgive me, Brook Lynn, but I won't give you dirt on him, either. I don't know what he's shared with you and what he hasn't. I won't betray his confidence."

Silence.

Would Brook Lynn hang up now?

"All right. How can I help you?" the girl asked again, and this time a layer of warmth wrapped her tone.

Uh, talk about confusing. But if the spunky blonde who'd managed to snag the town dragon was finally willing to listen… "Well, Beck and I kissed last night and now—"

"You *kissed*?"

"They kissed!" Jessie Kay demanded.

Argh! "Would you please stopping butting in? You are the most frustrating person on the planet right now."

"Sorry, sorry," Brook Lynn said. "Where are you? No, you know what, forget I asked. You're at Beck's office. Duh. Caller ID. In just a few minutes, Beck is going to get a call. Soon after, he'll leave. And soon after that, I will arrive—I'm currently at Two Farms—and we will finish this conversation in person."

Click.

Okay. Wow. But true to the girl's word, Beck received a call on his cell phone before he stuck his head into Harlow's—his—office.

"I have to go," he announced. He wouldn't meet her gaze.

"Oh. Is something wrong?" Did she sound too breezy?

"Nothing I can't handle." He was gone a few seconds later—and she realized she missed him already.

What the heck is wrong with me?

As she began to pace, she noticed Cora received a call, as well, and left soon after. Then Brook Lynn arrived with her sister and, yep, Kenna Starr. The best friend. Harlow was too worked up to care about the potential hate mob.

The girls invaded the office, each pulling a chair up

to the desk. Brook Lynn appeared giddy, Jessie Kay suspicious and the redheaded Kenna befuddled.

"How did you get Beck to leave?" Harlow asked.

"Had Jase call him for a bro-mergency," Brook Lynn said. "Meaning Jase is finally telling him how Tawny Ferguson has been coming to the house, asking questions about Beck. She's there now, in fact."

What!

I mean, whatever. Wasn't as if an old flame of Beck's mattered. He never went back for seconds. "You *are* here to help me, right?" Harlow asked, hesitant.

"Yes," Brook Lynn and Jessie said in unison.

"Yes?" Kenna asked. She was a beautiful woman, her hair like living flames, her eyes steel gray and her pale skin adorably freckled. And, lightbulb! She would be the perfect model for Midnight Romp, one of the characters in West's game. Fierce avenger by day, seductress by night.

Harlow was making a mental note to ask her to model when Brook Lynn said, "So…how was the kiss?"

"Oh, she liked it, no doubt about it," Jessie Kay piped up. "She didn't have to tell me that part. I just know from experience."

A twinge of jealousy. *Not important, either.*

"Jessie Kay is right. I liked it. But now I don't know what to do about it," Harlow said. "I would have done more than kiss him, but I want forever and he wants a single night, so we called it quits and now he's treating me like I'm the devil."

Kenna opened her mouth.

"I'm not," Harlow insisted, and Kenna closed her mouth. "Not anymore."

"This sounds made-up. Beck is *always* nice," Jessie Kay said. "Even to his leftovers. Again, I know this from experience."

"I guess I really ticked him off. But I have no idea how."

Jessie Kay tapped a fingertip against her chin. "I have a suspicion, but I need more info before I voice it. Tell me how he's treating you, exactly."

Easy. "He snaps at me. He glares at me, and he's stopped opening my car door for me. He doesn't call me *lollipop* or *dove*."

"Wait. Let's backtrack just a bit. We want to help Harlow Glass...why?" Kenna asked.

"There's a good chance she isn't the girl we once knew," Brook Lynn explained.

Not quite a shining endorsement, but she'd take it.

"So we like her now?" Kenna asked.

"We're deciding." Brook Lynn settled deeper into the chair. "But either way, we *are* helping her today."

"Can you?" Harlow asked, not daring to hope. "What was your suspicion, Jessie Kay? You never said."

"Well, I think he still wants you, despite your desire for forever. And since you denied him, and he thinks he can't give you what you want, he's acting like a baby whose favorite toy was taken away."

The storm raging inside her stopped, just stopped, the sun suddenly shining brightly.

"Game changer, right?" Jessie Kay asked. "Do you now just want Beck to be nicer to you—or do you still want him to commit to you?"

"Both?" *Could* he commit? Why did he go for so many women? Just because he could, or was there a deeper reason behind his he-slut behavior, the way there'd been a deeper reason behind her bullying?

What did she know about Beck's past? The loss of his mom, the rejection of his father, the family members who'd kicked him out. The foster system. No telling what he'd seen, heard and experienced as he was shuffled from one home to another.

Mental note: study problems foster kids might develop later on in life.

Fingers snapped in front of her face. She blinked, found Jessie Kay leaning over the desk in a bid to gain her attention.

"Where'd you go?" the girl asked.

Harlow propped her elbows on the desk, rested her chin against her knuckles. "That's not important. What is? Boys."

"Boys?" Brook Lynn echoed.

"They're all I know, but Beck is all man, and I'm out of my league with him. My last date took place my junior year of high school, and I rarely ever went out on a second with the same guy, and never… Well. You know."

"Never what?" Jessie Kay perched at the edge of her seat. "My mind is going to some strange places right now."

If she said it, there would be no going back. These girls would know one of her secrets, and as Brook Lynn had said, they hadn't yet decided if they were her friends or not. They could betray her, strike at her while she was down the way she had once struck at them.

Just do it. Tell them. How they responded would reveal their true intentions toward her. And perhaps ruin what little happiness she'd managed to eke out for herself, but whatever.

"I'm… I've never…been with anyone, okay?" she finished in a whisper.

"What!" Jessie Kay yelled. "No way my sweet little ears just heard such a lie. Are they bleeding? They feel like they're bleeding."

Would throwing a pen at her be considered an act of bullying?

"Are you sure you haven't slept with someone?" Brook Lynn asked her.

"You mean is there a chance I slipped, fell on a man's penis and then just forgot all about it?" Her tone was as dry as a yearlong drought. "No. No, I'm not sure."

"But…a virgin," Kenna gasped out. "You were the parking queen."

"I don't know if you've been told, but parking doesn't always lead to sex."

The redhead frowned. "I distinctly remember Scott Cameron, Tyler Bishop and Cory Yinny saying—"

Harlow threw her hands up, exasperated. "I'm sure the boys said a lot of things, but I've never gone further than second base. And I'm not embarrassed about it." She was glad she'd waited. Back then, sex would have been about control rather than connection. A power play, without any involvement from the heart. "Everything you heard was an exaggeration."

If anyone could understand the falsity of rumors, it was Kenna. Her rep had been just as tattered as Harlow's. More so, even. After one drunken night at a party, she'd gotten pregnant and had instantly become the town man-eater. But look at her now. Engaged to one of the richest men on the planet.

"Does Beck know you haven't yet played your *V*

card?" Jessie Kay asked, as if they were discussing a diagnosis of cancer.

"No." Unless he'd guessed last night, which was totally possible. As experienced as he was, he could probably count how many men she'd kissed. "I'd prefer it if you guys weren't the ones to spill the truth to him." In high school, boys had reacted one of two ways. In challenge, wanting to be the one to win the prize, or in amusement, wanting to shame her into finally giving it up.

But again, Beck wasn't a boy. He might decide to have nothing to do with her.

Hadn't he already?

"Don't look at me," Jessie Kay said, holding up her hands. "I don't plan to tell *anyone*. I'd laugh so hard I'd puke before I ever even got the *V* word out. Not because of the *V* thing, of course, but because it's you."

Thanks. "That's great. Wonderful. Meanwhile you guys haven't helped me *at all*."

"Well, when I wanted to get Beck into bed," the blonde began, "I just—"

"Argh! No. Getting him into bed isn't the problem. It's keeping him there." Though, if he went out with another woman tonight, slept with her after kissing Harlow, would she still welcome him there?

No. Of course not.

Probably not.

"Then I'm out," Jessie Kay said. "Though I *did* go on a date with Daniel Porter the other night and he asked me out on a second."

"He's hot," Kenna said, giving her friend a thumbs-up.

Pulling teeth would be easier than getting answers from these girls. "Enough about Daniel!"

"Someone's a she-beast today." Jessie Kay nudged her sister. "How'd you keep Jase?"

"He says I am the sunshine in his darkness. What? I am."

"That's great for you, but I'm not exactly anyone's idea of radiant." Harlow's shoulders slumped.

"You could try cooking and cleaning for Beck," Jessie Kay suggested. "Guys love that kind of thing. Or so I've heard."

She shook her head. "I firmly believe guys should clean the messes they make, without help from a girl. Amen."

"All right. How about you, Ken," Jessie Kay said. "How'd you keep Dane?"

"According to him, I breathed."

That. That was what Harlow wanted. To be special. Treasured. Beck made her feel that way, of course, but only in spurts. And spurts just weren't good enough. "Clearly, breathing isn't going to be enough for me."

"Then allow me to be a voice of reason," Kenna said. "Be yourself. Do and say what comes naturally to you, what is right to you and for you. If he isn't what you need, if he won't step up to the plate, then he's not the one for you, and he's not worth your time and effort. Move on."

Finally! Advice. And it was good. The kick in the pants she'd needed. But it worried her, too. Was *she* what Beck needed? So many questions had come to light during the conversation. Too many, it seemed. Why he was the way he was, and if the guy who so obviously hated change would ever be able to change himself.

Unfortunately, there was only one thing that would answer them all: time.

CHAPTER THIRTEEN

BECK STOOD IN a back corner of the hotel ballroom, surrounded by the very definition of luxury. Multiple chandeliers, each boasting thousands of heart-shaped crystals, were framed by an elaborate tin ceiling. The walls were draped with plum-colored velvet and twinkling lights, the floor a spectacular though dizzying pattern of ebony and ivory. There were twenty-five tables placed throughout, bouquets of roses and candles for centerpieces. Classic elegance, Brook Lynn had called it.

The kids on his soccer team gazed around with wide eyes, muttering "ooh" and "ahh."

Tonight they were celebrating a winning season, and despite ranging in age from eight to twelve, each of the team members was dressed in formal attire. Something he, West and Jase had arranged and Brook Lynn had overseen.

Beck wore a tux tailored to fit him exclusively, and yet the tie felt like a noose around his neck. He wanted Harlow here, with him, but he was glad she wasn't anywhere nearby. A terrible tug-of-war had erupted inside him, each side pulling him in a different direction.

He couldn't have her without committing to her. He had to have her, but he couldn't commit to her. It was the surest way to lose her forever. Already she suspected he wasn't good enough or stable enough for her. And when she realized she was right, that he *wasn't*, nothing he did or said would convince her to stay with him.

If he even wanted her to stay with him.

Damn it! If he made it through the banquet without punching a wall, he'd consider it a win. He shouldn't be thinking about her. Shouldn't care that she'd ended things before they'd even begun. He could move on, finally go back to the way things were. But he didn't want to go back. Somehow she'd become his new normal. And oh, shit, he *was* going to punch a wall.

Jase stepped to his side, stopping him, and handed him a glass of champagne. "You look like you could use it."

"This, and about a thousand more."

"Still upset about Tawny?"

Tawny. Apparently the curvy blonde had been coming to the house ever since their date, plaguing Jase with questions. *Has Beck been seeing other women? Has Beck ever been in love? How does Beck feel about kids?*

Yes. No. And girl, please. Kids were not in his future and never would be. He'd even considered getting snipped—still might do it.

"No. I'm over it." He'd sat down with Tawny and had a gentle heart-to-heart, telling her they weren't a couple and they weren't ever going to be a couple. As he'd spoken, she'd tried to crawl into his lap and stuff her hand down his pants.

He'd had to get stern, telling her they weren't having sex again, either, and he'd been clear about that from the beginning.

When she'd left, close to tears, Beck had drained a beer before tossing the bottle against the wall and watching it shatter.

"Then what has your panties in such a twist?" Jase asked.

Beck would still rather cut off both his nuts than dump his problems in Jase's lap. "I'm fine."

Jase frowned at him.

"I'll be fine," he corrected.

Brook Lynn arrived and cuddled into the big guy's side, smiling at Beck with saccharine sweetness. "Did I tell you I saw Harlow today? Whatever you're doing, keep it up. She looks *miserable*."

The words were a knife to the gut. "When did you become so vicious?" When did he?

He'd been an ass to Harlow today. And why? Because she hadn't given him what he wanted?

Well, he hadn't given her what she wanted, either, yet she'd remained civil. "I don't want Harlow miserable."

Brook Lynn studied him more intently than he liked. "So…you'd like to see her happy, settled?"

"Yes." She *deserved* to be happy and settled, to have her dreams of having a husband and family come true. The permanence Beck couldn't offer.

Can't…or won't?

His hand fisted.

"Good. I was testing you, and you just passed." Brook Lynn beamed up at him. "I have the *best* idea. You and I are going to work together to find her the perfect man. We'll start with your friends, of course, guys you trust who can give her what she needs."

A growl rose from deep inside Beck's chest, lingering in his throat before trying to push free of his mouth. Find Harlow another man? Not in this lifetime.

Brook Lynn nibbled on her bottom lip. "Are you

upset? You look upset. You did say you wanted her happy, right? I didn't misunderstand, did I?"

"You didn't." Each word felt as if it'd been yanked through a meat grinder.

"Good. She wants a nice, stable guy. Who doesn't? She's certain stability will make her happiest, and I agree. So think about those friends of yours, like I said, and figure out who will be a good match for her. We'll discuss your choices tomorrow." With that, Brook Lynn pulled Jase onto the dance floor.

Beck rubbed at his chest to ward off the sudden ache. A waiter passed with a tray of champagne glasses. He drained the one he had and replaced it with a new one, draining it, too.

From across the room, West spotted him and soon worked his way over, offering Beck another glass.

Beck grabbed it so fast the liquid swished over the rim. "Thanks," he muttered, and the champagne went down the hatch in a single gulp. He tended to panic anytime his friend was in possession of alcohol. His gateway.

"Repay me by getting out there and doing your thing."

"What's my thing?" he asked, desperate to forget Brook Lynn's "best" idea.

"What do you think? Dancing with the single mothers."

In other words, flirting. For once, he wasn't in the mood. "I'd need the entire bottle of alcohol for that."

"Why? You're usually the belle of the ball."

"Not tonight."

"Because you're intimidated by me in my tux? Good to know. But one of the single moms brought her sister, and I've decided I want her. I need you to step up to the plate and take one for the team, intimidated or not."

The words *I want her* weren't shocking coming from West. Beck had heard something similar from the guy once a year for the past eight years. The very reason he could predict the outcome. West would win the girl—he always did. He would spend all kinds of time with her, dote on her and lavish her with gifts. Then he would dump her in exactly two months, for some made-up reason, and hate himself for months to come.

"Which one?" Beck asked. He wasn't going to watch passively. Not this time. He could barely keep himself afloat right now and wasn't willing to risk another spiral for West, another woman brokenhearted.

West pointed to a pretty thirtysomething with a short cap of blond hair and blue eyes. "Her."

"Sorry, my man, but I saw her earlier. Now I call dibs."

West almost looked relieved. "What about Harlow?"

The ache in his chest deepened. "What about her? We're friends, that's all."

"Friends with benefits?"

"Just friends." *Even if I miss her the way I'd miss a limb.* "The blonde—"

"Don't worry about it. She's yours." West patted his shoulder. "I won't stand in your way."

He'd known that would be West's reaction. Just as he'd known if West asked him, he would have backed off the blonde without a fight, despite his misgivings about how the guy's plans would play out.

Beck grabbed two more glasses of champagne from a passing waiter and drained them. After that, the evening passed in a bit of a blur. He ate when dinner was served, gave a speech praising every member of the team. He flirted and danced with Donna... Dana? Whoever. West's blonde. She was an ER nurse, newly divorced with no kids, and she was looking to add a little spice to her life.

"If you're still looking," he said, "does that mean you haven't found it with me?"

Her smile was wide, playful. "Not yet."

"But because you're such a sweet girl, you're willing to let me keep trying?"

"I'm a giver like that."

"Then I better bring my A game."

She chuckled. "You mean you actually have a B game?"

"And a C game. But I only play that way when I'm really desperate."

"You mean you aren't desperate for me?" She pretended to pout.

"Honey, I bypassed desperate and went straight into drooling when you walked through the door." The words came easily to him, as usual, but fell from his tongue hollowly. He used to enjoy this kind of bantering, the tease before the big show. Now he wasn't sure when he'd ever been more miserable.

Donna/Dana ran her fingers through his hair, and he almost pulled away. He remembered how Harlow had done the same last night. How his scalp had tingled and his blood had heated. How she'd looked when she'd done it. As if she were drunk on pleasure...on him. As if he were something special, not just a random guy she might enjoy.

"Tell me about yourself," Donna/Dana said.

"And bore you to death? No way. I'd rather hear about you."

As she prattled on, his mind drifted in a direction he didn't want it to go. Brook Lynn expected him to find a guy for Harlow. A lover. A potential husband. Could he actually do it? Should he?

Committed women were invisible to him. He'd never forgotten the shame he'd felt with Carol, the foster mom, knowing she was cheating on her husband with him. His guilt had only grown over the years as he'd watched one family after another crumble because of infidelity.

Maybe…maybe the answer to all his problems was doing exactly what Brook Lynn requested. If Harlow got serious with another man—Beck swallowed a curse—his craving her might finally go away.

"Beck?" Donna/Dana said, nuzzling his cheek. "You still with me?"

He stepped back, widening the distance between them, and kissed her knuckles. "Do you really think there's anywhere else I'd rather be?"

"Well, I certainly hope not."

More and more families left the party until only West, Jase and a sleepy Brook Lynn remained.

"I'm driving your car, Beck," West said. "How do you want the rest of this night to go down?"

He looked at Jase, who was holding Brook Lynn so close, so tight. Brook Lynn leaned against her man, knowing he would protect her with his life. He looked at West, who was willing to drive him and Donna/Dana to her place, then wait in the car so he would have a ride when he finished. Even willing to drive him and Donna/Dana to their place—where Harlow would get a front-row seat to the show. He looked at Donna/Dana, who was smiling up at him, as tipsy as he was, probably willing to do anything he asked. She wouldn't stop him before he got her clothes off, his body on fire for her, and ask for more than he could possibly give.

West nudged his arm. "So what's it gonna be?"

HARLOW HAD SPENT an entire evening on her cell phone, using up data to research problems abandoned kids could have later in life, until she thought she'd pegged Beck. Severe detachment disorder. Having lost everything he loved time and time again, he'd learned to stay distanced from everything and everyone.

Her heart had ached for him as she'd fallen into bed to sleep like the dead, only to be awoken by—

Bang, bang, bang. "Open up, Harlow."

That.

Eyes burning, she donned her robe and stumbled to the door of the RV. From a nightmare of Beck plowing his way through a parade of women to Beck standing at her door in the flesh—in the middle of the night.

Bang, bang. "You have two seconds to show yourself, then I'm kicking my way in."

"I'm coming, I'm coming. Hold your horses." She opened the door—and gasped. A small patch of light glowed from the porch lamp and washed over Beck. He was in a tux. A gorgeous, wealthy man almost too fine to touch, like something out of a magazine. His dark hair stuck out in spikes, and his eyes simmered with fire and determination.

"Fool woman." His lips were compressed into a thin line, his words slurred. "I could be a stranger here to murder you."

"Are you drunk?"

"Only a 3.65 on the Richter scale…or maybe a 6.53… What does that matter?" He barreled his way inside, gently pushing her back. He closed the door with a kick of his leg. "You gotta protect yourself better, popsicle."

New nicknames. A thrill to hear when she shouldn't have cared. "What are you doing here? It's, like, two in the morning."

He nodded as if she'd just made his point for him. "It's two in the morning, and you work for me. I told you there would be times I'd want you to draw in the middle of the night."

"So you want me to draw?" she asked, stepping back to give herself breathing room. His nearness bothered her, made her ache for what she'd had before—what she could never have again. His mouth and hands on her, his body grinding against hers.

"No, I don't want you to draw. Don't be ridiculous. I want to talk, to tell you what Brook Lynn and I decided." His gaze raked over her, everything about him suddenly relaxing. He leaned back, bracing himself against the wall, and smiled over at her, slow and wicked. The devastating smile she could not resist. "I want to take those nightclothes to dinner and then I want to take them off you."

She shivered. "They…uh, they aren't hungry."

"Doesn't matter. You should have worn something else." He stepped toward her. "You're making me forget why I'm here."

Careful. He would make *her* forget her reservations. "You and Brook Lynn decided…what?"

He stopped, a flash of rage in his eyes, quickly gone. "Let's not talk about that right now." He started up again, prowling toward her, backing her against the kitchen counter. Heat radiated off him, and a whimper escaped her. "I missed you tonight. I wanted you with me, hated that you weren't."

Could he hear the swift pound of her heart? "Where were you?"

"A banquet for the soccer team West and I coach. Shhhh, don't tell." He placed a finger over her lips, and she fought the urge to lick him, relief and desire pouring through her. "Women go crazy when they find out."

No kidding. She just happened to be one of them. "I already knew you coached underprivileged kids. I've been handling bits and pieces of your business, remember?" Like fielding calls from moms who suddenly couldn't recall when the next practice happened to be, even though it fell on the same day every week. "Did the kids have a good time?"

"The best. And I sent Donna/Dana away. I didn't want her."

"Donna/Dana?"

He nodded. "She would have slept with me and wouldn't have asked for more."

Jealousy delivered a strong kick to her insides, but it was followed by the sweet caress of surprise. He'd nixed a potentially easy bedmate—while drunk—to come be with Harlow, who was as far from easy as could be?

"Go on," she urged, melting against him.

"I'd rather enjoy you while I can." He nuzzled his nose against her jawline and played with the lapels of her robe. The silk brushed against her flushed skin, tickling her. "I'm sorry I was so rude to you. You've got me tied in so many knots I'm not myself anymore." He nipped at her ear. "And damn me, but I'm starting to think that's a good thing."

Her already weak knees threatened to buckle. She would have fallen, but he caught her and set her on the counter. His big hands settled on her bare thighs. Her robe was short, but seated as she was, it was micromini.

He pushed her legs apart and stood firmly between them, as if he had every right to be there. "You are so beautiful." His gaze remained on his fingers as they continued to trail up and down those lapels. With every upward glide, he parted the material even more.

She wasn't nude underneath, but she might as well have been. She wore only a tank and a pair of panties. Little protection against such potent desire. "I'm not. Beautiful, I mean. I'm really not." She didn't want him to see how not-beautiful she really was, but she couldn't bring herself to stop him from exposing a bit more of her skin. Not yet.

"You are more mysterious than the Voynich Manuscript, you know that?" he said. "Maybe that's how you've managed to keep me hooked. I want to solve the puzzle you've created."

"You like puzzles?"

"I never have before."

"But you want to solve me?"

He didn't seem to hear her, his gaze on her shoulders and the robe about to fall. "Such pretty skin."

Stomach twisting, she covered herself at last. "Why don't we watch TV, hmm?" She motioned to the only television set—in the bedroom.

"I'd rather watch you." As he clasped her ankle and lifted her bare foot, she gasped, only to moan when he began to massage spots she hadn't known were tender. "Tell me the last time you went on a date."

"In high school." Once she'd healed from her injuries and realized no one in town would ever forgive her, she'd spent all her time at the farmhouse, transcribing medical documents for her mom, whose eyesight had deteriorated over the years. Unfortunately, Harlow hadn't been able to keep the job after her mom died, unable to admit she'd done any past work without putting *all* of her mom's contributions in question.

"As I suspected," Beck said, "which means the bar is set pretty low."

"Definitely. High school boys are pigs."

He pressed deeper into her arch, dragging another moan out of her. "What's your longest relationship?"

"Only a few weeks." She eyed him warily. "I used to move from boy to boy, depending on who wasn't paying any attention to me. If the one I wanted had a girlfriend, well, he soon didn't."

"There were boys who didn't pay attention to you?"

"Only the smart ones," she said, surprised by his takeaway from her speech.

"But you changed. What changed you?" he asked softly, pushing for answers, always pushing.

Argh! Her body temperature dropped from white-hot to bone-cold, and she pulled away from him. He let her, taking hold of her other foot. "I should have known you'd circle back to the Incident yet again."

"The incident. Meaning a single circumstance. Tell me," he said.

"No. I don't want to talk about it."

"Have you *ever* talked about it? Or have you let it fester?"

She pressed her lips together, refusing to reply to even that. If she gave the slightest bit, he would take more and more until she had nothing left.

"What if I tell you a secret about *me*?" he asked. "Something I've never told anyone else."

In a snap, desperation hit her. She would do *anything* to learn more about him—even an exchange. "Yes. Okay. Tell me a secret, and I will tell you about the Incident. But only the bare minimum facts."

He snorted and shook his head. "As if I'll give my secret away so cheaply. You'll tell me every detail."

"Five details for five of your secrets."

"Ten details, two secrets."

"Four details, four secrets," she countered.

"Twelve details, no secrets," he insisted.

Her eyes narrowed. "Tell me *all* your secrets and I'll tell you one of mine."

"You'll tell me everything about it?"

"Everything," she agreed with a sigh.

His smile stretched wide. "You've got yourself a deal, baby."

He hit a particularly tender area, and she released another moan, her back arching, her breasts straining against her top.

"That feels… Oh… Oh!"

Voice nothing but mist and seduction, he said, "I could make you feel even better…all over. If only you'd let me."

Desire thrummed, more insistent, until she teetered on the brink of ultimate surrender.

This flower is dead…

With what little willpower she could scrounge up, she pulled her foot from his grip and crossed her arms over her chest, hiding the twin beads trying to play peekaboo. "You go first," she muttered. "All your secrets."

"And let you welsh?"

She gave him the look most of her teachers had given her over the years. Authoritative yet pitying. "And let you tell me lame secrets about your sexcapades?"

"Well, well. Miss Glass certainly has my number. In more ways than one." For one drawn-out moment, all he did was stare at her lips. "First secret. As a teenager, I was arrested twice."

"How naughty of you." An outlaw who lived by no rules but his own. She should have guessed.

And oh, wow, my romance-novel roots are showing.

Gaze intense, studying her every nuance, he slipped his fingers up her calves, played a game of tickle and retreat at her knees. "Once for theft, and once for beating the crap out of a guy, though there should have been dozens more arrests after that. I needed money, so I fought men twice my size and age. Anyone others were willing to pay to see beat down."

"That's good info to have," she said, aching all over, "but hardly your best-kept secrets. I'm sure Jase and West know."

"You're right. They do." He rubbed his jaw, and she heard the light scrape of stubble. "You don't want to know about my sexual conquests, and you don't want to know about my record. What *do* you want to know?"

Hands itching for contact, any contact, she plucked at the collar of his shirt. "Tell me about one of the worst foster homes you lived in."

He stiffened, and several moments ticked by in silence. This was it—the moment of truth. If he deflected, she'd know he wasn't ready for this. If he didn't, well, he would surprise her.

He surprised her.

"There are several to choose from," he said. "There

was one… The dad had a problem with his temper and knew how to hide bruises. He hit me, whipped me with branches and paddles. Sometimes just looking him in the eye set him off."

Bile rose, swift and sure. "Oh, baby." She wrapped her arms around him, hugging him tight, offering all the comfort she could. "I'm so sorry." At first, he remained stiff. Second by second, he relaxed until he was hugging her back, holding on so tight she'd wear the bruises tomorrow, but she didn't care, loved being his lifeline.

"There was another foster home," he whispered. "A worse one. The mother would sneak into my room at night…"

The sickness intensified, a blistering burn. "How old were you?"

"Fourteen."

Too young. Far too young. Rage came out swinging. "I'll kill the bitch!"

"I was big for my age."

"Like that matters. What she did was wrong in every way, and she knew it. I won't just kill her. I'll torture her in ways you can't even imagine."

He kissed her collarbone once, lingered, then kissed again before pulling back to cup her face, his palms rough and callused, utterly perfect. "You want to know another secret? You are one of the best things to ever happen to me, Harlow. So sweet."

"Sweet for wanting to torture the worst piece of scum ever to walk the earth?"

"Yes." His thumbs stroked her jaw, heating her skin, the fire he so easily stoked stirring and blazing with new life.

The need to comfort him, to make up for the traumas

of his past, smoldered beneath it, vibrant and undeniable, an obsession, an addiction without end.

This amazing warrior wasn't a he-slut, she realized. He was a man trying to survive the hand he'd been dealt. How dare she judge him? How dare she make him feel bad for his choices?

She'd handled things poorly with him before, but she wouldn't this time. Denying him—denying them both—had been the wrong way to go. She wanted him more than she'd ever wanted another, so why not have him? Why not enjoy him?

Afterward, if the worst happened and he cut her loose, well, the worst happened. She would have tried for happily-ever-after. She would deal.

"Beck," she whispered, and rubbed her nose along his jawline. "You are one of the best things to ever happen to me, too, and I want to be with you."

He went still, even seemed to stop breathing. "I'm not the best, I'm the worst. You don't."

"You *are* the best. And I do. I really do. Let me prove it." Fighting past her shyness, she placed her palm between his legs and stroked up…down, and oh, wow, he was big and hard and perfect. So amazingly perfect.

He sucked in a breath. "Harlow."

Her name on his lips never failed to enchant her. "Please, Beck."

A groan that did not sound human sprang from him. "Yes, beauty. I'll give you what you need. What I need." He cupped her breasts and despite the robe and tank, the effect he had on her had to be obvious. "I'll give you…" He frowned.

"What's wrong?"

"Someone else." He stumbled back, out of reach.

"Someone else?" Her brow furrowed with confusion. "I don't understand."

"I'm not what you need. You said so."

Her blood cooled, the words she'd once uttered in haste now coming back to bite her. "You are."

"No. I decided I'm going to do whatever is necessary to make sure you're happy." He stumbled to the fridge to grab a beer.

"Uh, are you sure you need that?"

"Never been surer." He popped the top and drained the contents. And he did seem steadier as he placed the bottle on the counter, removed his jacket. He tugged off his tie as well, and unfastened the first three buttons on his shirt, as if the material choked him.

"Is the heat on?" he asked. "Why is the heat on in the middle of summer?"

"It's not on."

Three more buttons.

"Are you feverish?" His lips *had* burned so sweetly. She flattened her hand over his forehead, his skin as hot as his lips, but it wasn't clammy or sickly.

He leaned into her touch, his eyes closing, but all too soon that golden gaze was back on her and narrowing. "I'm tired," he said, and he sure sounded it. "I should go to bed."

Though her body shouted in protest, her mind sighed in relief. They desperately needed to discuss what had just happened—about what she wanted to happen still—but it would be better if he were sober.

"All right. I'll walk you home."

He shook his head. "Don't want to leave. Not yet. You suggested we watch TV, remember?" He linked their fingers and led her into the bedroom. A short journey, and yet an eternity seemed to pass. He settled atop the mattress.

He's in my bed. Trembling, she drew the comforter over him. "Forget the TV and get some rest."

"Stay with me." He caught her hand, tugging her beside him.

He's in my bed—with me. Her mind had trouble processing the extraordinary event. Women all over the world experienced the wondrous phenomenon of being held like this, but Harlow never had. It was a first, and it took only a second to realize she did not want it to be an only. The heat of him cocooned her, buffering her from the world that had once been so cold to her. His strength anchored her, his hard planes offering resting places for her soft curves. His intoxicating champagne scent fused with her natural fragrance—became their scent.

"Tell me your secret." His warm breath fanned over her forehead. "I have to know more about you. It's a compulsion. A necessity."

"Not now." She would ruin the moment.

"Please, shortcake."

"I… I'll tell you in the morning." When the alcohol was out of his system. "All right?"

"You promise?"

She drew in a deep breath, held it. Exhaled slowly. "I promise."

He kissed her temple. "Sleep, then."

She didn't want to fall asleep. She wanted to stay awake and enjoy the feel of being held, almost cherished. But his arms tightened around her, intractable steel bands, as if, in this vulnerable moment, he feared losing her, and it didn't take her long to drift away with a smile.

Whether he'd admitted it to himself or not, she mattered to him.

CHAPTER FOURTEEN

HARLOW BLINKED UNTIL the fuzz cleared from her eyes, her bedroom coming into view. All was as she'd left it, save for the man's shirt and tie hanging from the edge of the curtain rod over the window.

What—

Something shifted on the bed, warm breath fanning her neck. She stiffened, slowly turned her head—and came face-to-face with a sleeping Beck.

Beck!

That's right. He'd come over in the middle of the night, wanting but not wanting her to draw a picture. He'd crawled into bed and pulled her beside him, holding her close. His arm was still draped over her middle, his lashes casting spiky shadows over his cheeks.

His soft expression made him appear boyish, carefree, and inside her, a well of tenderness bubbled over. She remembered their talk, his hands on her skin, and she instantly went up in flames, her desire for him returning—had it ever really left?

Why not pick up where they'd left off?

Yes, oh, yes.

As stealthily as she was able, she crawled from the bed and tiptoed into the bathroom, took care of business and brushed her teeth, then crawled back into bed. Beck, who hadn't stirred, now curled around her, as if he'd been waiting for her, his warm breath a caress against her neck.

"Beck," she whispered, hoping to ease him awake.

He sighed softly, inserting a leg between hers and draping a hand over her rib cage. Anticipation caused her to tense. If he moved that hand up just a few inches…

Up…up…it slid, and she held her breath—*do it, please do it*—but he stopped just before he actually cupped her. Hot tremors swept through her, and she swallowed a whimper.

"Beck. Wake up." *Please.*

His thumb brushed upward again and again, sending heated shivers through her. More desperate by the second, she squirmed against him. When the not-quite-enough torment continued, she inched downward, forcing him to cup her at last. All the while his thumb continued to brush up—but still he made no contact with her distended nipple.

The air deflated from her lungs. "Beck," she repeated, arching up, rubbing against his thigh—yes, yes!—practically driving herself insane with the promise of more.

The movement of his thumb slowed as it drew closer, closer to where she needed it most—but not close enough.

Argh! "Beck. I mean it. Wakey, wakey, eggs and bakey."

Again his thumb brushed up—and this time…this time he stroked her. A cry of delight parted her lips, lances of pleasure shooting through her. Realization, too. He couldn't be doing this in his sleep. He just couldn't. The effect was too masterful, the touch too skilled.

She flipped open her lids—and found him smiling at her with wicked intent.

"YOU SMELL LIKE cinnamon and mint, baby. Did you brush your teeth hoping I'd kiss you?" The thought wrecked him. *She'd* wrecked him.

"Yes. Yes."

Beck knew he should resist. He'd come here with every intention of telling her the plan. He would be setting her up with someone else. But look where he'd ended up. In her bed, wrapped around her, desperate for her.

He couldn't resist her. He'd always been a sexual man, but never like this. She'd somehow caused him to devolve, stripping him of etiquette and turning him into little more than an animal.

"You want me, even though I won't commit to you?" Let there be no misunderstandings between them. "You're willing to be with me?"

She stiffened. "Even though."

Guilt pricked at his gut-wrenching desire. Her reaction, despite her words… He should *definitely* get up, dress and leave. He nuzzled her neck instead, the need for her, only her, undeniable. "I'm going to make you feel so good, baby."

"This," she said, arching into his touch like a needy little kitty, "is a wonderful start."

This was only the beginning. "Good." He lifted his head. "Do not move from that position."

"But—"

"I mean it." He dragged himself out of bed and padded to the bathroom, where he quickly brushed his teeth, using her brush and paste. She wouldn't be the only one with minty-fresh breath. That done, he returned to the bed, any lingering resistance dying as he peered down at her. A flawless treat, ready to be devoured.

Urgency rode him hard—*take her, now, now*—but he stood in place. "So there are no misunderstandings, I need you to tell me how far I can go."

She licked her lips. "You can put your hands…your mouth on me. Give me pleasure. I dreamed about you… ached for you all night."

Ruthless need battered at him as he crawled toward her. "Pleasure…as in sex?"

Now she hesitated. "I don't… I…"

All right. He'd take that as a no. No matter. He could do plenty with his hands and mouth. And she could do plenty with hers. "I believe we ended last night with your hand right…here." He placed her palm flat against his erection, hissed at the razor-sharp desire careening through him.

"Yes," she moaned, squeezing him. "You're so big."

He gently bit into her bottom lip, drawing the tender flesh between his teeth. "The better to please you." He pushed up her tank, baring her breasts. Her beautiful, rosy-tipped breasts—

"Wait." She began to struggle against him, frantic. "Don't. I'll leave the shirt on."

But it was too late. He saw the scars. A collage of them began just below her collarbone and stretched all the way to her navel, even covering her breasts. There were jagged pink lines and patches of puckered skin, as if someone else's skin had been sewed to her. The sight almost proved to be his undoing, not because it was ugly—nothing about her was ugly—but because of the pain she must have endured.

A wave of tenderness overtook him, and he kissed

the tip of one scar…the tip of another. He had to know what had happened to her, and he had to know now. But when his gaze flipped up to her face and he realized she was staring just over his shoulder, that she'd gone stiff as she waited for his verdict, his rejection, he decided he couldn't do it. Not now.

"You only grow more beautiful with every second that passes, baby. How is that possible?" He lowered his head again, kissed the edge of one of the scars and this time he traced his tongue over the puckered edge.

Slowly the tension melted from her. She wound her arm around him, her nails soon digging into his back. "You don't have to lie. Not with me."

"I'm not lying. In fact, I will never lie to you. Not about this or anything else. You promised me, and now I promise you." He fit his lips over her nipple and as he sucked, she cried out, her hips lifting from the bed. "Like a wild strawberry, sweet and addictive, and I can't have just one." He turned his attention to the other, sucking it hard, harder, then flicking his tongue back and forth to soothe the ache. The little bead swelled under his ministrations, a silent plea for more.

"Beck." A gasp, her hips undulating with need.

He yanked the tank over her head. Every obstacle had to go. Strands of inky hair fell over her shoulders, the pillow, and as he ran his fingers between her breasts, down her stomach, he felt the evidence of more scars. Far more than he'd realized. He kicked off the covers, baring the rest of her. Some of the scars were bigger than others, clearly deeper.

Aching for her, he kissed another scar, then another, his fingers still traveling down, down…finally tunneling under her panties. His eyes nearly rolled back into his head. She was wet. No, not just wet. She was soaked, and she was white-hot, burning him so deliciously.

She'll taste as sweet as candy.

As he rubbed...rubbed...spreading her moisture, building her desire, stoking his own desperation, he croaked, "Part your legs for me, Harlow."

The moment she obeyed, he thrust a finger deep, and oh, hell, she was tight. Sweat beaded on his brow, the urge to rip off her underwear and sink inside her a tangible thing.

Control! "Can you take another one?"

"Yes. Please, yes." The way she clung to him, as if he were as necessary to her as breathing, only magnified the sensations blasting through him, and in that moment, *she* was necessary to him.

Precious girl. As he thrust in a second finger, she gave a strangled cry and lifted her hips. An instinctive action, and an irresistibly greedy one. The heel of his palm pressed where she ached most, and as her body's shivers vibrated into his, that very necessary control slipped farther and farther away.

"Touch me," he demanded.

"But...aren't I already?" Then understanding hit her and she eagerly shoved his underwear out of the way.

What had been a delight only seconds before became a glorious torment. While her rhythm lacked any kind of finesse, her unfettered excitement and enthusiasm touched him deep inside, where no one else had ever been.

He knew women, knew their reactions, and knew Harlow wasn't gifting him with pleasure by rote, but through the most primitive compulsion. The same was true of him. With her, he was too swept up to stick to routine—a hand here, his mouth there, give this so he could take that. He thought only of branding his woman now, now, now, hanging on and never letting go. Owning her—the way she owned him.

"I know you can take another." He wedged in a third finger, and she gasped. She moaned. Her head thrashed atop the pillow, ribbons of jet-black silk tangling around her face.

"Too much? Am I hurting you?" It would kill him, but he would stop.

"Just need...a moment...to adjust."

He waited, his every muscle vibrating with the urge to move...*have to move*...but her enjoyment mattered more to him than anything else. "You feel so good. Never felt anything better." His thumb caressed in circles, pressing...pressing closer to the heart of her.

Her knees parted farther, and she dissolved into the mattress, close, so damn close, to release. That's when he removed his fingers.

With a disappointed cry, she latched on to his wrist. "No! Stay! It doesn't hurt anymore."

"I'll be back, don't worry." Nothing would keep him away.

Reluctantly she released him, and he spread her essence down his length, moistening it from base to tip. He put her hand back on him—put his fingers back inside her. She sighed with contentment, gripping him hard and tight, just the way he liked.

"Look at me," he commanded.

Those baby blues were almost too hazed to focus. Her pupils were blown, nothing but twin pools of desire, drowning him...but what a way to go. "As I thrust

my fingers in you, ride my length up. As I pull out, ride
my length down."

"Yes, yes."

As he slanted his lips over hers, thrusting his tongue
against hers, he thrust his fingers deep, deeper inside
her. Her groan filled his mouth, and her hand, her sweet,
sweet hand, rode up his length. He pulled his fingers
back, and she stroked down. A growl rose from somewhere in his chest, a place he'd never known existed,
where a spark of possession had never quite died.

Mine.

The claim would have freaked him out—did freak
him out—but he was past the point of caring. His skin
was pulled too tight over muscle and bone; any second
he would burst apart at the seams.

"Faster," he said, and the sounds of their panting
breaths filled the room. He would have sworn the very
air around them electrified.

Her hips followed his every motion while his followed hers. He deepened the kiss, slid his fingers back
in and at the last second, angled his wrist. Her grip
tightened on him, and she cried out in wonder, her inner
walls spasming.

As the pleasure washed over her, she made the most
sublime sounds, gifting him with an expression of such
exquisite satisfaction he knew he would be haunted by
it all the days of his life. Then her nails sliced across
his back, branding him as her property, and he, too,
spiraled over the edge.

Completely emptied out, he collapsed beside her, and
he wasn't sure how much time passed before he had the
strength to rise, find a towel and clean her up.

She draped her hands over her eyes, her cheeks

flushing to a gorgeous rose. Embarrassed? After what they'd just done?

The tenderness returned, redoubled, and he tossed the rag aside. He pried her fingers from her face and smiled at her. "You are a treasure, you know that?" He smoothed a lock of damp hair from her face. "Never change."

She gripped the covers, those ocean-water eyes languid with satisfaction—and dread. "Is this the part where you blow me off?"

Her lips were red and swollen from his kisses, and it took him a moment to get his attention off them and onto her words. "Blow you off? You're my friend, rabbit. You're stuck with me."

"Well. That's something, at least." Gaze downcast, she stood and dressed in the tank and shorts. "Last night you mentioned something you and Brook Lynn wanted to do for me."

His airway instantly tightened and sweat beaded on the back of his neck. He swiped up his shirt and tugged it on, and realized he was trembling as he haphazardly buttoned it. He didn't bother fastening his pants.

"Let's talk about it later, okay?" Way later…or never. Yeah. Never sounded good.

"That's what you said last night. Beck, what's going on?" Worry darkened her features. "Tell me before I have a panic attack."

"No reason to panic, baby. It's nothing bad." He'd said he would never lie to her, and he wouldn't. He hadn't. What he and Brook Lynn planned *wasn't* bad for her.

He was another story.

"Beck."

He pulled at his collar, saying, "Brook Lynn thinks it will be a good idea if we find you…a man. Someone better than me." The material ripped, and he dropped his hand to his side. He could only grit out the rest of the explanation. "Someone who will meet all your needs."

She stumbled back as if he'd kicked her, the color draining from her face, leaving her pale and waxen. "You and Brook Lynn think…" A wealth of hurt peered at him as she floundered for a response. "You want me to be with someone else? Already?"

Never! he almost snarled. He hated the thought of her with someone else, and there was a good chance the guy would end up in the hospital before all was said and done. "I want you happy. You deserve to be happy. This is for the best."

Hurt gave way to anger. "Whose best?"

"Well, it sure the hell isn't mine," he shouted, then immediately hung his head in shame. He had no right to yell at her. Blame rested on his shoulders, and his alone. "I'm sorry."

"Stuff your sorry." She pointed to the door. "Get out."

No. No way in hell was he leaving her like this. "If you don't want another man, don't be with another man. But—"

"Out!"

He shook his head, desperate to get through to her. "I'm not leaving until you give me what you promised. Your secret."

"I'm not telling you anything," she spat.

"You promised."

"That was before I knew your plan to pawn me off on someone else."

Ripped apart inside, he said, "If I could commit, it would be with you, Harlow. I've never wanted a woman the way I want you, but I'm just not hardwired that way. I can't do a relationship, I don't want a family. You still want those things—right?"

She was silent for a moment. Slowly, she nodded.

Her agreement wasn't a surprise, but was still somehow a blow he hadn't been prepared to take. "Like I said, I can't give those things to you." He hated those words. They were final. The end of this, whatever it was. He wanted to fall to his knees and beg her to forget he'd said anything.

But he didn't. Love and lose. It was the story of his life. Even if he could love her, he couldn't stand to lose her.

Harlow opened her mouth, closed it. Silent, she studied his features for a long while. Whatever she saw removed the starch from her shoulders.

"Do you think you'll cheat on me?" she asked.

"No! I know I wouldn't. I know the toll infidelity takes on everyone involved, and I will never be a part of it. But I won't put myself in a position to be responsible for someone else's happiness."

"I'm responsible for my own happiness."

She said that, probably even believed it, but he would one day do something to upset her, and she would regret being with him. She would leave him. "Your secret," he insisted.

"You never want to talk about anything else," she snapped.

"Tell me what happened to you, and I'll stop asking."

"No."

"Tell me."

"No!"

"Damn it, Harlow. Tell me! You owe me."

She glared at him, her chest rising and falling so quickly he feared she would faint. "You really want to know? Fine! Someone threw gasoline on me and lit a match."

She'd been *set on fire*? "Harlow," he said, her name nothing but a broken whisper. He reached for her.

"No! Keep your sympathy," she spat, jolting back. "I don't want it."

"Too bad. Your stupid pride can't comfort you—but I can."

"You? How can you comfort me, Beck? Right now, you're my tormentor."

He bit back a curse. "Tell me who hurt you." He would find the guy. The girl. Whoever. What happened after that, happened.

The anger drained from her, and she wrapped her arms around her middle. "My mom and I went shopping in Dallas. I always wanted to shop back then. Had to keep up appearances, you know." She gave a bitter laugh. "If I wasn't the best, I wasn't happy. But I wasn't happy, anyway. I was rude to everyone that day, as usual. The salesgirls. Our waiter when we had lunch. Even my mom. It was as we were walking back to our car. The sidewalk was so crowded. People were every-where, and someone bumped into me, knocking me back. I felt a splash of something wet, then a searing pain on my stomach. I fell backward and rammed into someone else and was pushed farther back, getting lost in the crowd, the burning only growing worse. Then people started shouting and running all around me. My mom tried to get to me, but there were too many in the way. I fell, and people ran over me, crushing me, but they put out the flames, at least."

"Did you see who did it?"

"No, but I can guess. Someone I'd wronged that day."

Not good enough. He wanted a name, and if it took him the rest of his life, he'd get one. There were ways. "Tell me what happened next."

"The crowd cleared and my mom finally reached me. She had worked with Dr. Vargus for years, Strawberry Valley's only doctor up until two years ago when Dr. Chastain came along. The two got me patched up as best they could and set me up with a specialist to do the skin grafts. We decided not to talk to the police because Mom feared I would be crucified, told I deserved it. Because I did."

"No," he said, furious on her behalf. "You didn't."

Maybe she suspected just how close he was to yanking her against him, because she moved to the door, twisted the knob. "Now you know my secret. You can go."

"Harlow—"

"I won't be going into work today. I'm taking the day off."

"Fine, but you're not quitting." They weren't together, but he still couldn't stand the thought of losing her. Not yet.

Not ever.

"I didn't say I was quitting, just that I was taking a day off."

"Okay. All right." He owed her that much, at least. "But I want you to carry your phone everywhere you go. Before you argue, don't. You may not be at the office, but you'll still be on call."

"Fine."

"And we *are* going to finish this conversation."

"You mean the one where you tell me you'll be setting me up with other guys?" Her voice held a thousand notes of bitterness, one of fury and countless of hurt.

He ground his teeth, pinched the bridge of his nose. "Yes."

"Great. I can't wait. Now get the hell out."

CHAPTER FIFTEEN

HARLOW GATHERED HER paints and trudged the short distance to her childhood home. With Beck and West at the office, and Jase off somewhere with Brook Lynn, the place was empty. She was certain her key would fail, that she'd have resort to tossing a rock through a window, but she decided to give it a try anyway. *Click.*

Shocked, some of her anger draining—this had to mean something, right?—she headed straight to her old room, which was saturated with a scent she now recognized as Beck's. An-n-nd back came her anger. Her emotions were clearly in turmoil, and she desperately needed an outlet. The few canvases she had in the RV weren't enough. Nor was the RV itself.

She covered the floor and all the furniture with plastic, dragged in the stepladder she found in the hall closet and squeezed the desired paints onto her palette.

Shaking with the need to create, she worked her brush furiously over the walls.

Whatever the dark slashing lines ended up becoming, Beck would surely hate it, just because it was different. Not that she cared. The alternative to painting was staking him to an anthill. Before staking herself! She'd abandoned her rules for one night—one hour—in his arms. And yes, he'd pleasured her in ways she hadn't known were possible. His kiss, expert. His touch, masterful. His body, tailor-made for hers. She'd been lost, adrift, and he'd been her only anchor. Breathing had mattered only because she'd shared his breath.

And then, the ecstasy and agony she'd experienced when he'd kissed her scars… He'd been so reverent, so adoring, had even called her a treasure. But all along he'd planned to gift wrap her for another man.

With a screech, she threw a glob of black paint at the wall.

He'd said, *If I could commit, it would be with you. I've never wanted a woman the way I want you. But I'm just not hardwired that way.*

Then and now, the words popped the balloon of her fury, leaving only confusion. Why did he believe he couldn't commit? Did he not realize he had *already* committed to her? At least in part. He could have ditched her at any time, but again and again he'd cared for her. And hadn't he admitted to missing her when she wasn't with him?

Maybe, just maybe, he wanted to be with her for more than a night. Maybe he was just afraid to put a label on it. He had attachment issues in spades, after all. And why not? Throughout the course of his life, he'd lost everyone and everything he'd ever loved. Except for West and Jase, of course, but he might not realize just how deeply his commitment to them ran. Might only disdain commitment in the romantic sense.

Tears welled in her eyes, a sense of hopelessness driving her to throw another glob of paint. Stability still mattered to her, would always matter to her, and she wasn't going to get it from Beck. But what he'd said was true. Pride wouldn't comfort her. Pride wouldn't keep her warm at night, or pleasure her so sweetly.

To be with him, she might have to sacrifice her dreams and definitely put her pride on the line. She'd have to fight for him, and fight dirty. She'd also have to watch him date other women while she pretended to go along with his silly plan to date other men. She shuddered with distaste.

I want him. Only him. I maybe even...

Her mind shied away from the *L* word. Love was all-consuming, all-encompassing, an action just as much as an emotion. Love gave rather than took, placing another's needs above her own.

A strange buzzing noise drew her attention, and she frowned as she looked around. A red light flashed in the corner of her cell phone. Since Beck had gifted her with it, she'd only used it for research, but she'd had one before her mother died. She knew a text had just come in.

As she climbed down the stepladder and backed away from the wall, she surveyed what she'd created so far. A midnight sky with a full blood moon. Thick purple-tinted clouds rippled, and she could almost feel the vibration of thunder. Several bolts of lightning glowed ominously.

Not bad. Even with the chaotic black holes she'd unintentionally crafted.

She cleaned her hands with a rag and grabbed her phone, her jaw clenching as she read the screen.

Baby: What did 1 ocean say 2 another ocean?

Beck must have programmed in the nickname, the jerk. Seeing it caused tears to return to her eyes. This man amused her, challenged her on a level she hadn't known she needed, and whether he would admit it or not, he utterly adored her. She couldn't give him up. She just couldn't.

Decision made. She would fight for him, whatever the cost.

As a heavy weight lifted from her shoulders, she typed, What?

Baby: Nothing, they just waved

Her lips twitched.

Her: Ugh! The cheese!

Baby: Don't B such a beach

She laughed out loud.

Baby: U just LOL'd. Don't deny it.

She spun around, making sure he hadn't sneaked into the room.

Her: I laughed at U, not w/U

Baby: Harsh. Hey, would U rather get UR foot stuck in a bear trap or invite me over 4 din 2night?

"That depends," she told the phone. "Are you going to try to set me up with another man while we're together?"

But she typed: Sure, come over. I've decided 2 get on board w/UR plan.

Just not the way you hope, she silently added.

She waited one minute, two, but he never replied. *Don't like my ready agreement, Mr. Ockley?*

A girl could hope. And Harlow did. It was the only life raft in the middle of a great and terrible storm.

She added:

Here R my requirements 4 my new man. 1) SV resident 2) Employed 3) Honest 4) Kind 5) Hates beige

Again, there was no response.

So she continued:

Oh, & 1 more thing. Any date U set up, U have 2 attend. Alone. I don't like strangers. U'll B my bodyguard.

Smiling, she set the phone aside and approached the only wall she hadn't yet covered with paint. Perhaps it was time to create a sunny summer day.

"BECK."

Jase's voice wrenched Beck out of the dark mire of his thoughts, and he glanced up. "What?"

Jase and West occupied the seats in front of his desk. They'd seen him this morning, soon after he'd left Harlow's RV to call a private investigator he'd used in the past. His determination to find out who'd hurt her hadn't lessened. He'd been stomping around the house, cursing under his breath, and they had followed him to work to do some sort of intervention.

"At least he looks human again," West said. "Or he did, for a few minutes. Now he's back to beast mode."

Beck set his phone aside and tried not to think of

Harlow's last round of texts. Tried…and failed miserably.

She'd already forgotten the pleasure Beck had given her.

She expected him to watch another man seduce her—and not end up in jail? The pencil snapped in his hand, and he tossed the pieces across the room.

"And we've lost him again," Jase muttered.

Beck ran a hand through his hair, gritting out, "Thanks to Brook Lynn, I've got to find Harlow a date."

"*That's* what this is about?" West exclaimed. "Dude. Just tell Brook Lynn no."

Jase gave him a pitying smile. "You want to tell her no, fine. But she'll just take matters into her own hands."

Beck leaned back in his chair and stared up at the ceiling. "I won't tell her no. Harlow wants a husband, and I want her happy."

"The way I hear it, she wants a commitment from you," Jase said, "but that doesn't necessarily mean marriage."

"What's your beef with marriage, anyway?" West asked, clearly forgetting his own beef with it. "We all know marriage for the sake of marriage never works, but two people who care for each other can succeed at anything."

"Uh, that's not actually true," Beck said. West had cared about Tessa, and Tessa had cared about West, but he'd still lost her.

Beck had never believed the accident report. Loss of control due to rain? No. He'd seen the hopeless despair in Tessa's eyes when she'd left the apartment he and West shared. His friend had gotten high and forgotten to throw her a GED party, and she'd finally snapped, driving her car into a street lamp. Hadn't helped that she'd never recovered from her assault. She'd often talked about needing a break from the misery. A cry for help neither of them had heeded.

Why set himself up for similar pain?

"I don't want to talk about this," he said.

Jase picked up one of the photos Beck had framed and brought to work. One of a young Harlow sitting in a tire swing, smiling at whoever held the camera. Her mother, most likely. "I'm the ex-con, but you two have a way of making me feel like a shining star of mental health."

"Anything for you," West said, patting him on the back.

"Just shut up and help me pick a man for Harlow." Beck gripped the arms of his chair with so much force he expected the entire thing to crumble. Right now, the only hope he had of returning to the life he'd once known was losing interest in her, and the only way to make that happen was to follow through with Brook Lynn's plan. "Only the best for her."

He hated this, but he would do it right. And in the end, Beck wasn't the best. Not for her, not for anyone. He simply wasn't enough.

"What about Mark Timberlane of S&S?" West splayed his arms, all *meet your solution*. "He runs his own company, makes a ton of money and is recently divorced."

Can't shake the life out of my friend for doing what I asked. "He's not the one."

Jase unveiled a slow grin. "Please. Do tell."

"Did you not hear West? Mark is recently divorced.

He didn't fight to keep his marriage together, which means he has no real sticking power. Therefore he's not the one for Harlow. Next."

"What about the new guy who hired me to do the video game?" West suggested. "He saw some of Harlow's sketches and had a mindgasm."

"No." Beck had spent a lot of time with the guy, coaxing him into choosing West rather than some other computer genius. "He's indecisive."

"And that's a hard limit for Harlow?" Jase laughed outright. "Face it, my man, you don't want her with anyone but yourself."

Beck leaped to his feet, his hands curling into fists. The urge to punch a hole in the wall was strong, overwhelming, and what the hell was he doing? He eased back down, the answer pretty plain.

"What about Dorian Oliver?" Dorian didn't live in Strawberry Valley, but he met Harlow's other criteria.

West whistled. "The guy's perfect for *anyone*. If I swung that way, I'd be all over him."

"I remember Dorian." Jase cracked his knuckles. "Keep him away from Brook Lynn. Women look at him and experience that, what's it called, insta-love."

True, but he wasn't a player. Like West, he was choosey. But unlike the pair of them, he preferred commitment. He'd married his high school sweetheart and would still be with her if she hadn't died from cancer.

Beck had spent a summer with him years ago, both of them fostered by the same family. They'd liked each other from minute one and had kept in touch over the years.

Fighting the urge to throw his phone across the office, Beck picked it up and made the call.

HARLOW EXPECTED BECK to come knocking at her door. Not because she'd agreed to spend the evening with him, but because of what she'd done to his bedroom walls. When the entrance swung open, however, he wasn't glowering at her. He smiled and held out a bouquet of pink and white flowers.

"For you."

What the...? "Uh, thank you?" Trying to coax her from her earlier upset? She accepted the gift, a sweet scent teasing her nose. "What are they for?"

"Do I need a reason?"

Yes! But she nibbled on her bottom lip and shook her head.

"They reminded me of you," he said then. "Soft and pretty, delicate and dewy."

Killing me. "Have you not been home?"

"No, why?"

"Well, uh... I kind of painted my—*your* bedroom walls."

He frowned. "Kind of?"

"Fine. *Definitely* painted."

"Why would you do that? I liked my room the way it was."

"So? You'll like it better now."

"I won't."

"Well, you can suck it," she said, flipping her hair over her shoulder.

The frown morphed into a scowl. "Grab your paints. If you have to work all night, you'll work all night, but those walls will be beige by morning."

"Not even in your dreams. You were willing to keep the mural when you first moved in."

"But now I'm used to beige."

Frustrating man. "We'll talk about the walls tomorrow."

"Harlow—"

"Brook Lynn came by, saw what I'd done, and asked if I'd paint a mural at her house." A zombie mural, of all things, for easier target practice. "*She* knows talent when she sees it."

"Did you tell her no, you already have a job?"

"Please. I said yes so fast I broke records. I will work for food."

He went still, sniffed the air. "Do you have a pie in there, Harlow?"

"No," she said, and his shoulders drooped with disappointment. "I have *two* pies. I haven't painted the mural yet, but I demanded an advance."

He pushed his way inside, a drug dog on the trail of the biggest bust of his career. "Blueberry and apple. Good girl."

She filled two bowls, then joined him at her small table. One bite, and they both moaned. Waiting had been difficult, almost impossible, but somehow she'd managed it, wanting to share this moment with him. And now she was glad she had.

He winked over at her, his golden eyes sparkling.

She smiled at him, unable to help herself.

He reached for her, only to drop his hand before contact. Stiffening, he looked somewhere over her shoulder. "So... I found you a guy."

Denial rose like a tidal wave. "So soon?"

"Yeah. His name's Dorian. I'll get you a laptop so you can look him up on Google. Chicks are doing that nowadays."

"Great. Wonderful."

"You should see the pictures people have posted of me. In fact—" He withdrew his phone. "We'll look now."

"No, thanks. Let's keep this about Dorian," she said, just to poke at him.

His eyes narrowed, but he stored the phone. "I've known him since I was fifteen. He's a fireman, and according to the girl who lived next door to our foster family, totally hunkalicious. He's smart, kind and honest to a fault, but he lives in the city. If that's a deal breaker for you…"

"No," she said. Beck wanted to play this game, so they would play.

"Take some time, think about it." He threw down his fork, the metal clanging against the glass bowl. "We don't have to talk about this now. I know it upsets you."

Upsets *her*? "No, no," she said. "Tell me more about him."

Beck pushed his bowl aside, as if he'd lost his appetite, a reaction that thrilled her to her soul. He couldn't stand the thought of her with another guy, could he?

He scratched his chest, saying, "Want to watch TV? There's gotta be something good on." He tromped back to the bedroom and threw himself on the bed.

"Damn it," he said a few seconds later. "I've got pie on my shirt."

"Go shirtless." Please.

To torment him, she finished her dessert—and enjoyed another slice—before joining him in the bedroom. He'd gotten comfortable, kicking off his shoes, and yes, he'd removed his shirt. The sight of him arrested her. He was more than pure seduction and total temptation—he was a dream come true. His pecs were rock-solid, his stomach roped and lined with a goodie trail that made her mouth water.

How was she supposed to keep her hands to herself?

Better question: How was he?

Almost defiantly, she toed off her shoes and climbed in beside him. "Move over, cover hog."

He obeyed without protest, even stretching out his arm in an invitation for her to cuddle close. An invitation she accepted, resting her head against his chest. His heart was racing, pounding like a war drum, pandering to her hope.

She would *not* make the first move. She wouldn't! But she also wouldn't make this easy on him. "I like the name Dorian."

"Most girls do." His finger jabbed at the remote, switching channels.

"It's sexy."

Another new channel. "It's stupid. Door-e-ann is the name of a great-grandmother."

"Or a famous male stripper I can ply with singles."

Yet another new channel, this one a skin flick, filling the room with sounds of heavy breathing, rustling sheets and whining mattress springs, making her pulse jump and her insides go liquid.

"Have you seen this one?" he asked.

"No. Tell me about it."

He set the remote aside, traced his fingers up and down her arm as she tried not to stare at the sea of naked flesh. "The plot is super complicated. You'll have to watch closely."

"I can see how insert tab A into slot B would confuse you," she muttered. Dang him! Her pulse jumped faster. Did he *want* her to attack him?

Realization settled. He did. He 100 percent, no-doubt-about-it wanted her to attack him. If he could get her to make the first move, he would feel he had permission to make one right back. How devious.

I will outlast him. She swiped the remote and switched off the TV. "Let's play a game."

"Good idea." He toyed with the ends of her hair. "I know how much you like to imagine yourself as other people. The stripper, for instance."

"You can stop right there. I am *not* stripping for you."

"As if I don't know that. I'm suggesting a role-play. You're a stripper who's just fallen off the pole. I'm a doctor, and I need to give you a very thorough exam to ensure you're able to return to work tomorrow."

Her whoremones cheered. But self-preservation won out. Most girls would be *offended* by his proposal.

She smacked him in the chest, considered performing a titty-twister, but resisted. "I'll save that game for my new boyfriend, thanks."

His lips pursed. "Fine. Let's play the quiet game."

"I lose. Let's talk. Daniel Porter is back from his military tour, and he's superhot." Both statements were true; she simply left out the part about Jessie Kay going on a date with him. "He lives in Strawberry Valley. Maybe I should call him instead of meeting your friend Dorian."

Beck clamped the back of her neck in a hard clasp before releasing her. "I've seen Daniel around town, and I'm pretty sure I heard a rumor he stole a doughnut from Strawberry Valley Community Church."

"Wouldn't that make him perfect for me, considering I'm a reformed pie thief? Anyway, the church gives doughnuts away for free."

"I still don't trust him. I'll look into him, but until then, I don't want you anywhere near him."

Protesting too much, baby? "I hate to break it to you, Mr. Ockley, but you aren't the boss of me."

"Actually, Miss Glass, I am. You work for me. Basically, I own your soul."

She gave him another smack in the chest. "I mean you're not the boss of my personal life."

"How dare you." He caught her wrist and, with a firm tug, pulled her across his body and tickled her under her arms. "I'm the boss of your personal life. Say it."

"No," she managed as she laughed uncontrollably. "Never!"

"Say it."

"Stop…stop…please stop." She flung herself to the other side of the bed, but he just followed her over, the tickling more intense. "I'm going to pee my pants!"

"That will be embarrassing for you. What are the magic words?"

"You're…you're in charge…"

The tickling instantly stopped. "Of?"

Harlow's chest heaved, and she struggled to catch her breath. "You're in charge of…of…" When finally she felt capable of movement, she dived to the floor, calling, "You're in charge of nothing!"

A mock growl left him, and he stood. "You'll pay for that, dumpling."

She scrambled to her feet and backed away from him. Struggling not to laugh all over again, she held out her hands to ward him off, but he just kept coming. From the corner of her eye, she spotted the second pie. The apple. The one he hadn't yet tasted.

She swiped it up, saying, "Come any closer and the pie gets trashed!"

Abject horror shone from his face. "That's taking things too far, Harlow Glass. Too far!"

"You're right, you're right. I'm sorry." Gently she returned the pie to the counter, blew it an apology kiss, and then used her hands to form the letter *T*. "Time out."

He crossed his arms over his chest. "You can't call a time out, not in matters of love and war."

"Shows what you know. I just did." She walked to the fridge, thought for a moment, and grabbed two of Beck's beers, popping the tops and turning to face him. "Time in. Come any closer, and the beers get trashed."

He barked out a laugh, but quickly blanked his features. "Not my favorite beers," he said, rubbing his chin with two fingers. "Anything but my favorite beers... But I just can't seem to stay away from you." One step, two...he approached her.

"I'll do it. I'll pour them out." She held them over the sink.

"Do it, and things will get ugly. I won't be responsible for my actions."

"Oh, yeah?" She placed her thumb over the tops, shook the bottles and, as his eyes widened, sprayed him with the exploding liquid.

When the fizz ran out, he licked the drops from his mouth. "Well, now," he said, his tone even. "I guess things are gonna get ugly." And then he advanced.

He easily confiscated the beers and repeated her actions, shaking them and spraying her with what remained. Laughing hysterically, Harlow tried to escape. He merely backed her into a corner, dropped the bottles and held her in place with one hand while switching on the sink faucet with the other. He doused her from head to toe with water, and after she'd screamed and laughed in outrage, he stepped back to study his handi-work, nodding with satisfaction.

When he focused on her breasts, his satisfaction dovetailed into white-hot desire. "Your nipples are hard." Husky voice, a little slurred, as if the beer had gone to his head.

Her amusement died, and she began to pant. "Look away."

"I can't." He planted his palms on the cabinets be-side her temples, caging her in. Counter behind her, aroused male in front of her. "Say yes, and I'll lick you clean from head to toe."

Her mouth went dry, and her knees shook. *Yes, yes, a thousand times yes.* A moment of pleasure awaited her...but only a moment.

He'd just set her up with another man; she had to re-sist him. "No," she whispered. "My date..."

Fury clouded his eyes before he spun away from her. "Your date. Right."

"You did this, Beck. You. No one else."

"You should thank me. He's Mr. Perfect. Everything I'm not."

"What does that mean?"

"Doesn't mean a damn thing."

Feeling sad for him—for them—she sighed and said, "I think that's the problem. It never does with you."

CHAPTER SIXTEEN

BECK PEERED UP at the ceiling of his bedroom, morning light seeping through the crack in the window curtains. He'd spent the night tossing and turning, missing the feel of Harlow in his arms.

After they'd cleaned the RV, he'd returned to the farmhouse to shower and change. The need to go back, to make things right with her, had been strong, but he'd somehow resisted. The girl was turning him inside out—which was the very reason he had to continue on this current path.

Except, tired and grumpy, he thought, *What the hell?* He brushed his teeth, changed and made his way to the RV. Since she had no problem using her key to invade his house, he had no problem using his key to invade hers. He quietly made his way inside and found her in the bed. She lay curled on her side, her face toward his, a beam of light spotlighting her, turning her into the real Sleeping Beauty. He reached for her, caught himself just before contact and swallowed a curse.

He gathered everything he needed to cook his famous morning-after breakfast, and as the bacon began to sizzle, she sat up like a zombie rising from the grave. At his laugh, her eyes snapped open.

Utterly adorable—and damn it, he had to look away.

His body was strung tighter than a bow. Any more pressure and he would snap.

"Beck?"

"The one and only."

"What are you doing here?"

"Cooking. I hope you're hungry, princess."

"For bacon? Always. But I'd rather have you," she grumbled.

He had to grip the counter to remain in place. "Your date is tonight, remember?"

"What!" she gasped out. "How could I remember when you never told me? So soon?"

"Why not?" The longer he put it off, the crazier it would make him.

"Just… Screw you." The patter of footsteps. The slam of the bathroom door.

"Not a morning person," he called. "Got it."

She emerged as he finished loading two plates with eggs, bacon of course, hash browns, pancakes and more bacon. They sat across from each other at the small table, and he pushed her plate in front of her.

"Well, well," she said. "I didn't sleep with you, but I get the blow-off breakfast anyway. Is it my birthday?"

"Technically, you have slept with me. Though I'm not sure why I keep coming back. I had to spend that night listening to you snore—"

"I do *not* snore!"

"Honey, you sound like a freight train."

"You are such a liar." She threw a fork at him. "Tell me you're a liar!"

"And actually become a liar? No. You're welcome, by the way. For my exalted presence and the breakfast. When is your birthday, anyway?"

"December third."

"That's coming in fast."

She shrugged before admitting softly, "It'll be my first birthday without my mom."

Hello, ache. I missed you. "Well, it'll be your first birthday with me, you lucky girl, and I hereby vow to make it the best one of your life."

Looking more vulnerable by the second, she said, "Just how are you going to do that?"

He grinned slowly. "Are you thinking naughty thoughts, Miss Glass? Wanting me to give you something *personal*?"

"Oh, shut up and let me eat," she said, grabbing another fork.

"Uh, uh, uh." He snatched the plate away from her. "Not until you tell me what you want for your birthday."

"Gimme that food before you get stabbed."

"Tell me."

"A wedding ring. How about that?"

Brat. "I'd be willing to give you a practice wedding night." He set the food in front of her, saying in falsetto, "'Thank you, Beck. You look so handsome this morning, Beck.'"

Harlow dug into her food, ignoring him.

"'Why, Beck Joseph Ockley,'" he continued in his impression of her, "'you always have the best ideas.'"

Harlow glanced up. "Your middle name is Joseph?"

"Yep. What's yours?"

"Adrianne."

He'd had a forkful of eggs on the way to his mouth, paused, then slowly lowered the utensil. "Did you say… Adrianne?"

"Yes." She chomped into a piece of bacon. "Why?"

"Well, I had no idea your initials were *HAG*."

Horroified, she gasped out, "Don't you dare call me hag."

He smirked at her. Was there any woman more adorable?

Dorian would go crazy for her.

Good humor suddenly gone, Beck attacked his food with a vengeance. When he finished, he felt sick, but he stood, carried his plate to the sink.

Without looking at her, he said, "Your date will be here at seven. Be ready."

"Don't worry, I will. And I'll wear something sexy. One of the racier dresses you gave me."

He barely contained his scowl. "One of the immodest ones you refuse to wear for me?"

"Definitely."

"Great." Either she was more confident now, or she simply hoped to torture Beck. "I'll wear a suit."

"As my bodyguard, it'd be more appropriate for you to wear camo."

"Hag, it won't matter what I'm wearing. If I decide to take out your date, he'll never see me coming."

AFTER BECK TOOK OFF, Harlow called for reinforcements. To her surprise and delight, Brook Lynn and Jessie Kay showed up at five to help her get ready for her three-person date-slash-torture session.

"By the time we're done with you," Jessie Kay said, "Beck is gonna wish he'd lost his penis in a tragic bull-riding accident."

"Let's hope." Like a harem girl within the pages of a romance novel, Harlow was buffed, waxed and oiled, her hair curled and coiffed. Despite her earlier bravado, she pulled a cashmere sweater over the revealing sheath dress she selected, hiding her scars.

When the girls finished with her, she twirled in front of the full-length mirror she'd had installed in the bedroom, pleased with how she'd turned out. The icy color of the dress brought out the blue in her eyes, and even her hair. Three healthy meals a day had added a natural rosy tint to her skin and blessed her with the feminine curves she'd always envied in others.

"If he can do more than drool," Jessie Kay added, "he's a stronger man than I am."

Brook Lynn rolled her eyes. "As if there's ever been a stronger man than you."

"This is true."

Harlow would have given anything to be part of their family. They had such an easy camaraderie. They supported each other, loved each other, no matter what.

Brook Lynn glanced down at her vibrating phone and sighed. "That's Jase again. He says I'm needed home stat. I swear, ever since he learned Dorian Oliver is coming to town, he's been freaking out."

"I should probably stay here," Jessie Kay said. "You know, as Harlow's moral compass."

"You are not inviting yourself on tonight's date— or into Dorian's pants," Brook Lynn told her. "And if you're a moral compass, I fear for the world."

"What about you and Daniel Porter?" Harlow asked.

Jessie Kay looked to the floor, hiding her eyes. "We're still dating, but not exclusive. He just got home from a yearlong military tour and isn't ready to commit."

Ugh. He might not be ready, but Jessie Kay surely

was. *Been there, living that.* Harlow reached over and squeezed her hand. "I'm sorry."

"It is what it is. The story of my life."

"You two are depressing." Brook Lynn tugged her sister to the door. "Come on, let's go before you make Harlow cry a river."

They were gone a few seconds later, and Harlow wiped her suddenly sweaty palms on her thighs. This was her first date as an adult woman. Why had she insisted Beck come along? Now she had to rebuff this Dorian guy without looking as if she were rebuffing him, while encouraging Beck without looking as if she were encouraging him.

Easy.

A hard rap exploded at the door, making her gasp. It was six forty-five, and Beck had never been early for anything. She figured the girls had forgotten something and had come back to get it, her smile of welcome fading as the door swung open to reveal Beck dressed in a pin-striped suit, as promised, looking gorgeous and sophisticated and totally out of her league.

A man she'd never met stood next to him, Brook Lynn and Jessie Kay hovering in the background, gaping at him. Jessie Kay even fanned herself and pretended to faint.

Beck whistled with appreciation. "Lord have mercy, hag. You've fried my brain. I can't even stay mad at you for desecrating my bedroom walls."

"Hag?" the stranger asked.

"A nickname that will likely get some part of Beck removed in the near future," she said. "And I did not desecrate his walls. I made them better. They were beige."

Stranger laughed, and she would have sworn fairies wept. "I think I'll stick with Harlow, then." He extended his hand. "I'm Dorian Oliver."

As they shook, she took his measure. He topped out at six foot, an inch shorter than Beck. He had a lion's mane of pale hair, his eyes a startling mix of smoke and sunset, and his face...

His features were the most symmetrically perfect she'd ever seen. "I want to sketch you," she blurted out.

Beck stepped in front of him, thin white brackets of strain around his mouth. "There's no time for that. We have dinner reservations."

"We?" Dorian asked from behind him.

His gaze never left Harlow. "Did I forget to mention my darling requested a bodyguard?"

His darling? "I've changed my mind about that," she said. "You can stay—"

"Too bad." Beck gave her the evil eye. "There are no take-backs."

"Don't worry about it," Dorian said. "Don't hate me, but I actually considered asking him to join us when he first called to set us up. I've never done the blind date thing, and I wasn't sure I'd like it." He winked at her. "I'm a big fan right now."

Flattered, she smiled at him. "I feel the same. I'll just...um..." Brain dead much? "I'll fetch my purse and we can be off." But all she had to do to "fetch" her purse was reach back and curl her fingers around the handle. So much for a needed reprieve.

Both men offered a hand to help her down the step. Glancing at Beck, all *you did this to yourself*, she accepted Dorian's, twining their fingers.

"I have an idea," she told him. "We'll pretend Jerk-bag isn't with us."

Dorian released another magical laugh, and Beck grunted.

"I'll drive," he announced when they reached the driveway full of cars.

"Excellent. Harlow and I will sit in back and get to know each other better." Dorian helped her inside.

Before he could walk around the car and take his own seat, Beck stopped him. The two engaged in a heated conversation for what seemed forever, their voices muffled. She couldn't understand what they were saying, but was it too much to hope Beck had realized his mistake and was telling the guy to go home?

Apparently it *was* too much to hope. They got inside, Beck behind the wheel, Dorian in back with her, as planned.

"Anyone want to tell me what that was about?" she asked.

"No," Beck said.

"Jerkbag gave me a lecture about minding my manners," Dorian said, amused.

"Were they too good?" she quipped.

Beck reached back and squeezed her knee, making her squeal. Then he had the gall to say, "Are you trying to make me have a wreck? Control yourself back there."

She pushed his hand away and leveled a smile at Dorian. "So. How did you and Beck meet?"

"Same foster home."

"A good one, I hope." What had these boys endured over the years?

"It was one of the best." Dorian smiled fondly. "I

was happy for the first time in my life and didn't want to leave."

She placed a hand over her heart. "Do you realize you just opened up to me and revealed a little about yourself? Are you a unicorn-shifter?"

"I don't know what a unicorn-shifter is." Beck expertly turned a corner. "But I open up all the time."

"Yeah, but I have to use pliers."

They reached the restaurant, a quaint little Italian place just outside city limits, and Dorian exited to hurry around and open her door. Street lamps surrounded the parking lot, chasing away most of the night's shadows. The parking lot was surprisingly empty considering an open sign flashed neon red over the entrance.

"Thank you," she said.

"What about *my* door?" Beck asked as he emerged.

"Why don't you stay in the car?" she suggested. "Enjoy a little peace and quiet."

"That's the thanks I get? After I rented out the entire restaurant?"

Dang him, she melted. He'd put her comfort— Wait. *I'm falling for this?* She was on a date with a man he'd selected for her, for goodness' sake. "I'll send you a fruit basket tomorrow." She raised her chin. To Dorian, she added, "Sorry about this. I'm being rude, ignoring you, but—"

Dorian chuckled as he drew her several steps ahead of Beck. He leaned toward her, whispering, "Look, I know there's something going on between you two. West called me earlier and told me you belong to Beck and I'm to keep my hands off you while helping him realize the terrible mistake he's making."

West was rooting for her?

"Speak up so the rest of the class can hear." Beck trudged in front of them, opened the restaurant door.

Giddy, and feeling just a little evil, Harlow leaned her head against Dorian and petted his arm. "Isn't it obvious? We're getting to know each other better…and maybe even falling in love."

ROUND ONE DID NOT end in Harlow's favor, and she pouted the entire drive home. Besides the three of them, there had been two other people in the restaurant: their waitress and the chef. Both happened to be females. Of course. Beck had claimed the table across the room, and when he hadn't been flirting shamelessly with the waitress, he'd been in back flirting shamelessly with the chef.

Without the pressure of having to rebuff Dorian, Harlow was able to relax and enjoy herself, doing a little flirting of her own, hoping to fan the flames of Beck's jealousy. He'd hardly seemed to notice, and as the night had worn on, he'd only become more charming with the staff.

Now, with the evening coming to a close, Beck parked in the driveway of the farmhouse. Dorian helped her out, saying, "I'll walk you to your door."

Beck got out in a hurry and patted him on the shoulder. "There's no need for that, my friend. I've got it from here."

"How kind of you," Dorian said.

"Isn't it? We had a great time, by the way."

Harlow glared at Beck. "Will *we* be calling him for another date?"

Beck flashed his teeth in a grin utterly devoid of humor. "We'll discuss it."

Dorian tried to mask a laugh with a cough. "Well, I certainly hope you do, Harlow Glass. I don't remember the last time I've had so much fun."

She flipped her hair over her shoulder, the ends slapping Beck in the face. "You are a man of great taste. Unlike some people I know."

Beck gave the guy a push toward a cute little '65 Nova. "I'll call you tomorrow and let you know the verdict."

"Please do," Dorian replied.

"Actually, bypass the middleman. You have my number," Harlow reminded him, and he winked at her before sliding into his car.

"You gave him your phone number?" Beck thundered.

Shouldn't grin. "Do you have a problem with that?"

At first he offered no response, watching as Dorian's car roared to life and meandered out of the drive. When the taillights at last disappeared around the corner, Beck whirled on her and shouted, "Hell, yes, I have a problem with that. I shouldn't have to tell you this, pumpkin, but he's not right for you. I could tell within five seconds. Why couldn't you?" He wrapped an arm around her waist and led her toward the RV. "I did you a favor, sending him away. He would have tried to kiss you at the door."

Maybe, but only for Beck's benefit. Even if she hadn't been enamored with someone else, she and Dorian would not have been right for each other. Beck nailed it. They'd lacked chemistry.

"Did you ever stop to think I might *want* to be kissed?" she asked.

"Baby, you should fall to your knees and thank me for being here to save you from yourself."

She stepped in his path and placed her hand on his chest, stopping him. It was then she felt the barely suppressed tension in him, the knotted muscles and the swift pounding of his heart.

"A kiss isn't a big deal, Beck. Is it?"

Glowering, he said, "It certainly should be."

I'm getting somewhere with this man. Have to be. "Has it ever been a big deal for you?"

"Only with you." He was on her a second later, pressing her against the cool RV wall. His lips smashed into hers, his tongue driving into her mouth to demand its due.

She told herself to pull away, to push him away—something. They hadn't come to any kind of understanding, and he'd just arranged for her to go out with another man. But she wrapped her arms around his neck and held on for dear life, even tilting her head and welcoming him deeper. The desire always simmering below the surface of her skin boiled out of control, spilling over, consuming every inch of her.

Her legs trembled, her knees weakened. He balled the hem of her dress and pulled it to her waist, right at her panty line. Warm, sultry air brushed against her tingling flesh.

"You wet for me?"

"Yes," she whispered.

"Only me?"

She pressed her lips together, refusing to answer.

A muscle jumped beneath his eye. "Let's see." He moved his hand to just under her navel and slowly traced his fingertips down, down, sliding under her panties.

The anticipation was too much. "Beck. Please."

"Wider." He nipped at her ear and, not content to wait, kicked her legs apart. As she gasped, he wedged one of those big fingers inside her. He groaned, and she moaned, arching forward, seeking more.

"Soaking," he praised. "Let me taste."

She thought he would pull his finger out, maybe lick it, and that would have been the hottest thing she'd ever seen. But he dropped to his knees, and her breath hitched. This was hotter.

"Hope these aren't your favorite." With a single tug, he ripped the side of her panties, baring her to his view.

Tremors of excitement, of need, cascaded over her. The moon was out, and the porch light was on, both casting muted golden ribbons their way, but the wall of the RV cast a wide shadow the ribbons couldn't reach, hiding them from prying eyes.

"Wish the sun were shining," he said, and he sounded drugged. "I want to see you bathed in light."

"Beck."

He leaned in, his warm breath fanning over her. His tongue flicked out, touching her for the first time, and she cried out in delight. Her hips moved of their own accord, following his motions.

It was… He was… *Can't think.*

"So sweet," he praised. "You are like honeyed cocaine, baby."

He'd aroused her before, and he'd made her come, but the arousal had never been this ragged or intense. Her new cries, panting breaths and whimpers echoed through the night, a song of desire.

"Beck, I'm so close."

"You hold out as long as you can." His voice lashed

with command. "I'm not even close to being done with you."

Hold out? She tried, oh, she tried, but his tongue worked her harder and faster, worked *black magic*. Then he brought his fingers into play, sinking two inside her, stretching her, and she saw stars behind her lids, screaming as she finally fell over the edge of desire.

As she quaked with aftereffects, he pushed to his feet. He towered over her, his expression one of absolute hunger, the playful side to him utterly vanquished, his gaze devouring her face the way his mouth had just devoured another part of her, practically consuming her whole.

"I want you." He unbuttoned his pants, lowered the zipper. "Here, now."

Yes. "Beck, I…" *Stop. Think.*

He gripped his length with one hand, wound a lock of her hair with the other. "Say yes, Harlow. I'll take care of you. I swear I'll take care of you."

But for how long?

Crap! Crap, crap, crap. Ice-cold waves washed over her, invading her bloodstream, dousing the fire he'd stoked, and she realized she was right back where she'd started: going nowhere fast.

"Beck…" She had to tell him the truth, and she had to make him understand why she wanted what she wanted. "I can't do this. I'm not casual about sex. I've never been casual about sex. I… Beck, I've never been with a man, and I can't—I won't—give my virginity to a one-night stand."

He stiffened, shook his head as if he'd misheard her. "But…you can't be…" He scrubbed a hand over his face, different emotions playing in his golden eyes. Anger. Longing. Relief. Even possessiveness?

"I've been up-front about my long-term goals from the beginning. I plan to give myself to the man I'm committed to, and no one else." *Be that man. Please.*

He released her, refastening his pants as he backed away. Considering she'd nearly gone up in flames a few moments before, the forced separation almost killed her; she had to swallow a cry.

"I… I'm sorry, Harlow," he stammered. "I didn't know, or I never would have pushed you…" He looked so lost, so broken. "You're a prize, and you're worth more than what I can give you. I'm sorry," he repeated. Then the stubborn male turned, walked up the drive and disappeared inside the farmhouse.

CHAPTER SEVENTEEN

A WEEK PASSED. An entire week without a phone call or text from Beck. Actually, no, that wasn't true. Harlow received a text from him the morning after she'd revealed her virgin state. He told her to take the day off, that he had things handled at the office.

As one day bled into another, he stayed away from her as if she'd told him she had an infectious disease—or that she was the only woman in the world who could get pregnant with eye contact. Not once had he shown up in the morning to drive her to work, so she'd holed up in the RV to sketch, leaving the game sets and characters she finished on the desk in Beck's bedroom.

Through it all, two things had given her hope, making her think she'd lost a battle rather than the actual war. He still hadn't changed the locks on the door, and he hadn't painted over the artwork decorating his walls.

But her hope was dwindling fast. He'd left last night and he hadn't come home. Had he gone on a date?

This morning, she'd finally broken down and called Brook Lynn, seeking more advice, which was how she'd ended up at Two Farms for lunch with the entire girl gang.

"He's been a beast," Brook Lynn said as she buttered a roll. "Gripes about everything, yells at everyone."

Jessie Kay nodded. "You'd think you told him your

hoo-ha is actually a Venus flytrap and his penis will be severed if he has sex with you."

"Do you have to say that word while we're eating?" Daphne asked.

"Which one? *Penis*?" Jessie Kay bellowed. Some patrons gasped. Some glared at her. Others shook their heads, all *bless her heart*. "The word *penis* is not the equivalent of *maggots*, you know. Though it probably should be."

"And now I've lost my appetite," Daphne said, pushing her bowl of chicken potpie away.

Kenna threw a piece of fried cheese at Jessie Kay. "Have some class and call it a baby maker or something."

Everyone at the table went still.

"Are you trying to tell us you're pregnant?" Brook Lynn demanded.

"No!" Kenna burst out. "What? We're waiting until we've had a few years together. You can call it the trouser snake, for all I care."

Trouser snake? Really? "What about man meat? Or even the middle leg?" Harlow suggested.

Jessie Kay nodded thoughtfully. "Or we could go with something simple like the peen. If we wanted to get technical, we'd have to go with the meatsicle. Or the anaconda, but that's on a case-by-case basis."

Daphne tried for a stern expression, only to ruin it with a snort. "I am not playing this game. But if I were, I'd suggest we call it the weenie wonka."

How had they ended up on this subject? "Ladies." Harlow clapped her hands to gain their attention. "Can we please return to bad-mouthing Beck?"

"The guy who's been serving out Mr. Happy Meals

to satisfied customers for years? Yes. Please continue." Jessie Kay gave a regal wave of her hand.

And I actually asked her for help? "Why would he ignore me since learning of my…you know…untouched state?"

"He hasn't talked about it," Brook Lynn said, an apology in her voice. "To be honest, I had no idea what was going on until you called."

Great! "Why did you agree to help him find me a new man, anyway?"

"I didn't agree—I suggested it."

"What? Why?"

"To tick him off and make him admit he wants you all to himself." Brook Lynn grinned. "He pulled me aside the other day and told me not to set you up with anyone. He would be handling all the details."

"Well, he's not handling them. Where'd he go last night?"

The blonde winced.

Don't say date. Don't say date.

"To the city…for a double date with Dorian." Brook Lynn patted her hand. "I'm sorry. I only know because Beck called Jase late last night and said he wouldn't be coming home."

Her shoulders drooped, what remained of her hope dying a quick and brutal death.

A bell tinkled over the door, and she glanced over to see Scott Cameron coming into the restaurant. He gazed around, as if he were looking for someone specific, only to stop on her and smile coldly.

So not in the mood. Besides, did he never work?

Scott removed his baseball cap and approached their table. For the first time in years, she got a good, long look at him up close and personal and noticed he wasn't the athlete he used to be. He had a slight beer gut and a— What was that called? Muffin top? Without the hat, there was no hiding his receding hairline.

"Um, hi, Scott," Brook Lynn said. "Is there something we can help you with?"

"You can tell me why you're hanging out with the wicked witch of the Southwest."

Jessie Kay bristled. "You're right. She's a witch. But she's our witch, so you better back the hell off before I decide to get creative with my butter knife."

Harlow gaped at the girl. *She's...defending me?*

"Besides," Kenna said, nose in the air. "Our girl is taken. Your juvenile efforts to gain her attention won't work."

"Taken? By that Beck guy? Please. Everyone knows he'll stick it to anything breathing. Isn't that right, Jessie Kay?" Scott laughed as both Jessie Kay and Harlow hissed at him. "Besides, you ladies gotta stop expecting a man to sweep you off your feet. *You're* the ones who are supposed to handle the broom."

Oh, no, he didn't. "How about I shove a broom right up your—" A hand slapped over Harlow's mouth.

"Family establishment," Brook Lynn whispered at her, only then removing her hand.

Scott opened his mouth to say more, thought better of it and stalked off, snagging a table at the other side of the room. Their waitress raced over to pat his arm while casting Harlow a hate-filled scowl. Okay. It was safe to say her next order would contain spit, at the very least.

"Thank you," Harlow said to Jessie Kay.

"Well, you *are* a witch. I meant that with every fiber of my being."

Harlow clutched her chest. "The warm tingles are overwhelming. Tell me. Is this love? This feels like love."

Brook Lynn snorted.

"Our waitress can't be more than twenty," Harlow said. "I didn't go to school with her, wasn't ever rude to her, so why does she loathe me?"

"Haven't you heard? She and Scott are dating." Kenna swiped up the last roll in the basket. "Bet he's ranted and raved about you. My guess is she called him the moment you arrived and that's how he knew to come here."

Can I never catch a break?

"Forget about her," Daphne said. "I want to know what you're going to do about Beck."

There was no need to think about it any longer. "Nothing," she replied, then sighed as depression settled heavily on her shoulders. "He made his choice, and it wasn't me."

"He's just confused," Brook Lynn said.

"He's fighting his feelings for you," Kenna added.

Hadn't girls been telling themselves those kinds of lies since the beginning of time?

"Plus, have you really put much effort into winning him?" Jessie Kay asked. "I haven't seen you go to the house to flash him. Not once. And when I secretly checked his text messages a few nights ago, I didn't see one dirty picture of you. From other girls? Yes. Like, a lot of other girls. Seriously, I had no idea so many in this town were of the *Fatal Attraction* variety."

"I want names," Harlow growled.

Jessie Kay smirked at her. "I think smoke is actually curling from your nostrils."

Kenna slapped her friend's arm. "You shouldn't tease her about the dirty pictures."

"Ow." Jessie Kay frowned at the redhead. "I wasn't teasing."

"Well, you're tormenting her."

"Am not!" Jessie Kay's frown deepened. "I'm just trying to light a fire under her, get her spurred into action. Unlike you two, who want to throw her a pity party."

Had she put much effort in? Harlow wondered. He'd stayed away from her, sure, but she'd stayed away from him, as well. He hadn't called or texted her, but she hadn't called or texted him, either.

The thought instantly lightened her mood, and though she was trembling, she withdrew her phone. "All right, girls. I've never gone X-rated before. Help me?"

Jessie Kay rubbed her hands together. "Darlin', you came to the right place."

Brook Lynn, Kenna and Daphne groaned.

"One day, when you look back over your life, you'll realize this is where things started to go horribly wrong," Brook Lynn said.

"Don't listen to the haters." After a bit of table wrestling, Jessie Kay managed to stuff a napkin in her sister's mouth. "These gals were tutored by me, and look at them now. All three of them are in healthy relationships."

"*Despite* your tutelage," Kenna muttered.

"Tell them, Daph," Jessie Kay said.

"She *has* helped me nail down Brad Lintz," Daph admitted with a sigh.

A Glass Pass survivor, as well as the owner of Lintz

Automotive, and the sheriff's son. Good. He deserved a happy ending.

"For this to work," Jessie Kay said, "we've got to call that Dorian guy, like, right now. He's a key ingredient to my—I mean *your*—success. I'm only ever always thinking of you. So do it. Call him and tell him to come to Two Farms."

"But—"

"Aw, you're shy. That's so cute. No worries, I'll do it for you." Jessie Kay swiped Harlow's phone, scrolled through her contacts and found the right number. She placed the device at her ear, waited. "Dude! Even your voice is pure sex. But listen. I'm Jessie Kay, Harlow's best friend. You and I made eye-babies the other day. Yep….Yep…Mmm, keep talking. I mean, no, no, stop talking and listen. We need you to come to Strawberry Valley right now. Two Farms. It's a matter of life and death. PS, don't tell Beck." She hung up, pulled at the collar of her shirt. "That boy is dangerous."

"And we need him…why?" Brook Lynn demanded.

"You'll see. Now. The next part is a bit tricky. We're *all* gonna have to be a little tipsy." She signaled their waitress. When the pretty brunette dragged her feet to their table, she said, "Bring us that big bottle of Macallan locked behind the bar."

The girl's eyes grew big and round. "But that's… almost a *thousand dollars*." She whispered the last, as though scandalized.

Harlow nearly had a heart attack. "We do *not* want that bottle. Not now, not ever."

Jessie Kay hiked her thumb at Kenna. "We do, and it goes on her fiancé's tab. He can afford it."

"He can," Kenna agreed.

"And don't you dare open the bottle and bring it to us in glasses," Jessie Kay added. "You'll just pour it into another container before it ever reaches us and fill our glasses with the cheap stuff. I used to work here. I invented that trick. We want the bottle unopened, and no glasses. We're doing this old-school."

"What?" Daphne said. "With that fancy bottle? Why?"

Jessie Kay got real serious real fast. "We're going to have ourselves a good old-fashioned ho-mance and share the bottle. It'll bond us. Whiskey sisters for life."

To Harlow, it sounded like a little slice of heaven. Who cared about the money? If Kenna's fiancé refused to pay, Harlow had organs she could sell on the black market. Sisters? Yes, please. "I'm in!"

BECK REALIZED HE'D come full circle. Once again he was seated at the window in his bedroom, peering out at Harlow's RV. He'd gone to see her about an hour ago, pulled by an invisible chain he couldn't cut, but she hadn't answered the door. He'd let himself in like the concerned neighbor he was and discovered she wasn't ignoring him; she just wasn't at home.

It was the middle of the day, which was intolerable. She had work to do, damn it. Where was she, and who was she with?

He'd stayed away from her far too long, and it had affected him physically. As he'd already realized, she'd become his new normal, which meant he couldn't sleep without her in his arms. He couldn't eat, his stomach tied in too many knots. Not even Brook Lynn's pie had tempted him.

He'd handled things poorly. Harlow was his friend,

and he never should have run out on her after her big confession. But he'd been so surprised…so turned on. So possessive, wanting to be the first and only man to have her. He'd almost signed on for forever, picked her up and carried her to his bed.

A bed he'd shared with too many women to count.

He'd known from the beginning she deserved far better than he had to offer, but that thought had cinched it. She was untouched, pure…and he was tainted.

Despite the red flashing through his vision, he knew he had to find her another guy faster than originally planned. Like, tomorrow. Committed women were invisible to him, he reminded himself. His attraction to Harlow would finally fade. He needed it to fade. He couldn't go on like this.

So. It was time to take things to the next level. No more dates for Harlow. Instead, he would set up a party and invite every bachelor he knew, and she would then speed-date each and every one; at the end of the night, she would pick her favorite.

He would invite everyone but Dorian.

Yesterday Beck had set up a double date for the two of them, thinking his friend needed to be consoled by another woman. Consoled, not distracted so that he'd stay away from Harlow. But Beck had been a major asshole all night and scared both women away.

His phone buzzed, and he swiped up the device, grateful for the distraction of the text—until he found a picture of Harlow attached. As the image burned past his retinas and into his brain, he jumped to his feet. His sweet little hag was sitting in Dorian's lap, and the rat bastard was smiling.

The caption underneath read, Lok Beck! Loooook what I fond! A nice slice of jucy man meet!!!!!!!!

The typos were adorable, and he hated himself for thinking so. This was not a humorous situation. Harlow was ruining her future, settling for momentary pleasure with a guy who wasn't right for her.

R U drunk? he typed.

Her: Only a 9.99. Or maybe 9.99.

Him: Where R U?

As he waited for her reply, he studied the picture in more depth, not allowing himself to focus on Dorian or Harlow, only on the things around them. A wall with wooden slats. A picture of two crumbling white farmhouses tilted on its side. He'd seen that picture before... Where, where...

Two Farms.

His phone buzzed again.

There's a party in my pants. Want 2 come? <— See what I did there???????

An animal growl rose from deep in his chest. If Dorian touched Harlow while she was in this aroused, drunken state, his hands would end up in Beck's trophy case.

He made his way to West's bedroom, the door already open. "I need you to come with me to Two Farms."

"Why?" West glanced up from the motherboard he

was building from scratch. He often worked from home and thankfully today was one of those days.

"Harlow's drunk, and Dorian's taking advantage of her."

Rather than appearing enraged on Harlow's behalf, West looked to be fighting a grin. "He's never been the type to take advantage of a drunk woman. If she's had more than a single glass of something, he'll back off."

Beck whipped out his phone and showed his friend the picture. "Does this look like he's backing off?"

"Fine." West glanced at the calendar app displayed on his phone, resting beside the computer parts. "I can spare half an hour. Just give me a minute to dress." He stood, and for the first time Beck noticed the guy wore only a pair of boxer briefs.

Minute after minute passed, his friend searching for the perfect pair of jeans. Beck snapped, "I'd like to leave sometime this year."

"Which is why I'm hurrying." West held up two shirts, one all black, the other black with the words Boyfriend Material scripted over the center. "What am I in the mood to wear?" he wondered aloud.

"Dude. I'm seriously about to take away your man card."

"That's fine. I've got two."

Beck grabbed the shirt with text, tossed it on the floor and wiped his shoes on it. "This one's dirty. Wear the one in your hand."

"Well, well. Someone's certainly cranky today."

Someone had an ass-kicking to deliver.

A buzz sounded from West's desk. Beck walked over and swiped up his friend's phone, just in case Dorian had decided to circumvent Beck. Maybe ask for a condom. When he saw a message from Jessie Kay, he tossed the phone at West.

"You might want to see this."

West peered down at the screen, features tightening with anger as he studied the pictures the girl had sent. One of her and Daniel Porter, and one of her and Dorian Oliver. The text read, Need an honest unbiased opinion. Which 1 should I choose????

"Let's go." West was already striding toward the door.

Now that was more like it.

As they settled in Beck's car, another text from Harlow came in. He almost couldn't bring himself to look. Almost.

GUSS WHATTTT? Dori—that's wat I cal him now— scarred Scott away 4 me. He's may new hero. I ow him. What should I giv him???? Do U kno if he liks cherries?

Beck put the pedal to the metal.

CHAPTER EIGHTEEN

ALL HELL BROKE LOOSE.

Harlow and her whiskey sisters had indeed drunk straight from the bottle, and after they'd finished the good stuff, they'd turned to the hard, cheap stuff. They'd talked and laughed too loud and almost gotten kicked out of Two Farms. Then, about an hour ago, Dorian arrived and Jessie Kay explained the *life or death* plan—make Beck wish he were dead—or you know, married.

Dorian had taken a page from Beck's playbook and given Mr. Calbert, the owner, a wad of cash to rent the restaurant for the rest of the day, and the other patrons were escorted out. Except for the superadorable Daniel Porter, whom Jessie Kay had texted and asked to join them.

"It's been five whole minutes," Brook Lynn said. "Time for another picture. Kenna! Camera!"

Ever obedient, Harlow posed on Dorian's lap yet again while Kenna snapped more pictures and Dorian told her all about his double date with Beck.

"I'm serious," Dorian said. "The guy had zero interest in his girl and talked about his 'little hag' all night."

"That's cool, I guess." If *cool* was the new word for *awesome*. She couldn't even bring herself to be offended by the nickname.

"Okay, y'all. I've got a brilliant idea about digital

strip poker," Jessie Kay called, motioning to Harlow's phone. "Tell Beck all about it, so he can tell West."

Harlow started typing as Jessie Kay explained the rules.

I'm gona get nakid.

That should cover all the details right? Send.

"Now," Harlow said to Dorian. "Tell me more. About the date, about Beck, about everything." Was the room spinning?

Holding her up to prevent her from falling, Dorian said, "If you want him, he's yours, and even if he's loath to admit it—even to himself—he'll be the best damn boyfriend you've ever had. I remember the way he used to look at couples who were clearly in love. He wanted what they had, just couldn't admit it then, either. Stick it out, and he'll realize the truth. Growing up in the system can really mess you up. He just needs to heal."

Yeah, but how much time? Would she end up broken in the process?

Maybe, but wounds could be kissed better.

"You Strawberry Valley girls must be addictive," Dorian remarked, peering at Jessie Kay, who was now dancing around the room. "I've been warned away from the Dillon sisters."

"Jase is gaga over Brook Lynn, but who told you to stay away from Jessie Kay?"

The front door burst open before he could reply, and Beck and West came storming into Two Farms like avenging angels. Harlow's heart kicked into a frenzied beat. The plan had actually worked? Beck scanned the room and when his gaze landed on her, he closed in.

Meanwhile, West marched over to Jessie Kay.

"Showtime." Dorian helped Harlow stand.

The swiftness of the action caused her stomach to lurch. "Curses! I think I'm going to be sick."

Beck reached her a second later and gently extracted her from his friend. "Time to go. Now."

Sick could wait. The man of her dreams was here! She threw her arms around him and tried to climb him like a mountain.

He held on to her while lecturing Dorian. The words were lost to her, a strange buzz in her ears. Beck anchored her against him and petted her hair, and she must have passed out after a few minutes, held so comfortingly in his embrace, because the next thing she knew she was floating… No, she was being tossed here and there in the deep end of an ocean. Her stomach gave another lurch, and she moaned.

Floating again…a hard jostle.

"Don't worry, baby," Beck said. "I've got you."

She was on her knees in a cornfield, she realized. Beck held on to her hair as she leaned over and threw up every drop of liquid she'd consumed that day, and maybe five days prior. When she finished, darkness descended over her mind and she was floating again…cool clouds settling beneath her, a chilled wet cloth wiping over her brow, her mouth.

"Beck," she moaned.

"I told you. I'm here. I'll always be here for you."

With those words echoing in her mind, soothing her in a way nothing else could have, she drifted off to sleep.

GROANING, HARLOW HISSED at the sunlight streaming in through the window.

Was she sick?

Oh…crap. She was worse, she thought, memories from last night downloading straight into her brain. She was still alive.

"Here. Take these."

Beck's voice, but it was far too loud. Slowly she turned her head toward him. He stood at the edge of the bed. *His* bed. He held out two white pills and a glass of water.

Why was he being so nice to her? "Thanks," she muttered, swallowing the pills and a gulp of ice-cold water. Her stomach protested at first but soon settled down.

He set the glass on the nightstand and eased beside her. "We need to talk."

"I know. I'm sorry about yesterday and Dorian and—"

"Harlow," he said, stopping her with a finger pressed against her lips. "What are you apologizing for? I'm thinking about making whiskey a necessary part of your diet. Do you have any idea how handsy you get?"

Wait. "You're not mad at me?"

A flicker of pain in eyes now dark with regret. "If I were mad, would I have called every guy I know to throw a party in your honor?"

Wait. What? "A party?"

"In your honor."

"With every guy you know in attendance?"

His fingers curled around the comforter, pulling so tight he nearly ripped the material. "We're still on the hunt for your forever man, aren't we?"

It was like taking a knife to the gut. Or a hammer to the head.

He still planned to set her up with someone else.

Tears burned the backs of her eyes, but she blinked them away. "When is the party set to begin?"

A muscle jumped in his jaw. "In just a few hours."

The hard lump growing in her throat nearly cut off her airway. "How did you get everyone to agree so quickly?" And why the hurry?

"I was owed a few favors."

And he'd decided to call them in—to get rid of her sooner rather than later. "Well, then. A party we shall have," she said, trying to sound excited, sounding hollow instead.

He offered her a bright smile, but for once, it lacked any kind of light. "Great," he said. "I made it a lunch event rather than a dinner one, so we can spend the evening talking about your impression of the guys."

"Great," she echoed. "Unless I decide to go home with someone."

He went stiff as a board. "You will not put out on the first date."

"Like you can really stop me."

Ignoring her words, he said, "I went shopping in your RV and picked out a dress, brought it and all your makeup over. You can get ready here."

"Thanks. A girl couldn't ask for a better friend."

"We *are* friends." He reached out, ghosted his knuckles along her jaw.

The touch, slight though it was, blindsided her, as always, sending electric pulses arcing through her, making her ache and burn. When would his effect on her fade?

"Friends," she agreed.

Staring at her intently, he said softly, "I want to be

more, Harlow. You know that. But I'm not a forever guy."

"Why?" Need made her desperate, and desperation made her reckless. "Why do you give so little of yourself?"

He smiled his most indulgent smile, and it made little parts of her die inside, but as she stared at him, she began to notice a brittle edge to the expression. "Honey, I give the best part of me."

"No. No." She banged a fist against the bed. "Stop deflecting. Stop charming. You're breaking my heart. The least you can do is tell me the truth."

All at once, it was as if a light inside him died out, his eyes suddenly a never-ending pit of darkness. "I'm… messed up."

"So am I!"

"Harlow," he said, voice raw, almost guttural. "You don't understand."

"No, I don't. We could be happy together. You just have to give us a chance."

"Harlow." He combed his fingers through her hair, urging her forward, hugging her close to his chest as if she were precious, and in that moment, that second, she fell totally and completely in love with him. The knowledge shone brighter than the sun, sending shadows of the past fleeing.

She loved him. Loved his kindness and the complexity of his personality. She loved the way he looked at her, his dark eyes a little wild, a lot hungry. She loved the way he held her.

And maybe—maybe he'd fallen in love with her, and just hadn't realized it. He'd spent more time with her than any other woman. He enjoyed being with her, and he did everything in his power to take care of her. He was jealous of Dorian and had come to her rescue.

"We can be messed up together," she said, realizing then she would never give up, would never let him go. He belonged with her, and she belonged with him. That wasn't going to change—a fact that should please him.

"What if I give you everything," he said, "and it isn't enough? *I* am not enough. What if you leave me anyway?"

Lightbulb! He had attachment issues, yes, but he also feared rejection. He'd faced it with his dad, probably even countless families who'd overlooked him in favor of adopting some other kid, maybe even from the kids at the many different schools he'd attended.

"I wouldn't leave you," she said. *I can't. I love you.* Would the admission scare him further?

His features, still infinitely tender, were torturous to behold. "The future is more unstable than dynamite, baby."

"Yes, but you can't live your life by what-if."

"I can spend my life *preparing* for what-if." His grip tightened on her before he let go and stood. "Sometimes suspecting the outcome is better than knowing what actually happens."

"No. That's the coward's way, Beck, and you'll never find satisfaction living that way, only discontent." No peace, only worry.

A hardening around his eyes. "Maybe, but there have been times discontent has been my only friend."

"Well, good news. This change won't hurt you, it'll only help you." *I will give you everything. I will prove once and for all you are the one I want—the one I will always want.*

She would have to step out of her comfort zone without the aid of whiskey, but the potential payoff would make any momentary discomfort worth it. This man, and the life they could have together, was worth everything.

"Harlow—"

"No. Don't say anything." He'd only hurt her, dig the knife a little deeper, and he needed time to think about all she'd said. She stood and kissed his cheek. "Get out of here so I can shower. I've got a heart to win." *Yours.*

A muscle jumped in his jaw. He cupped her shoulders, holding on so tight she'd wear the bruises for days. But then he let go, and she missed his strength. He left the room without another word, shutting the door softly behind him.

Harlow barricaded herself in the bathroom, where she brushed her teeth—twice—and showered. When she emerged, she found the clothes Beck had picked out for her hanging on the back of the door. He must have brought them in while she'd sudsed up, because they hadn't been there when she'd entered.

Sly Beck. The glass stall had been so fogged with steam she'd missed him—but she'd bet he'd gotten a nice sneak peek at her.

Silly Beck. He'd made her next play that much easier.

The dress he'd brought was one she hadn't yet worn. The low bustline would reveal the top edge of her scars, but maybe it wouldn't matter. The white lace would cling to her curves.

Something she liked about Beck—even when he hoped to foist her off on other men he didn't actually want her to be with, he still helped her look her best.

She dried her hair, applied her makeup. Just as she was putting on the finishing touches, the doorbell rang.

She sucked in a breath. The guests had already begun to arrive.

Now or never.

A knock sounded at the door. "You ready, baby?"

As I'll ever be. She raised her chin and opened the door. Beck stood before her, showered and dressed in a sexy black T-shirt and jeans, and her mouth watered. He was casual sophistication, the man every other longed to be. The one every woman desired. As he looked her over, his gaze heated, blazed, the very air around them blistering.

Slowly she turned for him. "What do you think?"

"You are so beautiful," he said, voice ragged. He cupped the back of her neck and dragged her close, so close, and held her against his chest. "You are too beautiful for anyone here."

She gripped the sides of his belt loops. "Tell me something, Beck."

"Anything." He looked at her as if he breathed for her alone. As if his heart couldn't take its next beat without her. As if he cherished her.

Tremors swept through her. "Did you see what's underneath this dress while you were in the bathroom?"

"It's all I've been able to think about," he admitted.

It was a baby step, but a step nonetheless. "It's not too late to send everyone home." She rose on her tiptoes, brushed the tip of her nose against his. Even with her hooker heels, she needed a boost.

A predatory glimmer in his eyes. "I need you to pick someone else. You have to pick someone else." Again his tone was ragged, quelling the hurt his words would have otherwise caused. "Pick him today."

"What if I already have?" She kissed the corner of his beautiful mouth. "What if I pick you?"

He closed his eyes, and his breathing was as choppy as her own. "You were once the girl who only wanted what she couldn't have. What happens when you have me?"

"I'm not that girl anymore. I keep you."

"Will you?" His lids flipped open, revealing desperation, even anger. "You wanted me to stop deflecting and talk about myself. Well, here you go. I'm the guy who's lost everything he loves one too many times. I've never been enough for the people who are supposed to love me back. How could I be enough for you?" He shook his head. "So you'll pick someone else, and the cravings will stop for us both. We'll remain friends."

Heartbreaking commands steeped in more of that awful fear. Fear she couldn't fight for him. Only he could wage that war.

A cough drew their attention, and they broke apart almost guiltily, though Beck maintained contact, locking his arm around her waist.

"What?" he snapped at the interloper.

Jase, she realized, whose smile projected only sadness. "Your friends are here, and apparently each guy assumed he would be on a private date with, and I quote, the most beautiful woman God ever created."

That's how Beck had described her? No pressure.

"No one realized this would be a *Bachelorette* situation," Jase continued, "and everyone is a little weirded out. If you don't get out there soon, no one will have a chance to meet Harlow because everyone will have left."

"We're on our way." As soon as Jase vanished around the corner, Beck pulled her close for another bone-crushing hug and kissed her temple. "I'm sorry. I just… I'm sorry."

Stay the course. "How did you get these men to come? Everyone in Strawberry Valley hates—"

"They aren't from Strawberry Valley. You were fine with Dorian living in the city, so I figured you'd be fine with these guys living in the city." He hooked a stray lock of hair behind her ear. "Once they see you, they'll be willing to move."

Romantic words. Sweet words. Hated words. "You're sure this is what you want?"

He inhaled deeply, exhaled slowly. "No, but I'm sure it's what I need."

Another baby step, but not enough. Not nearly enough. "All right." They would soon find out just how much he liked what he thought he needed. "I'll pick someone."

He turned away from her, balled his fist and even raised it to the wall as if he longed to punch. "Good," he said, arm falling to his side without inflicting any damage. "Let's do this."

He led her out of the hall and into the masses.

HARLOW STOLE THE SHOW.

Beck enjoyed this peek at the confident girl she'd become. Enjoyed it as much as he hated it.

At some point during the party, after he'd introduced her to eleven different single men, feeling a bit like a pimp, she'd stopped leaning on him, stopped clutching his hand. Eventually she'd let go of him altogether and even stopped glancing his way. Several guys had made her laugh.

Now she held court. Unable to look away, Beck leaned a shoulder against a corner wall. She graced the center of the living room, men circling her, enchanted as she told a story about beating up the neighbor boy for stealing apples from her orchard. Her mother had sent her to her room, and when she came back to check on her sweet little princess to make sure a lesson had been learned, she found Harlow building a Lego Death Star "to destroy the entire farm."

Never told that story to me. But oh, he could well imagine what a terror Harlow had been. Might have even given him a run for his money. Or joined him, so they could conquer the world together.

"I'm ready for this to be over." Jase sidled up to his side. "She found the right one yet?"

"No." Though Harlow could have any—or all—of them.

Some of them might be planning to take her away from me even now.

He downed the rest of his beer.

West came up behind him. "I'm going to politely disagree, Beck, my man. I think she's most into Cooper."

Cooper Hayes. No. Hell, no. Harlow would not become Harlow Hayes. "Alliteration?" *Not on my watch.* "I'll die first."

"I'll pretend you're not coming up with creative objections out of desperation if you'll tell me why the hell you invited him," Jase said.

"A moment of insanity."

"One that hasn't let up, I see," West muttered.

Coop took Harlow's hand, kissed her knuckles and

led her away from the crowd. He stopped in a private corner and said something to make her laugh. Beck claimed Jase's whiskey and drained it, then focused on his breathing. In. Out. Good.

"I'm going to ask this only once," West said. "Are you sure this is what you want? What you need? Her with another man. Do you really believe your feelings for her will fade? Think before you answer," he said as Beck opened his mouth. "Because I'm going to take you at your word, and if that word is yes, *I* am going to lay claim to her. Because honestly? I would marry her if it meant easing you of this torment."

West and Harlow? Never!

Coop reached for her, and she backed up. She caught herself and stood still while Coop sifted strands of her silken hair between his unworthy fingers.

She'd no longer backed away from Beck, now only ever leaned into him. But for how much longer? When would she begin to seek comfort from another man?

He watched, mesmerized, as she twirled the strands of hair to remove them from Coop's grip. Despite the little hiccup—the guy had moved too fast for her—her smile was genuine and as sweet as sunshine as she spoke to him.

Was she falling for him?

She can't. She's mine.

The words echoed in his mind, and for once, he didn't try to fight them, just let them fill his awareness, testing their truth. *She's mine. Mine. Miii-nnne.*

Was she?

He hated the thought of her with another man and really hated himself for pushing her in that direction. He was happiest when they were together. He suffered when they were apart—and it wasn't ever going to stop, was it?

He expected panic, a frantic need to flee, to get the hell away from the woman threatening to destroy life as he knew it, but as he drank her in, the eyes he loved to drown in, the skin he would sell his soul to touch, all he felt was gut-wrenching desire.

Change? Bring it on.

He'd been a coward, just as she said. He'd denied the truth, too afraid of the possibilities. But he never would have allowed her to pick another man, he realized. As hard as he'd been pushing her in that direction, he'd been creating obstacles. Even today, he'd warned each and every guy. Pain awaited anyone who hurt her, even in the smallest way.

Mine. And it was time he took what belonged to him.

"Out," he bellowed.

All eyes darted to him.

"Out. Now."

"Finally." West grinned before pasting on his scariest scowl. "You heard the man. Out!"

"Don't make *me* tell you to go." Jase acted as a bulldozer and began herding the guys toward the door.

Frowning with dismay, Harlow followed after Coop.

"Not you, baby," Beck said, striding across the room.

Her eyes widened at his approach, and damn, she was lovely. Innately sensual. *And all mine.*

Without a pause in his step, he took her hand and led her into the hall. For her, he would willingly put himself into the barbed, gilded cage known as a relationship. He just couldn't let her go.

"What's going on?" she demanded.

"What should have happened weeks ago." He kicked

his bedroom door closed and swung her around, crowding her against it. The dark tension he'd suffered with all these many weeks finally abandoned him, replaced by a tension of another sort.

"Beck." Her lips parted on a gasp, one he caught with his mouth, desperate to taste her. But she didn't kiss him back; she shoved him away. Or tried to. He wouldn't budge. "No." She shook her head. "I'm not letting you do this to me. You kiss me when the mood strikes, then tell me to be with someone else when fear hits. Well, I refuse to be treated that way. I'm leaving." She spun, placing her back against his chest as she tugged at the knob.

"Scared now that you're getting what you asked for? Well, that's just too damn bad, baby." He kept his hand flat on the wood, ensuring it never opened.

"Getting what I asked for?" She glared at him over her shoulder. "You came on to me, then told me to find someone else. Now you're coming on to me again. What will happen tomorrow?"

"I won't be pushing you at anyone else. Not again." Not *ever* again.

A tremble started in her chin, then spread to the rest of her.

"Don't cry. Please, don't cry."

Defeated, she pressed her forehead against the door. "You've always been good at saying the right things, but not so good at doing them."

"I'm sorry. I didn't realize how hard it would be to see you with other men. I was *seething* inside and wanted to commit cold-blooded murder. You're mine, and no one else is *ever* allowed to have you. Tonight I'll prove it. You asked for a relationship, a commitment," he said. "You insisted on both, in fact, and if that's the only way I can have you, that's the way it'll be. We're together. I won't ever lie to you, and I expect the same from you. Is that acceptable to you?"

Slowly she turned. Shock, wonder and hope stared up at him, razing wounds deep in his chest. "Beck…"

"Say yes. Nothing else matters right now."

"I— Yes," she whispered.

Good. "Now take off your clothes."

CHAPTER NINETEEN

SOMETHING ABOUT BECK'S words bothered Harlow. *If that's the only way I can have you, that's the way it'll be.* But at the moment, she reeled too wildly to care. She and Beck were an actual couple. He was in this, with her all the way.

"I know you're inexperienced in these matters." The hot intensity of his gaze belied the low gentleness of his tone. "But I'm on the verge of a meltdown. I need you naked as soon as possible. Take off your clothes, baby."

With trembling hands, she reached for the top of her dress. All she had to do was slide the material down, but she hesitated. As vulnerable as she was feeling, she didn't want to do this alone.

She dropped her arms to her sides, whispering, "*You* take them off me."

An expert, he hooked his fingers inside the bustline and, with a single tug, had the material pooling at her feet, leaving her in undergarments and hooker heels. "Step out of the dress."

The moment she obeyed, he had her bra unhooked. The garment fell away, his fiery gaze locked on her breasts as her nipples puckered with painful precision.

"These sweet little jewels were made for me alone." He cupped her, tracing his thumbs over the distended peaks. He'd always been a seductive force, but today, this moment, he was raw carnality made flesh—and utterly irresistible.

"They're small," she said, knowing he'd been with big-chested beauties like Tawny.

"They're perfect. They're all I've wanted since I met you. *You're* all I've wanted."

He dropped to his knees, reverently removed her shoes one at a time then tongued the waist of her panties until he had the material firmly between his teeth. He dragged the tiny scrap of fabric down, down, finally reaching the floor.

Skin heated. Goose bumps broke out. A quiver teased her deep, deep inside as languorous pleasure flooded her limbs. All she wanted to do was melt into him, meld onto him.

"I want to see you, too," she said.

"You will. Trust me." He stood, his hands sliding around her, one at her nape, the other at her lower back. He dragged her flush against him, lowering his head, claiming her mouth in a single swoop. His tongue thrust against hers, taking, demanding, and when she met him with a thrust of her own, he went wild, feeding her the most rapturous passion. The kiss should have sated her in some way, but it only stoked her appetite higher.

Beck backed her toward the bed, and when her knees hit the side of the mattress, she went down. He didn't follow her right away but stood between her spread legs, his breaths coming shallowly, hollowly, tension tightening his features. His pupils were so large his eyes appeared black—twin stormy nights.

He gripped the collar of his shirt and yanked the material over his head, baring his gorgeous chest. His pecs were muscular, decorated with sinew, his nipples small and brown, his stomach roped with strength. She wanted to follow his golden-tipped goodie trail with her tongue.

"Let me." She sat up and, with her gaze locked on his face, unfastened his pants. He wore boxer briefs, his erection straining past the top. She thought about the time he'd gone to his knees before her—thought about the things she could do to *him*—and moistened her lips.

His fingers curled more firmly around her nape. "Kiss me," he croaked, and she knew he yearned for her to do it. "Kiss me and never stop."

"Yes." She pushed his underwear down, freeing the rest of him, then leaned forward and *liiicked* the tip.

He shuddered, his fingers combing through her hair, fisting the strands. She licked again and again before swallowing him down, as far as she could go.

A hoarse groan left him. "That's the way, baby. Just like that."

Lifting her head, she said throatily, "I've never done this before. Tell me if I do something you don't like."

"If you're doing it, I'll like it." He traced his fingertips over the rise of her cheek, his features infinitely tender. "Take me down again and let your tongue ride the underside, then suck me hard on your way back up."

She did as instructed and drew a deeper groan from him. Emboldened, she did it again and again, quickening her pace.

"Doing so good, baby. Making me so hot."

His groans became increasingly ragged…until all he could do was pant, the air growing heavy with his arousal, and her own. His reactions caused a passion fever to burn through her. But he fit her chin between the curve of his fingers and thumb, slowly lifting her head.

"I'm not done," she said.

"That keeps up, and I will be. Lie back."

BECK HADN'T BEEN with a woman he actually knew in—ever. He hadn't realized the tender feelings he'd already had for Harlow would add shocking depth to the experience, a layer of awareness he couldn't deny he relished.

She eased onto the mattress, her luscious body open and vulnerable to him. "Beck…"

The purr of her voice did things to him. Maybe because he knew she didn't always sound that way. Maybe because he knew no one else had ever made her feel so needy, that he alone possessed the power to tempt her.

And she alone possessed the power to unman him.

He kicked off his shoes, stepped out of his jeans and underwear and crawled over her, peering down at her, drinking in the languid desire he saw shining in her heavy-lidded eyes.

She ran her hands, those smooth, elegant hands, up his arms, and the touch meant more than any that had come before, affecting him deeper than skin, blood and bone. He trembled under that touch.

"Second thoughts?" she said, a bit unsure.

"Never." Sweat trickled from his temple, dripped on her lovely shoulder. "It's been a while for me, and I want this to be perfect for you."

Her smile was pure sweetness, like sunlight in the middle of a raging storm. "It's with you. It's perfect."

She meant that. He knew she meant that. He trusted her in a way he'd never trusted another.

"But," she said, nibbling on her bottom lip, "what did you mean by 'a while'?"

He fed her the gentlest kiss he was able, one of reverence as much as passion—passion he barely kept banked. "I mean since the day after I met you."

When she gasped, he could hold off no longer. He kissed her again, letting all that passion loose at long last. Her tongue sparred with his, not just accepting his aggression but returning it. He got lost in the kiss, thrilled in it as it swept him away and consumed him. He didn't have to worry that she would want too much from him. He'd already offered everything. He didn't have to watch the clock or wonder how he'd make his escape when the deed was done. He was right where he wanted to be with the only woman he wanted to be with.

"What do you need me to do?" she asked breathily. "Whatever it is, I'll do it."

"Just keep breathing, baby."

As TURNED ON as Harlow was, aching as if she'd never known a single moment of satisfaction, she expected to burst into flames. But hearing those words—*Just keep breathing, baby*—she almost burst into tears.

Had any man ever pleased a woman as much as Beck pleased her?

He opened the upper drawer of his nightstand and set one, two, three condoms on top.

"Um, perhaps you're overestimating my stamina," she said.

"Or you're underestimating mine." He kissed and licked his way to her breasts, paying extra attention to her scars, kissing them all better. He sucked one nipple, then the other, switching again and again until she was writhing.

"Let's see how much you liked having your mouth

on me, shall we?" He thrust a finger inside her. "Oh, baby. You liked it. A lot."

"I really did." She circled his wrist, holding his hand where it was. "Don't stop. Please, don't stop."

"I'd die first. But you need something else inside you, and I'm going to give it to you."

"Yesss. Yes. Please."

"Grab the headboard."

She obeyed, closing her hands around the wrought iron, and with his hips he nudged her knees farther apart. Farther. Farther still. She attempted to wrap her legs around him, but he was having none of that and spread her as wide as she could go.

"I want to see you," he said. "I have to see you. All of you."

Cool air brushed against her most intimate parts, and she shivered. Slowly, languidly, he looked at her, and like that, the rest of the world ceased to exist. They were the only two people alive; it was the sweetest agony she'd ever known.

He returned his finger, then added another. She was stretched, burned, but not enough. She needed more, needed him. Always him.

"You said...something else."

"You're so pretty here," he said silkily, "I decided to play a little more."

He hooked one of her knees over his shoulder, dipped his head and sucked where she ached...ached so badly... Her thoughts careened, split, her pleasure intensifiing, her head spinning.

She closed her eyes, so vulnerable to this man who'd stolen her heart...who would now own her body, and her future. And she nearly came out of her skin when he angled his wrist, the pressure increasing right along with the burn. But the pleasure far exceeded both, and she undulated her hips, sending him even deeper.

"You might just be the death of me, baby."

"Don't worry," she panted. "You'll take me with you."

He continued to play. She thrashed, and she begged. She released the headboard to comb through the silk of his hair, but he told her to assume the position, so she obeyed, the promise of completion beckoning. Completion he never gave her.

"Stop tormenting me!" she finally screeched.

His husky chuckle was strained, a dark caress against her sensitized skin. "If I'm going to come harder than ever, so are you."

He scissored his fingers, and it was almost enough to send her over, but almost wasn't good enough, and as she hovered at the blunt edge of satisfaction, the agony nearly lost all hint of sweetness. It was painful, being denied what she needed most, and a whimper left her.

He gave her one last lick before pulling out of her completely.

So empty. "No, no," she rushed out. "Put them back in."

"I'll give you something better, just like I promised." As he loomed above her, light from the overhead fan fell over him, the sweat that had created a fine sheen on his skin glistening. He looked as maddened as she felt.

Under her watchful gaze, he ripped open a foil packet with his teeth. He braced his weight over her with one hand and rolled the latex into place with the other. His fingers found her again, but rather than spearing into her, they guided his shaft into place.

"I don't want to hurt you." He kissed the corner of her eye, the rise of her cheek, the tip of her nose and slid in an inch. The burning stretch was a promise of what was to come, and she wanted—needed—more.

She planted her feet in the mattress and arched up, taking him another inch.

"You're so tight," he rasped. "Let's give you a minute to adjust."

A minute would be an unbearable lifetime. Passion had long since torched her inhibitions, leaving her most primitive instincts to guide her. *Want more? Take it.* She grabbed a hank of his hair and forced his mouth to hers, the desperation of the act drawing an appreciative growl from low in his chest; his tongue darted out to duel with hers. She was already wet, already white-hot, and this was only making her wetter and hotter, but it also seemed to be chipping away at his control. His hips began to move in shallow jerks, sending him a bit deeper...just a little deeper...

"Beck!"

"Doing so good. Taking me so perfectly."

"You're so big," she said.

He gave another chuckle, the sound half amusement, half torment. "You'll thank me for my size in a few minutes."

"Braggart! Just do it."

He pushed in a little harder, sinking halfway inside her, and wow, okay. No wonder he'd wanted to go so slowly. The pain threatened to overshadow the pleasure again, and she thought she might curse at him. But she knew if she so much as flinched, he would stop and try to prepare her better, and there was no way she could allow that to happen. She wouldn't survive it. Besides, this man belonged to her. She would have him, all of him. Now.

Seeing no other recourse, she dug her nails into his ass and yanked his lower body forward while arching up her hips. He slammed all the way to the root, and a scream burst from her, as much from surprise as from a mixture of pain and pleasure. But he was in her now, filling her. He was joined with her; they were one.

The vulnerability she'd felt before? Nothing compared to this.

"You okay? Tell me you're okay." At least he was right there with her. Tension ravaged his features, revealing a vulnerability of his own—and an animal hunger he would probably kill to assuage. He was a man on the cusp of having exactly what he wanted, and yet satisfaction still hovered just out of reach. How much longer would his tenuous control last?

A tremor moved through her, and she said, "Keep going." The pain was already subsiding. Purring, she rubbed her legs up his sides. "Finish me."

He anchored his hand just under her knee, angling her and applying pressure as her lower body curled into him, then he began to move. In, out. Slowly at first, a mere teasing of what could be, rubbing, rubbing the most intimate parts of her. Then he gave a hard jerk of his hips, going in deeper, impossibly deep, wringing a delighted gasp from her.

"You like that?" He came up on his knees, pressed her other leg to the side and up, opening her completely. He thrust.

"Beck!"

His thumb found her sweet spot and circled, circled. Pleasure crested inside her. So close. Almost there. His thumb pressed with more force. Yes! Satisfaction hit, and hit hard. She screamed, utterly consumed by ecstasy.

"Look at you," he said, and he sounded awed—a little feral. "Look at you, baby." And then his pounding thrusts came faster, so much faster, the tether to his control finally frayed beyond repair.

He was wild, almost brutal, and she loved it. Loved looking at *him*. Loved being the object of his passion. His eyes glittered wildly, the tension in him clearly mounting. His lips were red and swollen from her kisses. He was a fantasy without equal. And he was hers.

"Harlow," he cried out, surging in one last time. He gripped her hips with delicious, bruising strength, the tension gradually fading from his features as he came.

He collapsed over her, quickly rolling to his side so that he wouldn't crush her. Without his strength to hold her, her body was too weak to wrap around him and she, too, collapsed against the mattress. They lay there for a long while, facing each other, the ragged sound of their breathing filling her ears.

"That was…" she said.

"World-changing?"

"Merely okay," she finished, trying not to smile.

He gave her bottom a light tap. "If you aren't careful, Miss Glass, I'll start again, and I won't stop until I've made you admit the truth."

"No, no," she said with mock horror. "Anything but that." Then she chewed on her bottom lip. "*Will* we do it again?"

"Definitely."

"When?"

"Impatient?"

"Yes!"

"You'll be sore."

"I don't care."

He smoothed the hair from her cheeks, only to gaze at his hand and stop, as if the appendage had done something it shouldn't have. A flash of fear crossed his face before he donned a blank mask. He rose from the bed, disposed of the condom.

"What's wrong?" she asked, worry chasing away her languid satisfaction. She sat up, clutching the sheet to her chest, no longer quite so relaxed with her nudity.

He climbed in next to her and turned her, drawing her back to his chest. He wrapped his arm around her, one of his legs fitting between hers. "Round two will have to wait. I'm tired, and I need a nap. Go to sleep. We'll work out all the details when we wake up."

Details? "What details?"

He kissed the shell of her ear. "We'll discuss them when we wake up. Now go to sleep."

But after that, how could she?

CHAPTER TWENTY

BECK'S WORDS PLAGUED Harlow every minute of naptime. They plagued her while the two of them ate dinner alone in the kitchen and Beck hand-fed her. While they climbed back into bed and watched TV. While they made love again. While Beck slept peacefully.

By the time morning arrived, the fog of desire had faded, her thoughts clearer than they'd been in a long time—since meeting him, in fact.

We'll work out all the details in the morning, he'd said. And before making such sweet love to her, he'd said, *If it's the only way I can have you, that's the way it'll be.*

It—meaning commitment.

Realization *hurt*. Beck hadn't jumped into this relationship with her because he loved her or even liked her. He hadn't even committed because he couldn't stand the thought of being without her. He'd done it because it was the only way he could sleep with her.

In other words, he felt as if she'd backed him into a corner.

What kind of future would they have if he felt trapped by her? What would happen when he came to resent her for it? When, not if. Sharp thorns of bitterness would set in, that's what, and each would be aimed at her. Hatred would soon follow. Could she really do that to him? Could she really do it to *herself*?

She and Beck had been doomed before they'd started, hadn't they?

But if she left him, if she walked away, she would be fanning the flames of his fears. Could she really do *that*?

They needed to talk.

She carefully extricated herself from his embrace and padded into the bathroom, trying not to panic as she brushed her teeth, dressed in one of his shirts and a pair of his sweatpants.

"Harlow?" Beck's voice, tinged with upset. Because she wasn't beside him?

Hope bloomed, the only rose in a deadly winter. *Please, please want me the way that I want you.*

She schooled her features to reveal only calm, then opened the bathroom door. "I'm here."

He'd thrown his legs over the side of the bed, but at her greeting, his head jerked in her direction, his upset fading. He was breathtakingly naked, his muscled chest on display, his impressive lower half hidden by the sheet they'd shared.

He smiled at her, a wicked invitation to experience round three. His hair lay in total disarray, the golden tips gleaming in the morning light. His stubble was slightly denser, and her skin already ached for its tickle.

"I think it's clear I hadn't planned to wake up alone in this bed," he said.

Do it, before you chicken out. "Does it make you happy to think about a future with me, Beck?"

His smile dimmed a little. "First, I'm seriously thinking about considering giving you a spanking. Afterward

I'll show you where I wanted you to be when I opened my eyes—and what I wanted you to be doing."

Her stomach knotted and cramped. "Please. Answer my question."

The smile faded completely, and he rubbed his chest. "Why do a Q and A when there are so many other things we could be doing? Better things."

Let's try this another way. "Last night, you mentioned going over details we hadn't yet covered. What details?"

He patted the mattress beside him. "The only detail I'm concerned about right now is your distance. Get over here."

"What details?" she insisted.

"And your clothes," he continued as if she hadn't spoken. "Take them off."

"Beck. I'm begging you."

He stood, looking like a warrior of old, ready to claim the spoils of battle.

Claim me.

"I'm going to chalk this up to your inexperience," he said, gripping the base of his erection, "but men like sex first thing in the morning, and I'm going to prove it."

She almost went to him. It would have been easier and far more pleasurable. "Do you feel trapped?" she asked point-blank.

A muscle jumped beneath eyes gone wild. He closed the distance, framed her face with his big hands. "Why are you doing this?"

Not an answer. "I have a right to know."

"I committed myself to you, didn't I?"

"Yes, but only because it was the sole way you could sleep with me."

The muscle beneath his eye jumped even faster. "And you can't be happy with what I'm offering?"

"What *are* you offering, Beck? You've never said. Marriage sometime in the future?"

His lips pursed, and his hands fell away from her. "I'm offering here, now. And tomorrow. Which, by the way, is more than I've ever offered anyone."

"But what about the day after tomorrow?"

He rubbed at his chest. "I don't know."

The flames of hope were dying, one after the other. "You're telling me we're doing this on a trial basis? That's the detail you wanted me to know, isn't it?"

Almost defiantly he snapped, "Every relationship operates on a trial basis, Harlow. No one ever knows if theirs will be forever, especially in the beginning."

"But they know what they're willing to give and what they'll continue to withhold." She drew in a breath. "Does it make you happy to think about a future with me?" she asked again.

"Enough. Let's—"

"Does it?"

"You don't want me to answer that, baby."

"I do. I really, really do."

"Very well." He ran his tongue over his teeth. "When I envision the future, I see doom and gloom. That's it. That's all I've ever seen."

Confirmation of her worst fear—it was worse than taking a bullet to the heart.

Her choice was simple: lose him now or lose him later. Rip the bandage off or let the wound underneath fester.

Can't break down. Not here, not now. "I want you with every fiber of my being, but I won't stay with a man who feels like I've trapped him, who sees only doom and gloom with me. You'll come to resent me."

"Don't do this," he said, and in that moment, there was something scary about him. As if the shutters were coming down, blocking her out. "You know what?" He laughed with bitterness rather than humor. "Part of me expected this. You had me, and now you don't want me anymore."

"Part of you *expected* this? Is that why you felt comfortable enough to 'commit' to me?" she sneered, using air quotes. Her own fears and pain were making her ugly right now, but she didn't care. "Because you were so sure I'd leave you and you wouldn't have to be with me for long?"

"Stop. Just stop." His tone was dark, dangerous. "Let's close our mouths before one of us says something we'll never be able to take back. We'll go to work and cool off."

She shook her head. "I'm not going anywhere until you answer my other question. Do. You. Feel. Trapped?"

"Harlow."

"Do you?" she screeched.

"Yes," he snarled, glaring at her. "Are *you* happy now? I'm in a cage, and you put me there. But I don't want you with another man, and I will do anything to ensure you're mine. Even this."

Even this. *He's destroying me, piece by piece.* "Well." *Head up, blink back tears.* "I wish that were enough for me, but it's not."

He flinched as if she'd hit him. "You mean *I'm* not enough for you."

"No, that's not what I mean."

He stormed over, latched on to her upper arms and

shook her. "You aren't leaving me, Harlow. I won't let you."

"I…am," she said, fighting sobs. They brewed in her chest, frantic to escape. *Have to get out of here.* Now. She lurched from his grip.

Glaring at her, he swiped up her dress, her shoes and held on to them, as if they were the only reasons she hadn't run yet. "Don't you dare do this."

"I have to. Don't you see? I'm not going to trap you. I'm not going to doom you. I'd rather you hate me while free than resent me while caged."

He took a step toward her, his nostrils flaring as he breathed, his chest heaving. "If you walk out that door, we're done. You can pack your things and get the hell out of the RV, off my land."

A stream of tears burned her cheeks. "I don't want to do this."

"Then don't. Stay here."

"But I have to," she finished, and walked out of the room.

HARLOW HOPED BECK would realize she was worth any risk, that she offered happiness rather than gloom, but he was a man, and that particular species could be as dumb as a box of rocks. So, of course he never came came to the RV, and by the evening, she was forced to pack her meager belongings.

She prayed he needed more time, even daydreamed about him showing up after she secured a room at the Strawberry Inn—for double the usual rate, since the owner hated her and apparently had a "bitch" fee—but he never did that, either.

In the ensuing days, she left her room only to apply

for jobs. Style Me Tender and Swat Team 8 weren't bringing in enough revenue to justify a new hire, and Two Farms and Strawberries and More grocery—both of which had advertised for help—had turned her down flat.

As the days continued to pass, her savings began to dwindle. She realized she had a choice to make. Stay another week at the inn, without food, before finding a new place to set up camp, or find a new place to set up camp now and eat for a few more weeks. She opted for the latter and finally found a place on Dane Michaelson's two-hundred-and-fifty-acre ranch.

She had to spend precious money buying a new tent, which sucked because sleeping on the hard nylon floor after basking in the decadence of the RV for so long truly drove home the depths to which she'd fallen from grace. Once again she had to boil pond water to drink and wash with an outdoor hose.

But really, the times she would spot Beck in town with a beautiful woman on his arm, and he would look right through her, those were the times that hurt most. He'd written her out of his life completely. Just. Like. That.

If he could dismiss her so easily, she was better off without him… And yet still she cried herself to sleep every night. And when a cold front blustered in, her tears actually froze on her cheeks. She ended up spending the rest of her earnings on a sleeping bag, a wool coat and flannel socks.

If she wanted to eat again, she'd have to set traps or find a job, and fast, but only one other place was hiring. The inn she'd vacated needed another maid.

Would Carol Mathis, the owner, be willing to give her a chance?

Harlow made the hour-long walk to Main Street, noting multiple Happy Halloween signs and posters for the upcoming Berryween Fall Festival. Soon the entire city would be transformed into a spook-lovers' paradise. Booths would be erected, each one decorated with some type of haunted theme. Games would be played, food would be sold and devoured. She wondered if Beck would bring a date, maybe even win the stupid woman a stupid stuffed teddy bear.

Tears filled Harlow's eyes.

And, oh, crap! There were Brook Lynn and Jessie Kay, out delivering breakfast sandwiches to the locals. Her stomach performed eager, hungry flips, paining her. She darted into a shadowed alley. The girls had asked Virgil and Mr. Rodriguez about her—she'd heard them—but she wasn't ready to talk to them. Maybe they'd curse her, maybe they'd support her. Either way, she was still too raw to deal.

She wished she could pour her emotions into her art, but she'd left her paints behind.

A waft of smoke billowed in her direction and tickled her throat. Coughing, she turned and met the gaze of Daniel Porter, who was in the process of stubbing out his cigarette.

"Harlow Glass," he said with a nod.

"Daniel. Uh, hi." The last time she'd seen him, she'd been a drunken mess. "You're looking well."

He didn't offer the requisite "You, too," even though it would have been polite. And she wasn't hurt by that. Not anymore. Because of Beck, she'd been introduced to true pain. A snub like this? Not even a blip.

Though Daniel had been in town for several weeks, he'd continued to cut his dark hair military-short, and even in the shadows his features appeared chiseled from stone. His shoulders were broad, his chest ripped underneath the tightness of his shirt, and he had several tattoos peeking out from the sleeves.

"Look, I'm glad I ran into you," she said. "I'd like to apologize for my behavior as a kid. You were—are—a beautiful human being, and I had no right to say otherwise." He'd had a problem with acne, but who hadn't back then? "It's not like I'm perfect or have any right to judge. You should see my chest. I have so many scars I make Frankenstein look pretty."

He stuffed his hands in his pockets. "Sure. I'll take a look at your chest."

She sputtered, and a smile teased the corners of his mouth.

"You finally score that Beck guy or what?"

"Yeah, I did, but it didn't do me any good." Did Daniel actually care or was he asking because he'd heard about Jessie Kay's night with Beck? "I didn't steal him from Jessie Kay, if that's what you're implying. They were already over when I met him."

He went still. "What do you mean? Did she date him?"

Oh, crap. No one had told him? "I'm, uh, not going to comment. Jessie Kay is my friend, she's said so a couple of times now, and—" Crap, crap, crap. His expression was only growing darker.

"You'll have to excuse me." He stormed away.

What have I done?

She wanted so badly to call Jessie Kay, but she'd left her phone in the RV, knowing she wouldn't be able to afford the monthly payments. A quick peek revealed the Dillon sisters were gone. Dang it! She raced to the inn.

Carol, an attractive woman with salt-and-pepper hair, hazel eyes and the lined skin of someone who'd lived a happy life, manned the counter, the landline at her ear.

She noticed Harlow and scowled, saying into the phone, "Let me call you back after I've taken care of a sudden cockroach problem." She slammed the phone into the receiver. "I thought we'd gotten rid of you."

"I need to borrow your phone. Please."

"Sorry, but it's out of order."

"You were just using it."

"And it just broke."

Harlow shifted from one sandaled foot to the other, frantic, looking for help. But the only other person in sight was Carol's youngest daughter, Holly, a gum-smacking Goth who hadn't stopped flipping the pages of her magazine.

While the youngish Holly hadn't been a victim of Harlow the Bully, her older sister, Dottie, had. Carol had clearly not forgotten all the times Dottie had come home sobbing because of something Harlow had said.

Guilt stabbed at her. But dang it, she had paid for her crimes a thousand times over in the past two weeks alone.

"Fine," Harlow said. "If you won't let me use the phone, will you give me a job?"

"A job? For you?"

"I'll work hard and never cause any trouble."

Carol snorted.

"I'll work for less money than anyone else."

Finally. Interest. Smiling with glee, Carol abandoned the counter to walk a circle around Harlow. "Well, well.

Look at you, desperate enough to scrub my toilets. Even though you once called this inn, my home, a dump of the lowest order."

Harlow could feel herself caving in, her shoulders slumping, her head bowing. "I was wrong." The place rocked, reminding her of home. Overhead was a chandelier made entirely from deer antlers. Strawberry-themed paper decorated the walls. Gray stone surrounded the fireplace, and there were scuffs on the wood floors.

"Well, before I agree to sign you on, you're gonna have to show me you've got what it takes to work here." Delight colored her tone, sending a cold chill down Harlow's spine.

She took heart, however. This was the furthest she'd come in the "interview" process.

"Come on. There are thirty rooms," Carol said, leading her through multiple hallways, portraits of strawberries hanging in every direction. They came to an open door, a cleaning cart in front of it. "If I decide to give you a chance, you'll be responsible for every single room, every day. Guest or no guest."

"Momma?" The voice drifted past the door frame.

Harlow tensed as Dottie entered her line of sight. A bit on the short side and a little plump, she looked like a child's doll with her dark corkscrew curls and freckled skin. She'd registered on Harlow's radar when she'd aced a test Harlow had failed.

For that, I called her hateful names and ensured everyone in school treated her like a pariah.

Dottie's gaze landed on Harlow and narrowed. "How dare you show up here. Get out!"

"I'm sorry," she said, a lump growing in her throat.

"I'm sorry for everything I did to you when we were teenagers."

"Watch me as I *don't* believe you. The day you were born, the devil crapped his pants, knowing he'd finally met his greatest competition." Dottie focused on her mother. "Why is she here?"

"Harlow came begging for a job," Carol said, her glee escalating. "You, of course, will be her boss, and if she doesn't meet your high standards, you can kick her out."

Dottie opened her mouth, closed it with a snap. "Fine."

The two weren't going to give her a chance, were they? No matter how good a job Harlow did, she would be found lacking. Well, no matter. She would suck it up. Maybe she'd earn a few bucks in the process.

"Have fun, you two. Or not." Carol left them to their duties.

"I need to make a call. I'll be quick." Harlow rushed to the phone on the desk.

"Slacking already," Dottie said, her anger only intensifying.

Voice mail picked up. "Jessie Kay, it's Harlow. I ran into Daniel and I'm so, so sorry, but I mentioned you'd once dated Beck and he acted like he didn't know, and I'm sorry."

Dottie snatched the phone and slammed it into the reciever. "One more infraction like that and you're toast."

"You're right," she said. "Put me to work. I'll do whatever you say."

"Oh, I'll put you to work, all right."

And she did. The girl directed Harlow like a plow horse, harsh words her whip.

Is that all you've got?

You should be better at cleaning up shit. You've slung enough of it over the years.

I could do better with my eyes closed and my hands tied behind my back.

By the end of the day, Harlow's pride stung—nothing new there—and her body ached, muscles she hadn't even known she possessed now heavy and shaky.

"You did okay today," Dottie said, folding towels and stacking them on the cart for tomorrow. They were in the laundry room, the air pungent with the scent of cleaners and disinfectants. "I'm not going to fire you."

Shock swept through Harlow, nearly knocking her off her feet. "Really?"

"Is this the part where you ask for preferential treatment?"

"No. Of course not! But…does the job happen to come with free room and board?"

Dottie snorted, and Harlow took that as a *no way in hell.* "We start at six a.m. Don't be late."

"I won't." Harlow hesitated in the doorway. "I meant what I said. I really am sorry for everything I—"

"Don't," Dottie snapped. "Save your apologies for someone who cares. We were kids. I'm over it."

No. No, she wasn't even close to over it.

Harlow sighed, wondering what kind of life Dottie had led. If she was married with kids, involved or single. The gossip train so rarely mentioned her. But now wasn't the time to ask. "I'll see you tomorrow."

Harlow spent the rest of the evening moving her camping gear to a piece of land owned by Strawberry Valley Community Church, as close to the center of town as possible so she could make her early-morning shifts while still maintaining the cover of trees offered by the surrounding forest. She did her best not to think about Beck—what he was doing… Who he was doing it with.

In the middle of the night, however, while the locusts sang and the crickets chirped, serenading her as she shivered from cold, she couldn't help but crave his arms around her.

Fought a war, lost—and in turn lost the most important part of my life.

This was her new reality. Working, camping. Wishing Beck were with her, missing him with every fiber of her being, wanting to hate him, wanting to rant and rail at him for not realizing relationships could be a blessing, a gift, then wanting to scream at him for letting her go.

THE NEXT MORNING, Harlow made it to the inn with fifteen minutes to spare. Her eyes burned; they were dry, probably swollen from her tears and definitely gritty with fatigue. Her hair was a mess, her clothes dirty.

Dottie was already in the storeroom. She took one look at Harlow and tossed her a pair of scrubs. "Your uniform."

Good morning to you, too. "Is there a place I can shower first?"

Dottie pointed to the right. "The employee bathroom has a stall. And we'll be sure to deduct the hot water from your check."

Of course.

By the time Harlow showered, changed and appointed herself a locker, Dottie had the first room halfway cleaned. They worked alongside each other for one hour—two—not a single word spoken.

Finally, as Harlow stuffed a pillow inside a new case, she said, "Are you married?"

"Why? Are you hoping to steal my husband?"

Okay. No small talk. Noted.

Another hour passed. Dottie broke for lunch. Harlow hadn't brought any food and had no extra cash to buy anything so she just kept working. Her stomach growled, remembering the sandwiches, pies and peppers Brook Lynn had once made her.

I miss that girl so bad. Even now, Harlow could hear Brook Lynn's musical laugh. Wait. Hear? She peeked her head out of the room to see the petite blonde striding down the hallway, carrying what looked to be a casserole dish, Carol keeping pace beside her.

Pride urged her to hide—*Can't let her see me like this.* But pride was nothing more than a fear of being found lacking, and if her time with Beck had taught her anything, it was the pitfalls of succumbing to fear.

She was done hiding. She had a life to live, and she was going to live it. Brook Lynn spotted her and smiled—a genuine smile—and Harlow released a breath she hadn't known she'd been holding.

"Thank you for walking me to my room, Carol," Brook Lynn said.

"It's just one of the many services I offer here at the Strawberry Inn." Smug, Carol added, "Speaking of services, we now offer a new one. Our most elite customers will be allowed to watch Miss Glass clean their room."

Well, well. Even better.

"What an amazing reward package," Brook Lynn said. "I'm absolutely going to take you up on it, so, if you'll excuse us." She entered the room and shut the door in Carol's face.

"How did you find me?" Harlow asked.

"I've had my ear to the ground. Yesterday Virgil Porter spotted you heading into the inn, so he made sure to have a nice long chat-up with Carol. He found out you'd accepted a job and called me."

"Does Beck know?"

"No. Word hasn't reached him. Yet."

Carol hadn't done much gossiping, then. She was probably as embarrassed by Harlow's presence as she was gleeful. "I'd like to keep it secret as long as possible."

"In a town this size, as long as possible usually only equals an hour, but maybe this will help the showdown sure to come." Brook Lynn held out the plastic container. "My famous apple-and-carrot casserole."

"For me?" Harlow thumped her chest, just to be sure.

"And anyone you'd like to share it with."

She grabbed the casserole and hurried to the couch. She removed the lid and the fork taped to the top. "You might want to look away," she said, digging in. The sweetness of apples and carrots hit her taste buds, and she closed her eyes to savor.

Brook Lynn sat on the coffee table. "Jessie Kay wants you to know Daniel broke things off with her, but you aren't at fault and she's not upset."

Her enjoyment plummeted.

"It's really not your fault," Brook Lynn insisted. "He refused to be exclusive but didn't like that she was hanging out with Beck and Jase after...you-knowing them."

Harlow set what little remained of the casserole aside. "Did she cry?"

"No, she rallied. She's got a date with Dorian tonight. But enough about my sister. Beck is miserable, you know."

Hope quickly dovetailed into despair. "I don't want to talk about him." But…maybe she should. She was still raw, yes, but she needed help.

"I'm not leaving until I know what happened. I came here willing to bribe you. You can't deny you've accepted that bribe, it's smeared all over your face, so start talking or I momma-bear-claw that casserole right out of your stomach."

CHAPTER TWENTY-ONE

BECK HAD NEVER been so close to losing his mind.

Harlow had vanished. After she'd left him, she'd moved into the Strawberry Inn, one week quickly turning into two. He'd hung out in town as much as possible, needing to see her—needing her to see him—but sightings of her had become fewer and for the past week, there hadn't been a single one.

Seven entire days without knowing where she was or if she was okay.

He'd scoured every inch of his land. He'd talked to—yelled at—the locals. He'd called the PI who'd finally, at long last, found the person responsible for her attack, and asked the guy to search Oklahoma City, thinking, fearing, she might have hitched a ride to get as far away from him as possible. If anything had happened to her...

He would want to die. But first, he would kill whoever caused the hurt. The way he'd wanted to kill the girl who'd set her on fire. Stacy Kellogg. Once a clerk at a little boutique in Dallas. Now dead, but not by his hand. Two years ago, she lit a coworker on fire, was caught, but hung herself before being sentenced to jail time.

Beck's movements were jerky as he tugged on his pants, buttoned up his shirt. He'd thought he would give Harlow a few days to cool down, to think about things and realize she was miserable without him. She was supposed to come crawling back and plead with him to forgive her for leaving in the first place. She was supposed to forget her questions and his answers and accept what he could offer.

Damn her!

He was skipping work—again—to go hunting for her. If necessary, he would tear this town apart. He just— He had to see her, had to talk to her and perhaps shake some sense into her. He couldn't go on like this.

He missed her. Missed her smile and her laugh. Her spirit. She challenged him. Made him step up and be a better man.

One taste hadn't been enough. For the first time in his life, he'd had a woman once and it had only made him want her more. Her scent in his nose. Her body flush against his. Her breasts in his hands. Her—everything. Only her.

Another change, the biggest of all, and one that freaked him out now that she was gone, making it a little harder to breathe, but it was a change he couldn't regret. If he had her, nothing else mattered.

As he swiped up his socks, Brook Lynn stormed into his bedroom without knocking. She stopped directly in front of him to poke him in the chest. "You idiot!"

"Exactly right." A fact he'd lamented many times the past week. "But I'm not sure what crime I committed against you."

Brook Lynn poked him a second time. "You see doom and gloom with Harlow. You think relationships are a cage. No wonder she left you."

His every muscle tightened, ready to spring into action. "You talked to her?" He yanked the socks into place, demanding, "Where is she?"

"I'll tell you," she said, pure Southern tenacity, "after you sit your butt down and listen to me."

Jase heard the commotion and flew out of his bedroom. "What's wrong, angel?"

"Beck is an idiot, that's what."

"Where is Harlow?" Beck demanded, losing patience. "Tell me before I do something we'll both regret." If he had to shake Brook Lynn, he would. He would probably lose both of his hands when Jase ripped them off his arms, but that would be a small price to pay.

"Sit!" Brook Lynn shrieked.

All right. So she'd turned into a shrew. Got it. He sat.

"I get that you three boys have problems because of your pasts," she said, pacing in front of him. "But do you really think you've cornered the market on them? That Harlow doesn't have her fair share?"

Jase held up his hands, all innocence, and backed out of the room. "Sorry, my man. I'd jump on this grenade for you, but...I don't want to." He smacked into West, who'd just come out of his own room to investigate. "Run," Jase told him, and he did.

"Some friends you are," Beck called.

"Well," Brook Lynn insisted.

"No?" he said.

"That's right. No. Harlow has problems, too. While you had to deal with crappy parents and foster care, she had to deal with her father's cruelty and death, then her mother's death, a woman who was her only means of support, all while the entire town hated on her. You think that was easy for her?"

"No," he said more firmly. "Now where the hell is she?"

"Maybe she's in your stupid cage," she snarled, stuck on the word. "A cage? Seriously?"

His teeth gnashed together. "*Feelings* are a cage." One he'd successfully avoided for most of his adult life. Then Harlow had come along and showed him just how unfulfilled he actually was, how unsatisfied. He wanted to hate her for it, but damn if he didn't like her more.

"Well, at least we now know you have feelings," Brook Lynn grumbled. "What about the doom and gloom you see in your future?"

"It's not specific to her, but to me. I don't know how to expect anything else."

She rubbed the back of her neck. "You could have been a little more clear to your girlfriend. It would have saved us all a lot of trouble."

Niether one of them had been in the right frame of mind. Accusation had taken the place of listening.

"Harlow is miserable without you, Beck."

"Good." If he had to suffer, she should, too.

"Good? Good! For a bona fide he-slut, you sure don't know anything about women. Harlow would give up anything to see you happy. Anything! Even her own happiness."

"If she's so concerned about me, why isn't she here?" The question exploded from him with more force than he'd intended.

"Tone," Jase shouted from somewhere in the house.

Beck winced. Yelling at his friend's woman? Really? He would flip his ever-loving lid if one of the boys did the same to Harlow. "Sorry," he mumbled. "What else did Harlow say to you?"

Brook Lynn took a moment to huff and puff before admitting, "Mainly that you two want different things."

Different things? Like hell. "She asked for commitment, and I gave it to her."

"Your version of it."

"Yes." He gripped his knees with so much force he might need a wheelchair for the rest of the day. "She told me I wasn't enough for her."

"Do you even have ears?" Exasperated, Brook Lynn threw her arms up. "According to Harlow, she told you what you were offering her wasn't enough. And rightly so. What you're offering wouldn't be enough for *anyone*."

Screw it! "Where is she, Brook Lynn? I've answered your questions, and now I demand answers of my own."

She gave him a pitying look. "You told her you felt caged, and when she set you free, you *blamed* her for it. She cried, Beck. She went back to living in a tent."

Razors cut through his chest, and he replayed the fight through Harlow's eyes. She'd been scared, her own fears driving her. She'd only wanted reassurance. His admittance they had a chance at something good.

He closed his eyes and exhaled. As the air left him, his upper body just kind of sagged with defeat. Damn it. If she'd mentioned feeling trapped, he would have set her free, too.

"Are relationships always this difficult?" he croaked.

"Only the ones that matter." Brook Lynn sighed. "Look, it's not too late to salvage this. She's hurting, and that's a guarantee you'll have to grovel before she'll listen to a word you have to say, but if you don't convince her you're in the relationship of your own free will, that she's an important part of your future, one you can't live without, you'll lose her."

I can't lose her.

"She *is* an important part of my future."

"Don't tell me, tell her." Brook Lynn gazed around his room and grimaced, obviously noting the empty beer bottles he'd discarded. "You aren't just an idiot, you're a pig, and it's a wonder you managed to snag someone as classy as Harlow." With that, she strode out of the room, shutting the door behind her.

He'd messed up. What if he couldn't win Harlow back?

No. No, he couldn't think like that. She'd gifted him with her virginity. That meant something to her. To them both.

He raced after Brook Lynn, calling, "Where is she?"

Brook Lynn leaned against the kitchen counter and accepted a coffee mug from Jase. She blew on the liquid, taking her sweet time.

"Please," he said. "With a cherry on top of me."

She smiled at him, still not in any kind of hurry. "I suggest you pack a bag and move into the Strawberry Inn for a while."

His control frayed, ready to snap at any second. "This is my house. I'm not going anywhere. Just tell me where the hell she is."

"Tone," Jase snapped a second time.

Brook Lynn patted Beck on the cheek. "Did I mention the inn has a new maid? And get this. She seems to have a soft spot for idiots."

HARLOW STUFFED A pillow into a fresh case. She'd been washing, dusting and vacuuming all day, and if she wanted to keep this job—which she did, she had to—she would be washing, dusting and vacuuming all evening. Her arms, back and thighs ached. Her feet screamed in protest. Despite the blast of the air conditioner, which she'd cranked to high, perspiration created a film over her skin.

"You didn't do it right." Scott Cameron reclined in the center of the king-size bed, as smug as a pasha being serviced by his least favorite concubine. "Do it again."

Though she would have preferred to smother him with the pillow, she removed the stuffing and once again fit it inside the case. In the past few hours, half the town had moved into the inn, it seemed. Scott, Virgil Porter. Jessie Kay. Daphne and her daughter Hope. Kenna. Four girls she'd tormented in high school. Another guy who'd gotten the Glass Pass. Word of Carol's promised "elite package" had spread fast.

"And wipe the mirror again," he said. "I see streaks."

"You know, Scott," she said, "if you spent half as much time pleasing your girlfriend as you do tormenting me, she'd be the happiest girl on the planet."

He glowered. "Trust me. She's plenty pleased."

"You sure about that? The few times I've seen her, she's looked miserable."

Before he could respond, Dottie peeked her head through the crack in the door. "We've got another customer waiting for you to clean, Glass. Room twelve."

Great!

"But she isn't done in here," Scott complained.

"You've had her for over an hour," Dottie retorted, surprisingly snappy. Usually she was sunny smiles, all "yes, sir" and "yes, ma'am." "Your time's up."

Amid Scott's protests, Harlow dropped her rag on

the floor and at last abandoned the sinking ship. "Thank you," she told Dottie when they were alone in the hall.

The girl *hmphed* and flounced away. No name-calling? Well, if that wasn't progress, Harlow didn't know what was.

As she made her way to room twelve, Carol came around the far corner and joined her. "Oh, Miss Glass! Isn't this amazing? At this rate, I'll have Holly's orthodontic work paid for without having to mortgage my home or freelance contract killing. Someone once asked me to do that, you know."

"How wonderful for you."

"Isn't it? Carry on, carry on." Carol patted her shoulder before skipping off.

"Glad my humiliation could help."

"Yes, yes, keep up the good work." Carol nodded enthusiastically before disappearing around the corner.

Harlow reached her destination and raised her hand to knock, but the door was already open. Another eager customer. Yippee. Who was it this time?

She stepped inside with a resigned, "Hello?"

A bag rested on the bed, small, black and masculine. A minute after the water shut off in the bathroom, hinges creaked—and out stepped Beck, wearing nothing but a thin cotton towel.

Heart hammering, she stepped back and bumped into the door, shutting it and sealing herself inside. Curses! He looked good. Too good. His hair was darker when it was wet, the strands stuck to his brow and cheeks, dripping droplets of water onto his shoulders and the hard ridges of his chest.

His gaze narrowed on her. "I heard my hag had changed careers, and decided to come see for myself."

Her body began to ache for a reason that had nothing to do with work, readying for this man, as always. Tremors rocked her, and she did her best to hide them. At least the fatigue that had plagued her for the past few hours vanished in a blink, replaced by sizzling energy.

Run to him...

No! Never again. "I'm not cleaning your room while you watch," she announced.

"Good. The room isn't dirty." His smile was dark, humorless. "I'm afraid you'll be cleaning something else."

He'd come to sleep with her? After everything that had happened between them? Bastard! "If you say your *body*, I will smack you."

"As you can see, my body isn't dirty, either."

Disappointment poked at her, and it only made her angrier. "Then what?"

"What else?" He tapped his temple. "My mind is absolutely filthy. If you knew half the things I'm thinking right now...the things I want to do to you..."

"Of course you want sex. You're incapable of meeting anyone's emotional needs."

Pain ravaged his features. He reached for her. "Harlow."

"No. I'm leaving," she said, nails cutting into her palms, drawing blood. "We broke up, and you started seeing other girls."

"I'm not seeing other girls."

"Too bad for you. Maybe I'm seeing other guys." She turned, grabbed the knob.

He was behind her in a blink, planting his hands flat on the door, keeping her sealed inside with him. "You're not going anywhere, baby. Apparently we have ourselves a bit of a communication problem, and we're going to work through it here and now."

Too close! His body heat enveloped her. His scent invaded her nose, her every cell. "You're wrong. There's nothing to work through."

"If that were true, baby, I'd have no reason to go on."

She went still. He put his mouth at her ear, whispered, "I'm sorry. I'm sorry I let you go. Sorry I didn't come after you. I was stupid, and I was wrong."

Tears in her eyes. "It's too little, too late, Beck."

"I refuse to believe that."

"Your women—"

"Nothing happened with them. I escorted them around town to make you jealous, and then I took them home. I hated every second, and I promise you, it will never happen again."

"I don't care."

"Are you seeing other men?"

"No. *I'm* no longer in high school."

His relieved breath tickled her nape. "I'm in uncharted territory here. I was bound to mess up."

Stay strong! "You don't see happiness in your future."

"Baby, I meant I have only ever expected doom and gloom. I was afraid to hope for anything else, but with you, I *am* happy."

"I… I don't care."

But he wasn't done. "When I told you I felt trapped, that I felt like I was in a cage, well, I meant it."

"I don't—" Oh! She reached back, grabbed a hank of his hair and tugged.

"Ow!" He pried her fingers loose, then picked her up and tossed her on the bed. He pounced on her a second later, pinning her down, clasping her wrists over her head and spreading her legs by hooking his feet against her ankles and pushing.

She tried to bite his chin. "Let me go."

He dodged, the action shaking his body against hers—she had to press her lips together to stop a whimper of sudden need.

"The cage refers to my feelings for you, baby, not you as a person," he said, and she once again went still, not daring to hope. "I don't want to care about you this intensely, but I do. I don't want to crave you this strongly, but I do. I don't want to depend on someone else for my happiness, but I do. And I think… I think you don't want to crave me this strongly or depend on me, either, but you do. We're both scared, baby, and we're looking for ways to protect ourselves. But I'd rather look *with* you."

The tears returned to her eyes, stinging. He had feelings for her. He truly had feelings. He cared for her intensely, craved her strongly and depended on her for his happiness. He was scared, he'd said, and honestly, he was right. She was, too. In the wake of his admission, she found the strength to face the truth. When she'd imagined having a family, she hadn't factored in the vulnerability she would experience, or the fear of one day losing all she'd come to love.

"All my life I've considered feelings for another person a prison." He released her hands to cup her jaw. "I will never be able to control how you feel about me. I will never be able to force you to stay with me, to accept what I have to offer, and it terrifies me."

"Beck…"

"I want you to give us another chance, Harlow. I need you to. Please."

"But we're both so broken." A relationship wasn't just about finding the right person but also *being* the right person. "How can we make anything last?"

"We make a decision to fight for what we have."

In a fight, someone always came out the loser. "Neither of us *knows* how to fight."

"I know I want you, and that's enough for me. We'll be honest with each other. We'll talk when we're feeling overwhelmed, and when we fight we won't walk away. We'll hash it out and make up in bed." He kissed the corner of her mouth. "With us, only one thing matters. And it's this. Am I enough for you?"

He gazed deep into her eyes, a moment charged with electricity, a moment of shocking intimacy, every emotion unveiled. Longing, relief. More fear.

And as he peered at her, she thought she even saw... love.

Suddenly, no answer had ever been clearer.

"Yes."

CHAPTER TWENTY-TWO

BECK HELD HARLOW in his arms for a long while. Just held her, making no move to seduce her. He'd not forgotten her words. *You're incapable of meeting anyone's emotional needs.* He would meet hers if it killed him, and it just might.

He burned for her. But he also liked the intimacy of the moment. Hell, he loved it.

"Beck," she said. She'd pulled her hair into a ponytail, several tendrils having escaped confinement to frame her face. Her skin was free of makeup, her eyes glittering like diamonds, her lashes so long they curled into ebony fans. Her cheeks were flushed, her lips lusciously red.

She could have been dolled up, but it wouldn't have mattered. No matter what she wore, or didn't wear, she met a need he'd never expected to have. A need for her specifically. Her smile. Her scent. Her wit. Her warmth. Her thorns. No one else would do—now…maybe not ever. Once you'd had perfection, everyone else became a pale imitation.

"Yes, baby."

"I want you."

"No. There'll be time for that later."

"I *need* you." She reached up, toyed with the ends of his hair. She smelled faintly of disinfectant, but not even that could hide her innate fragrance of strawberries, surely driving him deeper and deeper into insanity, where only she existed. "I've missed you so much."

Killing me.

"Kiss me," she demanded.

The world could have been burning around him and he wouldn't have been able to stop himself from obeying. *Nothing* could have stopped him. He'd been without her too long, and while he could go several minutes without breathing, he couldn't go without this woman for another second.

"Beck… I've missed you so much."

"Baby, I've wanted to die without you."

He pressed his lips into her and like that, urgency rode him hard, lightning flashes of demand riding the tides of a desire he couldn't control.

His tongue dueled with hers, the taste of her sweet and luscious, better than he remembered. He nipped his way to her jaw, to the pulse hammering at the base of her neck. the softness of her skin enrapturing him, reminding him of all the other places she was soft as silk and hot as hell.

"You are mine, and I am yours. I won't forget again." He lifted his head to peer down at her. The beard stubble he hadn't shaved this morning had left thin lines of pink around lips that were already plumped by his kiss, redder than usual, and velvet-soft—a fine wine guaranteed to go straight to his head.

Her pupils expanded until only a rim of ice-blue remained—still enough to drown in. "I won't, either."

Triumphant, he yanked her top over her head, tossed the material aside. The white cotton bra she wore had a front clasp, and he kissed his way down her chest to rip it open with his teeth. She gasped as he tongued one of her nipples, then the other, plumping and reddening them, too. Her hips began to writhe against him, the core of her instinctively seeking the fullness he'd taught her to crave.

He removed her shoes, tugged off her pants and panties, leaving her bare. Opening her slender thighs was a compulsion, one he obeyed. She was already wet, glistening, and he licked his lips in anticipation.

"The things I'm going to do to you…" Weeks without her. Weeks of longing and imagining and cursing and dreaming. They would not be leaving this bed until they were both sated.

She placed her foot against his chest. "You doing things to me is great, but I'm going to do things to you, too. I want to be the best you've ever had." Confident words, belied by a tremor in her voice.

"You already are." Where her skin touched his, he sizzled, especially over his heart, the organ currently trying to beat its way out of his chest. He took her ankle, lifted and pressed a kiss on her calf. "All you have to do is look at me, and you surpass everyone else."

She breathed his name. "Stand up. Please."

He obeyed, and she moved to her knees. He cupped her breasts, her chest rising and falling faster and faster as she reached out and tugged at the waist of his towel. The moment the material loosened, she tossed it aside, baring his entire length.

"So hard," she praised, grazing her knuckles from the head to the base. "So big."

"That's what you do to me."

"Let's see what else I can do to you." She swung her legs over the side of the bed and stood beside him. He fit his hands around her waist. If she desired another location, to another location they would go. But she pressed against his shoulders, urging him to sit.

As he gripped the comforter, she slowly lowered herself onto his lap and straddled his legs. Her core, hot and drenched, brushed against his shaft, and he hissed in a breath.

"I need you to move, baby."

"Like this?" She slid up, up languidly, then slid down, down slowly.

"Faster."

She went even slower.

He groaned, and she laughed with feminine power.

"I like seeing you tormented."

He bucked his hips up, trying to change her rhythm. When he failed, he rasped, "Faster, baby. You'll like it."

"I like it now."

"Baby…"

"Feel free to stuff any complaints into my suggestion box."

Deciding to fight dirty, he reached between her legs and speared two fingers deep inside her, drawing a gasp of pleasure from her. "This box?"

She gasped. Down, down she slid, slow, so slow, purring her delight.

He removed his fingers, the moisture she surrendered nearly his undoing.

"Beck."

With his gaze locked on hers, he licked his flesh clean.

Fire blazed in her heavy-lidded eyes. She trailed her hands up her stomach, kneaded her breasts, pinched her nipples, then burrowed through her mass of hair to remove her ponytail band.

Could come just watching her.

She lifted the dark locks high, higher, then dropped them, the ends falling over him, caressing. Ecstasy and agony.

She was a fantasy, her undulations growing more and more frantic. "I have to… Soon… Dying… Beck, please! It's been too long."

"I'll take care of you." He pulled her in for a soul-wrenching kiss, their tongues rolling, their bodies grinding together. He'd come soon, could already feel the first sizzle of satisfaction blistering the base of his shaft.

He twisted and tossed her to her back. A gasp from her, those slumberous eyes finding him and begging him to finish her. He was tempted, so damn tempted to take her bare, something he'd never done with another.

"Are you on the pill?"

She shook her head, inky tendrils tangling together.

"I'd like you consider it." He swiped a condom from his bag, sheathed his length in latex. "I'm clean. I get tested every six months, was tested recently, in fact, but I'll get tested again. If you're on the pill, there won't have to be anything between us."

"I would like that," she said and moaned. She arched her hips. "I don't mean to tell you how to do your job, really I don't, but if you don't stop talking and *get inside me* I'm going to cold-blooded murder you!"

"Complaints can go in my—"

"Beck!"

His chuckle was a dark promise as he hooked his arms under her thighs and lifted her hips. With enough force to rattle the entire bed, he slammed all the way into her. The pleasure… It was almost more than he could bear, but he did it again and again, moving in and out of his woman. Because he had to, because he couldn't tolerate the thought of doing anything else.

The headboard banged against the wall. The pictures shook. He pounded harder, need driving him, obsession and addiction hanging on for the ride, a promise of more.

She gasped his name, writhing and thrashing.

"Let me watch you." He pressed his thumb against her sweet spot and, just like that, she erupted, screaming, trembling, squeezing his shaft from base to tip.

He slowed his thrusts, sinking in a mere inch at a time. "Nice and easy now." Sweat trickled down his temples as he plucked at her nipples.

"Beck," she gasped, the pleasure in her voice hitting his system with the strength of an entire bottle of whiskey. She hadn't yet come down from her climax, and the new pace drove her straight into another, her belly quivering, her core drenching him with electric heat. "It's…it's… Oh, oh! I can't stop. It's not stopping."

Her back arched, sending him deeper, and as he hit as far as he could go, his control finally snapped. Nice and easy? No longer possible. He hammered at her with everything he had.

A knock sounded at the door.

Had he locked it? He couldn't remember, just knew he would kill anyone who stepped through it.

He hammered, hammered, hammered, the bed rocking, rocking, the pictures banging, banging.

Another knock rang out. A woman's voice seeped through the cracks, "Harlow?"

The thought of getting caught must have thrilled a secret part of his naughty beauty because she shot straight into another climax, and this time she milked him hard enough to send him over the edge of pleasure…pleasure that consumed him from head to toe. He roared, pouring every drop of tension into the condom, his muscles clenching and unclenching, the fire in his veins at last cooling.

"Harlow. You've got another room to clean," the woman said.

Harlow gasped and scrambled out from under him. "I'm, uh, coming," she called.

"In more ways than one," he muttered. He removed the condom and tied it off. "I'll dress and we can head home." He wanted to hold her. He wanted to feel her breath against his skin, and share secrets into the darkest part of the night.

"No way. You heard her. I have to get back to work." She tugged on her clothing.

He gave a single shake of his head. "You're coming back to work for me."

"Sure. I'll continue my work on the character sketches, but I'll start *after* my shifts at the inn. I like standing on my own two feet, and besides that, I refuse to leave Dottie in the lurch."

He gnashed his molars. *My fault.* More work for her meant less time for him. "What about us? I'm in this thing one hundred percent."

She smoothed the wrinkles from her top, plucked the ponytail holder from the floor and combed back her hair, taming it in a knot on top of her head. "I am, too, but we're going to have to take it a day at a time."

What the hell? He didn't like having his words

thrown back at him. "Let's take it a week—a month—at a time."

She smiled at him, soft and sweet and a little sad, but she didn't back down. "I don't want to hurt you again, and I certainly don't want you to hurt me. We need to learn more about each other and actually, you know, date or something. I mean, we've slept together twice, but we've never even gone out."

"That's not true. We've been dating ever since you stole my pie." But he got where she was coming from. She'd shared bits and pieces about her past, but there was still so much he didn't know about her. Did she hope to have kids? Or would that be another wrench in their relationship?

"While you took all your randoms to dinner, you've never taken *me* anywhere. Like I'm an embarrassment or something." A tremor in her voice.

He'd hurt her. However unintentionally, he'd hurt her. "I'm taking you out tonight. Don't make any other plans."

She sighed. "Doesn't have to be tonight. I'm not trying to rush you, Beck. Not anymore."

"Tonight," he insisted. "And every night after."

Another sad smile. "I'm not hogging all your spare time, and I'm not putting a label on us. Not officially."

"No label?" He exploded. "That's what you've been pushing for since day one."

"Girls are allowed to change their minds."

He was in her face a second later, practically breathing fire. "Do you plan to see other men?"

"No." Her glare was sharp enough to cut glass. "Will you see other women?"

"No," he said. "I told you I wouldn't. I have no desire for anyone else."

"Even though I won't be sleeping with you again? Not until we're labeled?"

He unveiled his slowest, wickedest grin. "Think to hold out on me, do you, baby? We'll see how long you last now that you know what it's like to be filled. We might have scratched an itch today, but you'll be begging for me soon enough."

She returned his grin, a woman who'd come to learn the power she held, making his gut twist. "Or you'll be begging for me."

CHAPTER TWENTY-THREE

HARLOW EMERGED FROM the room, spotted Dottie leaning against the wall, fanning her flushed cheeks, and blushed. There wasn't time to issue a warning—*cover your eyes...or not, yeah, probably not*—before Beck came up behind Harlow wearing only a towel. He pushed something into her pocket.

"Your phone," he said, and nipped her earlobe. "As my girlfriend, it's your duty—no, your honor—to send me hourly—half-hourly—reports about your day. I'll be waiting. And yes, I just labeled you."

Tingles pricked the back of her neck. "It's only a label if I accept it. And are you sure you want to know about the joys of scrubbing toilets?"

"More than anything. I'll prepare to be riveted."

Pulling away from him might have been the toughest thing she'd ever done, but she managed it.

"I want one of those," Dottie said as Harlow closed the door, ensuring Beck wouldn't overhear the rest. "I moved to the city for a few years and got married, but we divorced after only six months. If there's a trick to keeping a guy like that, you have to tell me."

"There's no trick." She hooked her arm through Dottie's and led her down the hall. "If being yourself isn't enough, the guy isn't worth your time." As Dottie's shoulders slumped with disappointment, Harlow said,

"You're amazing. Never let anyone convince you otherwise. Now. Do you have a particular guy in mind?"

A blush stained Dottie's cheeks.

"You do! Who is it?"

The girl pressed her lips together in a firm line.

"You can trust me, you know," Harlow said. "I'm not going to use the information against you. I've learned my lesson about treating people that way, and I would honestly rather die as some zombie's dinner."

Dottie took a deep breath before admitting softly, "Daniel Porter."

"He's a good choice, though I happen to know he's a bit commitment-shy. But who knows? You could be the girl to win him over, and he *is* currently single." Jessie Kay had moved on, Brook Lynn said.

"He's also here," Dottie whispered with a dreamy sigh. "He came in about half an hour ago to rent a room…and requested your service."

"Why don't you do the cleaning?"

"I would, but he paid extra for you," the girl grumbled.

No way she'd go in there alone, leaving Dottie to fear the worst. "Well, I'll definitely need your help."

Dottie licked her lips, nodded reluctantly. They found a cleaning cart and pushed it to room twenty-five. A tremor rocked the girl as Harlow reached up and knocked.

"Remember, just be yourself," Harlow whispered. "You are a treasure, and you deserve to be treated that way."

Daniel pulled open the door a few seconds later, looking gorgeous in a black shirt and a faded pair of jeans. Dog tags hung at his neck, a tattoo peeked from the sleeve of his shirt, and his feet were bare. He was totally bad-boy hot, and Dottie certainly noticed, her tremors intensifying.

"We're here to clean your already-clean room," Harlow said with sass, and he moved back, allowing them to step inside.

He hadn't brought a bag, and he hadn't hung a single piece of clothing in the closet or disrupted the sheets or even used one of the towels in the bathroom.

"Wh-where would you like us to start, Mr. Porter?" Dottie's voice was low and sweet and layered with nerves.

"I'd like to speak with Harlow, if you don't mind. In private."

"Of course." Dottie hung her head and padded toward the door, but Harlow grabbed hold of her wrist and held her in place.

She'd just garnered the slightest bit of Dottie's trust. Being alone with Daniel would jeopardize such a fragile bond.

"Whatever you say to me," she said, "I'll just repeat to my partner, so save me the trouble and talk while we work."

Daniel sat at the desk while Harlow messed up his perfectly made bed in order to remake it. She claimed one side and Dottie, who wouldn't pull her gaze from the sheets, claimed the other.

"Last chance to hear what I've got to say without an audience," Daniel said.

"Talk," Harlow replied.

He gave a clipped nod. "Since Jessie Kay was hanging around the new guys so much, I had a few contacts look into them. Jase went to prison for manslaughter,

West did a few stints in rehab and Beck has a juvenile record. He fought. A lot."

I know. He told me. "Almost everyone in town knows about Jase. He served his time, and he's a good guy. As for West and Beck…" Harlow walked to Daniel's chair, placed her hands on the arms and leaned into his face.

"If you're about to kiss me in thanks," he said, "don't. I like you as a friend. That's why I'm here."

Warm pleasure spread through her. *Look at me. I bagged another friend. At this rate, I'll have the town in the palm of my hand by Christmas.* "One, I'm into Beck. Two, Beck would never hurt me. If you start spreading rumors to the contrary, I might have to serve a little time in prison myself—for premeditated murder. I wouldn't like hurting you. We're friends, you just said so, but I'd do it nonetheless."

Daniel studied her for a long while before nodding his understanding.

"Thank you." She hugged him—she just couldn't help herself—before turning to Dottie, who was wide-eyed with surprise. "Finish up here, will you?"

"Y-yes."

In the hall, she texted Beck, the need to reach out to him—to torment him—too strong to deny.

What R U wearing??

His reply came a few seconds later.

Now that I'm talking 2 U? A smile.

Wish U were wearing ME??

Only more than anything ever.

GOOD! U can wish but U can't touch. Bet U'll B the 1st 2 cave.

Really?? Good luck resisting THIS.

A picture accompanied the text, and a blush crept over her cheeks. He'd actually sent her a picture of his bare butt. Except another picture came in a few seconds later, only it was panned farther out, revealing the "crack" she'd previously seen was actually the line between his pressed-together knees.

His next text read, Dirty minded girl.

Grinning, she skipped to the next room. As she cleaned, she mentally checked out, operating on autopilot—dust, scrub, vacuum, make bed. Rinse/repeat with the next set of rooms. The only time she came alive was her break, when she texted Beck.

Her: This toilet is so big...so hard...

Beck: Yeah, baby. Yeah. Tell me more.

Her: It's so wet.

Beck: Now UR just being cruel. What's it wearing? Describe in minute detail.

She laughed. This man...oh, this man.

When she knocked on the door of her final room, she realized she'd worked twelve hours straight. A first for her, and it felt good. Look how far she'd come. From impoverished and down on her luck to making a living without help from anyone. She now had two jobs, one an outlet for her art, her greatest passion. Well, maybe not her greatest. Not any longer. She had Beck…for the moment, at least.

The temporariness of their arrangement was the only wrench in a seemingly glorious future.

Tawny Ferguson opened up and glared all kinds of hatred at her. Scott Cameron—her cousin—stood behind her, grinning a big bad wolf grin.

You've got to be kidding me. "I just came to tell you I'm done for the day. Your room will have to wait."

"Ha! You're done when we say you're done." Tawny eyed her up and down and sneered. "When Scott called and told me you were here, well, I rushed right over and managed to snag the last room. I expect to get my money's worth."

Or, you know, revenge. "You expect to punish me for dating Beck." There was no way Harlow would allow these two to critique and complain about everything she did.

"He's not yours, bitch." Tawny drew back her hand. To slap Harlow across the face?

Scott caught his cousin by the elbow, stopping her.

"Let Harlow make the first move. Carol will be forced to fire her."

"Bitch," the blonde snapped again. "Beck will get tired of you soon enough."

"Maybe, but we both know he's already tired of you." Harlow retreated a step, intending to go.

Scott released his cousin to grab Harlow's wrist, keeping her in place.

"Let me go," Harlow demanded. "Now."

"Let her go, or die." Beck's voice growled from down the hall.

Gasping, she spun. He strode toward her with Dottie at his side. Worry clouded the girl's face. Rage darkened Beck's. Scott let her go as if she'd just caught fire.

"Beck," Tawny said, fluffing her hair. "It's wonderful to see you."

"I cleaned this room earlier," Dottie said.

"Yeah, but my cousin paid for—" Scott began.

"The works? I just reimbursed her." Beck threw a wad of cash at the twosome before claiming Harlow's hand and focusing on Scott. "My girlfriend's shift is officially over. I suggest you leave. If you're still here in the morning, I'll take that to mean you'd love to continue our previous chat." Tawny he simply ignored, and the girl withered before Harlow's gaze.

Almost feel sorry for her.

Almost.

As Beck tugged Harlow away, taking her the way he'd just come, she sought Dottie with her gaze. "Thank you," she mouthed.

The girl offered a hesitant but genuine smile.

"You okay?" Beck asked.

"I'm fine, really, but thanks for the white-knight rescue."

"Just one of the many services I offer in my boyfriend package." He released a heavy breath. "Scott is lucky I've learned the value of restraint."

"Yeah," she said. "*So* lucky."

He stopped and faced her, his lips quirking at the corners. "You mocking me, baby?"

"Me? Never." The old-fashioned ambience of the place framed him—lace doilies surrounded each of the strawberry photos, everything surrounded by pink-and-yellow-striped wallpaper. He was a male made even more masculine around beautiful, feminine things, his strength all the more evident, and keeping her hands off him required major effort. "You're worked into a foaming-at-the-mouth man-frenzy, and I love it."

"I bet you'll love this, too." He backed her into the wall. Only a whisper away, she breathed his breath as he breathed hers, the knowledge causing her to inhale and exhale harder and faster, her heart drumming frantically.

"I'm waiting," she said, arching her hips to rub against him. "Make your move so I can turn you down."

His nostrils flared. "You're already on the verge of begging for more."

"So are you."

"I am. So, if you want to go on that date, we have to leave now. Otherwise I'm going to carry you to our room."

Her knees almost buckled. "I… I want to go on our date," she forced herself to say. No matter the aches in her body, dating him was important to her.

A moment passed before he gave a stiff nod. "Very well." He backed away from her, extended his hand. "Where have you been staying? We'll grab your things."

Oh…crap. A flare of panic hit her as she twined their fingers. "That's not important right now."

Immediate suspicion crossed his features. "Where?" he insisted.

She didn't want to answer and wouldn't lie. Besides, the stubborn man wouldn't quit until he knew the truth. "First on Dane Michaelson's land, then behind the church," she admitted on a sigh. "In a tent."

He ran his tongue over his teeth. "Brook Lynn hinted as much. I didn't want to believe her."

His eyes closed, his face suddenly ravaged with pain. "I never should have kicked you out and forced you back into a tent. I'm not sure I'll ever be able to forgive myself."

She touched his face, making him look at her. "We both made mistakes."

"You merely reacted to mine, but I vow to you here and now, you'll never have to spend another night in a tent ever again. I've set up a trust for you."

"A trust? Are you kidding me?"

"No. And you're going to take the money and like it."

"I most certainly will."

He waited for her to finish the sentence, to add "not." But she didn't, and he realized she had, in fact, accepted. "Okay, then. Glad we got that settled."

"If you want to spend your money on me, I'll let you," she said. Pride wasn't going to stand in the way of her future any longer.

He laughed and muttered, "I will never understand you, will I?" then kicked into motion, dragging her with him. "You're staying with me if I have to tie you down."

"Kinky, but there's no way I'm letting you do that."

"I look forward to your attempts to stop me."

Harlow knew her hard limits and knew if she and Beck wrestled, she'd be the one to cave. "Fine. I'll stay in your hotel room."

"With me."

"Alone."

Brow arched, he cast her a glance. "Are you not confident in your ability to resist me?"

No! Even now she burned for him. To distract them both, she said, "If we go on a date tonight—"

"If?"

"We have to actually go out," she continued. "To dinner, at the very least. And you have to pay for everything."

"Pay for everything? Baby, I only ever go Dutch."

Hardly. "Everything," she insisted.

"Fine. I'll pay for everything. Do you see how accommodating I can be?" He released a heavy sigh. "If only you were as easygoing as I am, willing to compromise about the room."

She swallowed a grin. "Very well. You can stay in the room with me, but you'll have to sleep on the floor."

"Certainly. After we have the most amazing sex of your life."

Incorrigible male. "I don't put out on first dates." Instead of stopping at the very room under discussion, he dragged her out of the inn. The sun was in the process of setting, the big ball of fire turning the sky into a canvas lit up with different shades of pink, purple and gold.

As they strolled down the sidewalk, realization hit. "Wait," Harlow said. "Where are we going?"

"On our date, of course."

She dug in her heels. "We can't go on our date right now. I'm wearing scrubs."

"It's not my problem you decided to dress down for the occasion."

Note to self: when Beck goes to war, he fights dirty. "As I'm sure you know, a girl is more likely to fall for a man's seduction if she's feeling sexy."

"Since you've already decided not to put out, that hardly matters in your case." He paused in front of

Two Farms, peering down at her with sizzling hunger he couldn't quite contain. Voice low and husky, he said, "Have I told you yet how *sexy* you are right now?"

"Incorrigible," she muttered.

"Just desperate for you." He lowered his head, feeding her the kiss every girl dreamed of receiving, deep and intense, as if he'd never tasted anything so sweet and he had no intention of ever stopping. But just as she reached for him—*so weak, not even trying to resist*—he pulled away to lead her inside, leaving her panting, reeling.

"Table for two in back. Preferably a shadowed corner so no one will be able to see what I'm doing with my hands," he told the hostess, a girl in her early twenties who stood there staring at him for several long, embarrassing moments.

Know how she feels. Harlow tapped the girl on the shoulder and in a stage whisper, said, "He has gas." She shrugged then, as if to say, *What can you do?*

The girl withered with disappointment. "This way, y'all."

Beck tapped Harlow's butt cheek as they followed, whispering, "Really, darling? You went with noxious odors?"

His next tap had a bit more bite, and she giggled like the carefree girl she'd never before been.

Several of the patrons noticed Beck and waved him over. He pretended not to notice.

The hostess motioned to a small round booth in the corner. Harlow slid to the center, and Beck moved in close beside her; they accepted their menus. Though Harlow had lived in Strawberry Valley all her life, she'd eaten here only once, with Brook Lynn and the girls. She remembered nothing about the food.

Beck's heavy arm wound around her shoulders. "I'm sure you're dying to know how my dates usually go and lucky for you, I'm going to tell you. I order for both of us, I ask questions about your past, and then we go back to your place or mine."

"Mostly yours," she grumbled.

"But that isn't how this date will go down."

Insulted, she gasped out, "Well, why not? And just so you know, this date is now shaping up to be the opposite of awesome and I will share my review with all the women in town."

The waitress was close in age to the hostess and arrived with an overbright smile, doing her best to keep her distance while still being heard. "What can I get you guys to drink?" It was clear she'd pulled down the collar of her shirt and pushed up her boobs to accentuate her massive cleavage.

Beck's attention went straight to her eyes. "We'll start with your best red. We'll have today's special, whatever it is, and other than the delivery of each item, assume we're fine and stay away."

The girl appeared relieved as she ambled off. Harlow couldn't believe Beck had been so rude to a female. He hadn't even laced his words with innuendo.

Did he have a fever?

"I thought you weren't ordering for me," Harlow said.

Beck cupped the back of her neck, a possessive action she loved, toying with her hair. "Here's how this evening is going to go. I'm placing my balls in your court, and yes, I hope you take that several ways. You can question me about my past, and I will answer truthfully, no matter how personal you get. You may continue until the end of the meal, when I will take over."

Unrestricted access to his past? Even for a limited time? Yes, please. "I agree to your terms. But you only get to ask me one question a day." That way, he would have something new to look forward to—other than sex.

"Two questions."

"Zero."

His lips quirked at the corners. "All right. One question a day."

Excitement and anticipation built to a crescendo as the waitress rushed back over with the wine. Harlow confiscated the bottle and shooed her away. As soon as she and Beck were alone, she let the red gush into the glasses and decided to start with easy questions to warm him up a bit.

"What's your favorite color?"

He kissed the top of her eyelid. "Since meeting you? Ocean-water blue."

I may be putting out, after all. "Favorite food."

"You."

Heat spilled over her cheeks. "Beck."

"What? I said I'd be honest."

"Then you should have gone with pie."

"Baby, you're sweeter than pie, and that's a fact."

Moving on, before she took his mouth with her own. "What's your favorite memory?"

"Being inside you." He swirled his wine before tossing it back.

"One-track mind," she said, and tsk-tsked. Also a dangerously bone-melting answer, just not the kind of info she was looking for. "Worst memory. And if you say losing me, I will probably kiss you, and then I will definitely slap you."

"A warning like that is also known as encouragement," he said with a wink. But he set his glass aside and drained hers.

"The memory's that bad, huh?"

When his fingers laced with hers, she felt a tremor flow through him.

"Beck," she said. "Whatever it is, I won't judge you, I promise."

His lips lifted in a humorless smile. He leaned into her, saying quietly, "I'm sure you heard the rumors about Jase. He went to prison for beating a guy to death when we were eighteen…but here's what you don't know. I was with him when it happened. I was part of it."

The pronouncement didn't exactly shock her, but it did give her pause. Sweet, flirtatious, helpful Beck had beaten a guy to death? "Why? I mean I heard Jase defended a girl's honor."

"He did. We all did. We had a friend. Tessa. Jase and I loved her like a sister. West *loved* her. One night she went to a party, and a guy assaulted her."

Harlow's scars began to ache in sympathy. "I'm so sorry."

"We went after the guy, beat him and just didn't stop. He died from his injuries. Jase took full responsibility. Nine years behind bars. I could have come forward at any time to alleviate his burden, but never did."

"Why?"

"The three of us, we've always lived by a code—do whatever's asked by the others, no questions. For the longest time, we had no one to rely on but each other.

We each knew loss and regret and needed someone we could count on no matter what."

Her mother had been the one she counted on, supporting her through the worst of times. She understood the need.

"You suffered your own punishment, I'm sure. Violence of any kind leaves a mark, whether on the skin or in the soul."

Beck squeezed her hand, almost hard enough to bruise. "What you endured hurts me in a way I never imagined possible. You did not deserve what was done to you."

The waitress arrived with their dinner, piping-hot bowls of chicken and dumplings. Delightful scents combined with perfect harmony: bread yeast, sweet vegetables and the cream in the sauce.

"Is what I did a deal breaker?" Beck asked as soon as the girl was out of earshot.

Was it? He'd committed the crime as a teenager. Eighteen, old enough to know better. But what if he held *her* crimes against her? She hadn't killed anyone physically, but she'd certainly killed a few spirits.

"No," she said and he breathed a sigh of relief.

"Eat, Harlow. Please." He caressed her cheek. "You've lost weight."

Weight she couldn't afford to lose. She took a bite, then another, then paused as she recalled the clock on their conversation. "You still wrestle with guilt over the crime," she said, a statement, not a question. "And over Jase. Right?"

"Yes."

Learning about his past was helping her connect the

dots to his present—and his future. Maybe he didn't think he deserved a happily-ever-after.

"Do you—" He pushed her bowl closer to her, and she took another bite before finishing her question. "Do you think you'll ever get married?"

"There was a time I would have said no. Now? I won't rule out the possibility."

It was progress. More than she'd dreamed, considering he hoped to protect a fragile heart that had been battered and bruised countless times as he was taken from foster homes he'd come to love. As Jase was taken from him, and he couldn't allow himself to help.

"Do you want kids?" When she'd imagined herself married to Prince Charming, she'd also imagined a brood of rug rats.

But if she didn't end up with the right man, that dream family would simply fall apart, wouldn't it?

"I never wanted kids with a one-night stand, but again, I won't rule out the possibility any longer." He arched a brow. "Deal breaker?"

"No." As much has she loved him, she wasn't sure anything would be a deal breaker.

He smiled at her.

She swallowed the last bite of her meal and opened her mouth to ask her next question.

"Sorry, baby, but it's too late. You're done eating. It's my turn now."

Well, crap. She should have eaten slower. "Ask your one question," she said.

"For the information I crave, we need to be alone." He leaned into her and nibbled on her earlobe. "Let's go back to the inn."

CHAPTER TWENTY-FOUR

BECK MADE A PALLET on the floor.

Harlow demanded to know his question again and again, but he said, "In a minute," every time. Under her watchful gaze, he slowly stripped to his underwear.

"Those muscles don't fight fair," she grumbled.

"And you think those legs of yours do?" He got as comfortable as possible, considering desire burned in his bones.

She snuggled comfortably in bed and switched off the lamp, throwing shadows over the room.

"While you're up there on that cold, hard bed, I'm down here on these soft-as-silk sheets." Silk, sandpaper—whatever. "It's like you're punishing yourself when I only want to pamper you."

"Nice try, *Becky*, but I'm not buying the bull you're selling."

He covered his smile, realized she couldn't see him and let it stretch wide. "Becky? That's the nickname I get?"

"Hate it?" Relish dripped from her tone.

"Darling, it's absolutely perfect. Come down here and let your good friend Becky keep you safe all night."

She snorted. "Ask your question already. I'm about to fall asleep."

With darkness surrounding them, he kept his voice

whisper-soft, almost like smoke. "What's your dirtiest fantasy?"

The rustle of covers. He couldn't see her, but he could easily imagine she'd just rolled to her side in an effort to assuage the ache between her legs—one only he could end.

"I like to fantasize about you and me…"

Just like that. Hard. As. A. Rock. He stroked his length up, down. "Go on."

"We're in one of the rooms here at the inn…and I'm wet, throbbing…"

"What do I do?" he croaked.

"You slowly…sweetly…make the bed for me."

He barked out a laugh. "Evil woman. I said *dirtiest* fantasy."

"You've seen these sheets. You know they're filthy. Besides, watching you clean would be total girl porn."

"Me doing *anything* should be Harlow porn."

"It is. It really is. You're my fantasy. But what's Beck porn?"

Anything Harlow, and that was the honest truth. She moved, and he hardened. She breathed—hell, she looked at him or entered a room, and he wanted her. Just her. Just to be near her like this. She eased something inside him, as if the missing part of his life had finally been found.

And maybe—maybe this time he could keep her. She hadn't run when he'd confessed his greatest sin.

"Did you enjoy your first official date with me?" he asked, choosing not to answer her last question.

"I did. You were charming—"

"I'm always charming."

"And witty. And what do you mean, always charming? You most certainly are *not*."

"Hey, it's not my fault you're unable to recognize charm every time it bites you."

"Ha!"

He blew her a kiss, even though she couldn't see him. "Go on to sleep, Harlow. Get some rest." *You're going to need it.*

Covers rustled again. "Beck?" she whispered.

"Yes, Harlow."

"I'm glad you're here."

"Me, too." Though it took him hours to fall asleep, when he did, he was smiling.

THE NEXT DAY began poorly. Beck woke up to find Harlow had already taken off, crushing his need to kiss her goodbye.

Mood souring by the second, he dressed in his usual suit and tie and, before heading to the office, stopped to talk to Carol about Scott and Tawny. He learned the two had already checked out—saving their lives—and asked that any new customers be turned away, as Beck would be paying double for every room. The less Harlow had to do, the more energy she would have for other activities.

At work, he watched the clock, waiting for time to tick by and cursing its ability to slow to a crawl.

By 5:03 p.m., he was certain Harlow had finished with her chores. But why hadn't she called him?

"You should be embarrassed," West said, plopping into the chair in front of his desk.

"Why?"

"You're even more of a goner than Jase, and I'm pretty sure his balls have shriveled up and died."

"They most certainly have not," Jase said. "I know, because they are currently hanging in Brook Lynn's trophy case."

Beck leaned back and folded his hands over his middle. "You're one to talk, Westley."

"What's that supposed to mean?"

"There's a certain sassy blonde you like to stare at… This ringing any bells for you?"

West glowered at him. "Don't be ridiculous. I don't want Jessie Kay."

"Keep lying to yourself. Maybe one day you'll even believe it."

Eyes narrowing, West said, "If I wanted Jessie Kay, I wouldn't be on the prowl for my next relationship, now, would I?"

When West decided to "be in a relationship" he always picked a woman he found attractive but didn't actually enjoy being around. Jessie Kay seemed to fit the bill. Why not go for *her*?

"Anyone particular in mind?" Beck asked.

"No one I'm willing to discuss."

"Too bad. Where's she from? Strawberry Valley or the city?"

West glowered. "The city. Why?"

"Curiosity." If West decided the girl was the one— and continued with his date-and-dump pattern—he'd have her moved to Strawberry Valley by the end of their first month together. But this time, Beck suspected there would be more to the relationship than usual. Like keeping Jessie Kay at a distance.

Beck glanced at the clock—5:08 p.m. Harlow had

a second job, damn it, and as her boss, he deserved a little consideration.

He jumped to his feet. "I'm sorry, but I have to go. We'll continue this conversation after you've made up your mind...between the girl in the city and the one you *really* want here in Strawberry Valley."

West hurled anatomically impossible curses at him as he stalked from the office.

Beck didn't bother with his car, just barreled down the street on foot. Mr. Porter and Mr. Rodriguez were playing checkers, as usual, and called out a greeting.

"Going back for your girl?" Mr. Porter gave him a thumbs-up. "Good for you, son. Good for you."

"Make sure you take her flowers. The ladies love them some flowers," Mr. Rodriguez said.

Right. Beck backtracked, buying a bouquet from the florist a few streets over. But when he reached the inn at last, he found no sign of Harlow. He watched TV for an hour...two. He paced their room for an eternity. Finally, he caved and texted Harlow—where are U???—but he never received a reply.

He was just about to hunt her down when a knock sounded at the door. "Room service," a woman called, and he nearly came out of his skin when he recognized her voice.

He practically ripped the door from its hinges. Finally he could breathe. She stood with one arm anchored overhead, the other on her hip. Gorgeous girl. She grinned, making everything right in his world.

He cupped the back of her neck and pulled her in for a swift kiss—swift because she walked away from him.

"Thank you for the best greeting ever," she said.

"I brought you flowers."

She whirled, her eyes wide. "Flowers? Again?"

Thank you, Mr. Rodriguez. "Again." He lifted the bouquet from the nightstand and passed it to her.

As she sniffed the petals, her eyes closed and a smile lifted the corners of her lips. An expression he would kill to see again. Every day. He walked to her, almost in a trance, but she must have sensed his intention to take her in his arms, because she backed away.

"Oh, no, you don't. I'm starved," she said. "Order room service while I shower?"

"You don't want to go out on another date?"

"I'm too tired. Besides," she said with a wink, "I like having you all to myself."

He clasped his chest, just over his heart. "You're killing me, baby. You know that, don't you?"

"Oh! You'll be happy to know I finished a few sketches while I was on my break." She withdrew a stack of napkins from her pocket.

Grateful for the distraction, he studied each one, utterly blown away by her talent as usual. "This one looks like Kenna. And this one looks like Brook Lynn."

"I know. I'm sorry. I can change them, but I just thought—"

"No. They're perfect. *You're* perfect."

As she shut herself in the bathroom, their gazes remained locked until the last possible second, the moment charged with heat and grit.

He shook with the force of his need for her, nearly ready to say to hell with it, storm the door and take her up against the shower wall.

Her way. Do it her way. Too important to mess up.

He'd calmed by the time the food arrived. But when Harlow emerged from the bathroom on a cloud of fragrant steam, wearing one of his T-shirts and a pair of panties, his greatest temptation and his fiercest torment, he just about creamed his damn jeans.

After she ate, they settled on the bed to watch TV. Beck was careful not to touch her, his control simply too fragile.

Hours passed, but he wasn't certain which programs played on the screen. Need had him by the throat. Or the balls. He hated it. He loved it. And when he could take it no more, he made his pallet on the floor and lay down.

"You ready for your next question?"

"I am," she said, switching off the TV and lamp, shrouding the room in darkness.

"What's your favorite thing about me?"

"I'd have to go with…your mustache. It's practically a recreational vehicle in this town."

"I hate to be the one to break this devastating news to you, baby, but I don't actually have a mustache."

"Well, you've got the shadow of one, and there have been a few times I've felt the prickle of it." A tremor of need shook her voice. "I liked it," she whispered.

Hunger became starvation, and it required all of his considerable strength to remain on the floor. He liked her playful side. He liked her sense of humor. Even celibate—*whimper*—he was happy as long as he was with her.

"Beck," she whispered.

"Yes, baby."

"My favorite thing about you is your heart. It's softer than I ever realized, and I treasure it."

"WHAT DID YOU want to be when you grew up?" Beck asked. This was their third nightly session, and again, he'd looked forward to it all day, watching the clock, cursing it. Only one thing had distracted him, and only for a short time. The call from West. The guy had gone on a date with his potential relationship from the city, but decided against going further with her for a reason that had nothing to do with Jessie Kay, he'd insisted when Beck pressed the issue.

Please.

From the nightstand, a lamp glowed, allowing him to watch Harlow atop the bed. She rolled toward him, a lock of midnight hair hanging over the side of the bed, teasing him. "You'll laugh, but…"

"Tell me." He had to know. Every. Little. Detail.

"I wanted to be a trophy wife. But only because a life of leisure sounded way cooler than the things my friends wanted to be," she rushed to add. "Doctor? Blood is gross. Reporter? Hounding family members of someone who just died? Never! And if you say 'what friends,' I'll smother you with one of my pillows. I had a posse back then."

"A posse, huh? Did you often ride off into the sunset together?"

He hadn't laughed, but she launched one of those pillows anyway, smacking him in the face. "I had it all figured out. I would paint during the day while my very rich, very good-looking husband worked at his office. He owned the company and even the building, of course, and everyone feared him. Except me, because even though he was a bear, he was putty in my hands."

"Of course."

"Our chef would prepare dinner," she continued, "and the maids would clean up after us."

All doable. He would enjoy making her dreams come true. "And now?" He stuffed the pillow under his head.

"Now I absolutely do *not* want to be a trophy wife. I told you. I like earning my own way."

"I bet I could change your mind."

"You wanting to pamper me, Becky?"

"Desperately. If only you'd let me…"

Silence stretched, and tension grew.

"What about you?" she asked, a hitch in her breath.

"I'd make an *amazing* trophy wife."

She snorted. "I mean, what did you want to be when you grew up?"

He could have refused to answer. This wasn't about him. But when had he ever been able to resist her? "For a while, I dreamed of being a cop. I was going to bust some serious caps and take some names. Then I was arrested for theft, then assault, and that dream died real fast."

"What'd you steal?"

"Food, mostly. My fosters at the time were big on taking the checks they got for keeping me around, but not on feeding me."

She extended her arm, offering her hand. As he reached up to twine their fingers, she said, "I hate that you weren't treated fairly."

"I turned out all right."

"But you are not without wounds."

"None of us are," he said. "But for the first time in my life, I think I'm healing."

"TELL ME MORE about your parents," Beck said the next night.

Miracle of miracles, Harlow had made a pallet next

to his with zero prompting from him. They faced each other, were basically curled into each other, and he'd never been so pleased with so little. But he wanted more. He *needed* it. As close as she was to him, so close he breathed in the soft fragrance of her skin every time he inhaled, his hands fisted because he remembered all too well the silky feel of her hair tangled between his fingers.

He missed her so bad he hurt physically.

Unwilling to leave her this morning, he'd blown off work. Well, his own. He'd accompanied Harlow, stepping in and helping her with chores. He'd teased her and laughed with her, even scolded her. She worked too long and too hard, refusing to slow down, and he'd quickly gotten tired of people coming to the inn just to humiliate her. And since he'd taken over most of the rooms, the would-be patrons had holed up in the lobby and dining hall and Carol had demanded Harlow clean both.

His temper had nearly snapped. Would have, if Harlow hadn't stormed to the register where Carol was helping an out-of-town guest, yelling, "Enough! I'll clean, but I won't entertain. Not without a significant pay increase. So unless you want to triple my check or fire me, I'm done for the day!"

Her confidence had grown by leaps and bounds, and Beck liked to think he'd had a positive influence on her. While Carol wasn't the sharpest tool in the shed, she recognized a moneymaker when she saw one, and she hadn't fired Harlow. The girl brought in too much business with or without the personal cleaning entertainment.

And Harlow, well, despite the setbacks, she truly

seemed to enjoy her life. As she'd worked today, she'd teased him right back, and he cherished every second.

"You were cuddled when you were sick, I'm assuming," he said now.

"Yes," she said. "My mom was the best. She loved me, and I was never in doubt of that."

"Did she know you were the town bully?" he asked carefully, not wanting to raise her hackles.

"Yeah. My dad knew, too, and he'd yell at me for it anytime a teacher or parent would complain, but that would only make me lash out worse."

"He was a hypocrite."

"Yes, but I thought his attention, any attention, was better than the times he ignored me."

Poor Harlow. She'd been adrift, conflicted and in turmoil. Beck knew the feelings well. He'd felt them every time his dad had dropped him off at one of his aunt's houses, saying he'd call, but never calling, saying he'd be back soon, but never showing up. Meanwhile, his uncles had enjoyed playing ball with his cousins.

"Even though my dad was a deadbeat, I loved him almost as much as I hated him," he said. "I always hoped the guy would change his mind about giving me up and rescue me from the system. At least, I hoped the first year…a little the second…but by the third I knew the truth. I would never see my father again."

Harlow patted his hand, her gaze holding him captive, what should have been a gesture of comfort sending pulses of pleasure along his already-sensitized nerve endings. His entire body vibrated with need.

"I hate what you went through," she said, "but I love that you understand me."

"Trust me, baby, I understand." And he did. He enjoyed sharing his past with her, which surprised him, but he also enjoyed her empathy, touched by how much she actually cared. It was something he wasn't used to getting from anyone other than Jase and West, but it was something he craved almost as much as her luscious little body.

His fingertip grazed her palm, and she sucked in a breath. "Beck…" Need drenched her voice, reminding him of all the other times she'd whispered his name, breathed it straight into his ear, shouted it. If she scooted closer, or, hell, if she so much as drew in a shaky breath, he would know all the waiting had agonized her, too. He would be on her in a blink—

She scooted closer.

"Harlow." He swooped in, thrusting his tongue into her mouth, tasting, owning—being owned. His control burned out, and as she clung to him, he rolled her to her back, pinning her down with his weight.

He'd been starved for her and wanted his hands everywhere at once. He cupped her breasts first, kneaded the plump flesh and ghosted his thumbs over the distended peaks of her nipples. "Missed these perfect little beauties."

Moaning, she raked her nails along his scalp. "Feels so good, Beck."

He stroked his way to her ass, cupping her there, jerking her against his erection. The friction maddened him. "I'm going to take you hard, baby. It's been too long."

"Yes…yes…"

He yanked off her shirt, then his own. A single tug broke the front clasp of her bra. He dived back down for another soul-burning kiss—but the cool air must have roused her from the passionate frenzy because she stiffened.

"Wait. What are we doing?" She rolled away from him, panting. "We can't have sex. Not yet."

He swallowed a roar. For a while, only the sound of their breathing could be heard, but as time passed at a crawl, the intense ache between his legs gradually faded.

The one in his chest did not.

He could not resist her, and yet she seemed to have no trouble resisting him. No relationship could survive such an unsteady foundation.

Once again, the future did not look bright.

CHAPTER TWENTY-FIVE

DOTTIE CAME KNOCKING on Harlow's door bright and early next morning, offering to give her the entire weekend off.

"Why?" she asked, hearing Beck rustle around behind her. As she rubbed the sleep from her eyes, the bathroom door closed with a soft snicker.

Something was wrong with him. He'd tossed and turned all night and snapped at her when she'd wished him a good morning. "Well, tomorrow no extra services will be offered so that the staff can attend the Berryween Festival. I'm going as a toddler with a tiara. Basically I'll be wearing a formal gown and throwing lots of fits. How about you?"

"Oh, uh, I'm not sure I'm going." And she wouldn't pout about it. First she hadn't had the money to waste on a costume, and now it was too late to buy one, everything sold out. "But why give me today off?"

"My way of saying thank you for giving me private time with Daniel."

"Oh." *Oh!* "Did something happen?"

A blush spilled over the girl's cheeks. "No, nothing like that, but we talked and it was awesome, and he's still here so I get another chance and I've never been so excited." Dottie threw her arms around Harlow's neck and hugged her. "Thank you," she said, and skipped away.

As the shower started up in the bathroom, Harlow's happy smile faded. Her body ached so badly, had been on fire since Beck had reentered her life, but last night had taken her to a new level of torment. She'd thrown herself at him, thinking to hell with her plan to get to know each other better. He'd kissed her with such hunger, and she'd come close to begging him to take her.

Of course, that's when her fears had peeked out of the mire, and she'd ruined everything. The sooner she slept with him, the sooner their relationship focused on sex rather than intimacy. Their late-night chats would end. The quiet moments of teasing and learning—the moments she craved with every fiber of her being—would be gone forever.

When he emerged from the bathroom, he wore a white T-shirt and dark ripped jeans. He looked so young and beautiful, a model fresh off the runway.

"I'm happy to report I have the next two days off," she said, toying with the hem of her shirt.

He ran a towel through his hair, his gaze landing anywhere but on her. "I heard."

Nervousness mule-kicked her stomach. He hadn't been this standoffish since they'd called off their breakup. "You've been spending more and more time here, helping me clean rooms—" a fact that still thrilled her "—so why don't we go to your office this morning? You can get caught up and I can finish my sketches."

Still he didn't face her. "Good idea."

"Afterward, I'll have to go to Brook Lynn and Jessie Kay's house to finally paint the mural I owe them."

"Not a problem."

Short and sweet answers were not his style, and it made her even more nervous. She hesitated for a moment. "Tomorrow is the Berryween Festival. Would you like to… I don't know…go with me, even though I don't have a costume?"

"Sure." He sat at the edge of the bed and pulled on his shoes.

How enthusiastic he *hadn't* sounded.

She showered and, wanting to look her best, dressed in one of the summer dresses Beck had returned to her. The ice-blue beauty with a deep V-neck and flirty skirt. She forwent a sweater, despite the cooler temperature, no longer concerned by her scars. She was what she was, and Beck liked her—but he didn't give her the usual heated once-over, didn't speak to her as he escorted her to the office, and it made her nervous. He didn't even speak to her as he worked or afterward when he drove her to Brook Lynn's house.

"What's wrong?" Brook Lynn asked when she entered.

At last Beck focused on her, watching her intently, waiting for her answer.

She merely offered a half smile. *Won't lie, but won't admit the truth, either.* "Did you get all the paints and brushes from the RV?"

"I sure did. Well, Jase did," Brook Lynn said. "We have a system. I want, he procures."

Jase, who sat on the couch in the living room, flipping channels on the TV, nodded. "Through any means necessary."

Brook Lynn beamed. "I'm awarding you ten points for giving the perfect response."

"I think I deserve twenty," he said.

"Then I'll have to deduct five for silly thinking."

He snorted.

"What does he do with these points?" Harlow asked in a whisper.

The feisty blonde waggled her brows, and something deep inside Harlow contracted. Sex. Of course. But that kind of game was okay for them to play, because Jase loved Brook Lynn with all his heart, and he wouldn't allow the romance to die just because they were intimate.

"Come on. I'll show you where I want the mural." Brook Lynn led her into the hallway, where the borders had already been taped and the floor covered in plastic. "*Now* you can tell me what's wrong," she said, moving in front of Harlow.

"Well, for starters, I'm a mess," she admitted softly. "I told Beck I wanted to stop having sex while we got to know each other better, but everything I learn makes me like and admire him more, and I love him so much but don't want to tell him and scare him away, and I don't want to lose him, but what if I sleep with him like I really want to do, I mean really, really want to do, but I lose him anyway because we stop snuggling and talking, and all we can think about is sex, and what if—"

Brook Lynn slapped her hand over Harlow's mouth. "Oh, wow. I would introduce you to Run On Sentence, but I see you've already met." Her hand fell away and she said, "That guy is crazy about you. But, no, you can't control what he does, feels or thinks. You can only control what you do. If you really love him that much, don't let fear make your choices for you. It's only ruining the time you have together. Start actually living. Otherwise you'll look back and wonder why you didn't njoy the time you *did* have together. And physical intimacy doesn't preclude emotional intimacy. Not when rue, heartfelt emotions are involved. Have a little trust n the man. And yourself! You won't let the snuggles nd talking end."

"That's actually a good point."

"Duh. That's the only kind I have."

Bottom line: Harlow had to stop making her choices based on how she assumed Beck would react and start naking the right choices for herself.

"Okay," she said with a nod. "All right. I'm going o go for it, and if everything blows up in my face, I'll olame you and seek revenge. Now get lost so I can paint our mural and then seduce the man of my dreams."

BECK SHIFTED ON the couch for the thousandth time. Harow had been painting for several hours, and he missed er the way he would have missed a hand, as if she had omehow become a necessary part of him. Maybe she ad. Hell, she definitely had.

"Women adore romance," Brook Lynn suddenly nnounced. She and Jase were on the couch as well, uddling together in the far corner, their dog asleep in Brook Lynn's lap. "Did you know that, Beck?"

"Since I'm pretty sure I've dated more of them than ou have, I'm going to go with *yes*."

"You haven't dated and you haven't romanced. You've screwed. Do you get what I'm saying?" she sked.

"No, but I'm sure you'll tell me."

"Being romantic means cuddling. Sharing secrets."

He looked to Jase and sighed. "Where is she going vith this?"

His friend shrugged. "Got me. I'm not a detectiv for the mysteries of women. I'd have more luck as unicorn wrangler."

Brook Lynn slapped Beck's shoulder. "Just stop an think. You're known as the one-and-done man. Now while you aren't sleeping with your girlfriend, you'r romancing her. But what happens when you start sleep ing with her again? The romance goes away. At leas in her mind, it does."

Well, well. Harlow had clearly confided in Broo Lynn. He liked that she had a friend, but did not lik the fact that she hadn't told *him*. Instead, she'd pulle away last night, choosing to be alone with her fear while stoking *his*.

And okay. He hadn't confided his fears to her, ei ther. Instead, he'd internalized his hurt and snappe answers at her all day.

"Do you still feel like you're being kept in a cage? Brook Lynn asked.

"Cage?" Jase asked.

"Still harping on the cage." Beck heaved a weight sigh. "Perhaps it's time for you to get over it, consider ing you were never actually invited inside it."

"Who's in a cage?" Jase demanded.

"Besides, maybe I've been a good little schoolboy, Beck said, ignoring his friend. "Maybe I've learned lesson."

"What? That feelings aren't so bad?" she asked.

"Hardly. If I'm going to feel, I have to make dam sure she does, too."

Brook Lynn leveled an evil grin on him. "I'm look ing forward to the day you realize your cage has bee filled with all of us all along." Before he could reply she added, "Now I'm changing the subject, and you're letting me. Are you going to the Berryween Festival tomorrow?"

"Yes." His next official date with Harlow.

"Jase and I are going as Adam and Eve. What about you and Harlow?"

"We're going as Beck and Harlow."

Brook Lynn snorted. "Be serious."

"I am."

Horrified, she said, "Wow. I know you guys are new to town and everything, and you have no idea how things actually work around here, but seriously. I had no idea you sucked such giant donkey balls."

Beck glared at his friend. "Are you going to let your woman talk to me that way?"

"Yes" was Jase's only response.

Laughing, Brook Lynn kissed the guy on the mouth. "I love you."

"Not as much as I love you."

Beck's chest constricted with some unnameable emotion. Disgust—had to be disgust. "Let's shut up and watch TV."

"Let's!" With a bubbliness that irritated him, Brook Lynn clapped and said, "I've been storing episodes of *The Walking Dead*. We can marathon, and I can teach you how to survive the coming apocalypse."

ANOTHER FEW HOURS passed before Harlow finally rounded the corner. Beck had to shake his head to clear away images of blood and gore from the TV show, and the clenching he'd experienced earlier returned, only worse, his heart curling up like a fist and banging against his ribs. Definitely wasn't because of disgust.

Splatters of paint marred Harlow's lashes, arms and clothes, her skin flushed a lovely rose.

Her gaze skittered to him, an almost shy smile lighting her face.

"All done?" he asked.

"I am. Want to see?"

"Me! Me!" Brook Lynn jumped to her feet and clapped, waking the dog. Sparkles barked as his mommy rushed forward and grabbed Harlow's wrist. "I do!"

"The paint is still wet. You can look, but don't touch," Harlow said.

Currently the story of my life.

Brook Lynn raced past her and into the hall, where she squealed like a little girl who'd just found the present of her dreams underneath the Christmas tree.

Harlow, who'd remained in place, released a relieved breath, twin spots of pleasure darkening her cheeks. "I wasn't sure she'd like it. I mean, I know she asked for zombies on the wall, but I thought she'd realize her horrible mistake when she spotted all the blood and guts."

Jase smiled, his affection clear. "My girl is weird."

"You're just jealous I have a plan for the zombie apocalypse and you don't," Brook Lynn called. "Now I have the perfect wall for practicing expert slaying techniques."

"You're right, angel. I'm jealous," Jase called back. "Twenty more points?"

Harlow met Beck's gaze as he straightened. Her pupils expanded as she took a step toward him. "You ready to go?"

He held out his hand and, without a moment's hesitation, she twined her fingers with his.

He nodded to his friend on the way out, then helped Harlow into the car. Night had long since fallen, the moon half-hidden by clouds with no stars in sight.

Trees whizzed by as he sped down the road. "We need to talk, baby."

"I know," she replied softly.

"We haven't been honest with each other, and it's putting a strain on us both."

"You've lied to me?"

"No. Absolutely not." He frowned at her. "You should know better."

Her shoulders hunched in, and she rubbed at her face. "You're right. I'm sorry."

Better. "If this relationship is going to work, you have to tell me when you're scared about something. And I have to tell you the same. We have to rely on each other, Harlow, not on outside parties."

"Yes. You're right, again." She peered down at her hands, twisting the fabric of her skirt. "I wanted to be with you last night, so badly I nearly couldn't breathe."

"Why did you stop me?" He knew the answer, but he wanted to hear her say it.

"I was so afraid we'd have sex and the talking and sharing I've come to love so much would stop. And I worry the lack will be the death knell of our relationship."

"In case you haven't noticed," he said, tenderness welling in his chest, "I've enjoyed the talking and sharing, too."

"Really?"

"Really. You are ridiculous and weird, frustrating and challenging."

"Hey," she said with a frown.

"But you are the most entertaining person I've ever met and everything I learn about you makes me lo— like you more." No damn way he'd almost dropped the *L* bomb.

"That's good," she said, "because I'd rather die than give up that part of our relationship."

He reached over, cupped her leg just above her knee where the dress had ridden up to reveal a mile of succulent thigh. "Our relationship means a lot to me, too, baby."

Moonlight glinted off crystalline blue irises he couldn't help but fall in.

Honk.

A flash of another car's lights. Driving. Right.

"You just said the *R* word without vomiting. I'm impressed," she said. "But you mentioned fears of your own."

He nodded. "The more you come to mean to me, the more I'm certain I'm going to lose you, and I hate it. If you leave me, Harlow…"

"Now you're thinking the worst of me. You won't lose me, Beck. I'm yours for the taking." She unbuckled again and leaned over to nibble on his ear. "Pull over, and let me prove it."

He let go of her knee to grip the wheel, his knuckles soon bleaching of color. "Are you sure?"

He could feel her nod against his skin. "I want you, and I don't want to wait."

He whipped the car to the side of the road, edged deeper into the trees. When the engine died, the dash lights faded, darkness sweeping over them. Their deep, panting breaths filled the car, a fine film already rising over the windows.

"I can't ever get enough of you." He lifted her over the console, and as she straddled his waist, he said, "I want you so much I probably need therapy."

"How about immersion therapy?" She rubbed against him, pulling a ragged groan from him. "Get inside me. I've been so empty without you."

He was already hard as a rock, but her words careened him toward the edge, affecting him more intensely than the touch of any other woman. "I don't want you empty, baby." He wedged a hand inside her panties and found her hot and damp. Perfect.

She tugged at his fly, the heat of her palm meeting his swollen flesh. He could only rasp out a tattered, "I want you on the pill *soon*."

"Yes. Tomorrow."

He shucked his jeans to his knees and yanked down the top of her dress, freeing her breasts. He tore at her panties, saying, "I'll buy you new ones." As he thrust a finger deep inside her, he crashed his mouth into her. Fire raged in his blood, flickered over his skin.

Desire shouldn't be this ferocious, this consuming. He'd always been able to walk away at any time, naked or not, inside a woman or not. But he couldn't walk away this time, didn't want to. He had to get inside Harlow, had to fill her, brand her, lay siege to her. Lay claim. His life depended on it.

In the shadows, her eyes glittered like diamonds as she pulled away to say, "Where's the condom?"

"Pocket."

Next thing he knew, she was digging inside it. A moment after that, the sound of foil being ripped masked his panting breaths. She arched back long enough to roll the latex down his swollen length, every touch propelling him to a new level of need.

He gripped her hair, stilled despite the agony, and peered into her eyes. "We're together officially, Harlow. Say it."

Melting over him, she nipped at his bottom lip. "We're together. Now…always."

"Always," he echoed, and gripped her hips, placed her at his erection's tip, and thrust up while she drove down on him. There was a moment of sweet relief, her inner walls clenching him with wet heat, and he knew he was finally where he belonged. But the relief didn't last long, the relentless madness coming back to haunt them both.

"Beck." She dug her nails into his scalp and kissed him, hard and dirty, taking his mouth the way he was taking her body—laying claim.

He swallowed her moans, her sweet little purrs that sounded both pained and carnal. Bracing her knees wider at his waist, she took control of the rhythm, hard and fast, using him for her pleasure, and he loved it. Loved the feel of her. Loved the strawberries-and-cream smell of her. Loved—his mind shied away from his next thought, even as his body edged ever closer to satisfaction because of it.

Refusing to go off first, he worked his hand between them. When he reached her drenched center, he pressed. She cried out, began to rub in seeking circles against him, just to get closer. And when up and down failed to do a good enough job, she rotated her hips left and right, the pressure on his swollen shaft absolute perfection.

"Beck…faster…"

"That's it, baby. That's the way." Harder and harder he pressed against her.

What began as a little tremor soon swept through her like an avalanche. She came, shouting his name, and with a roar, he followed her over the edge, pouring his climax into the condom.

He wasn't sure how long they quaked together, or how long passed before they calmed, but he cherished every second. He held her so tightly he was almost afraid he was hurting her. Almost.

"That was…"

"Only the beginning," he finished for her.

CHAPTER TWENTY-SIX

GOING DAYS WITHOUT physical intimacy with Beck, all because Harlow had feared their relationship would fall apart afterward, had been stupid. Beck was right. They had to trust each other, and they had to share with each other. They wouldn't survive otherwise.

After their explosive encounter in the car, he drove her to the farmhouse. He led her into his private bathroom, where they showered, cuddled in bed together, and talked in hushed, secret tones.

"Since you can't ride my nonexistent mustache everywhere," he said, "what kind of car would you like? And don't tell me a car is too expensive a gift to—"

"Please. I like gifts. Gimme. But a car is a car. I don't care what kind."

He made a noise of disbelief. "A car is not a car, Miss Glass. You take that back right now."

"Never!" She squealed when he tickled her, finally admitting, "I don't even have a driver's license."

"What?" he demanded, and she shrugged.

"I had one, but I let it expire in high school and never got it renewed."

"You have a reason to get it renewed now."

And the funds, apparently. "True, but I haven't driven in years. I'll endanger the entire town."

"Just means you need to practice. You can drive us to the Berryween Festival."

"You'll be placing your life in my hands."

His eyelids grew heavy, hooding the dark, carnal gaze underneath. "Baby, there's no place else I'd rather be."

She curled around him, resting her head on his shoulder, drawing little hearts over, well, his heart. "I'll keep you safe. I was only in, like, six fender benders back then, and only, like, five of them were my fault."

He chuckled, his warm breath tickling the top of her head. "I'm feeling safer already. I'm also thinking I should give you a bumper car instead of the key to my Jag."

"No take-backs," she said. "You offered the Jag, so I'm driving it. I've developed a need for speed."

"In the past two minutes?"

She nipped at his nipple. "Seems like forever."

He cupped her bottom and squeezed. "Careful. You keep that up, and you'll find yourself flat on your back, Beck Jr. deep inside you."

"You mean the Baconator?"

He barked out a laugh. "You've named my penis the Baconator?"

"What? I like bacon."

"Well, I'm naming your breasts Strawberry Pie and Strawberry Shortcake." Rolling her to her back, he cupped the strawberry twins, licked one nipple, then the other. "Hey, girls. Did you miss me?"

Moaning, Harlow ran her fingers through his hair. "They missed you *so* much."

"Good. Wrap your legs around me, and I'll give them

a more intimate hello," he said, and when she stiffened suddenly, he lifted his head. "What's wrong?"

Habit urged her to say the typical, "Nothing. I'm fine." But if she trusted him, she would share with him. "I've heard you say that very thing to other women."

His brow furrowed with confusion. "How do you know?"

"When I was camping on my—your—land, I would come to see the house every night and there you'd be. And it doesn't bother me anymore, it really doesn't. I don't know why I reacted that way. I'm sorry."

He peered at her for a long while, his expression intense but unreadable. Finally he said, "Wrap your legs around me, Harlow."

She did—without stiffening—fitting her body around his, placing her core right against his massive erection. His hiss of breath blended with her deliciously agonized gasp.

"Do you know what I remember about those women?"

She shook her head, not sure she really wanted to know the answer.

"Nothing. And do you know what I'll always remember about you?"

Melting into the mattress while somehow dissolving into him, she scraped her nails down the plane of his back and said, "Tell me."

"Absolutely everything."

He gently pinched her chin between his fingers, making sure her gaze remained on him, perhaps wanting her to know, to see, that he meant what he said with his entire being.

He loves me. He has to love me. But as screwed up as his life had been, he might not recognize the emotion.

Harlow smiled up at him. "I believe you. Now shut up and earn some points of your own. You win ten for every orgasm you give me."

Those eyes of melted butterscotch glimmered. "I won't be satisfied until I've received fifty points, so get ready, because I'm not going to stop until I've hit my goal—and even then it's iffy."

THE NEXT MORNING dawned dark and hazy, rain clouds smeared across the sky, fat and gray, creating the perfect atmosphere for a spooktacular festival. Tents—also known as graveyards—were set up all along Main, offering food and games, everything from Brain Smash to Pin the Guts on the Zombie.

Harlow, grateful to be alive after driving a car for the first time in years—so slowly half the town honked at her and Beck asked if she'd taken lessons from the good people at the senior citizen home—sipped a sweet tea and leaned against Beck as they strolled down the street. He had his arm around her, proud to be with her no matter how many incredulous stares they received.

When she'd woken up, he'd had two costumes laid out. A sexy lion for her—fake ears with a thick, blond mane, a scrap of faux fur over her breasts and a short skirt complete with a long, curling tail—and a sexy jungle safari lion tamer for him.

When she wobbled on her faux-fur high-heel boots, he laughed and said, "Trouble walking on your own, baby? I *did* earn eighty points, after all."

"Only because I graded on a curve." But he'd definitely be earning more points today. His costume consisted of a sleeveless orange hunter's jacket over a bare chest, ripped jeans and combat boots. Oh, and she couldn't forget the whip draped over his shoulders.

"No, you had to give me double points for those last two—"

She slapped a hand over his mouth. "Don't you dare say it. Besides, you shouldn't gloat. I earned three *hundred* points for those last two...you knows."

He plucked her hand away and smiled so tenderly she almost melted. "That you did."

She glanced around to distract herself from his sexiness. People and kids dressed as everything from a zombie clown to a snow queen crowded inside different tents. Red and black balloons stretched from buildings on the left to buildings on the right, forming an arch in the center. Though the street had been blocked off to vehicular traffic, an old-timey green truck inched along the center, the current Miss Strawberry Valley standing in back, dressed as a sexy strawberry and waving.

Well over a decade had passed since Harlow had actually attended the festival. As a teenager she'd been too "cool," and as an adult she probably would have been stuffed in the dunk tank. Oh, how times had changed. She soaked up every moment of this.

"Harlow! Harlow! Over here!" Brook Lynn called. She wore a flesh-colored bodysuit with strategically placed fig leaves. She waved from inside the You've Got It Coming booth, a crowd stretching out a mile long to buy bowls of casserole, different sandwiches and slices of pie.

Harlow waved back. Jase, Jessie Kay and Daphne were working inside the booth, as well, and when they heard her name they glanced up to smile at her. Jase wore a similiar flesh-colored bodysuit with a single fig leaf between his legs, and oh wow, he looked good. His muscles stretched the suit's fabric, making it ripple.

Jessie Kay had come as a sexy zombified version of *Alice in Wonderland*, and Daphne as a sexy Harpy with glittery wings.

As Harlow acknowledged each of them, so happy she could burst, Jessie Kay called, "If you're hungry, get over here. I promise not to spit in your food."

"No, thanks. I'm good for now." Besides, if she cut to the front of the line, the crowd of ax murderers and skeletons would mob her. Ever since she'd started working at the inn, they'd been more tolerant of her. Maybe because they'd had closure…or because they'd gotten to spoon-feed her a little of her own medicine. Whatever it was, she would take it over being the town pariah. But there were just some things she dare not risk.

West, who flanked Harlow's other side, mumbled, "That woman is a menace."

"Who? Jessie Kay?"

"As if there's anyone else even half as dangerous."

Dangerous? "She's awesome," Harlow snapped, defending her friend. "One of the best people I know."

Beck kissed Harlow's temple. "He's just bitter because he hasn't been able to get into her pants yet."

"Watch your mouth," West said. His tone was firm, but not so firm she worried they'd break out in fisticuffs anytime soon.

Beck held up his hands in surrender. "How are things going with your relationship search, my man?"

"You're finally ready to settle down?" Harlow asked. "Well, make sure any girl you date knows you have no taste and wouldn't recognize perfect girlfriend material if she bit you. Oh, who am I kidding? She'll figure it out on her own after a few minutes in your presence."

Beck laughed.

"You guys annoy me," West grumbled.

Carol Mathis, dressed as a vampire's bride, ambled past Harlow and nodded, publicly acknowledging her presence. Dottie, looking gorgeous in a pink sequin gown with teardrops painted under her eyes, kept pace beside her mother. She smiled and waved, and Harlow eagerly returned the greeting.

When Dottie disappeared around a corner, Harlow's gaze collided with Scott. He stood across the street, dressed as a cowboy, watching her from the Dead Again booth.

Beck stiffened, gritting out, "I swear that man wants me to help him."

"He isn't cursing at me. I'd say he's backed off," she said.

"Doesn't matter if he's backed off or not," West said. He'd gone all out with his pimp costume, wearing a rainbow-colored faux-fur coat and bell-bottoms, even carrying a gold cane. "He still looked at another man's property, and that's a crime deserving of torture."

With the bitter twinge in his voice, he sounded as if he knew a little something about that.

"Property?" she said.

"I prefer the word *toy*," Beck said, and nipped at her ear. "Let me play with you."

Tawny and Charlene bounded over. Both women wore lingerie. Or scraps of material trying to pass themselves off as lingerie. They each held a gourmet corn dog from Brook Lynn's booth, and Harlow made a mental note: next stop, Brook Lynn's booth, whether the town revolted or not. *I want.*

"Hi, Beck. Hi, West," Tawny said, her gaze locked on Beck. She twirled a lock of pale hair between her fingers and licked at the tip of her corn dog.

If she gave that tasty treat a blow job, Harlow might just go nuclear.

"You're looking good, Beck," Charlene said. She was a young, newly divorced brunette who'd once helped Harlow terrorize the town, becoming the new queen bee when Harlow retired.

"Gotta say, you are absolutely adorable as a pussy-cat tamer," Charlene added, shooting Harlow a gleeful smirk. "You can wrangle me anytime. Again."

Tawny nodded enthusiastically. "I second that."

Harlow stiffened.

Beck offered the pair a cold but gorgeous smile and they preened happily, not seeming to realize the danger zone they'd entered. "Have you guys met my girlfriend, Harlow? Nowadays I spend all my time with my girlfriend, Harlow." Just for good measure, he added, "My girlfriend—Harlow."

"Hi. I'm his girlfriend. Harlow," she said with a little wave.

Tawny bared her teeth in a scowl.

"Harlow Glass," a voice boomed. Scott's voice. She turned, right along with Beck and West. "No one wants you here. Go home."

Beck vibrated with barely suppressed violence as Scott, who'd said his piece, tipped his hat and ambled off.

"I'm fine," she told Beck. Her boyfriend. "He's not worth ruining our day."

"You're not worth it, either," Tawny said, now radiating smug satisfaction, "but that hasn't stopped you from ruining ours."

West smiled a seducer's smile—one Harlow had never seen him use before, and oh, wow, it might possibly have beaten Beck's for World's Most Devastating. The girls certainly weren't immune. They released dreamy sighs and instinctively stepped closer to the man.

"Ladies," he said. "We don't know each other well enough, and that's a mighty shame. Though I do recall introducing my tongue to yours, Charlene, when we were drunk—or was that you making my head spin?" He stepped toward them, widening his arms to snake around both their waists, the beefcake in a bitch-sandwich. Taking one for the team? "Why don't we start with you two telling me every detail about your childhoods and end with your crush on me," he said, drawing them away.

Charlene went eagerly, while Tawny threw a devious glance at Harlow before heading off.

Beck didn't say another word and neither did Harlow, who was too afraid she'd start cussing.

A lady keeps the corridors of her lips clean, her mother used to say.

Not feeling so ladylike now, Momma. Her claws were out, and they were hungry for blood.

A Ferris wheel had been erected down the street, the first the town had ever had. There was a line almost as long as the one at Brook Lynn's booth, but Beck bypassed it without apology. Not that anyone seemed to care. He even received several pats on the shoulder.

"Best festival yet," someone said.

"You sure know how to give good festival," someone else said.

That's right. He, West and Jase had paid for everything. No wonder no one minded that he'd cut the line.

"We're next," he told Sunny Day, who stood at the front collecting money.

"Is that so?" With oil money to burn, and a temper legendary in five states, Sunny wasn't one to give in easily.

"That's so. How much?"

The piercing in her nose gleamed, a diamond shiny even without the help of the sun. "Twenty. Each."

"The sign says five dollars a ride," Harlow pointed out.

She smacked her gum. "Take it or leave it."

"We'll take it."

Harlow finished off her sweet tea with three big gulps, and oh, gross! Tea leaves must have settled at the bottom of the cup, because the drink left a bitter aftertaste for the first time.

Beck threw the cup in the trash, then dug two twenties from his pocket. Sunny pocketed the cash, unabashed. Never mind the festival's profits were supposed to help add a gymnasium to Strawberry High.

With a few button pushes, the wheel soon came to a stop.

"Everyone but Mayor Trueman and his *assistant*," Sunny said, using air quotes, "can stay put."

The mayor was not the most liked person in town nowadays. A few days ago, word about his affair with his "assistant" spread, devastating his wife.

Beck dragged Harlow to the empty cart, ensured

her tail was out of the way before buckling in, and then waited until they were in the air to speak.

"I can't change my past," he said as the wheel started its slow ascent and Harlow had no means of escape.

"I know." She peered out at the town; the higher they lifted the more she saw. Sweeping hills, flat plains, fields of wheat, cotton trees shedding the small white blooms, valleys with strawberry vines drying out for the cold months ahead.

"You can't change yours, either."

"I know that, too." The air smelled so fresh up here. The dew of coming rain dampened her skin. A cool breeze blustered past and she shivered. With Beck, run-ins like this would happen again and again. Women would always throw themselves at him. Always desire him.

"Talk to me." Beck drew her firmly against his side, shielding her from the worst of the wind. "Tell me what you're feeling."

A thousand different things. Upset. Remorse. Regret. Resignation. Determination. But at the forefront? "Jealousy," she admitted. "You're mine, and yet they know intimate details about you. They probably discuss you, and even hope to get you back into bed again."

He kissed her temple, lingering over her skin. "They will never succeed. I've had a taste of you, love, and I am utterly addicted."

Love. The endearment rocked her, as precious as it was life changing. Did he mean it the way she prayed he did? Did he actually love her as she'd suspected?

"I know we discussed this, but I need to hear the answer again. Do you ever compare me to them?" she asked.

"All the time." At her outraged gasp, he laughed. "They lose. Always."

Slowly she relaxed against him. As the Ferris wheel made its descent, it seemed as if half the town watched her and Beck's cart. He received a few winks, even more thumbs-up. Giving everyone a show, Beck anchored two fingers under her chin, turned her head and kissed her.

The crowd cheered, and the wheel began another ascent, throwing Harlow's stomach into her feet, making her light-headed and deliciously dizzy. At the same time, passion burned through her, white-hot. With Beck, passion always burned through her. He tasted so good, his heat a soothing balm to her tattered soul, and by the time he pulled away, she was panting, squirming in her seat.

He rubbed his nose against hers, his thumbs brushing over her cheekbones in a featherlight caress. "You're not thinking of leaving me, are you?"

"I'd rather die," she said, putting everything on the line.

A flash of relief in eyes now hot with more than desire. "I probably shouldn't tell you this, but we are open and honest with each other, so you need to know a different answer would have meant I started playing hardball and let you see my dark side."

"You have a dark side?"

"Pray you never meet him. He spanks."

She chuckled. "I'm beginning to think you've got a secret fetish."

"Secret? Love, I've been thinking about it since the moment we met. Just been waiting for the green light from you."

"Well, I will let you spank me the day you let me spank you."

"So…today?" he quipped.

Her smile stretched from ear to ear. "You are incorrigible. You know that, right?"

"I believe the word is pronounced *irresistible*."

"And you have no shame," she added.

"But you love me anyway." As the words echoed between them, he frowned and shifted away from her.

Did he not like the thought of her love? Despite the fact he'd used the endearment with her twice already?

Her stomach roiled so hard she gasped, and as the wheel continued to climb, the roiling only grew worse. In all her life, she'd only been sick only a handful of times. Her mom used to say she had the immune system of a champion. But the times she *had* gotten sick, she'd fervently prayed to be wiped from the planet forever; the fever, chills, sweats, and trembles so violent she'd looked as if she were having a seizure had been almost too much to bear.

This was somehow worse.

She clutched her stomach, beads of sweat popping up on her brow. She could actually feel the blood draining from her face and knew she was deathly pale, judging by the horror suddenly radiating from Beck.

"What's wrong, love?"

"My stomach hurts. Bad." Bile rose.

"Get us down," he shouted to Sunny. "Now."

The girl held out her arms, all *what am I supposed to do? Pull you off with my she-strength?*

Beck flattened his palm on Harlow's belly and gently rubbed. "Just hold on a little longer, baby. I'll get you home."

Nausea churned faster, harder, and she gagged. She judged the remaining distance with dread. Not even halfway down yet. She wasn't going to make it, was she?

"Beck," she said on a moan.

He understood. He ripped off her cat-ears headband, tucked her hair under the collar of her shirt and held on tight to her waist, saying, "Lean over as far as you can. I won't let you fall."

At any other time she would have been humiliated. Right then she hurt too much. So she did it. She leaned over and vomited her guts out, spraying whoever stood below their cart.

CHAPTER TWENTY-SEVEN

BECK HAD NEVER been so scared in his life. Over the years, he'd been beaten, sexually used and manipulated by a foster mom, abandoned and forgotten. But this—this was far worse. He'd never had a woman of his own, and he'd never had to worry about anyone but himself. Jase and West had always been self-sufficient. If one of them had gotten sick, they'd sucked it up and yelled at anyone who dared approach. Only in the privacy of their rooms had they curled into balls of pain and rocked back and forth, moaning and softly begging for mercy. The manly way.

But by the time his friends returned home later in the evening, their laughing voices echoing all the way to the bedroom, Harlow had grown far worse. She'd begun to dry heave, too weak to make it to the bathroom or even hold herself up. Beck had to carry her and anchor her against his chest, afraid she'd drown in the toilet otherwise.

"You're going to be okay," he told her. "You have to be okay."

She was too weak to respond. She could no longer even hold open her eyelids.

When a few minutes passed without another incident, he carried her to bed and tucked her into the softness of the sheets. Her face was puffy from strain, her skin waxen and clammy. Locks of hair clung to her damp cheeks and neck. He dressed her in a clean T-shirt but it, too, stuck to her skin.

Brook Lynn and Jessie Kay entered the room and flanked his sides.

"I heard she threw up on the mayor," Jessie Kay said. "I thought it was the most awesome prank ever. I didn't realize…"

"She'll be okay," he repeated. More to himself than to them.

Brook Lynn patted his arm. "Why don't you take a shower, get changed. Let us take care of Harlow for a while."

"No. I'm not leaving her side." This woman was the center of his world. He'd let her in, or maybe she'd burrowed her way inside. Either way, she belonged to him and with him, and damn it, he needed her to get better, and he needed to see her do it.

She'd been fine one moment and deathly ill the next. She wasn't feverish or exhibiting any other symptoms.

"Is there some kind of virus going around?" he asked, desperate for answers. He couldn't help her until he knew what was wrong.

"No, otherwise I would have gotten it long before now," Jessie Kay said. "I always get sicker faster and far worse than everyone else. Could she have eaten too much junk food?"

A soft moan rose from Harlow—right before she vomited up a river of blood.

The crimson splatter on the sides of her mouth had to be the most horrifying sight he'd ever seen. Beck sprang into action. He scooped Harlow into his arms, her body utterly boneless, and shouldered his way into the hall. "Jase! West!"

Both friends came running.

"Help me get her to the emergency room."

Jase swiped up his car key, and West held open the front door, then the car door.

"Go to St. Joseph's." He wanted Harlow to have the best medical care, experts in every field at her disposal, and as much as he loved Strawberry Valley, he wasn't sure about the medical facilities.

As fast as they drove, they reached the city hospital in less than an hour. A true miracle, considering they didn't wreck or get pulled over. Along the way, West made some calls, so, by the time they screeched to a halt at the curb, doctors and nurses were already outside, waiting for them.

Several people reached for Harlow at once. Beck almost couldn't bring himself to let her go. But he did it, his stomach seeming to twist around a knife. She was placed on a gurney and wheeled away.

As Jase parked the car in the lot, West led Beck inside. They sat in the waiting room, and one hour after another passed, every second more agonizing than the last.

Beck checked with the receptionist at the front desk so many times she began to moan every time he approached. Brook Lynn and Jessie Kay eventually arrived with food and bottles of water. Brook Lynn tried to get him to eat or drink something, but he refused, too unsettled. She tried to engage him in conversation, but there was only one person he cared to chat with right now, and she wasn't available.

Finally, a nurse came out to ask their entire group

questions about her. What Harlow had eaten and drunk that day, what she had done. He answered as best he could, but when he asked questions of his own, the nurse rushed off without responding.

Another hour passed.

He couldn't lose Harlow. He just couldn't. He liked—no. Damn it, no. He *loved* her, and he wasn't going to hide from the truth any longer. He loved her with all his heart, all his mind and all his strength. He loved her, and he had come to depend on her. She was the best part of his life.

The only part that mattered anymore.

A burn of tears in the back of his eyes, He tangled his hands in his hair and tugged at the strands. Was it normal to be kept waiting this long? Damn it! Why the hell wouldn't anyone tell him what was going on?

He paced. He considered punching the walls. He tried to breathe as his imagination tormented him with a continuous replay of Harlow vomiting blood.

At long last the nurse returned to lead their group to a comfortable seating area away from the crowd. No matter the questions Beck threw at her, she replied with, "I'm sorry, but you'll have to ask Dr. Lowe."

"I'd be happy to ask him. If he'd be kind enough to show his damn face."

She beat feet. Finally, a short, squat man with a no-nonsense gaze and a stern demeanor joined them, saving the building from the fury of Beck's fists.

"My apologies for the delay. I'm Dr. Lowe," he said as he shook one hand after another. "I'd like to speak to Miss Glass's next of kin."

"I'm her boyfriend," Beck said. "How is she? What's wrong with her?"

The doctor pursed his lips. "I'm sorry, but considering everything I've learned, I will only speak with immediate family."

"Why? What did you learn? Did something happen to her?" Beck nearly grabbed him by the shoulders to shake the answers out of him. "Is she going to be okay? You have to tell me. Please."

"Tell *me*. I'm the sister," Jessie Kay said, pushing her way forward. "I'm Jessica Glass."

Dr. Lowe led her to the side, and Beck nearly burst out of his skin. He didn't have a right to know Harlow's condition because he wasn't her husband? Hell, no. Unacceptable. He would have joined the pair and demanded answers *now*, but Jase grabbed him by the arm, holding him in place.

"Let go, man. Now."

"Calm yourself." Jase motioned to the entrance. Two security guards stood in the doorway, and a fortysomething woman wearing a pantsuit entered, a notebook in her hand. A detective, guaranteed. He'd talked to enough of them after Pax's death to recognize one on sight.

The blood drained from Beck's head. If the cops were involved...

Something bad had happened to Harlow.

Panic flooded him as he shook off Jase's hold and raced to Dr. Lowe and Jessie Kay. "She's okay. She has to be okay. You tell me anything else, and I will lose my shit." His throat was closing, making breathing difficult. Dizziness hit him, and blackness winked over his vision. "She can't be...she just can't be... I need her!"

Gentle hands helped him into a chair. "Beck." Jessie Kay's voice reached him through the length of a long, narrow tunnel. "You really have to shut your mouth and listen to me, okay. I know you're thinking the worst, but Harlow *is* alive."

The most profound sense of relief dulled the worst of the panic. Able to breathe again, the dizziness fading fast, he lifted his head and met navy blue eyes brimming with concern. "Where is she? What's wrong with her? When can I see her? Why are the cops here?"

Jessie Kay rubbed his back, saying, "Let me tackle this a question at a time, all right? They've admitted Harlow to intensive care. I'm sorry, but she isn't even close to stable. Dr. Lowe said…he said she's slipped into a coma." Tears streaked down her cheeks. "You can't see her. Not yet. None of us can."

A coma. Harlow was in a coma. In intensive care.

But Jessie Kay wasn't done. "You know eyedrops? What people use to make the red fade from their eyes? Well, the active ingredient is tetra something…something chloride. I'm can't remember the technical mumbo jumbo, I'm sorry, but whatever it is, it's great for the eyes but apparently ingesting it causes blood vessels to shrink and blood pressure to drop."

"Are you telling me Harlow drank eyedrops?" His tone was hard and harsh, cutting and loud, but he didn't attempt to moderate it, and he didn't apologize.

"Not willingly, I'm sure. Someone must have put the drops in her drink. The doctor said vomiting would have occured within minutes of ingestion, and since she threw up on the Ferris wheel, it would have happened right before you guys got on."

"No. Impossible." Before the Ferris wheel, she'd finished off her sweet tea—sweet tea he'd also ingested when he helped Brook Lynn set up her booth. Harlow had nursed that damn cup for hours, savoring every sip, and she hadn't got sick. Neither had he.

Besides, who would do something like that?

"They've run tests," Jessie Kay said, treading gently. "Plus, her symptoms fit. Vomiting occurs within minutes, and sometimes even seizures and a coma."

Seizures. Coma. There was that word again. Sometimes people fell into comas and never woke up.

His heart shriveled in his chest. "The symptoms fit other things."

"Yes, but they were able to question Harlow before she sank into...well, she mentioned her tea tasted funny. Tea doesn't go bad unless mold is starting to set up, so they ran tests for certain kinds of poison."

"You're Beck Ockley?"

In a daze, he glanced up at the newcomer. The detective. "Yes," he responded, his voice hollow.

"I'm Detective June, and I'd like to chat with you."

She proceeded to ask him personal questions about his life, and about Harlow and her past, and about their relationship. He answered everything, leaving nothing out. Who cared about privacy at a time like this? Nothing mattered but saving Harlow's life. Nothing mattered but finding the one who'd poisoned her—and making him pay.

"Can you think of anyone who would want to do her harm?" the detective asked now.

He shook his head absently. "Everyone seemed to have gotten over their anger. They smiled and waved at her."

"Not everyone," Jase said. "Not Tawny Ferguson and Charlene Burns."

The detective focused on him. So did Beck. The guy

had done his rock-solid best to fly under the radar since being released from prison. As an ex-con with a history of violence, he was likely to be the first suspect in a case like this—Beck and West surely close seconds. The fact that he was speaking up meant more than Beck could articulate.

"That's right," West said. "Both Tawny and Charlene hate Harlow. I was with Beck and Harlow when the two women approached. Soon after, a man named Scott Cameron drew our attention elsewhere. After that, I escorted Tawny and Charlene away, but it wasn't long before they broke away from me to follow Beck and Harlow to the Ferris wheel, giggling about something. I'm sorry. I never thought—"

Detective June wrote something in her notepad and said, "They may not have intended this to happen. A lot of people have heard that putting eyedrops in someone's drink causes diarrhea, nothing more, but they are dead wrong. I'll speak with Strawberry Valley's police chief, and I'm sure he'll question Miss Ferguson, Miss Burns and Mr. Cameron. If you think of anything else he needs to know—"

"I'm not Harlow's sister," Jessie Kay burst out, as if she couldn't hold back the words any longer. "I just said I was to find out what was wrong with her. And I went twenty miles over the speed limit to get here. Don't arrest me."

Frowing, Detective June handed everyone a card. "Dr. Lowe, please call me when Miss Glass wakes up."

After the detective left, the doctor adjusted the lapels of his lab coat. "You're all welcome to stay in here if you'd like, but visiting hours are currently over. They'll begin again tomorrow at eight, and at that time, we'll let you see Miss Glass, one at a time." He strode from the room.

Just like that? Beck was supposed to stay away from the love of his life for an entire night? A woman who lay in a coma, hooked to machines? She could die before the sun rose. He could lose her. After everything, he could lose her, and it would have nothing to do with his past, or his issues, or not being enough for her.

Death didn't care about Beck's future happiness, or Harlow's young age and sweet heart. The bastard took without prejudice and left the survivors to deal.

I can't deal.

Until Harlow, he'd had only half a life. He'd had friends and work and lots of sex, but no love. No real purpose. He'd hated change, and perhaps that was one of the reasons he'd resisted Harlow so fervently, and yet, where would he be without *this* change? Without her?

He stormed to the door, not sure what he would do. Leave not only the hospital but Strawberry Valley, hoping distance would ease the pain, make him forget? Drink *himself* into a coma? Sneak into her room? Hunt down Tawny, Charlene and Scott—hurt them?

Arms banded around him, steel bands he would have to fight to break through. West and Jase had surrounded him, offering comfort.

He drew on their strength, and in a moment of startling clarity, he knew what he had to do. "I've got to go," he said, wrenching free of his friends.

"Beck, man. Don't leave," Jase said. "Stay. For her."

West grabbed his wrist. "If you're thinking about going after Tawny and Charlene, don't. If you're locked behind bars—"

"Don't you see?" He whirled on them, taking a moment to explain because he owed them and didn't want them to worry. "I've always expected the worst from everyone, so I've always cut and run. Except with you two, because I saw myself in you. But I see myself in her, too. I see her pain and her need to connect—needs I share—and I'm not going to hold anything back anymore. I'm not going to worry about the future, or what will or will not happen. I'm going to do what's right, what I should have done the moment I met Harlow."

CHAPTER TWENTY-EIGHT

HARLOW BLINKED RAPIDLY to clear the fog currently obscuring her vision. The lights in the room were too bright, tears dried and crusted around her burning eyes. Her ears picked up a slow *beep*, *beep*, and when she turned her head, she found a bank of machines with flashing lights and numbers, connected to tubes, and the tubes were connected to her arms. A woman and a man she'd never met stood beside her bed, discussing heart rate and vitals.

She frowned. She was in a hospital?

Yeah. Made sense. She remembered throwing up on Mayor Trueman and being carried away from the festival in Beck's arms. Now there was a strange heaviness to her limbs, a shakiness she wasn't used to experiencing.

"Beck," she said. Or rather, tried to say. Her throat was sore, her voice nothing more than a whisper.

The man in the lab coat heard her, however, and patted her hand. "Harlow, I'm Dr. Lowe. You're at St. Joseph's hospital in Oklahoma City, and you've been very sick. We removed a tube from your throat, which is why you're having a bit of trouble speaking. But don't worry, the discomfort will pass."

A tube down her throat—she'd needed help *breathing*?

"Where's Beck?" She needed Beck.

"We'll talk about him in a minute," Dr. Lowe said. He propped his hip against the side of her bed. He wasn't very tall, and was a bit on the heavy side, his features stern. "Do you know why you're here?"

"I was sick."

"Not just sick. Harlow, you were poisoned. Thankfully, you've responded to the medications very well. You'll make a full recovery with no lasting damage."

Her mind got stuck on a single word. "Poisoned?" But…but…how? And by whom? So few people hated her now. Right? And she'd done nothing to anger anyone. Had she?

"It was a prank gone horribly wrong, apparently. Someone from your hometown put eyedrops in your tea. You slipped into a coma four days ago."

Wait, wait, wait. "I don't understand." Four days?

"When confronted by your police chief, the culprits confessed to their crimes. I don't remember their names, I'm sorry. There were two women and a man. They've been charged with contaminating a substance for human consumption. They're lucky they weren't charged with attempted murder."

"Beck," she croaked. "Where is he?" He had to be worried. "I want to see him."

The doctor's expression remained impassive. "Let us finish checking your vitals, all right?"

For the next half hour, she was poked and prodded and questioned, and she did her best to keep her temper in check. Beck had to be more than worried about her; he had to be freaking out. As poorly as he'd handled her vomiting, she couldn't imagine what the coma had done to him.

Finally the exam ended, and the medical staff filed out of the room.

"Don't forget to send in Beck," she called.

The doctor stopped in the doorway. "I'm sorry to tell you this, Miss Glass, but there isn't anyone in the waiting room for you."

Harlow lay in the bed, heart stuttering in her chest. No one was out there? Truly? "Maybe he's in the cafeteria?"

His half smile was not reassuring. "Yes, I'm sure that's it." He shut the door with a soft click. "Give him time. He'll arrive soon enough."

No way Beck would have left her, even for a minute. Unless the thought of losing her—as he'd lost so many other people in his life—had pushed him over the edge. He might have abandoned her in an effort to protect himself.

No way in hell. She wasn't going to think the worst of the man she loved and trusted with her fragile heart. But she *was* going to find him.

She maneuvered her legs over the side of the bed and stood. Her knees instantly buckled, her weight too much to hold, and if not for the bedrail, she would have toppled. When she felt more stable, she transferred her grip to the pole with her IV and catheter bags. Her paper-thin gown gaped in the back, but she couldn't hold it closed *and* hold herself up.

With as much dignity as she could muster considering her backside was bared, she worked her way to the door, the hallway, calling, "Beck! Beck!"

The nurse who'd poked and prodded her rushed over to latch on to her and prop her up. "What do you think you're doing? You shouldn't be out of bed."

"Beck!" Thankfully, she managed to do more than squeak this time. "Where is he? I know he's here. He wouldn't have left me." Tears beaded in her eyes. "He wouldn't."

Taking pity on her, the nuse said, "All right, sweetie. We'll go have a peek in the waiting room." She helped Harlow bumble onward.

Six people sat in the cushioned chairs, watching TV or reading magazines, and one slept on the couch. But none of them were Beck, or any of her friends.

"He's…he's not here." The tears spilled over, and a sob bubbled up, nearly choking her.

"I'm sorry, sweetie. I really am. Men can be pigs."

"Not mine. He's—"

"Harlow? Harlow!"

Beck! She turned, practically collapsing with relief when he raced from the elevators. West, Jase, Brook Lynn and Jessie Kay were in tow.

A second later, Beck had her wrapped in his arms, his callused hands meeting the bare skin of her back, offering the comfort she'd so desperately craved. Her tears came more freely, but this time they sprang from relief. He was here, and he was with her.

"I'm so sorry I wasn't here when you woke up, love." He tied her gown closed at her waist, while still allowing a slit for his hand. "Dr. Lowe told us you'd come out of the coma but that the sedatives in your system wouldn't wear off for another few hours, giving us plenty of time to finish our errands before you actually woke up. But here you are, alive and well." In his eyes, unadulterated relief mixed with elation.

"I didn't want to believe you'd left me, that the fear of

losing me was too much." Her voice was small, needy, but she didn't care. Trust and share.

"I will never leave you, love. Never." He drew back only far enough to cup her cheeks. "You are *everything* to me. I just had to run a a a few errands."

"We all love you, Harlow," Brook Lynn said. "You're one of us, and we will always be here for you."

"You're our whiskey sister." Jessie Kay fist-pumped the sky. "Whiskey sisters, unite!"

She smiled at them, the girls who'd forgiven and accepted her and the guys who'd welcomed her with open arms. But her smile faded as she studied their formal attire. Tuxes on the men, glittering gowns on the women.

Even Beck wore a tux, looking sexy and almost too beautiful to touch. "Why are you so dressed up?"

"For a party," Beck said.

"Okay, you guys." The nurse clapped her hands to ensure she had everyone's attention. "This is sweet and all, but I've got to put a stop to it. Miss Glass needs to be in bed."

"Then let's put her in bed." Beck scooped her up, while West followed them, the IV pole in hand.

Harlow leaned her head against the strong shoulder she'd come to rely on. In her room, Beck gently laid her on the gurney and tucked the blanket around her legs. She would have pulled him beside her, but the nurse hooked a monitor to her chest before leaving.

"What party?" Harlow asked when the woman left, picking up the conversation as if there'd never been a lull. "Why did you leave? What errands did you have? And just so we're being open and honest with each other, whatever you say, I'm not going to think it's good enough."

His lips twitched at the corners. "Thank you for being open and honest."

"Welcome. Now answer me, please."

He brushed his knuckles over her jaw, the caress tender and reverent. "Since you fell ill, I've had to do some soul-searching about what I really want for my future."

Her heart monitor sped up, the fast beep embarrassing.

"Without you, my future would be bleak. Harlow Glass," he said, dropping to one knee and holding out a ring box. Inside glittered the biggest diamond she'd ever seen. "Will you marry me?"

Shock played havoc with her reasoning. "Excuse me?"

"I want to marry you, and I want to start a family with you. I want as many little Harlows as I can get. I want you to be my painter slash trophy wife. I want to take care of you, and to be taken care of by you. I want to share the farmhouse with you, and only ever cook my famous breakfast for you. I want to go to sleep with you every night and wake up to you every morning, and tug you into the shower anytime during the day."

"But...but..." This was more than she'd ever dreamed possible, her every wish coming true right before her eyes. "The cage..."

"You didn't cage me, love. You set me free." He slid the ring onto her finger. "The party is for you, to celebrate your precious life...and our engagement—if you'll have me."

She placed her hand over her racing heart, the diamond glinting in the light. "Beck."

"Say yes. Tell me we can do a small ceremony as soon as possible, finally make you mine legally, then do a big one later on. I'm not sure how much longer I can go without knowing you are lawfully bound to me."

"Beck," she said again, tremors sweeping through her.

"I love you, Harlow. Every part of me loves every part of you. There is nothing I won't do for you, and nothing I won't do to keep you. You're it for me. My one. My only. And it would be an honor—a privilege— to be the man you choose to spend your precious life with. To create a family with you. To watch your belly grow big with my child. To be what you need and what you want. Now and always."

Tears of joy filled her eyes. But he wasn't done.

"I won't allow fear to lead me anymore. I won't push you away, won't let you push me away. I am happy now, and I see happiness in the future. I'm holding on tight to you, baby, and I'm never letting go. I'm crazy, sick, devastatingly in love with you, and I'm sorry if I'm coming on too strong right now, but no, that's not true. I'm not really sorry. You're mine, and I'm yours. Our issues can go to hell where they belong. You and I, we belong together."

Jessie Kay opened the door a crack and stuck her head inside the room. "Say yes already. Listening from the hallway is harder than you'd think."

"And don't forget," Beck added. "If you say yes, you'll get to live in the farmhouse again. You can paint murals on every single wall. In fact, I'll insist on it."

As if Harlow needed more encouragement. This man owned her, and had from the beginning. "Yes," she said with a laugh. "Yes."

The others spilled into the room, cheering. Beck kissed Harlow right on the mouth, not seeming to care that she'd been in a coma and hadn't brushed her teeth since. He didn't seem to care about anything but her, because he treasured her, and he planned to spend the rest of his life cherishing her.

The way she would cherish him, through the ups and through the downs. "Just so you know," she said, "this is a big change. A true life-altering one."

"Love, as long as your feelings for me stay the same, everything else is inconsequential."

She gripped the collar of his jacket. "My feelings aren't something you ever have to worry about. I love you so much. You are and always will be more than enough for me."

"Not even poisoning and a near-death experience could keep her away from you," Jessie Kay said, patting him on the shoulder. He flinched, and she laughed. "What? Too soon to joke about?"

"I'll be ready to joke about this in…never," he said.

Harlow scooted over and patted the bed, and he crawled in beside her, drawing her to his chest.

"What's going to happen to Tawny, Charlene and Scott?" she asked.

"They're going to spend a little time behind bars," Jase said. "Felonies are a bitch, and not something you can sweep under a rug."

Harlow should have been overjoyed by the news, but she wasn't. She wasn't even mad at the threesome. Not really. Did she think she deserved what they'd done? No. Not anymore, and not ever again. Beck was right. She'd paid for her crimes, and she was a different person now. But the misery of others no longer made her feel better about the misery of her own life. Not that she was miserable anymore. Because of Beck, she'd never been happier.

"I'm going to agree to a supersmall, superfast wedding because I want to get rid of the H.A.G. initials as soon as possible. But I'm also going to take you up on your offer of a second, larger wedding," she said to Beck. "I want the women of Strawberry Valley to witness our vows, even though I'm pretty sure they'll attend in funeral attire, mourning the loss of their Beck."

As the others beamed at her, Beck kissed her temple. "I'm not their anything, love. I'm yours. Now and forever."

* * * * *

*If you enjoyed Harlow and Beck's story,
you'll love the next installment (Book 3) of
the* ORIGINAL HEARTBREAKERS *series—*
THE HARDER YOU FALL—*featuring Jessie Kay
Dillon and Lincoln West, the sexy bachelor who's
breaking all his rules for this rowdy Southern belle…
Available December 2015 from Gena Showalter
and HQN Books.*

Available now in the
ORIGINAL HEARTBREAKERS *series:*
"The One You Want"
(in the anthology ALL FOR YOU*)*
THE CLOSER YOU COME
THE HOTTER YOU BURN

Turn the page for a sneak peek at
THE HARDER YOU FALL

WEST BACKED JESSIE KAY against the wall, this woman who tormented his days and invaded his dreams. She wasn't what he should want, but somehow she was everything he could not resist, and he was tired, so damn tired, of walking, hell, running away from her.

"What are you doing?" she demanded, but there was a hitch in her voice and it hit every masculine instinct he possessed with adrenaline, jacking him up.

"What do you want me to do?" He braced his hands at her temples, caging her in. He wasn't the only one who'd been running from the sizzle between them, but tonight, he wasn't letting her get away. One look at her, that's all it had taken to ruin his plans, and now she would pay the price—and make the day better.

Different emotions played over features so delicate he was constantly consumed by the need to protect her from the world…and ravage her afterward. First came need, then fear, regret, hope and finally anger. The anger concerned him. The Southern belle could make a man's testicles shrivel with a look. But still he didn't walk away.

She ran her delicate hands up his tie and gave the knot a little shake, an action that was sexy, sweet and wicked all at once. "I admit it. I want you, West…" she whispered.

That was it. All it took. He hardened painfully, his erection straining against his zipper, reaching for her.

But she wasn't done.

"I want you...to go back to your date," she snapped, giving him a push—not that he budged.

His date. Yeah, kept forgetting about her. But then, he'd gotten used to forgetting pretty much everything else whenever Jessie Kay walked into a room. She consumed him, and it was irritating as hell, a sickness to be cured, an obstacle to be overcome, but damn if he wasn't going to enjoy it here and now.

He bunched the hem of her skirt, his fingers brushing the silken heat of her bare skin, and again her breath hitched, driving him wild. "You've told me what you think you should want." He rasped the words against her mouth, hovering over her, not touching her but teasing her with what could be. "Now tell me what you really want."

Navy blues peered up at him, beseeching him. "Don't do this to me, West. You're just going to use me."

"I'm going to make you come. There's a difference."

* * * * *

*If you like Gena Showalter's breathtaking
contemporary romance stories,
you'll love her Harlequin TEEN series,*
THE WHITE RABBIT CHRONICLES:

*ALICE IN ZOMBIELAND
THROUGH THE ZOMBIE GLASS
THE QUEEN OF ZOMBIE HEARTS*

*And coming soon
from Harlequin TEEN,
A MAD ZOMBIE PARTY*

*Keep reading for a sneak peek at
A MAD ZOMBIE PARTY!*

FROSTY

The Walking Dead

I CRAWL OUT of bed and rub my gritty eyes. My temples throb, and my mouth tastes like something furry crawled inside, nested, had babies and died. I'm on my way to the bathroom to brush my teeth with a gallon of bleach when I realize my surroundings are unfamiliar. I stop and turn, ignoring a flood of dizziness, and scan a bedroom that has pictures of flowers hanging on pink walls, sparkly shirts and skirts spilling from an oversize closet, and a vanity scattered with a thousand different kinds of makeup.

A sleepy sigh draws my attention to the bed, and memories rush in fast. I went to a club, picked a girl, and went home with her. I slept with her, and now I'm going to leave and prove I'm a Class A dick. But at least I'm at the top of my field. Counts for something, right?

Dark hair cascades around her pale shoulders. She is simply the newest in a long line of randoms I've selected for one reason and one reason only: each resembles Kat in some way.

But they aren't Kat, and after the deed is done I can't leave them fast enough.

My stomach tenses, and my hands fist, as hard as hammerheads. After a few shots of whiskey, I can pretend whatever girl I'm with is my sweet little Kitty Kat, and I'm touching her again, and she's loving it, begging me for more, and everything will be okay, because we'll be together forever. I imagine she'll cuddle close afterward and say things like, "You are the luckiest guy in the world. You're dating me, and I'm superhot, but I don't even know it, which makes me even hotter," and I'll laugh, because she's ridiculous and adorable and everything right in my world. In the morning, she'll demand I apologize for doing bad things in her dreams.

She'll make my life worth living.

Then morning will actually come, and I'll realize she won't be doing any of those things. She's dead, because I couldn't save her.

I hate myself.

Kat deserves my loyalty until the very end—*my* end. And this crap? I'm cheating on her memory with girls I don't even know, don't even like and will always resent. They are not Kat, they will never be Kat and they have no right to put their hands on her property.

It's wrong. It's messed up. I'm not this guy. Only assholes use-and-lose, and once upon a time I would have been the guy who beat a prick like that into blood and bone powder.

Ask me if I care.

Before this particular mistake wakes, I gather my discarded clothing and dress in a hurry. My shirt is wrinkled, ripped and stained with lipstick and whiskey. I look like exactly what I am: a hungover piece of scum. I don't bother fastening my pants. The combat boots I leave untied. I make my way out the front door and realize I'm on the second floor of an apartment building. I scan the surrounding parking lot but find no sign of my truck.

How the hell did I get here?

I remember driving to the nightclub, throwing back one shot after another, dancing with the brunette after I plucked her from her group of friends, throwing back more shots and…yeah, okay, piling inside her little sedan. I'd been too wasted to drive. Now I'll have to walk back to the club, because there's no way in hell I'm waking her up to ask for a ride. I'd have to answer questions about my nonexistent intentions.

As I stride down the sidewalk, the air is warmer than usual, the last vestiges of winter having surrendered to spring. The sun is in the process of rising, igniting the sky with different shades of gold and pink, and it's one of the most beautiful sights I've ever seen.

I give it the finger.

The world should be crying—snot sobbing—for the treasure it's lost. At least I don't have to worry about being ambushed by zombies. The scourge of the earth usually only slinks out at night, the bright rays of the sun too harsh for their sensitive husks to bear.

"What you doing here, pretty boy?" someone calls. His friends chortle. "You want to see what real men are like or something?"

I keep my head down and my hands in my pockets. Not because I'm afraid, or because I'm in a part of Birmingham, Alabama, most kids my age try to avoid, scared off by the graffiti on crumbling building walls, the parked cars missing hubcaps and wheels, and the plethora of crimes being perpetrated in every alley— drugs, prostitution, maybe an armed mugging or two— but because in my current mood, I will fight, and I will fight to kill. As a zombie slayer, I have skills and abilities "real men" cannot hope to defeat. Not even gang bangers. Taking on a group of punk kids would be like shooting fish in a barrel—with a rocket grenade launcher.

Yeah. I have one of those. Two, actually, but I've always preferred my daggers. Up close and personal is my preferred method of elimination.

In my pocket, my cell phone vibrates. I withdraw the device and discover the screen is blown up with texts from Cole, Bronx and even Ali Bell, Cole's girlfriend. Kat's best friend. They want to know where I am and what I'm doing, if I'm coming home any time soon. When will they realize it's too difficult to be around them? Their lives are pretty much perfect. The three of them are living the happily-ever-after I've wanted since seventh grade, when Kat Parker walked into my classroom for the first time. The happily-ever-after I will *never* have.

Cole and Ali have each other. Bronx has his girl Reeve. What do I have? Pain and misery, and they both suck.

A big brute of a guy suddenly steps into my path. I say brute because the shadow he's casting tells me he's my size, loaded with muscle and topping out well over six feet.

If he isn't careful, he won't be walking away from this encounter. He'll be crawling. But as I glance from his boots to his face, I lose the 'tude. Here is my friend and fearless leader Cole Holland in the flesh. I've known and loved him like a brother since elementary school. We've fought beside each other, bled with each other and saved each other. But I'm not in the mood for another pep talk.

"How'd you find me?" I ask.

"My superamazing detective skills. How else?"

"In other words, the GPS on my phone." Technology is a whore.

Cole's eyes are violet, freaky, and right now they are glued to the collar of my shirt. He arches a brow. "Lipstick?"

"I'm on the hunt for my perfect shade," I deadpan.

"Your skin tone screams for rose, not magenta." His deadpan is better than mine.

The old me would have been all over that kind of response. I used to love exchanging trash talk with my boy. Now? I'd rather be left alone. "Thanks for the tip. I'll keep it in mind."

"Come on." Cole pats me on the shoulder, and if I'd been a weaker guy, I would have been drilled into the concrete. "Let's go get something to eat. You look like you could use a solid meal for once rather than a liquid one."

As much as I don't want to go, I don't want to argue with him. Takes too much energy. His Jeep is idling at the curb, and I slide into the passenger seat without protest. A ten-minute drive follows, and neither of us speaks. What is there to say, really? The situation is what it is, and there's no changing it.

When we end up at Hash Town, however, I wish I'd opted to argue. Ali, Bronx and Reeve are at a table in the back, waiting for us. Reeve and I have never been close; she was Kat's friend, and like Kat, slaying has never been in her wheelhouse. She can't see or hear zombies, but she's seen us fight so many times that she accepts what other civilians cannot: the monsters are real, and they live among us.

Reeve lost her dad—her only living family and our wealthiest benefactor—the day I lost Kat. For the first time, I'm struck by a sense of kinship with her. Maybe this forced interaction won't be so bad.

She smiles in welcome. She has dark hair and even darker eyes and, in junior high, she and Kat used to pretend to be sisters from different misters. Now, it kind of hurts to look at her.

Who am I kidding? Everything hurts.

I take one of two empty seats and signal the waitress for coffee. I'm going to need it. "So…is this an intervention?"

"No, but it probably should be," Ali says. "You look like crap." Her mouth has always lacked a filter, a problem exacerbated by the fact that she refuses to lie about anything. Two qualities guaranteed to turn any conversation into a battlefield. But I wouldn't change her. I'll take blunt over charming any day.

Cole sits next to her and kisses her cheek, and she leans in to him, the actions natural to them both, wholly instinctive. Kat and I used to do the same.

A lance of pain rips through my chest.

"The good news is my crap is another man's best," I say. "You look good, at least."

"Obviously." Ali buffs her nails.

It's such a Kat thing to say—to hear—we both freeze.

I need a moment to steady my breathing. New conversations eventually kick off, friendly insults bouncing back and forth among the group. My attention remains on Ali, and she mouths, *I'm sorry.*

I hike my shoulders in a shrug. Ali is Kat's polar

opposite in appearance. In storybook terms, she's the innocent snow princess to Kat's seductive evil queen. Ali is tall and slender with a fall of pale hair and eyes so clear and blue looking into them is like staring into an ocean, while Kat is—was, damn it—short and curvy with dark hair and hazel eyes a perfect blend of green and gold. There'd been no one prettier, or smarter, or wittier, or more adorable, and if I continue on this path, I'm going to topple the table before tearing the building apart brick by brick.

The waitress finally arrives with the coffeepot and fills my cup. "Your order will be out in a few minutes, hon." She pats my shoulder and ambles away.

"We took the liberty of ordering for you," Reeve tells me. "Two fried eggs, four pieces of bacon, two sausage patties, a double helping of hash browns and a stack of blueberry pancakes." She nibbles on her bottom lip. "If you'd like something else…"

"I'm sure I can make do with so little." I'm not hungry, anyway. "How's Z hunting going?"

"Better than ever." Ali takes a sip of her orange juice. "We've stopped fighting and simply allow them to bite us. In minutes, our light cleanses them—and us—of all darkness, and they float away into the hereafter. It's a miracle to watch."

Slayers produce spiritual fire, the only weapon truly capable of killing a zombie. But after the leader of Anima experimented on Ali, shooting her full of untested drugs, she developed the ability to *save* the Z's with her fire. An ability she then shared with other slayers by using her fire on *them*.

Multiple times she's offered to share the ability with me, too, but I've always turned her down. I'm not interested in saving my enemy. Zombies bit Kat. If I hadn't lost her to a hail of bullets, I would have lost her to toxin. So, zombies have to die.

The downside? I suffer when I'm bitten. The pain affects my whole body and is unbearable. The urge to destroy *everything* in my path is overwhelming. I also don't heal without slayer fire or an injection of a chemical antidote—and I have to receive one within a ten-minute window of the bite or I'm toast. And since I don't want to acquire the ability to save zombies, it has to be the injection. Always.

"Do I sense a *but*?" I ask.

Ali takes a drink of her water and nods. "The more bites we allow, the longer it takes us to recover."

"Makes sense. The more bites, the more toxin your spirit has to cleanse."

"More coffee?" the waitress asks.

The girls jolt at the sound of her voice. I just nod. Like Cole and Bronx, my guard hasn't dropped since I walked through the diner doors. I've known the waitress's location every second and knew she was close enough to hear us.

The coffee is poured, and she walks away without giving us the *you are so weird* look. Normally we wouldn't discuss our business so openly, but we're kids (technically) and we've learned that everyone assumes we're talking about a video game.

"We need to come up with a new way to help the Z's and ourselves," Bronx says. "After a battle, I'm drained for a week."

The food arrives a few minutes later, the waitress placing steaming plates in front of each of us. My friends dig in as if they've been starved for months.

While I was out drinking and sexing it up last night, they clearly did some of that zombie hunting and fighting. The sleeve of Ali's shirt has risen, and I see the raised red bite marks on her arm, just above a tattoo of a white rabbit.

I look around and find bite marks on Cole and Bronx, too, and it hits me hard. They went into the field of battle without me. They could have been hurt, or worse, and I wouldn't have been there to help them. The Z-saving thing is new, as untested as the drugs Ali was given, and we don't know all the ins and outs. Something could have gone horribly wrong.

I swallow a curse. I need to get my act together. Like, yesterday. But I'm not sure I can.

* * * * *

Brook Lynn's Stuffed Pepper Bacon Goodness

4 poblano peppers, halved and seeded

½ lb bacon

1 jalapeño pepper, seeded

1 small white onion

4 garlic cloves

1 tbsp butter

1 lb hamburger meat

salt and pepper, to taste

8 oz cream cheese

cheddar cheese for topping, shredded

Roast poblano peppers in oven or on grill until soft.

Dice bacon, jalapeño, onion and garlic, and then sauté with butter in a large pan. Add ground beef and brown it, seasoning to taste.

Mix beef and bacon mixture with cream cheese and fill each poblano half. Top with layer of cheddar cheese and place in baking dish.

Bake at 350°F for 30–45 minutes. Enjoy!

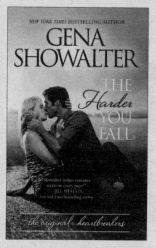

From *New York Times* bestselling author

SHANNON STACEY

Meet the tough, dedicated men of

BOSTON FIRE

and the women who turn their lives upside down.

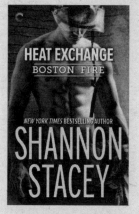

Aidan Hunt is a firefighter *because* of the Kincaid family. He's had the hots for Lydia Kincaid for years, but if ever a woman was off-limits to him, it's her. She's his mentor's daughter. His best friend's sister. The ex-wife of a fellow firefighter. But his plan to play it cool fails, and soon he and Lydia have crossed a line they can't uncross.

Available now wherever books are sold.

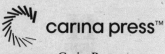

www.CarinaPress.com